Crown Of Reflection

Book One

Edwardo Stripe

About This Book

1st Edition 2026

Contents

Prologue

System Initialization

[SYSTEM NOTICE]

Host Status: Critical

Soul Transfer Pending

Artifact Bound: Crown of Reflection

Beginning Initialization..... Complete

Waiting for host confirmation...

Stripe woke up just enough to know he was still miserable and wasted. This was his life now. A non-stop solo party in the gutters.

His cheek was pressed against damp grass. The cold seeped through his thin shirt like the ground had teeth. A rusted metal edge dug into his back where the park bench underside met his ribs. He had crawled under it hours ago. Not for comfort. Not for safety. He did it because it kept the bitter wind off his face and the bright security lights from hitting him.

Under the bench, he could pretend the world was not watching him.

His bruised hand still gripped the vodka bottle. It was glass. Mid-shelf. He still had standards, even while he was failing at being alive.

He brought it to his mouth and drank like it was medicine. It was the kind of medicine that did not cure anything. It just made you stop caring that you were sick.

The city sounded far away, even though it was not. Cars passing. Distant laughter. A siren that rose and fell like a tired animal. He exhaled and watched his breath fog in the freezing cold.

The bottle tapped against the concrete when his arm went slack. That sound bent in his head until it stopped being glass. It became a padded glove thudding into canvas. It became a referee's palm slapping the mat.

His memory grabbed him hard, like it had been waiting for an opening.

He saw the cage. He saw ring lights hot enough to make your skin sweat before the fight even started. He heard the massive crowd roaring his name so loud it vibrated in his teeth. He felt the excitement and nervousness of an impending battle between two titans in their industry.

Stripe. Stripe. Stripe.

His opponent circled him. Bigger. Heavier. Confident, as if confidence were physical armor. His opponent had missed weight by 5 pounds and, as a result, had forfeited half his purse. Stripe slipped right. He threw the overhand right and followed with a left uppercut. It was the exact combination and the same rhythm his body still remembered, even if his mind was rotting in a bottle.

His opponent folded like someone had cut his strings. The arena exploded. The glory was all his. This is what he does best.

In the front row, she was there. Laughing. Hands covering her mouth. Her eyes were bright, looking at him like nothing bad could ever happen as long as he kept winning.

Later, in the quiet hallway outside the locker room, she grabbed his face and kissed him hard while reporters shouted questions that he ignored.

"You looked ridiculous with one glove still on," she said with a flirtatious hint in her voice.

He smiled in response to the happy memory.

Then a heavy kick slammed into his ribs and snapped him back into the freezing park. Air left his lungs in a harsh grunt.

He tried to curl tighter under the bench, but another kick landed. This time it hit higher, near his shoulder. The alcohol and sneak attack made a perfect mixture that prevented any real retaliation. He could see in front of him through the illuminated glow of the park lights.

Teenagers stood above him at the edge of the harsh park light. They had clean shoes and clean hoodies. They had the kind of careless, arrogant posture that only exists when you have never had to sleep with one eye open.

"Bro, what is this?" the first teenager laughed. "This motherfucker is really posted up under a bench."

"Nah, for real, look at this dude," the second one added, leaning closer. "He smells like he pissed himself."

"Jesus, he is gross. Yo, he got a bottle too," the third teenager pointed.

Stripe opened his mouth. Something came out that might have been a laugh, and might have been a wet cough. "You guys Uber. I ordered dignity."

They laughed like that was the funniest thing they had heard all week. One of them yanked the vodka bottle from his stiff hand.

Stripe reached for it instinctively. Not because it mattered, but because it was his. His broken body still understood ownership even when he had nothing else.

"Bro, he wants his drink back," the second teen mocked. "Look at him looking goofy as fuck." He lifted the bottle like a sports trophy, then tipped it out onto the dead grass. "Nah. You are not drinking that. It reeks."

Stripe tried to sit up. His muscles, soaked in cheap alcohol and starved of proper nutrition for months, refused to obey the command fast enough.

The thick glass bottle came down hard on his head.

It did not break the first time. It bounced off his skull and rang like a bad bell. Stripe blinked hard. He had been letting this exact bottle kill him for years. These kids were just speeding up the process.

"Again, again," the first teenager cheered. "Hit that dirty bitch again."

The second strike shattered it.

Glass exploded across Stripe's forehead. The thick base hit bone with a hollow sound that felt wrong, like a heavy door slamming shut inside his skull.

Warmth ran down his face. Cheap vodka and thick blood mixed together. His ears rang with a high-pitched tone. The park lights blurred into streaks of white.

Somewhere inside his fading head, the arena roared again. The ring lights flickered in his dying vision.

His wife's face appeared for a single heartbeat. Not as a prophecy. Not as a mystery. It was just a memory slamming into the present because his brain needed something familiar while it broke apart.

"Stripe!"

The scream overlapped the moment without explaining itself. It mirrored the exact way she had shouted his name after big wins, but it was distorted now. Stretched thin by pure panic and the horrific pain of the Moscow hotel room.

Another brutal kick landed. Then another.

He knew how to block them. He knew how to grab the kid's ankle, sweep the leg, and end this. But his body was a useless, broken shell. He was trapped inside his own decay.

The world narrowed until it was broken pieces. The bench above him became a dark, blurry ceiling. The grass became a resting place smelling of hot iron. That familiar smell of metal, but in a vast, overwhelming quantity.

The cruel laughter became far away.

"Yo, yo, we gotta go," the third teen panicked. "He is not moving." The teen's voice was veiled in panic.

"Nah, he is breathing. I think," the first one said, his voice trembling. "Bro, what do we even say if someone asks?"

"Say less," the second teen commanded. "He was tweaking and came at us. Self-defense."

Their voices layered over each other. Panicked and fast. They were already building a fake story while Stripe drifted out of it.

Then everything dropped out. It wasn't what he imagined death would be. The flashback and warm fuzzy feeling never came. Just cold darkness pulling him from his corpse.

White.

It was not hospital white, and it was not ceiling tile white. It was endless, blinding white, like the entire world had been erased and nobody bothered to redraw it.

Stripe blinked slowly.

A woman stood before him. Except she was not fully a woman.

His mind tried to draw lines around her shape and failed. Light folded around her form in a way that refused hard edges. There were curves, but they shifted. There was skin, but it was not human skin. His brain grabbed the closest approximation it could manage and rendered her as something feminine and unclothed. That was easier than trying to process something beyond structure.

It felt wrong to look at her for too long, like staring directly at the sun through a thin cloth.

"You are dead," she stated in a matter-of-fact manner. There was no room for negotiation in her voice. Just absolute authority.

Stripe frowned. "No, I am not."

He did not care for the finality and absoluteness in the situation.

She did not react like she had been insulted. She reacted like she had been inconvenienced. "You are."

"That is not how being dead works," Stripe argued. "I would know."

"You would not." Her voice a tiny bit louder than previously.

It was apparent no one had ever talked back to her in this manner.

Stripe looked down at himself. There was no pain. No blood. No broken glass. No empty bottle.

He lifted his hands. The constant, throbbing ache in his shattered knuckles was gone. The dull, heavy rot in his liver had vanished. His lungs did not rattle when he breathed. He felt light. He felt whole again. Then he realized the biggest ingredient to his personality was also missing. His anger was gone, washed away in the room of white.

He looked back up at her blurred, glowing outline. "If I am dead, why are you here?" His voice hinted at his confusion.

"I am a goddess," she replied, her voice echoing in the void. "I usher chosen souls into new worlds where their regrets may be addressed." Her voice had returned to absolution and authority.

Stripe squinted at her. "Okay. First, that is a lot of words. Second, why are you naked, and have you not even told me your name? This is crazy." He raised his eyebrow as he scanned her body up and down.

The light around her form shifted slightly, like it was trying to decide whether to be offended or highly amused. "You speak to me as though we are equals."

"You are the only person here. Who else am I supposed to talk to, the white void?"

Her presence sharpened. "You are dead." Her voice boomed through the infinite space of emptiness.

Stripe shook his head. "I have taken harder hits from bigger men."

"You were weakened," she countered. "Your body had deteriorated. You were no longer the champion you once were."

That stung much more than the word dead. Especially now that he remembered what being healthy actually felt like. Stripe lifted his chin anyway because he did not know how to do anything else.

"Prove it then." He put his hands on his hips in an exaggerated movement.

The goddess raised her glowing hand. The white space fractured.

Images appeared in the empty air around him like massive, floating panes of glass.

He saw the cold park. His body was on the ground. Glass was in his hair. Blood mixed with spilled vodka. He was pretty sure he saw brain matter near the concrete. Police lights flashed red and blue. The teenagers stood nearby, shaking, not crying for him but for themselves.

Another pane of glass materialized. A courtroom. A lawyer speaking about self-defense. Security footage showed the teens looking panicked at the park exit. Their fake tears could be mistaken for real by a jury. His arrest record displayed his previous history of violence. Fight highlights showing brutal knockouts are played on a screen. A judge's heavy gavel. Case dismissed. Meetings with shady men and receiving cash-filled envelopes.

Another pane shattered into view. The teenagers are being praised for their resilience. Receiving college scholarships. Smiling brightly for the cameras.

Another image formed in front of him. A funeral. Empty chairs. A cheap closed casket. No former teammates. No crowd. No one.

Stripe reached out to touch the wooden casket. His hand passed right through the glass. He was isolated.

Then, without warning, another pane appeared.

A kitchen table. Evening light pours through the window. A golden championship belt sat between two plates of takeout, as if it belonged there, just another household object.

Her laughter filled the room. "You are not putting that thing on the table again."

Stripe grinned at the memory.

Then it vanished. The white returned.

Stripe stared ahead. He exhaled, allowing his breath to empty his lungs. "This sucks."

"Do you still contest your death?" She almost sounded smug in her tone.

Stripe swallowed hard. "Nah, you made your point. I kind of went out like a bitch, though."

Silence stretched between them.

"You got a name, or do I just call you Goddess?" Stripe asked.

"Astraeia." Her voice was gentle and perfect.

"Really, that's a bit dramatic," he muttered. "By the way, you never answered me. Why are you naked?"

"I am not naked. You just cannot comprehend my true form." There was a hint of panic in her voice.

"A naked glowing woman who is see-through is what I comprehend. You're saying you didn't choose this look."

"..... You may select one divine blessing," Astraeia offered, ignoring his observation.

Absolute Strength. Perfect Regeneration. Arcane Supremacy. Instant Mastery. Great Sage.

Astraeia began explaining each ability. All of them were simple and overpowered. Then she got to the Great Sage. She talked for what felt like an hour. Four sentences in, Stripe's eyes glossed over, and he tuned her out."Utilizing your trauma as an indicator for power progression, the Great Sage can." She was interrupted mid-explanation of the complicated abilities the Great Sage provides.

"That one," Stripe interrupted. "I will take the long one. Please just stop talking."

"You comprehend it with just that small explanation?" she stated. Her voice betrayed the surprise she felt at his intelligence.

"Fuck no. But if its description is that long, it must be good." He paused, thinking about the name. "That sounds like some cheesy anime rip-off. Change it."

"You think death is a game," Astraeia said, her light flaring. "Fine. It shall be called Crown of Reflection."

"That sounds expensive, finally a name worthy of me. I fuck with it."

"You will never again experience intoxication," she declared. "Since you refuse to listen to me, the Crown will ensure you never have the luxury of tuning the world out again."

Stripe froze. The words hit him harder than the glass bottle ever did.

"Wait, what? Hold on. No, you can't do that. I need it." Genuine, absolute horror widened his eyes. He would have to feel everything. All the time.

He needed alcohol to get by. Without it, there was just silence and memories. This was the worst punishment for him.

Astraeia's form glowed as if she were chuckling, although Stripe doubted she would ever admit to it.

The white floor beneath him cracked and vanished.

He fell.

Chapter 1

Stripe hit the ground hard enough to feel the impact rattle all the way down his spine before his lungs remembered how to breathe.

He lay there longer than he needed to, staring up at a sky that looked clean. There was no smog. No towering skyscrapers blocking the horizon. Just an endless, piercing blue expanse dotted with clouds that looked like they belonged in a Renaissance painting.

The dirt beneath him was soft and cool, pressing into his shoulder blades in a way that felt almost polite compared to freezing, blood-stained concrete. The air tasted sharp. Clear. Too clear.

He inhaled, taking a deep, experimental breath.

He braced himself for the familiar, agonizing burn of cheap vodka crawling up his throat. He waited for the stale liquor fog throbbing behind his eyes and the dull, heavy headache grinding against his skull. He expected the sharp, stabbing pain of fractured ribs from the teenagers' boots.

Nothing. The years of alcohol damage to his ruined liver, bothering him, and the years of high-intensity MMA wear and tear were all gone.

"I can move my knees without them cracking and popping. This is insane," Stripe said to himself as he squatted up and down, enjoying his new knees. He did this until he collapsed on the ground. He lay there while his stamina recovered.

The pure, clean air fills lungs that feel brand new. There was no longer the slight sting of the city smog in the air.

He pushed himself upright and overbalanced, catching himself on his hands. His center of gravity was wrong. A heavyweight champion's body was a physical anchor, built on dense muscle, a thick neck naturally hunched from guarding the chin, and heavy, conditioned bones.

This new body felt light. It felt fragile. He felt like a welterweight who had skipped training camp. He could feel his lack of physical strength; his height was still around the same. Otherwise, he may have had to relearn to walk.

He looked down at himself. Boots. Standard brown leather. Underwear. Simple cloth. That was it: no wallet, no keys, no clothes, and no weapon.

He lifted his hands and turned them over. They looked wrong. He had smooth, unblemished knuckles. There were no thick, calloused scar ridges crossing the skin. There were no faint, permanent athletic tape stains from wrapping up before a cage fight. The tattoos he had spent thousands of dollars on were gone. The only familiar part of his body was the light brown skin tone he had in his previous world.

"Either this is heaven, or I'm about to get sued for indecent exposure in another universe," Stripe said aloud.

CROWN — Host body integration finalized.

The voice was loud and firm in his head. It was bland and almost robotic. There was no accent or any other uniqueness to it. It sounded as if ChatGPT had been uploaded into his brain.

Stripe blinked, tapping the side of his head. The voice didn't come through his ears; it resonated directly in the center of his skull.

"That is not a reassuring sentence," Stripe muttered. "Where is the naked glowing lady?"

CROWN — Current physical vessel assessed at Level 1.

He stood up straight, testing his footing in the soft dirt. The body responded. There was no stiffness in his joints. No chronic, nagging ache in his knees from years of wrestling and bad weight cuts. He did a quick shadowboxing combination: a jab, a cross, and a slip. The mechanics were there in his brain, but the muscles felt weak. Untested. He could still perform his moves with surprising quickness, but the physical force that used to be behind them did not exist any longer.

"You're in my head," Stripe said. His voice was annoyed and echoed through the quiet forest. It was loud enough to disturb some nearby birds perched in the trees.

CROWN — Affirmative.

"That feels invasive," he continued, frowning. "Do you have a volume dial, or am I just stuck with you narrating my life?"

CROWN — Internal interface operating within acceptable parameters. Volume adjustment is a low-priority function.

"I didn't ask for the customer service update," Stripe snapped. "Just tell me where I am."

A sudden, sharp rustle of movement in the tall grass cut off the Crown's response.

Stripe turned, dropping his hips and raising his bare fists. His fighting instincts took over before his conscious mind did. He squared his shoulders, looking for the threat.

A massive wolf stepped out from the brush about ten feet away.

But it wasn't just a big dog. It was pure, lean muscle covered in coarse, wire-like gray fur. It stood as tall as a man's waist. The yellow in its eyes glowed with a faint luminescence, signaling it did not belong in any normal forest. Foam dripped from the monster's mouth like a dog with a case of rabies. It was larger than any dog he had ever seen, even the giant wolves he used to see in nature documentaries.

When it shifted its weight, it moved with a terrifying, stuttering speed that shouldn't be possible. It left a faint afterimage in the air. Stripe's fighter brain failed to process the mechanics of its movement. It didn't step; it glided into striking range.

It was calculating the absolute best angle to rip out his throat.

CROWN — Wolf detected. Estimated Level 8 based on muscle density and overall physical prowess.

"I'm what?" Stripe asked, his voice tight.

Luckily, he had played a little bit of Final Fantasy, so he understood levels.

CROWN — Level 1 confirmed.

"So I stand a chance."

CROWN — Survival chance is five percent with current combat experience and stats applied.

Stripe exhaled through his nose, keeping his eyes glued to the beast. He didn't dare blink.

"This feels personal," Stripe whispered. "I thought the Goddess and I were getting along. She sends me to a new world and feeds me to a mutant dog?"

CROWN — Analysis of the conversation shows negative chemistry. WARNING. The threat is predatory in nature.

The wolf lowered its massive head, its lips curling back to reveal rows of jagged, yellowed teeth that looked sharp enough to shear through steel. The thick muscles through its shoulders tightened like coiled springs. Low, guttural growls vibrated in its chest.

Stripe bent, maintaining eye contact, sweeping his hand through the tall grass. He needed a weapon. A rock. A heavy stick. Anything. He grabbed the first solid thing his fingers found. It felt dense. Warm. Soft, but holding its shape.

CROWN — Keep eyes on the threat.

"That's the plan," Stripe fired back.

His fighter instincts loaded up the throw, his hips twisting to generate maximum kinetic force. He swung his arm side-armed with all his might.

But mid-swing, the squishy, awful texture registered in his brain. The heat of it. The undeniable mushiness. A horrifying realization hit his pride a microsecond before he let go.

The mass burst apart midair and splattered across the wolf's snout, covering its glowing eyes and bared teeth.

The horrific, rancid smell hit Stripe half a second later.

"You've got to be fucking kidding me," Stripe gagged.

CROWN — An improvised weapon composed of fecal matter is ineffective. Survival percentile is falling rapidly.

"Yeah! That makes sense!" he shouted.

The wolf shook its head, flinging brown streaks in every direction. It sneezed, trying to clear its snout.

Then it let out a deafening, terrifying roar that shook the leaves off the nearby trees. Anything in a few-mile radius would be sure to hear that roar.

CROWN — Berserk condition applied.

“Of course it is!” Stripe yelled, backing up. “Let me guess, it’s stronger now?” He said as if he had planned everything.

CROWN — Correct. I detect approximately a thirty percent increase in stats and aggression.

The wolf lunged. It cleared the ten-foot gap in a single, explosive bound.

Stripe dove sideways and rolled through the dirt, his lowered Agility stat making him feel like he was moving underwater. He scrambled frantically, his fingers closing around a thick, fallen tree branch.

“You brace the jaw,” Stripe gasped as he hoisted the wood. “That’s how this works.” He said in a very bad Australian accent, mimicking Steve Irwin.

CROWN — Clarify.

The wolf hit him before he could elaborate. The sheer kinetic force of the impact was like being hit by a speeding car. It knocked the breath out of his lungs and sent him crashing onto his back.

CROWN — Host HP 80/80 -> 62/80. Blunt force trauma detected.

Its mouth opened wide, snapping down just inches from his exposed throat. Hot, foul-smelling breath washed over Stripe’s face.

Stripe jammed the thick branch horizontally toward its foaming mouth with both hands, trying to create a physical barrier.

“I saw this on a survival show!” Stripe grunted, straining against the beast’s weight. “You wedge it so they can’t close their jaw!”

CROWN — Canine bite force exceeds branch durability threshold.

The heavy wood splintered and snapped under the crushing pressure of the beast's jaws, raining sharp splinters down onto Stripe's bare chest.

"That's not how it worked on television!" he screamed.

CROWN — Your memory may be distorted by intoxication at the time of viewing.

"Yeah, that's fair!" Stripe conceded.

He twisted his hips hard, bridging his weight to buck the beast off his center line, and rolled. Razor-sharp claws tore deep gouges into the dirt where his neck had just been. He felt the claws rake across his exposed ribs as he scrambled away.

CROWN — Host HP 62/80 -> 55/80. Lacerations sustained.

Stripe bit back a scream, ignoring the burning pain in his side. He scrambled to his feet, gripping the jagged half of the broken branch, and swung it like a baseball bat. With all of his might, the log cut through the air in an arc that was violent and fast. All of the force of his little level one body was behind this swing.

It smacked hard into the wolf's ribs with a dull thud.

CROWN — Damage inflicted. One point.

"One point is a lot, right?!" Stripe yelled hopefully.

CROWN — Negative.

The wolf barely flinched. It leaped unnaturally high into the air, its heavy paws slamming into Stripe's chest, taking him straight back to the ground.

They hit the hard dirt together in a tangle of limbs and fur.

Stripe shoved his bare forearm under the beast's jaw and pushed upward with everything he had. The beast thrashed, its hind claws scrambling and scraping across his stomach and thighs, tearing his skin open in fresh, bloody lines.

CROWN — Host HP 55/100 -> 12/100. Severe bleeding detected.

"You go for the throat!" Stripe roared, veins bulging in his neck. "Always the throat!"

CROWN — Current position prevents optimal access.

"I'm working with what I've got!" he shot back.

His arms started shaking. The terrifying realization hit him like a physical blow again. This new body was not strong. Back on Earth, he could bench press three hundred pounds. Here, a Level 8 wolf felt like a collapsing building pressing down on his chest.

"I used to throw men heavier than this!" Stripe gritted his teeth.

CROWN — Current strength output is insufficient for the lift maneuver.

"Really?!" Stripe spat, his arms buckling. "I couldn't tell!"

The wolf's jaws snapped, inching closer and closer to his face as Stripe's strength rapidly failed. His muscles burned with lactic acid. His vision began to blur at the edges.

CROWN — Host death imminent. Forcefully triggering reflection. Successful completion of the reflection will result in bonuses.

Stripe's head began to pound, and his thoughts became a blur.

He shut his eyes and rubbed his temples to drown out the pain.

Nothing worked; he was losing the battle to stay conscious.

An invisible force dragged him deep into his own mind.

--------STATUS----------

Name: Stripe
Level: 1
Race: Human
Class: None
Title: None
HP: 12 / 80
Stamina: 60 / 80
Mana: 0 / 0

Attributes

Strength 8
Agility 8
Endurance 8
Intelligence 8

Skills

None

Artifacts

Crown of Reflection

Chapter 2

The spiral accelerated the moment Stripe returned to his empty mansion in the hills. He walked through the double doors and locked them. The silence of the sprawling estate pressed against his eardrums with a physical weight. Every room was a preserved museum of a life that no longer existed. The imported oak crib sat untouched in the yellow nursery. Her favorite jacket hung over the back of the dining room chair. It was a snapshot of a perfect past. Stripe did not clean. He left her things in place.

He retreated to the custom bar in his entertainment room and began destroying his liver. The alcohol dependency transformed into a full-time occupation. He drank to silence the screaming in his head and blur the sharp edges of reality. He drank until his world-class physique began to soften and rot. Eventually, the quiet left too much room for memories to surface. Stripe decided to drown the silence out with noise. He threw the front doors open, allowing the worst elements of Los Angeles to flood his sanctuary.

The mansion became a nonstop party. The driveway was packed with exotic cars belonging to strangers. The living room was filled with blaring music that vibrated the floorboards. Strangers swam in his infinity pool, slept in his guest rooms, and drank his expensive liquor straight from the bottle, spilling it across Persian rugs. Stripe did not care. He wandered through the crowds like a ghost haunting a graveyard.

He surrounded himself with beautiful, empty women who flocked to the mansion for free alcohol and proximity to his fading fame. They wore expensive clothes and heavy perfume that smelled of artificial vanilla and desperation. None of them smelled like his wife. None laughed like her. None looked at him with an ounce of affection. His weakness led him to one-night stands with women who couldn't bear to spell their names. They offered physical stimulation and nothing else.

One night, Stripe sat slouched on a leather sofa in the corner. The music was deafening, the air thick with smoke. A young blonde woman with plastic surgery sat next to him, placing her hand on his thigh.

"You look so sad sitting over here all by yourself, champ," she purred, twirling her finger up his leg toward his inner thigh. "Why do you not take me upstairs? I can make you forget whatever is bothering you."

Stripe turned his head. His eyes were bloodshot and dead. He looked at her manicured nails, then at the greed in her eyes. He would never want to forget his wife. He needed a break from the noise, but he never wanted it to leave.

"I fucking doubt it," Stripe said, his voice flat. "I fucked women who were more beautiful than you at least three times yesterday. There's nothing you can offer me."

The disdain turned heads across the room. The woman flinched, snatching her hand back.

"You are a miserable, arrogant asshole," she spat, standing up and disappearing into the crowd.

Stripe took another pull from his vodka bottle. He knew his arrogance had curdled into something toxic and mean. He hated every person in the room because they were breathing while his angels were dead.

Sharks began to circle his fortune. Dave was gone; Stripe had fired the only manager who cared about his well-being. A financial manager named Vance took control of the accounts. Vance wore cheap suits and smiled too much. He realized Stripe was checked out of reality; the fallen champion never read emails, answered phone calls, or looked at bank statements. Vance saw a golden opportunity to get rich. Every few weeks, Vance showed up at the filthy mansion, navigating past passed-out strangers to find Stripe at the bar. He always brought a thick stack of documents and a fresh bottle of scotch.

"Just a few standard investment forms for you to sign, Stripe," Vance would say, sliding the papers over, his voice carrying false sincerity. "We are moving some assets around to maximize your returns. Very boring, technical stuff. Just sign on the dotted lines, and I will leave you to your party."

Stripe never read a word. Without his child, his entire empire was a useless burden. With a shaking hand, he blindly scrawled his signature across high-risk contracts, signing away the rights to his likeness and authorizing wire transfers to offshore accounts controlled by Vance.

"Thanks, champ. I will handle everything from here," Vance would smile, packing the briefcase.

Vance and his partners siphoned millions out of Stripe's accounts. They drained cash, then took out high-interest loans using the mansion and exotic cars as collateral, funneling the money through shell companies and cryptocurrency. By the time the financial structure collapsed, Vance had fled the country.

The reality crashed down on a Tuesday morning. The music stopped. The hangers-on drifted away when the free alcohol dried up. Stripe was alone in the filthy house, waking up on the living room floor with a blinding headache and a shaking need for a drink. An aggressive pounding echoed from the front double doors. Stripe groaned, pulling himself up off the sticky hardwood. His bare feet crunched on empty glass bottles and trash as he unlocked the doors.

Three men in windbreakers stood on his porch. The bold yellow letters across their jackets read IRS. Several police officers stood behind them on the stone steps. The lead agent stepped forward, holding a clipboard.

"Are you Stripe?" the agent asked.

"Yeah," Stripe grunted, leaning against the doorframe. He hid his depression behind a sarcastic mask. "What do you want? I am not signing autographs today."

"We are not here for autographs," the agent replied, handing over a stack of papers. "We are executing a federal seizure of this property and all associated assets. You have failed to pay federal taxes for three consecutive years. You are in default on massive loans. Your bank accounts are frozen. You missed your court dates, resulting in a judgment against you."

Stripe stared at the paperwork as the words swam out of focus. "What are you talking about? I have thirty million dollars in the bank. I paid this place off years ago." His voice shook.

"You have nothing in the bank. If you did, we wouldn't be here. We would have just taken it from there," the agent corrected without pity. "You have exactly one hour to gather your personal belongings and vacate the premises. If you do not leave, these officers will remove you for trespassing."

Stripe stood on the porch in a daze. He watched tow trucks attach heavy chains to his custom Ferrari and luxury SUV. Moving crews walked in, cataloging his antique furniture, massive televisions, and custom artwork. He walked back into the entertainment room, where an agent stood behind the bar holding Stripe's three golden unified championship belts.

"Put those down," Stripe demanded, his voice thick, cracking as he stumbled forward. "Those belong to me. I won those."

"These are considered high-value assets," the agent replied, dropping the priceless belts into a cardboard box. "They will be auctioned off to help satisfy your federal debt. Go pack a bag. Your hour is almost up."

Stripe did not fight. The violent monster that had beaten a man to death in a frozen alleyway was gone; he was hollowed out. He walked into the master bedroom, found a duffel bag, and packed a few t-shirts, jeans, and a heavy winter coat, leaving his watches and tailored suits behind.

He slung the cheap duffel bag over his shoulder and walked out the front doors for the last time. On the way, he opened the locked door to the baby's room, taking in the sight of his past life one final time. He walked down the road toward the city, leaving the physical embodiment of his life's work behind. He never touched the fighting league or streaming money because it reminded him of his sacrifices.

Desperation set in. Stripe rented a filthy room in a cheap motel in the worst part of the city, where the carpet smelled of mildew and a neon sign flickered all night. He needed cash to buy alcohol. He needed alcohol to silence the memories of his wife. Swallowing his remaining pride, he used a public payphone to call Marcus, the lead promoter.

"I am ready to fight again. I want my belts back. Give me a title shot."

Marcus answered with a heavy sigh. "Stripe. I heard about the house. I heard about the money. I was wondering how long it would take for you to call me begging for a handout."

"I am not begging," Stripe lied, his ego flaring.

Marcus let out a cruel, mocking laugh. "You are out of your damn mind. You have not trained in over a year. Your last fight was a disgrace. Sure, you won, but you weren't trying. The crowd doesn't want you anymore. I am not putting you near a title fight. You are a massive liability."

"Give me a fight," Stripe insisted. "Anyone."

Marcus saw an opportunity to profit from the dying name of a legend. "I have a kid. He is twenty-two, a phenomenal striker, and hungry. He needs a big name on his resume to build his hype train. I will give you $50,000 to step into the cage with him next month. No pay-per-view points. No win bonus. Just fifty grand to show up."

To a man who used to spend fifty grand in a weekend, it now sounded like a life-saving fortune to buy bottom-shelf vodka for ten years.

"Send the contract to where I'm staying," Stripe said and hung up.

Stripe did not hold a training camp. He sat in his motel room, continued to drink, and braced himself against the nightmares. He convinced himself that his raw talent and muscle memory were permanent.

Fight night arrived with a cruel reality. Stripe sat in the sterile locker room. The smell of bleach and athletic tape made his stomach churn. He was out of shape, a layer of fat covering his abdominal muscles, his face bloated and flushed from alcohol abuse. He had paid two random guys from a local gym a few hundred bucks to wrap his hands, and they did a terrible job; the tape felt loose. Stripe pulled a plastic water bottle filled with cheap vodka from his gym bag and took a swig to calm his shaking hands. An athletic commission doctor smelled the liquor and looked at him with pity, but the promoter had paid well; the doctor signed the clearance form and walked out without a word.

A production assistant stuck his head in. "You are up, Stripe!"

Stripe stood up and walked into the arena wearing a faded, generic black hoodie. The blinding lights were hot, and the crowd noise was a physical weight, but the context was inverted—eighty thousand people were booing him because they hated his presence. They remembered the untouchable king he used to be and hated him for falling so far after his wife's passing. Stripe stepped into the steel cage, already mechanized by exhaustion. The canvas felt unfamiliar beneath his feet. He leaned against the fence and breathed hard. His opponent bounced on his feet with boundless energy, looking at Stripe as if he were an irrelevant stepping stone.

The referee called them to the center. "Protect yourself at all times," he warned.

Stripe held his loose gloves up, but the kid smirked, refused to touch gloves, and walked to his corner. The bell rang. Stripe moved forward, intending to execute the same combination that won his titles in Moscow: slip right, overhand, finish with an uppercut. He saw the punch coming, and his brain commanded his legs to slip right, but his body refused to obey. The alcohol abuse had destroyed his central nervous system; his legs felt submerged in thick concrete, making him a full second too late.

The kid threw a head kick. Stripe's hands were low, and the young fighter's shinbone crashed flush against his jaw. There was a flash of white light, followed by complete darkness. Something clicked in Stripe. For a brief moment, he became his old self. The kid moved forward to press his advantage, throwing a flurry of punches, but Stripe swapped to a Philly shell and either absorbed them or pivoted away on pure instinct. Everything in his head had gone quiet the moment the kick connected.

Then, he was flat on his back on a cold medical table inside the locker room, retinas burning under fluorescent lights. His head pounded from a severe concussion, and his jaw throbbed. The kid had thrown another head kick, but Stripe had leaned back, watched the foot fly by, and countered with a massive overhand right to the prospect's unguarded chin. The kid went down, the ref waved off the fight, and Stripe collapsed as he walked to his corner.

He tried to sit up, but a heavy hand pushed him back down. Marcus stood over him in an expensive suit with a look of unadulterated disgust.

"Do not try to stand up. The doctors say you have a severe concussion. You are lucky that kid did not break your neck."

"Just make sure the money hits my account," Stripe slurred, clutching his head.

Marcus let out a hollow laugh and dropped a sheet of paper onto his chest. "That is your official termination notice. Your contract is voided due to a breach of the professional conduct clause. You showed up smelling like alcohol. You embarrassed my organization on global television."

"You owe me fifty grand," Stripe mumbled, his fingers crumpling the paper.

"The fine for fighting while intoxicated is fifty grand," Marcus stated, stepping back. "You are getting nothing. That prospect you knocked out was going to be the new you. You fucked that up and cost us billions in revenue."

Marcus walked out, leaving the door open. He had never intended to pay Stripe; he just wanted easy money off his legacy.

Stripe lay on the medical table in total silence, abandoned by his corner men. He touched his swollen jaw. His career was dead, his wealth gone, his reputation destroyed, and all doors were closed. The spiral had hit rock bottom, and he had somehow survived the fall. The streets of Los Angeles recognized only the currency of utility, and Stripe was no longer useful. He spent a few months sleeping on the couches of men who once claimed they would take a bullet for him, discovering brotherhood had a shelf life when the bank accounts were empty. One by one, those doors closed because wives were uncomfortable or the smell of whiskey ruined the furniture. Stripe picked up his duffel bag and moved under a concrete highway bridge.

He learned the stillness of the forgotten. Occasional jail stays or self-defense against troublemakers left him plastered across social media as a violent, drunk ex-champion. Sitting against stone walls in patched clothing, he counted pennies, using liquid medicine to numb his hunger.

On nights he saw highlight videos of his best knockouts on city walls, he drank even more.

One rainy afternoon, the wet cold drove him into the public library. His rags dripped onto the linoleum as his scarred hands typed the login for an email account that had been untouched for a year. A single subject line stopped his heart: a formal notification from the Boxing Commission inducting him into the Hall of Fame. They wanted him to stand in a tuxedo and accept a plaque for a life that ended in a Moscow hotel room.

The irony felt like a physical blow. He looked at his reflection, a bloated, broken man with a matted beard, worried about his next five dollars. He did not reply, logging out and walking back into the rain. He found a pawn shop three blocks away and traded his only remaining winter jacket for twenty dollars. Stripe took the insulting amount, went to a liquor store, and bought a mid-shelf bottle of vodka to maintain standards if he was going to die in the cold.

He walked into the park as the sun set and crawled under a familiar bench. He brought the bottle to his mouth and drank as if it were medicine. It was the kind of medicine that did not cure anything; it just made you stop caring that you were sick. His mind drifted; he knew his wife would find him pathetic, and his kid would think he was weak. These thoughts tore into him, and he decided right then that this would be the final time he drank.

When he woke up in the morning, he would go claim his money and his Hall of Fame spot and become the man he had promised his wife he would be. He was going to get his shit together and have the comeback of the century. Then, when he was on top of the world again, he would create a charity to stop gang violence and alcohol abuse. He lay there, coming up with his plan, motivated. This is the last drink.

The city sounded far away. He heard distant laughter and a siren that rose and fell like a tired animal. He exhaled and watched his breath fog in the cold. The bottle tapped against the concrete when his arm went slack, the sound transforming in his head into a glove hitting canvas, hot lights, and a roaring crowd. He saw the ring. He heard his name echoing through the rafters.

In his mind, he was back in his greatest triumph, seeing his wife laughing in the front row and kissing him in the hallway.

"You looked ridiculous with one glove still on," her voice echoed into the void of his memory.

He smiled at the sound of her voice. Then a kick slammed into his ribs and snapped him back to the park. Air left his lungs in a harsh grunt. He tried to curl tighter under the bench, but another kick landed near his shoulder.

Three teenagers stood above him at the edge of the park light. They had clean shoes and clean hoodies, carrying the careless posture of kids who had never slept with one eye open.

"Bro, what is this?" one of the boys scoffed. "This motherfucker is really posted up under a bench."

Chapter 3

Stripe felt his body responding better to his movements. But it did not help him in the situation he faced.

CROWN — "Reflection complete. Host muscle memory has now integrated into the host's new body."

The jolt back to reality felt like it hurt him more than it helped. He could tell he should have put more thought into his choice of ability.

"Sure do wish I had super strength or regeneration right now," he thought in his desperation.

The warning echoed in his skull. The wolf's massive jaws opened wide, a terrifying cavern of hot, foul breath and jagged teeth descending straight for his exposed throat. Stripe's muscles burned with lactic acid. He couldn't lift his heavy arms. He had nothing left to give.

THWACK. An arrow split the humid air with a sharp, violent hiss. It punched through the thick side of the wolf's skull. The massive beast's glowing yellow eyes rolled back. Its powerful jaw snapped shut with a horrifying clack just an inch from Stripe's nose. The massive body went slack, collapsing like a sack of wet cement onto Stripe's battered chest.

The remaining, precious breath was driven from his aching lungs. He lay pinned under the dead weight, staring up at the piercing, flawless blue sky.

"I threw shit at it," Stripe said with a light chuckle.

CROWN — "Correct."

With a strained, agonizing groan, Stripe shoved the heavy carcass off his bruised ribs and sat up. His body screamed in protest, warm blood leaking from the deep claw marks raked across his torso. At the edge of the quiet clearing stood a tall elf woman. She had long, flowing white hair that cascaded past her shoulders, and she wore pristine, elegant clothing that looked out of place in the dirty wild. Her crafted bow was lowered, but a lethal arrow was already nocked and ready. Her ears were long and pointed on the sides of her head. She was a picture-perfect beauty. It looked like she could roll into a modeling contract at any moment.

Her expression was not one of heroic admiration. It was sheer, unadulterated disgust. Sharp. Immediate. Visceral. Her striking golden eyes flicked from the wolf's feces-smeared face down to Stripe. He was sitting in the dirt, naked, bleeding, and covered in a horrifying mixture of the dead beast's blood and his own makeshift biological weapon. She didn't speak. She didn't ask if he was okay. She turned on her heel and walked back into the dense forest.

As she turned her back on him, Stripe felt a bizarre sting deep in his chest. It wasn't just his massive, bruised ego whining about a beautiful woman looking at him like he was human garbage. It felt much deeper than that—like a sharp, inexplicable wave of cold rejection from someone whose opinion mattered to him. He brushed it off as the severe concussion talking, but the hollow feeling lingered for a second too long. Her memory would be forever haunted by what she had just witnessed.

"That went well," Stripe muttered. "I really showed that thing who's boss."

CROWN — "Your contribution was minimal. You survived due to outside intervention."

"One point of damage is a solid start," Stripe argued back. "I was just tiring it out. I had it right where I wanted it," he said while flexing his non-existent muscles.

CROWN — "Deception detected."

Stripe ignored the artifact and forced himself to his feet. His legs shook. He looked down at the dead wolf. A thick, dark pool of blood was expanding beneath its head.

CROWN — "Recommend host secure clothing to prevent sexual deviant classification."

"Looks like we are going to be wearing wolf," Stripe said. "Time for some rapid skinning. I was sober for this part of the survival show, so I know what I'm doing."

CROWN — "Deception detected."

He crouched down, ignoring the throbbing pain in his side, and grabbed a jagged, sharp stone from the dirt. He began narrating his chaotic actions out loud as if he were an expert host on a prestigious wilderness survival show.

"You cut shallow along the belly," Stripe explained to the air. "There's like a natural seam or a line right here..."

CROWN — "False. No seam detected. Host is suggested to cut above the"

Stripe cut the Crown off with his own loud, confident narration. "There's always a distinct line," Stripe insisted. "Trust me, I remember this."

He was confident in his speech. He was wrong, but he spoke as if he were the best at cleaning a kill. He dragged the sharp rock down the wolf's soft belly. He pressed way too hard. He cut too deep. The foul stomach and coiled intestines ruptured open. The horrific stench rolled out of the carcass like a physical force, hitting Stripe right in the face. It was a vile, suffocating odor of half-digested, rotting meat and burning stomach acid.

"Whoa. That's new," Stripe gagged. The smell wrapped around him like it wanted to strangle him.

CROWN — "Intestinal tract compromised. Extreme contamination spreading."

"That was part of the plan," Stripe coughed. "I'm tenderizing it."

CROWN — "Technique inconsistent with optimal processing. This is an unmitigated disaster."

"No, watch," Stripe argued. "Then you just peel it back like a banana."

CROWN — "Analogy inaccurate."

He kept muttering half-remembered, incorrect instructions to himself while making the horrific mess worse. He sawed, ripped, and tore at the ruined hide with the dull rock. Through sheer, unyielding stubbornness, it began to resemble a recognizable pelt. He freed a heavy, jagged, bloody strip of hide. He wrapped it around his narrow waist, tying the bloody legs together to secure it.

"Boom," Stripe declared. "Functional, stylish clothing."

CROWN — "Odor levels have increased. You are detectable to all local predators."

"That's subjective," Stripe shot back.

He followed the distant, rushing sound of running water until he stumbled upon a wide, shallow river. He waded right into the freezing, rapid current. He scrubbed himself, trying to wash the thick blood and foul grime out of his fresh wounds, before dunking the makeshift pelt beneath the surface.

"You always rinse the meat before cooking it," Stripe reasoned. "Basic, fundamental rule of the kitchen."

CROWN — "Rinsing does not eliminate deep biological contaminants."

"It feels exactly like it should," Stripe insisted. "This is pretty much a shower," he said as he dunked his head under water.

The second his body submerged in the water, all the chemical funk on him turned the river a light brown. A few moments later, silver scales broke the choppy surface of the rushing water. Several large fish began floating belly-up right next to Stripe's wet legs. Stripe stared down blankly at the dead fish bobbing helplessly against his knees.

"That seems a bit overly dramatic," Stripe muttered.

CROWN — "Residual toxins from the ruptured wolf pelt, combined with your own biological matter, are contaminating the immediate water source."

He reached down and grabbed one of the floating, silver fish by the tail. His empty stomach rumbled.

"I don't smell that bad, Jesus," Stripe grumbled.

CROWN — "Consumption is not recommended."

"The Japanese eat raw fish all the time," Stripe argued, inspecting the catch. "It's called sushi, and it's expensive. This is fine dining."

CROWN — "Wrong species for raw consumption. Parasite risk is extreme."

Stripe willfully ignored the warning and took a confident, arrogant bite cleanly out of the side of the fish. His stomach revolted. The texture was sickeningly warm, rubbery, and foul. He staggered out of the river, fell to his hands and knees on the slippery, muddy bank, and vomited. He dry-heaved until his throat burned raw and his eyes watered.

CROWN — "Minor poisoning detected. Stabilizing host vitals."

Stripe wiped his mouth with the dirty back of his hand, spitting the vile, metallic taste into the dirt.

"She takes my booze away and leaves me this?" Stripe wheezed. "That feels personal."

CROWN — "Alcohol intoxication permanently disabled by divine modification."

"I heard you the first time!" Stripe yelled.

Glowing text appeared in his line of vision. A warm, rushing sensation flooded his veins, erasing the heavy exhaustion from his muscles and magically knitting the absolute worst of the deep lacerations on his chest closed. The profound relief was immediate and overwhelming.

CROWN — "Experience gained. Level 2 achieved. Title acquired: Toxic Fisherman."

"That title is absolute, total slander," Stripe protested.

CROWN — "Title reflects environmental outcome. Note: Host bodily fluids are now toxic and may inflict the 'Poison' status on external threats."

Stripe paused, wiping a thick string of spit from his chin. "Wait. Define 'bodily fluids'. Which ones exactly?"

CROWN — "All of them. Saliva, sweat, blood, and reproductive secretions."

"Great. Huge thanks," Stripe groaned. "So I'm an actual, walking biohazard. Now I'm even more disgusting."

CROWN — "Host gratification noted."

Before Stripe could argue the exact definition of gratification, heavy, dry branches snapped in the dense brush just a few short yards away. Several unkempt, armed men stepped into the clearing. They wore mismatched, dirty leather armor, carried rusted iron weapons, and looked at Stripe with hungry, violent intent.

CROWN — "Multiple hostiles detected. Estimated Levels 3 through 5."

The largest one, holding a notched broadsword, stepped forward with a cruel, ugly sneer.

"Oi," the Bandit Leader barked. "What specific crew are you with?" The bandit leader spoke with a gruff voice. It sounded as if he had smoked a pack of cigarettes a day.

"I'm not with anyone, though a few girls have tried," Stripe answered.

"Liar," a second bandit spat. "Just look at how you're dressed."

"Yeah, looks like a real dirty cutthroat," the third bandit added. "Probably raiding our prey. No wonder this area has anyone walking around."

Stripe evaluated the distance. They had lethal weapons; he didn't. But they were arrogant. Their careless stances were wide and sloppy. He stepped forward toward the closest bandit, raising his bare hands up in a submissive, defensive posture, keeping his empty palms open.

"Look, man, I am harmless," Stripe spoke with a cool, calm voice. "I don't even have a single weapon on me. Here, check me if you want."

The bandit grinned, stepping closer, lowering his guard to pat Stripe down. It was the absolute biggest, final mistake of his life.

Stripe pivoted. His left foot planted forward. His right foot anchored back. In a singular, explosive motion, he dropped his weight and launched his fist in a devastating, torqued arc with his entire body weight behind it.

The massive overhand right landed flush against the bandit's jaw with a sickening, audible crack.

But the loud crack wasn't just the bandit's jaw breaking. A blinding bolt of white-hot, agonizing pain shot straight up Stripe's unprotected forearm. Back on Earth, his guarded hands were wrapped in yards of expensive athletic tape, cushioned by padded gloves, and his bones were calcified from years of brutal, constant conditioning. In this fragile, Level 2 body, punching solid, unforgiving bone with bare, unconditioned knuckles felt like hitting a solid brick wall. His hand throbbed, the fragile skin splitting and the knuckles swelling.

He swallowed the sharp, blinding pain and didn't stop. In one fluid, seamless motion, he followed it up with a brutal, rising left uppercut that snapped the bandit's head straight back.

CROWN — "Sneak attack has landed with massive critical damage."

The man's eyes rolled back, and he began to crumple forward, unconscious long before he hit the dirt. Stripe slipped behind the falling man, wrapping his thick, powerful arm under the bandit's exposed throat, locking in a flawless, textbook standing rear-naked choke. He hoisted the limp body up to use as an effective human meat shield.

"Nobody fucking move!" Stripe roared. "I call the shots now!" Stripe screamed at the bandits with a raspy, authoritative tone.

CROWN — "Hostage value calculated at less than ten percent."

"Things are going to go, or I will break his neck right here!" Stripe yelled. "You don't want his kids not to have a dad! What about his loving wife at home?! Think before you fucking move!"

THWIP. A lethal crossbow bolt punched through the terrified hostage's skull, entering through the temple and exiting out the other side in a shower of gore. The man went limp in Stripe's tight grip, heavy as a dead stone, as hot, thick blood dripped down his lifeless face and onto Stripe's bare arm. The heavy body kicked once, a final, useless neurological spasm, before it stopped moving.

Stripe stared at the remaining bandits in disbelief.

"That was Greg," the Bandit Leader said. "He was the absolute worst of us. He killed kids and raped women." His voice didn't break or waver when speaking. This hinted that he was telling the truth.

The other bandits spat on the floor in response to Greg's death. Stripe opened his thick arms, letting the heavy, dead body slide out of his tight grip and slump onto the muddy riverbank.

"Yeah," Stripe said. "I guess I'm okay with this." His voice was a mix of surprise and acceptance.

The Bandit Leader raised his notched sword. The two remaining bandits drew their rusted blades, fanning out to encircle him. Stripe's experienced fighter brain calculated the impossible odds. His injured knuckles were bruised and throbbing in fresh, blinding agony. His torn chest was still bleeding. His stamina was shot from fighting a giant wolf, skinning it, and dry-heaving his guts out in the thick mud. Taking on three armed men with zero energy and bare, fragile hands wasn't a brave stand. It was an actual, undeniable suicide.

"Kill him," the Bandit Leader ordered.

Stripe didn't hesitate. He turned and ran.

> **[SYSTEM ALERT: Level 2 Reached | Title Acquired: Toxic Fisherman | 1 Stat Point Available]**

CHAPTER 4

Every step was a jagged reminder of how much his new life sucked compared to the old one. Back on Earth, his gait had been a weapon, a rhythmic and powerful engine that could carry a two-hundred-and-fifty-pound prime athlete across a canvas with terrifying speed. His movements were the result of decades of conditioning, a heavyweight frame built on explosive power.

Now, he felt like a toddler wearing a grown man's suit that did not fit. His Agility was a pathetic 7, and his Strength was a measly 6. To his fighter's brain, it was like trying to operate a Ferrari with a lawnmower engine. The gears were grinding, and the smoke was starting to billow from his lungs.

Branches whipped across his arms and face like jagged lashes as he crashed through the dense, unforgiving undergrowth. The forest did not care that he had unified world titles or that he had once been the most feared man in an octagon. It just wanted to trip him. It wanted to snag his ankles and deliver him to the men with the steel. Behind him, the heavy thud of boots thundered through the woods, accompanied by the clinking of gear and the sound of men who actually knew how to breathe while running. They were not fighting the terrain: they were part of it.

"He went this way!" Bandit One yelled. "I see the branches breaking!" His voice fluctuated with exhaustion.

"Don't lose him!" Bandit Two shouted. "That pelt alone is worth ten silver, and I want to see what else a freak in his underwear is carrying!"

"Yeah, that seems fair." Stripe wheezed, his voice a ragged edge of a cough. "I would not want to lose myself either. I'm a goddamn delight." He fluttered his eyes like a diva.

CROWN — "Multiple hostiles pursuing. Estimated Levels 3 through 5. Host Stamina is currently at 38 percent and dropping. Recommendation: Cease all attempts at humor. It is a high-cost, low-reward function. Focus on aerobic efficiency."

"Love that for me," he muttered, ignoring the burning sensation in his chest that felt like he had swallowed a handful of lit matches.

This body was new, unscarred, and functionally useless. It was a Level 2 vessel. The bandits were faster, stronger, and possessed actual weapons instead of just hopes and dreams. Every time his foot hit a loose patch of dirt or a slick root, he felt the absence of the dense, calcified muscle he used to rely on. He felt light, fragile. He felt like a welterweight who had skipped training camp to spend the month on a bender, only to wake up in a cage match against three guys with knives.

"You got any helpful advice, or are you just going to read me my obituary in real-time?" Stripe gasped.

CROWN — "Continue running. The probability of survival if you stop to engage is less than four percent."

"Bold strategy, Coach." Stripe snapped. "Really earning your keep in there."

THWIP. A crossbow bolt tore through the humid air, missing his shoulder by a fraction of an inch before slamming into a tree trunk. Stripe didn't flinch. His fighter's peripheral vision caught the archer's finger tension a split second before the release. He had spent years learning to read the subtle tells of an opponent's body, the shift of a shoulder or the narrowing of an eye. Even in this weak body, those instincts remained sharp.

"Did you see how I dodged that Matrix-style?" Stripe shouted, his voice cracking with a mix of adrenaline and exhaustion.

CROWN — "Projectile velocity suggests another shot is imminent. I suggest you stop narrating your survival and prioritize not having a bolt through your cervical spine."

"No shit!"

He cut downhill, the terrain dropping away into a steep, muddy slope. Loose dirt and dead leaves slid beneath his boots as he half-ran, half-fell down the incline. At the bottom of the slope, he spotted a small rock overhang jutting out from the hillside. It was not much, just a jagged lip of stone and frozen earth, but it was a place to vanish. He threw himself into the muck and pressed his body against the cold, damp underside, trying to become part of the mountain.

Above him, the pursuit reached the edge of the slope. He could hear the slide of dirt and the frustrated curses of the men following him.

"Split up!" the Bandit Leader barked. "He is a big bastard; he can't hide forever. Search the hollows!"

CROWN — "Survival percentile falling. Host survival probability is currently 18 percent. The scent of the rawhide is acting as a beacon."

I'm open to suggestions, Stripe thought, his heart hammering against his ribs like a trapped bird. He felt the cold mud seeping through his clothes, but he dared not move.

CROWN — "Maintain position until threat leaves the immediate vicinity. Suggested wait time is thirty seconds. Suppress respiration."

"That's not the encouraging number you think it is," Stripe whispered, his eyes fixed on the muddy ground inches from his face. "What then? I cannot stay under a rock all night."

CROWN — "Disengage from the threat area and arm yourself. With what, you ask? Greg the bandit's body has sufficient weapons and armor to slightly increase survivability. It is suggested that the host return and secure the gear. Scavenging is the most logical path for a Level 2 biological entity."

"That's gross." Stripe grimaced at the memory of Greg's lifeless eyes and the pool of blood flashing in his mind. "But fuck it. I've stayed in worse motels in L.A."

CROWN — "Thirty seconds have elapsed. The auditory signatures of the hostiles have moved forty yards to the north."

Stripe exploded from the overhang, scrambling back up the hill toward the riverbank where the initial encounter had gone south. He felt like a scavenger, a bottom-feeder. It was a long, humiliating way from the championship lights and the custom silk robes. Greg's body lay in a small pool of blood, looking pale, discarded, and too human. Flies were already investigating the ruin of the man's skull.

"This is definitely rock bottom," Stripe muttered, his hands trembling as he reached for the dead man's belt.

CROWN — "Bandit threats are circling back. They have realized the trail went cold. They will arrive shortly."

Stripe did not waste time being sentimental. He was a survivor. He grabbed a dagger off Greg's body; it felt heavy, cold, and real in his hand. It was honest steel. He yanked a damaged leather vest off the corpse, ignoring the wet sound it made as it separated from the skin, and took off running to the opposite side of the clearing.

He burst through a wall of thick, tangled brush and stumbled into a shallow, rushing stream. The cold water splashed up his legs, shocking his system and washing away some of the filth from the overhang. For a second, he considered stopping to wash the blood off his hands, but his instincts screamed at him to keep moving. He crossed the stream and pushed into the dense trees on the far side.

CROWN — "Scent disruption achieved. The running water has masked your biological trail. However, new threats have been detected within the immediate environment."

That sounds promising, Stripe thought. What now? A dragon? A giant spider? He slowed down, raising his head.

At the end of the stream, standing like wire-furred sentinels, were two giant wolves. They were massive, lean, powerful beasts with fur the color of storm clouds and eyes that glowed with a sickly, yellow luminescence. They growled, a low vibration Stripe felt in his own teeth, and eyed him like a poorly wrapped gift. Their gaze fell on the raw, blood-stained wolf pelt tied around Stripe's waist.

CROWN — "Mating pheromones detected on the pelt. Rival male species are currently enraged by the scent of a competitor. They perceive you as a trespassing Alpha who has claimed a kill in their territory. Aggression levels have increased by 400 percent."

"Of course they are," Stripe groaned, his knuckles tightening around the hilt of the stolen dagger until his hand shook. "I swear the Goddess planned this for her own entertainment. I'm a walking biohazard and a target for every horny dog in the forest."

The wolves launched themselves through the stream, kicking up sprays of white water. Stripe turned and staggered up the opposite bank, his boots slipping on the wet stones. He leaped for the lowest branch of a massive oak tree. The rough, ancient bark scraped the skin off his palms, but he ignored the pain. He hauled himself upward with every ounce of Strength his Level 2 body could muster.

"Up we go!" he grunted, his feet dangling for a terrifying second before he found a foothold.

CROWN — "Elevated position may reduce detection probability from ground-based predators. Your current scent profile is contaminating the foliage."

"Finally, something helpful. Tell me more about how I smell, it really helps the morale."

He pulled himself onto a thick branch fifteen feet above the ground, hugging the trunk for stability. His chest heaved as he forced his lungs to settle. Below him, the forest dropped into a deceptive, heavy silence, broken only by the rushing stream.

Then, the sound of snapping branches returned. Three bandits pushed into the clearing, swords drawn. They looked frustrated and tired.

"He crossed the stream here!" Bandit Two yelled. "Look at the tracks in the mud!"

"Spread out!" Bandit Three ordered. "Find the little rat! The boss is going to have our heads if we lose him now!"

Stripe froze against the trunk, trying to blend into the bark. One of the bandits walked directly beneath his branch. Stripe smelled the man's unwashed hair and the sharp, acidic tang of cheap tobacco. He could see the rust on his sword.

"He couldn't have gotten far... the mud is fresh," the man muttered, looking around.

The bandit's eyes drifted to the riverbank, and he stopped dead.

"What the hell happened here?" Bandit Three asked. "Look at the water."

Another bandit crouched beside the water, pointing with his blade. "Fish. Look at them all."

Dozens of silver-scaled fish floated in the current, bellies turned to the sky. They were not moving. The man reached down and picked one up, staring with wide-eyed confusion.

"Why are these dead? They aren't even bitten. It's like they just... stopped."

Stripe stared down from the shadows of the leaves, his jaw tight. A knot formed in his stomach. *That might be my fault,* he thought. *My sweat probably turned the stream into a sewer.* **CROWN** — "Correct. Your 'Toxic Fisherman' title is functioning exactly as intended. Residual toxins from your biological matter, specifically the sweat and blood from your recent struggle, are contaminating the immediate water source. You are an environmental hazard."

"Poison," the Bandit Leader said.

The third bandit stepped forward. He was bigger than the others, older, with a deep, jagged scar running across his jaw. He did not look at the fish or the tracks. He looked at the trees.

"Doesn't matter how he did it," the Bandit Leader snarled. "I can smell the bastard. He is near. He's got that putrid, half-rotted scent of a man who's been living in a wolf's gut."

His eyes swept the canopy, scanning with predatory intent. He was a hunter. He knew how prey behaved when cornered. Then, his eyes stopped. They stopped right on Stripe.

"I know you're up there, boy. I can see your boots."

Stripe did not move. He lifted his arm, took a mocking sniff of his armpit, and covered his nose with a grimace, looking directly at the leader. The Leader rested his heavy broadsword against his shoulder and flashed a grin that was all yellowed teeth and malice.

"You climb down now. And maybe I'll kill you quickly. Maybe I don't even let the boys have a turn. Otherwise, we start with the toes and work our way up. I've got all night."

Stripe exhaled, his knuckles tightening around his stolen dagger. He felt the cold energy of the Crown humming at the base of his skull.

"You know, usually when people meet in the woods, they're more polite," Stripe said. "How about you come up here, and we build a treehouse? I've got snacks, and I'm a world-class conversationalist."

The Leader’s smile vanished, replaced by stone-cold fury.

"Shoot him down!" the Bandit Leader roared. "Take the legs!"

From the shadows behind the bandits, a low, guttural snarling vibrated through the clearing. Pure, unbridled hunger. The Level 8 wolves had arrived, and they did not care about the bandits’ bounty. They only cared about the "Alpha" in the tree.

CROWN — "Host reflection imminent."

The familiar head-pounding headache returned. Stripe's whole body went numb with pain as he closed his eyes.

CHAPTER 5

The bass from the stadium speakers rattled the concrete beneath his bare feet. It traveled up his legs and settled in his chest. Eighty thousand hostile fans screamed for his blood. The noise was a physical weight inside the Moscow arena. It was deafening. Stripe loved it.

He soaked in the hatred like sunlight. He raised his arms high above his head. He wore a custom white silk walkout robe that cost more than most people in the arena made in a decade. His name was stitched across the back in pure gold thread. He was arrogant. He was wild. He possessed an ego so big that it's a surprise his body didn't explode under the pressure. He had earned every single ounce of it. He was the undisputed world champion.

He swaggered down the ramp. His corner team marched behind him in matching tracksuits. They looked nervous. The Russian crowd threw garbage. Half-empty plastic cups of beer bounced off the shoulders of his security detail. Stripe just laughed. He caught a flying cup out of the air, took a fake sip, and tossed it back into the dark sea of angry faces.

He danced his way to the steps of the octagon. He did not just walk into the cage. He owned it. The heat inside the octagon was oppressive. The television lights suspended high above the canvas were blinding. They baked the air until it tasted stale and metallic. Stripe rolled his shoulders and handed his silk robe to his head coach. He bounced on the balls of his feet. The canvas was rough and familiar. It smelled of bleached fabric, dried sweat, and the faint, iron-tang of old blood.

Across the cage stood his opponent. The man was a local hero. He was a massive, hulking heavyweight carved out of granite. He carried himself with a cocky swagger. The Russian treated his own confidence like an impenetrable suit of armor. He glared at Stripe from across the canvas with pure, unfiltered hatred. The crowd loved their fighter. They despised Stripe. Being a foreign fighter came with many disadvantages, but Stripe loved being the underdog.

Stripe smiled broadly around his custom gold mouthpiece. He stuck his tongue out at the massive Russian. The crowd booed louder. Stripe pointed a taped finger directly at the man and mimed sleep. He rested his hands against his cheek and closed his eyes.

The referee called them to the center of the cage. "You know the rules," the referee said firmly. "Protect yourself at all times. Touch gloves."

The Russian slammed his gloves forward. Stripe did not lift his hands. He just maintained his grin and winked. The referee sighed and sent them back to their corners.

The bell rang. The Russian charged forward like a runaway freight train. He wanted to take Stripe's head off in the first ten seconds. He threw a massive, looping right hook designed to end careers. Stripe did not panic. He did not flinch. He was a savant of violence. His arrogance vanished at the bell, replaced by cold, mechanical calculation. He saw the punch coming a mile away. The Russian telegraphed the strike by dropping his left shoulder a fraction of an inch.

Stripe slipped to the right. He moved his head just enough to let the heavy leather glove breeze past his ear. The rush of air from the missed punch ruffled his hair. The Russian was overextended. His balance was compromised. He had committed to a strike that hit nothing but empty air.

Stripe punished him for the mistake. It was raw mechanics. Physics in motion. Stripe planted his back foot hard into the canvas. He generated power from the floor. The kinetic energy traveled up through his calf, rotated through his hips, and snapped his shoulder forward. He drilled this counter for months after reviewing footage of the fighter.

He threw a devastating overhand right. The punch crashed flush into the Russian's exposed jaw. The sound was a sharp, wet crack that echoed over the roaring crowd. But Stripe was not finished. He never left the outcome to the judges. Before the Russian could begin to register the trauma of the first strike, Stripe shifted his weight. He dropped his left shoulder and drove a brutal left uppercut directly under the Russian's chin.

It was the exact combination he had drilled ten thousand times in the gym. It was a rhythm his body executed before his conscious mind processed the command. The connection was absolute. The Russian's eyes rolled back into his head. He folded. It looked like someone had cut the strings on a giant marionette. The massive man crashed face-first into the mat and did not move.

The fight had lasted fourteen seconds. The hostile arena plunged into shocked silence. Eighty thousand people stopped breathing. Then the explosion happened. The crowd erupted into absolute bedlam. Half of them cheered the spectacle. The other half screamed in outrage.

Stripe did not glance down at the unconscious man at his feet. He turned away before the referee waved off the fight. He leaped up onto the top of the chain link fence. He balanced effortlessly on the narrow metal rail. He looked directly into the front row. His wife was there, the love of his life. She was standing on her chair. She was laughing. Her hands covered her mouth, but her eyes were bright. She looked at him with the absolute conviction that nothing bad could ever happen to them as long as he kept winning. She was dressed in an elegant black gown that cost more than the venue rental. But she did not care about the clothes or the cameras. She only cared about him.

Stripe looked at her and felt the adrenaline wash away. She was his world. She was the only person on the planet who kept his massive ego anchored to reality. He loved her with a terrifying sincerity. He pointed a gloved finger directly at her and mouthed the words 'I love you' over the noise of the rioting stadium.

She smiled back and placed a single, delicate hand over her stomach. It was their private secret. She was pregnant with their first child. The thought of it filled Stripe with a protective warmth that rivaled the heat of the arena lights. He was going to be a father. He was going to give his child the world on a silver platter.

The medical staff swarmed the cage to tend to the fallen Russian. The referee grabbed Stripe's wrist and raised it high into the air. The announcer screamed his name. Stripe soaked it all in for a few more minutes. He was the king of the world. During the post-fight interview, he brought his wife on stage and had her put his shiny new title around his waist. This was one of the best moments of his life. But unfortunately, this very moment would lead to his worst. If only he hadn't brought her to the country or on stage.

Later, the hallway outside the locker room was a chaotic frenzy. Flashing cameras blinded him every time he blinked. A massive swarm of press and reporters shoved their microphones toward his face. Security guards yelled and pushed people back, trying to create a narrow walking path for the champion. Reporters shouted questions from every direction.

"Stripe! Did you expect a first-round knockout?"

"Stripe! Are you going to move up a weight class next?"

"Stripe! What do you have to say to the Russian fans?"

Stripe bounced on the balls of his feet, his eyes constantly darting over the shoulders of the press pool.

"Yeah, sure," he muttered to a reporter, barely registering the question. He offered one-word answers, his gaze scanning the chaotic hallway for the only face in the arena he actually cared to see.

She pushed her way through the thick wall of security detail. The massive guards stepped aside for her. They knew better than to block the champion's wife. She grabbed his face with both hands. She pulled him down and kissed him hard right on the mouth. The taste of her cherry lip gloss mixed with the faint taste of Vaseline and sweat on his own face. She pulled back and looked at him. Her eyes were sparkling with mischief.

"You looked ridiculous with one glove still on," she laughed. "Still, you did a good job during the interview."

Stripe smiled. He looked down at his hands. His team had removed his right glove, but the left one was still strapped tightly around his wrist. He was disarmed by her. He could knock out a heavyweight contender in fourteen seconds, but she could reduce him to a smiling idiot with a single sentence.

"I was in a hurry to get back to you," Stripe said, wrapping his good arm around her. "Reporters never give me a chance to breathe after a good night's sleep."

"Yeah, yeah. I can tell you're full of shit, but I will give you a free pass. Flattery will get you everywhere," she teased.

He kissed her forehead and disappeared into the locker room. Hours later, the atmosphere shifted. The sterile smell of the locker room and the metallic heat of the arena were gone. They were replaced by the suffocating, neon-drenched air of a highly exclusive Moscow VIP club. He was contractually obligated to attend certain events after a win. He loved these club visits. Free drinks and fan interactions.

The sensory shift was jarring. The club was located deep underground. The walls were lined with dark velvet and polished mirrors. The bass of the electronic music was so heavy that it rattled the crystal vodka glasses sitting on their private table. Strobing purple and red lights sliced through the thick fog machine smoke hanging in the air.

Stripe sat in a curved leather booth. He was draped in a tailored designer suit that hugged his athletic frame perfectly. He wore a massive diamond watch on his left wrist that caught the strobe lights and refracted them across the room. He was celebrating his title defense. He felt on top of the world. His outfit and accessories alone could be sold for enough to retire the average American.

His wife sat pressed against his side. She sipped sparkling water with lime. She leaned her head against his shoulder. He kept his arm wrapped securely around her waist. He felt untouchable. He was young. He was filthy rich. He was the most dangerous unarmed man walking the face of the earth. In a straight-up fight, he was confident no man in the world could touch him. Back in the USA, the only reason he had security was that gun violence was so high. He can't punch a bullet.

Then the perfect illusion shattered into a million jagged pieces.

Nikolai stumbled towards their section. The kid was a local thug. He was maybe twenty-two years old. He was dripping in Russian oligarch money and untouchable entitlement. He wore a silk shirt unbuttoned to his chest, exposing a thick gold chain. He was intoxicated. He carried a bottle of expensive champagne in one hand and a lit cigar in the other. His whole life had been wealth and power provided by Daddy's money. The worst kind of entitled.

He did not care about the velvet ropes. He did not care about the security guards standing near Stripe's table. Nikolai believed the entire city of Moscow belonged to his father, which meant it belonged to him. It was obvious to everyone around him that he had never been punched in the face. He pushed his way through the crowded VIP section. He lost his balance. He stumbled forward and bumped hard into Stripe's wife.

The impact knocked her shoulder backward. Nikolai's champagne sloshed over the rim of his bottle. The sticky alcohol spilled down the front of her elegant black dress. Stripe stood. The temper that fueled his fighting career flared. He expected the man in front of him to apologize. He was not expecting the man to double down.

Instead, Nikolai stood up straight. The young little shit did not look sorry. He sneered. He looked down at the spilled champagne on her dress. Then his gaze lingered. The look in his eyes as he stared at Stripe's wife was an insult in itself. Nikolai took a slow drag from his cigar. He blew the thick gray smoke directly into her face. He smirked. He spat out a filthy, degrading comment in heavily accented English. Stripe didn't know what he was saying, but he could tell by the tone that it was an insult.

The blood froze in Stripe's veins. The noise of the club seemed to vanish. His veins pulsed, and his fist tightened. His wife reached out. Her delicate fingers brushed against the sleeve of his suit jacket. She knew the look in his eyes. She knew the monster that lived just beneath his arrogant surface.

"Baby, please leave it," she pleaded softly. "He is drunk. He is not worth it. Let us just go back to the hotel."

But his temper was already ignited. The arrogance that served him so well inside the locked cage took complete control of his mind. He was the champion. Nobody disrespected him. Nobody spoke to his pregnant wife that way and walked away breathing normally. He stepped out from behind the leather booth.

Nikolai puffed his chest out. He thought his father's money protected him from everything. He did not realize he was standing in front of a man who broke bones for a living.

"You have a problem, Bitch?" Nikolai sneered. "Do you know who my dad is? He owns this country, and I own this club. You'd better sit down before you end up in a box."

Stripe did not answer him. He didn't need to. He had already decided what would happen next.

The strike was a masterpiece of raw mechanics. It was identical to the punch that ended the fight earlier that night. Stripe twisted his hips. He threw a straight right. He threw it harder than he would in the cage. He didn't need to conserve his energy. So he let it all out in a violent strike.

To Stripe, the punch traveled in cinematic slow motion. He watched the heavy gold chain swing around Nikolai's neck. He watched the glowing cherry of the cigar fall from the kid's fingers. He watched Nikolai's smug, punchable face twist when the inevitable impact approached. The fear in his eyes was easy to see. But there was no escape. Stripe did not hold back. He threw the punch with every ounce of malice and hatred he possessed. He aimed to destroy the target in front of him.

The physical connection was a work of art. Beautiful and horrifying. The heavy, thumping bass of the club music could not drown out the sound. It was a sharp, wet, echoing crack of bone shattering into several small pieces. Stripe's dense knuckles crushed Nikolai's jawbone. The force of the impact snapped the kid's head to the side. The skin tore. Teeth flew out of his mouth and scattered across the polished dance floor.

Nikolai crumpled. His legs gave out. He fell to the floor in a loose heap of designer silk. His head bounced off the expensive tile with a dull thud. A pool of dark crimson blood began spreading across the floor from his shattered mouth. His arms rose to his neck like a kid pretending to be a dinosaur. A small puddle of liquid appeared under his body, and the area smelt faintly of piss. Stripe folded Nikolai's clothes neatly. The issue was that Nikolai was still in them.

The VIP section plunged into a terrified, breathless silence. The strobing lights continued to flash. The electronic music kept pulsing loudly. But no one moved. The wealthy patrons stared in pure horror at the broken body bleeding out on the tiles.

Stripe stood over the oligarch's son. His right hand was throbbing. He adjusted the cuffs of his tailored suit jacket. He felt justified. A big part of him felt satisfied, almost as if he had done the world a service. Men in black suits rushed in, pushing Stripe off the kid. Stripe's manager grabbed him and was attempting to escort him out of the club. He was unaware of the severe nature of what had just taken place.

CHAPTER 6

CROWN — "Reflection complete. Host muscle memory has now integrated into the host's new body. Expect less awkwardness in your movements and more efficiency in your combat."

Stripe felt his body responding better to his movements. But it did not help him in the situation he faced. The jolt back to reality felt like it hurt him more than it helped. He could tell he should have put more thought into his choice of ability.

The bandits rushed into the clearing, angry and uncoordinated. They saw the wolves, and the wolves saw movement. The first wolf lunged, slamming into a bandit and tearing him down before the others could react. Teeth sank into his throat. The scream ended in a wet, choking sound. The giant, muscular wolf swallowed his throat. It happened so fast that the rest of the bandits didn't have a chance to save their friend.

"Jeffery, no! You fucking monsters!" the Bandit Leader screamed. Tears formed in his eyes. His voice screeched with pure, unfiltered rage.

Another bandit swung his blade, catching fur but failing to cut deep enough. The wolf twisted and tore into his thigh, dragging him off balance. The second wolf leaped onto a different man, knocking him backward and shredding his forearm before ripping into his neck.

The wolves' ruthless, brutal nature made the bandits shake with horror. They expected an easy human target, not a group of hunters. Chaos swallowed the clearing. There was no teamwork and no structure. Men shouted over each other in a panic. The wolves circled them, attempting to lure them into attacks and ruin their footing.

"Hold it!" one bandit yelled. Fear echoed in his voice.

"Move!" shouted another.

They were Level 5 bandits trying to contain two Level 8 predators in close quarters. Steel hit bone, and claws tore flesh. The bandits began dealing enough tick damage through the wolves' hard fur to slow the beasts' response time. The wolves encircled the bandits with an intelligence that only pack hunters show. Spit fell from their mouths, and the blood of the bandits soaked their fur. One wolf stepped forward to bait and attack, while the next attacked from behind, and the bandit recovered. This teamwork showed the wolves were experienced in killing human prey. This strategy worked well on the panicked bandits.

The first bandit fell when one of the wolves bit down on the base of his skull. This disrupted the formation of the remaining bandits. They were dropping fast. Had they gone on an all-out offense with the full team, they might not have suffered any casualties. A bandit stepped forward, swinging his sword as hard as he could. But the wolf had already moved. He got caught overextending to swipe at the wolf in front of him. His arm was caught by the second wolf, and he was dragged to the ground, screaming in pain. The wolf ripped his arm off, and the man went silent. His skull was grabbed by the other wolf, who proceeded to snap his neck in one quick jerk.

However, the bandits were brutal. They saw their chance at their ally's expense. The moment the wolf held him down and snapped his skull, the other bandits swung, killing one of the wolves. It attempted to scramble back when it saw the incoming attack, but it lacked the speed to do so. One bandit caught its front leg, disrupting its movement when the blade made contact. The second bandit stabbed forward with his spear in a flurry. The third man was stabbed from the side. The bandits figured out that stabbing worked better than slashing. The first wolf died under repeated stabs, but not before taking two men with it. Blood soaked into the ground from the dead wolf and his bandit prey.

As the spear tore into its flesh, its ally pounced on the spearman. It bit into his skull, causing his head to collapse. The man died mid-scream. Even full of holes, it managed to wrap its jaws around one of the attacking bandits' throats and tear it open. As it bled to death from its wounds, the bandit's throat fell from its mouth. The bandits and the wolves reached a stalemate. Two wolves had decimated the bandit group, leaving only one wolf and the bandit leader behind.

The second wolf lunged for the leader as he stepped into the attack. His great sword drove deep into the beast's ribcage, but claws raked across his wounded side, tearing open flesh that had already been bleeding. He killed it. The last wolf had just finished off the only other ally he had on the field. Stripe didn't get a good look at the exchange, but it appeared the man lost his arm. If he had to guess, the man missed an attack and was punished for it.

The bandit leader drew back his blade, ready to attack. The wolf was exhausted from the previous bout of combat. It jumped forward in a decisive strike but was knocked back by the giant blade. He followed up with a horizontal swing, and the wolf ducked under and bit his calf. Bloodshot out onto the floor; he was bleeding in intense amounts from the wound. He brought his blade back, slicing the wolf in half as it jumped back to gain distance.

When the dust settled, the clearing went quiet. Only labored breathing remained. Bodies were everywhere: bandits and wolves alike. Blood soaked the dirt. Stripe stayed frozen in the tree. He had not contributed, but he had survived. The leader wiped blood from his mouth and lifted his head. His eyes scanned the trees until they found Stripe.

"I know you're up there," the Bandit Leader snarled. "I can smell you."

The bandit screamed, his voice exhausted. Bloodshot from his thigh. The wolf had struck an artery in its final attack. Stripe did not move. The leader took a step forward and almost collapsed, catching himself on his sword.

"You think hiding makes you strong," the Bandit Leader said. His voice was angry and desperate.

"He cannot see me if I do not move," Stripe whispered. "It is like a dinosaur."

Stripe tightened his grip on the tree.

CROWN — "Incorrect."

The leader's voice shook, but not from fear. "Jeffery was leaving this life." He coughed, and blood spattered the dirt. "He had a place lined up. An orphanage. He wanted to help kids. I dragged him back to keep us from becoming evil. Now he's dead."

Every word came out labored and sincere. Stripe shifted on the branch, adjusting his footing. The bark cracked beneath his boot. Above him, something shifted. A coconut wedged between branches rolled loose. Stripe noticed it the moment it tipped forward, but it was too late to stop. It dropped past his shoulder. The large coconut fell fast and hard.

"Because of you, his wife and kids won..." the Bandit Leader started.

The bandit leader looked up too late. He didn't even have the chance to raise his arms in defense. CRACK. The sound was loud and fierce. The kind of thudding sound you hear as a sound effect in a cartoon. The coconut struck him square on the head. The leader stiffened, his grip loosened, and his eyes unfocused mid-breath. Then he collapsed face-first into the dirt without finishing his threat.

Stripe stared down in silence.

CROWN — "Damage estimated at one point. Threat deceased. Experience awarded. Partial credit: Wolf engagement. Environmental contribution credited."

Stripe blinked. He was the last man standing. In a world full of monsters, that is how victory was determined.

CROWN — "Multiple level-ups detected. Additional experience applied. Level 5 achieved."

Stripe stayed in the tree longer than necessary. His legs did not feel reliable yet.

CROWN — "No immediate threats detected."

Stripe exhaled. His muscles lost their tension, and he felt the exhaustion of running kick in.

"That is reassuring in a way that somehow isn't reassuring," Stripe said.

He climbed down, boots slipping against the bark. He landed in the clearing and almost slid in blood, catching himself against the tree. Bodies surrounded him: bandits tangled with wolves, armor torn open, fur matted with blood. The metallic smell hung thick in the air. Chunks of flesh and bone smeared into the ground. These were once living people, and now they were nothing but mush on the floor of a quiet forest.

Stripe walked toward the bandit leader first. Up close, the man looked different, less terrifying and more human. Stripe nudged him with his boot. Nothing.

"Damn, that is brutal," Stripe muttered. "Worse than how I went out."

His disgust showed in his voice. He turned his head and covered his eyes for a moment. He needed to gather himself. This was a brutal sight. He looked around the clearing again.

"Of all the ways," he said. "A coconut." A slight chuckle laced his voice.

CROWN — "Blunt force trauma to compromised cranial structure sufficient for termination."

Stripe sighed. "You could just say, yeah." Annoyance radiated as he spoke.

He crouched and opened the leader's belt pouch. Inside were several small metal discs, dull silver gray and heavy. Stripe rolled one between his fingers.

"What is this?" Stripe asked.

CROWN — "Currency for this world."

Stripe acquired a pouch for carrying the currency. He took it and attached it to the bandit's belt, then wrapped it around himself. It was the only piece of clothing that fit him. Then he took the leader's dagger, a simple, balanced steel. He tried lifting the greatsword, but it wobbled in his grip. Stripe dropped it.

"Yeah, no. That is a two-hands and a life insurance policy situation," Stripe said.

CROWN — "Strength insufficient for optimal wielding."

Stripe snorted. "You are just waiting to say that, aren't you?"

CROWN — "Negative. I do not wait."

Stripe moved to the other bodies, finding coin pouches, a ring, and a strip of dried meat wrapped in cloth. He avoided looking at Jeffery. The dried vomit streaked across the man's armor made something twist in his chest.

"I did not know about the orphanage," Stripe murmured.

CROWN — "Information unavailable at time of action."

Stripe stood. The clearing went quiet again as the wind moved through the leaves. Somewhere far away, a bird resumed calling. Stripe turned. Through the thinned trees, he saw something distant: stone rising white and gray above the forest. Towers, spikes, and a central keep. Stripe squinted.

"That is not a little village," he said.

CROWN — "City detected."

Stripe stared. The silhouette of hope shone in the distance. Staying in the woods was out of the question. He had no clue how he would survive another run-in with these wolves or bandits.

"That is a castle. Never thought I would see a real one."

CROWN — "Correct, the architecture indicates royalty of some standard."

Stripe threw on the bandit armor and took what he could carry. Then he started walking.

"Alright," Stripe said. "Let's get this out of the way."

He looked toward the distant towers. Before he decided to depart, he rummaged through the bodies of the bandits. They did not have much, but there were a few coins and other miscellaneous things. He put on the bandit ring. It was an ugly ring that reminded him of what a pimp would wear. There was a giant gemstone in the center that glowed in the light. But bling is bling.

[SYSTEM ALERT: Level 5 Reached | 4 Stat Points Available | Inventory: Bandit Ring added]

CHAPTER 7

The forest surrendered in degrees. The trees spaced themselves farther apart, letting sunlight hit the ground. The dirt path beneath Stripe's boots grew wider and deliberate. Wagon ruts hardened into the soil in parallel grooves, and hoofprints overlapped in dense clusters. People used this road enough to give it a confident direction.

Through the thinning canopy, the city revealed itself. The outer wall rose in pale, well-kept stone; the blocks aligned without gaps, the mortar pristine, and guard towers stood at measured intervals. Beyond the wall, the rooftops are layered over one another in uneven heights. At the center, a keep rose above everything else with vertical certainty. Stripe slowed, his feet shifting to a casual stance as he took in the scene.

"This place is gigantic. Not big like the cities back home, but big in a different way."

CROWN — "Urban density population is likely high."

"You don't have to turn it into a report. I can see that it's crowded." Stripe scanned the architecture. "Crown, I have a question. How do people here use the bathroom? Is there any plumbing?"

CROWN — "Unlikely. Observational data suggests historical methods. Visual evidence shows a combination of excrement in the streets and magical incineration."

"Like shitting in a hole or a bucket then tossing it out back? Is there a job assigned to someone to use magic to delete shit?"

CROWN — "Correct. Occupation is likely the correct assumption."

Stripe scrunched his nose, looking like a man who had just spewed his own business on a bush. As he approached the gate, the sounds of the city washed over him: merchants arguing, cart wheels creaking under heavy loads, and the ring of a hammer striking metal deeper inside the walls. A shimmer of magic flickered above a lantern as someone adjusted it with a minor spell. The air felt thick with activity.

Stripe looked down at himself. He wore a wolf pelt and ill-fitting leather chest armor. His bare arms carried fresh scratches from the forest, making his boots look like the most legitimate part of his outfit. A dagger sat at his hip that had not been his yesterday. He exhaled. He was better dressed than when he spawned in, but his appearance carried a new threat. He didn't look stronger; he looked desperate and crazy. Stripe smirked.

"We look professional."

CROWN — "Probability of suspicion remains high."

"To be fair, the only other people I have seen looked just like this."

CROWN — "Host observational data is accurate."

Two guards at the gate noticed him long before he reached speaking distance. Their posture shifted: weight settling, hands drifting closer to weapons, eyes narrowing. Stripe stopped several paces short of the gate to avoid looking like a threat. One guard studied him, his gaze raking up and down Stripe's body. The longer he stared, the deeper his scowl became. The first guard raised his chin.

"State your business, bandit."

Stripe lifted one hand. "Window shopping and possibly a shower."

CROWN — "Bodily cleansing is recommended. Host is unlikely to achieve platonic bonding with current odor levels."

The second guard gave him a flat look. Unlike the first guard, this one wore an unreadable mask. He was larger, older. With just a glance, Stripe pegged him as a veteran. If he needed someone to guard a perimeter, this was the man he would hire.

"That's not how this works." The second guard's voice carried absolute authority.

A breeze shifted, carrying Stripe's scent. It was a cocktail of uncured wolf hide, dried sweat, old blood, and the unmistakable stench of feces. The first guard leaned back. The first guard pinched his nose.

"Have you ever even bathed?"

The smell was so bad it felt visible. Imagine a sweltering day when the heat dances over the pavement, the haze a greenish-brown you can taste. Stripe sniffed his armpit in protest.

"It's not that bad."

CROWN — "It is that bad."

The Crown's voice lacked its usual robotic cadence. It was gentle, carrying a soft inflection. Stripe flinched as the voice landed wrong. The tone had changed. For half a second, it sounded almost human, possessing a softer inflection on the word bad. Stripe frowned.

"You sounded almost human there."

Then static tore through his skull. The sensation was sharp and invasive, like metal scraping inside his thoughts.

CROWN — "Error detected. Recalibrating sensory interface."

The world is distorted. The edges of Stripe's vision warped. Sound compressed. The second guard stepped forward, hand gripping his weapon. He did not know this bandit, but he would not allow a scene at his gate. The logical conclusion was to remove Stripe from the equation. The second guard drew his blade an inch.

"What's wrong with him?"

Stripe tried to answer, but his balance vanished. His knees gave out. Stone rushed upward, and darkness swallowed everything. This felt different than a Crown-forced reflection. Pure blackness surrounded him. It was a true void. Within that absence, a faint shape hovered just outside the center of his perception. Feminine. Indistinct. Familiar. He tried to turn toward it, but the moment snapped.

Cold stone scraped his shoulder blades. Stripe blinked. Two guards dragged him by the ankles through the gate. Stripe let out a groan.

"I didn't know they offered transportation at the gate. I think I have it from here, boys."

The first guard kept pulling. "You fainted, and you're wearing bandit clothing. That ring has the mark of the bandit king. Clothing seen harassing the forest routes."

Noise flooded back in. Fabric banners snapped in the wind. Traders shouted prices. Children ran past with wooden swords. Stripe turned his head as they dragged him. Near the inner wall, a beggar sat against the stone in patched clothing. He held a still posture, the kind Stripe recognized as belonging to someone who expected no interruption. Their eyes met. Recognition passed between two men who had slept on stone.

The man's eyes scanned the dirt on Stripe's body. He reached into his pouch and tossed a copper coin. It bounced off Stripe's chest and landed in his lap.

"Some people got it worse than me."

The pity in the homeless man's eyes was apparent. That annoyed Stripe more than being arrested for nothing. Stripe looked at the coin. He had silver in his pocket, but he did not know what it would buy. He did not know if it was enough for food or trouble. Money had once been abstract numbers managed by accountants, then loose change under bridges. Now it was metal disks in a forest world, where a beggar took pity on him. Stripe let his head fall back against the stone.

"From riches to rags again. I deserve this."

The guards dragged him toward a stone building inside the gate. Iron bars sat visible through the doorway. The door carried scratches suggesting it closed often and hard. The metal was thick and rusted. Stripe had been arrested in his past life, but had never seen metal bars this thick.

"Interrogation first." The second guard pointed toward a side room.

The Crown spoke again, its tone returned to normal.

CROWN — "System stability restored."

Stripe closed his eyes. *Welcome back. How was your nap?* **CROWN** — "Sleep is not equivalent to system restart."

The guard lifted his hand. Blue light gathered in his palm, then released. Water slammed into Stripe like a thrown river. The freezing blast washed dirt, sweat, and blood across the stone floor. Stripe gasped. The man sprayed him at full force, hitting every inch. Stripe rotated to endure the assault. Stripe shook the water from his hair.

"Holy shit, that water is cold."

The second guard pointed deeper into the room. "Step forward." Stripe moved. The guard pointed at the ground. "Squat and cough."

Stripe hesitated, then complied. The stone floor felt colder without the grime insulating him. He coughed. The guard leaned in to inspect. Stripe coughed again.

"The water's cold. I promise I'm not normally like this."

CROWN — "Deception detected."

Stripe closed his eyes. The guard chuckled. The second guard tossed him a towel.

"At least you smell better now."

CROWN — "No deception detected."

Stripe stood. "I'm surrounded by comedians."

A rough tunic hit his chest. He pulled it on. The guard marched him down a narrow corridor lined with iron-bar doors. Empty cells sat alongside cages filled with figures who did not bother standing. Reaching the last cell, the guard unlocked it and shoved Stripe inside. The door slammed shut with a metallic echo.

The cell was larger than expected, but held no comfort. Stone walls, scattered straw, and lingering sweat. A dozen prisoners looked up. Not all of them were human. An orc stood near the far wall with arms crossed, broad shoulders brushing the stone. Closer to the center sat a massive aquatic creature with a humanoid torso; it reminded Stripe of a heavyweight fighter covered in scales. Its skin held a sheen in the dry air. Its eyes were wide and flat, devoid of humanity, looking through people rather than at them. Near the corner sat a thin man with narrow teeth and restless hands. He smiled, revealing teeth sharp like a canine's.

Silence stretched in the cell. Stripe leaned against the wall. The orc lifted his brows.

"What brings you in?"

The orc was the largest man Stripe had ever seen, assuming the fish creature did not count. Tribal tattoos ran down the orc's face. His arms were massive, bearing heavy calluses from swinging something substantial. Stripe shrugged.

"The guards, duh."

The thin man snorted. The orc's scowl deepened.

"That's not what I meant."

Stripe scratched his jaw. "Wrong place. Wrong smell. I was profiled for how I looked, and now I'm in here." The orc studied him. "What are you, some kind of bandit?"

"That feels accurate given the circumstances." Stripe nodded toward the aquatic creature. "What's his story?"

"That's Oblong." The orc gestured with his chin. "He ate the heads of two men in a tavern after losing a dice game."

Stripe stared. Oblong tilted his head, eyes unfocused.

"That feels extreme for gambling."

"Yeah, considering there was no money on the line."

CROWN — "Subject displays limited cognitive engagement."

Stripe inched away from Oblong. "Stop talking."

The orc frowned. "You asked the fucking question."

Stripe tapped his temple. "Not you, the voice in my head."

The thin man let out a high-pitched snicker. "At least yours talks. Mine just laughs."

Stripe exhaled a long breath. "That's not comforting either."

Footsteps echoed down the corridor. Keys rattled. The cell door unlocked, and a guard pointed at Stripe.

"Interrogation."

Stripe pushed off the wall. As he stepped toward the door, Oblong's wide eyes followed him. Unblinking. Watching.

[SYSTEM ALERT: Level 5 Reached | 4 Stat Points Available | Inventory: Bandit Ring added]

Chapter 8

"Interrogation." The guard pointed at Stripe and waved him up.

Stripe pushed off the wall. Oblong's wide, dead eyes tracked his movement without blinking. There was no logic or reason behind the creature's gaze. The metal door slammed shut. The robed man stood across the table, candlelight flickering between them. His hands rested together as he studied Stripe.

Across from him sat a man in red robes. He had a long white beard and a wrinkly, covered face—the type of face you saw on veterans from the World Wars. A large burn mark covered his right side, looking as if someone had stabbed him with a hot iron. His body was thin, but the heavy robe swallowed up any other details. Stripe scanned the dark room. He could see the silhouette of large objects behind him. The air smelled of iron and rot. He might not be the smartest, but he could tell this room meant trouble.

CROWN — "Visual indicator clues suggest this room is likely for torture."

The robed man snapped his fingers. Candles along the stone walls flared to life, illuminating old bloodstains. Chains bolted into the ground bore weird carvings. A podium held an assortment of knives and pliers. One of the most disturbing items appeared to be a dildo with large spikes on it.

The Robed Man's eyes locked onto Stripe. "You are accused of banditry, public harassment by means of smell."

"That seems unfair." Stripe's voice cracked mid-sentence. "I didn't smell that bad. Also, I got this outfit from bandits. I am not a bandit. I didn't mean to poison the water either. It's all bad luck."

The Robed Man's tone carried no disbelief, only the cadence of someone taking notes. "Are you saying you killed armed bandits, took their belongings, wore their armor, and then walked to the city gate?"

Stripe shifted in the chair. The last room like this he sat in was AA. It was court-ordered, and he did not take it seriously. Stripe let out a dry laugh.

"I technically killed them."

CROWN — "False. The contribution was minimal. Environmental hazards killed the bandits."

Stripe grimaced. "Right. Technically, I only killed one. The rest just happened. I think the term is environmental hazard." He raised a finger to clarify his remark.

The robed man did not react, but his posture stiffened. Thick neck muscles bulged against his collar. The old man was ripped under that robe. The Robed Man tapped a finger on the table.

"Environmental hazards?"

Stripe nodded. "Some dogs and a coconut did the killing." He was positive the man understood him now.

"A coconut?"

Stripe did not elaborate. He wasn't sure how. Maybe they didn't even call them coconuts here. The Robed Man's posture shifted into something hostile.

"Hard to believe you had nothing better to wear than crude bandit armor while carrying blood-soaked silver."

Stripe shrugged. "I was technically naked before the bandit encounter. Look, I don't have the answers to the questions you are asking."

The word hung in the air. *Technically.* The robed man's eyes narrowed. He stepped forward. Slow. Deliberate. Annoyed. He picked up a pair of metal pliers from the table. The metal was pitted and dark with dried blood from previous interrogations. It smelled of rust and infected wounds. The Robed Man paced the room, his annoyance bleeding through his rigid posture.

"You rely on that word."

Stripe forced a half-smile and leaned back in the chair. "It's accurate."

The old man lunged forward with terrifying speed. He seized Stripe's hand, slamming it against the arm of the chair before Stripe could react. The pliers closed around the edge of Stripe's fingernail, and Stripe's muscles locked up. The cold, jagged teeth dug into his cuticle. He attempted to break the old man's grip but was no match for the pure strength restraining him.

CROWN — "Warning. Severe structural damage to digital extremities is imminent."

Stripe fought against the grip. "Whoa, whoa, whoa, chill out! I haven't lied. Don't I have rights? I want a lawyer!"

The pliers pulled. Pain exploded through Stripe's hand. White heat shot up his arm and into his skull. His breath vanished, and his body jerked against the chair. The nail tore free. Blood welled from the exposed nail bed. Stripe sucked air through his teeth. His vision blurred.

The agony clawed up his forearm and wrapped around his chest. He was used to taking hits to the jaw, but this was a slow, calculated destruction his fighter's brain did not know how to block. His finger throbbed with every heartbeat.

"That's fucked up," Stripe gasped. "I have rights, I think."

Every instinct told him to curl inward, but he forced himself still. He knew if he moved too fast, he would lose another nail. The Robed Man slammed his fist on the table.

"State your affiliation."

Stripe's pulse hammered in his ears. He swallowed, breathing hard. "Like a gang? What the fuck?" Stripe choked out.

Stripe was beginning to panic. He did not know what to say or do. He was tossed into this world with almost no explanation, and now he was being tortured for self-defense. The pliers clamped down on another nail. Stripe scrambled for the highest authority he could remember and tossed out a name.

"I belong to the church of the goddess Astraeia!" Stripe yelled.

The robed figure froze. The air changed as the candle flame wavered, then steadied. The Robed Figure stepped back.

"Affiliation will be confirmed."

His grip loosened. The pliers slipped from the nail. The figure snapped his fingers, and every candle in the room went dark. Darkness swallowed the chamber. Guards entered, grabbing Stripe's shoulders to haul him upright. Blood dripped from his ruined fingernail as they dragged him into the corridor.

Stripe said nothing, but the thought stayed with him. The Crown had not commented. Not once after his nail was ripped off. He expected it to note damage or suggest an optimal method of communication, but instead, it remained quiet. It was a dead, suffocating silence. He had just stumbled onto a massive cheat code by dropping that name, but the artifact going mute terrified him more than the pliers. Was it scared? Was it locked out by the magic of the room? He tried to mentally poke it, but felt nothing in return.

They shoved him back toward the cells. The door opened, and Stripe stumbled inside. The door slammed shut. Oblong's wide, dull eyes fixed on him. The orc noticed the blood. The orc leaned forward, probing for information.

"What did you say?"

Stripe flexed his injured fingers. The exposed nail bed throbbed with every heartbeat.

"Technically the truth," Stripe muttered.

The Thin Man cackled, his voice unnaturally high-pitched, almost mechanical. "That's hilarious. You're a funny guy."

Stripe leaned back against the wall. Beside him, an old man's breathing rasped directly in his ear. Another man sat on the opposite side of him. It was the first dark-skinned person he had seen in this world.

"It's been a long week," Stripe sighed. He closed his eyes, hoping the pain would stop.

CROWN — "Incorrect. It has been less than a day."

Stripe stared at the floor. "That feels wrong."

His body ached worse than any training camp he had ever attended. The thin man reached out to grab Stripe's wounded hand. Stripe pulled away. The man was covered in grime and brown stains. The Thin Man flashed a grin.

"Just a nail? Lucky."

The orc crossed his arms, his gaze shifting toward Oblong. The creature sat against the far wall, watching; it never blinked, trapped in a trance. The cell settled into uneasy silence. Stripe's hand continued to bleed. He kept flexing his fingers, trying to convince the nerves to calm down. The silence in the cell grew heavy. A sickening smell of rotting swamp water drifted from the aquatic creature. The tension thickened. The hairs on Stripe's arms stood up. Something was wrong with the rhythm of the room.

Oblong moved. Stripe barely registered the motion before the creature lunged. Its massive aquatic body surged across the stone floor, wet scales scraping against the ground. Its wide eyes locked onto Stripe's face: vacant and hungry. Stripe reacted on instinct, shoving sideways. His shoulder slammed into another prisoner, sending the older man stumbling into Oblong's path.

Oblong's mouth opened far wider than Stripe expected, its jaw flexing before it snapped shut.

Chapter 9

Oblong's mouth opened wider than Stripe expected. The jaw flexed, unhinging before it snapped shut around the older man's head. The old man punched the creature's neck. His screams died in the wet cavern of the beast's mouth. He kicked and scratched, but nothing worked. A heavy crack echoed through the cell, sounding like thick wood splitting. The man's body jerked. His arms flailed for a balance that was already gone. Then the head was gone. Not bitten halfway or torn to pieces. It vanished in one grotesque bite, as if Oblong's mouth existed for that single purpose.

Blood burst in a hot spray, splashing across Stripe's tunic and cheek. The headless body collapsed, twitching on the cold stone. Oblong chewed, its jaw working with dull patience. Stripe watched the outline of the swallowed skull shift in Oblong's throat before it disappeared. Oblong swallowed. Its throat expanded as the head traveled down the creature's neck. It leaned forward again, assessing the remaining corpse. Instead, it settled back onto its haunches with the calm satisfaction of a fed animal.

The cell erupted in sound. Someone shouted, another pointed, and a prisoner scrambled backward, slipping on the fresh blood pooling on the floor. Stripe stood frozen, breath flaring through his nostrils. The thick, metallic smell of copper hit him, mixing with the stagnant swamp-water stench radiating from the beast. Cold dread washed over him. He was locked inside a cage with an apex predator. The only sounds were wet drops of blood hitting the stone and the sickening crunch of Oblong chewing.

CROWN — "Partial kill credit awarded. Experience gained."

Stripe blinked. He hadn't realized he had pushed the man. "You are kidding."

CROWN — "Negative."

The orc exhaled, his jaw tight. He squeezed his fist, but did not leave his seat. "Stay away from him, he bites." The orc pointed at the giant fish.

Blood dripped down the creature's face. Stripe wiped the blood off his cheek with the back of his hand and stared at the headless corpse. The body twitched on the ground, unaware it was dead.

"Yeah. I got the memo." Stripe masked his shock. "Won't the guards come take that fish fucker out of here now?"

The orc let out a harsh laugh. "No. He saves them money by eliminating us. Fewer mouths to feed means less money spent."

Stripe mouthed the words What *the fuck*. "That is brutal. Seems unethical."

"Most of us are bound for execution or the mines anyway." The orc shrugged. In this world, you were an old man living life one minute, and dead on the floor the next.

Oblong's unblinking eyes drifted back toward Stripe. It seemed to weigh whether he was a problem or a meal. Blood pooled across the uneven stone floor. No one stepped into it. The space near Oblong remained empty. Footsteps echoed in the corridor. Two guards arrived and dragged the body out without a word. Time crawled. The thin man edged closer to Stripe, crouching near the wall.

"You got lucky again. Luck seems to follow you."

Stripe shot him a glare. He never viewed these events as luck. Stripe furrowed his brows. "That is one way to say it."

"If you had not moved, it would have been you." The thin man practically danced on his feet.

Stripe gave a single nod. The realization of his near-death settled over him. "Yeah, unfortunate for the other guy."

The thin man's eyes drifted toward Stripe's injured hand. He reached out. Stripe swatted him away. Stripe guarded his hand.

"Does it hurt?" The man scooted closer, invading Stripe's space.

Stripe flexed his fingers. Pain shot up his arm, but he masked it. You never show weakness in prison. "It is annoying if anything. I have had worse."

He shifted his hand out of sight. The thin man smiled and leaned closer.

"If you die... can I have your arm?" The request carried a sing-song cadence.

Stripe stared at him, jaw slack in disbelief. Everyone and everything wanted to eat him. "Let us not get ahead of ourselves. I still have a ton of youth and vigor in me." He paused. "But I guess I will not be using it if I kick the bucket." He forced a chuckle.

Stripe had bigger issues to deal with. Since his injury, Oblong remained obsessed with him. The fish never broke its dead gaze the entire day. Eating the man's head lessened the tension, but Stripe knew it would hunger again. Night fell inside the cell. The torches in the corridor dimmed, chilling the air. Prisoners lie down against the walls. Stripe stood his ground, watching Oblong. The creature did not sleep. It became still. It breathed in steady rhythms, eyes half-lidded but never closed.

CROWN — "Recommendation: eliminate threat during low-activity period."

Stripe shifted his weight. "You think I didn't think of that?"

CROWN — "Probability of being consumed during sleep remains elevated. Utilizing the host's historical knowledge suggests that the creature may be weak to PH imbalancing."

Stripe scanned the far corner of the cell. The communal bucket sat there, large and carved from thick wood. It was a grotesque necessity. He glanced toward the orc. The orc's eyes were open, locked onto Stripe.

"New guy. What are you scheming over there?" The orc sat up, his posture tense.

Stripe shrugged. "Fishing without a license."

The orc fell silent. The new guy was targeting the biggest threat in the cell. The veteran prisoner decided to sit back and watch. Stripe stood and walked toward the bucket. The thin man tracked his movements.

"You going to throw it at him?"

The man scooted closer, abandoning all sense of personal space. Stripe shot him a glare.

"I gotta get my lick back."

He popped his knuckles. He picked up the bucket and turned his back on the cell. There was no dignity left to preserve. A steady stream hit the bottom. The bucket carried substantial weight. His low-level body struggled under the load.

CROWN — "Unknown impact of pH alteration on aquatic physiology. Success probability is indeterminate. It is still the most highly likely plan of action."

Stripe took a breath, collecting himself.

CROWN — "Host secretion detected in mixture. Toxic Fisherman bonus is applied."

Stripe carried the bucket toward Oblong. It sloshed with each step, leaving a foul trail across the stone.

"Fish need PH balance, right? I remember that from somewhere." He recalled a fishing tournament he watched while on an alcohol bender. The details were gone, but the trivia remained. He tipped the bucket.

The foul liquid washed over Oblong's scaled face and body, soaking into the ridges along its neck and chest. Oblong was an aquatic creature trapped in dry air; its porous scales drank in the moisture. The toxic mixture bypassed its tough exterior, seeping into its bloodstream.

CROWN — "Target poisoned status applied via Toxic Fisherman. Target HP is dropping. Poison compounding with the target's pH imbalance. Improvised weaponry bonus applied."

The combination of Stripe's passive with the communal waste created a potent mixture. It mirrored the strength of a magical potion. Oblong's body jerked. A low guttural sound escaped its throat. Its scales twitched, and its muscles locked. It lunged forward, mouth agape and arms extended, before its limbs buckled under its massive weight. Green goo leaked from its eyes. Foam coated its mouth. It scratched at its neck, desperate to extract the pain. Nothing worked. It flopped to the ground, its massive body convulsing.

The thin man scrambled backward, pressing himself flat against the bars, panic seizing his face. The orc held his ground, but his sharp eyes widened in fearful respect. Oblong convulsed once more, jaws snapping without coordination. Then it collapsed onto its side. The heavy body struck the stone with a wet thud. It twitched twice, then stopped.

Silence filled the cell. Stripe stood over the beast, gripping the empty bucket. He had executed an apex predator. He was the scariest thing in the room.

CROWN — "Hostile eliminated. Experience awarded."

Stripe exhaled. His heart hammered in his chest, causing his nailless finger to throb. He was surprised it worked.

"No head this time." He delivered the line like an actor nailing a catchphrase.

The thin man stared at the body, his frame trembling. "You killed him with that?"

Stripe gave a single nod. "Environmental hazard." He tossed the bucket aside, projecting a false sense of confidence.

The orc studied Stripe, his tough facade fractured. "You killed that giant creature with piss and shit?" Astonishment broke his voice. His finger shook as he pointed from Stripe to Oblong.

Stripe took a seat on the bench beside the thin man. He crossed his legs and leaned back. "I have a certain set of skills."

A smirk crossed Stripe's face. He leaned back against the stone. His head hit the wall with an embarrassing thud. He masked the wince, trying to maintain the cool exterior. *I cannot believe that worked,* Stripe thought. *I'm going to be so cool in prison.* **CROWN** — "Calculating experience."

Chapter 10

The transition from the weightless void to the physical world was brutal. Stripe did not wake up peacefully. He felt something sharp and jagged dig into his forearm. The pain was immediate and white-hot. His survival instincts bypassed his conscious thought. He shot up in a frantic defense, ripping his arm away and throwing a heavy elbow backward before he even opened his eyes.

The thin man sprawled across the dirty straw, wiping a smear of fresh blood from his mouth. His pointy, canine teeth were stained red. Stripe shoved the man away.

"Chill the fuck out. I'm still alive."

The thin man let out a hiss and snapped his fingers. "Damn it."

The orc chuckled from the corner, a deep, rumbling sound. The heavy iron cell door swung open. The grinding of rusted hinges echoed down the corridor. A man in elegant white robes decorated with intricate gold threading and polished jewels stood outside. The fabric looked expensive, a jarring contrast to the filth of the dungeon. The person's face was obscured by a deep hood and poor lighting, but the aura radiating from them felt dense and powerful.

The guard stepped back. "This is the prisoner."

"Yes. He belongs to us." The Man in White stepped forward. "We will assume custody of him."

"Lucky bastard." The thin man muttered from the floor.

CROWN — "He wouldn't have waited again."

Her voice sounded different this time. It lacked the sterile, robotic detachment. It was softer, more human. Almost familiar.

"I know." Stripe nodded. "I was going to beat his ass to show dominance after this." Stripe paused, blinking away the lingering disorientation of the reboot. He rubbed his temples. "Wait. You sound different again."

CROWN — "Incorrect. The optimal manner of speaking has been consistent through all conversational engagements."

Stripe scratched his head. He felt like he was going crazy.

"Let's move, prisoner." The guard tapped his baton. "Or would you rather stay until your execution date?"

Stripe scrambled up, ignoring the throbbing pain in his bitten arm, and exited the cell. The prison was dark and damp. Stone walls covered in thick black mold surrounded them as they navigated the claustrophobic corridors toward the surface. Stripe stayed quiet. He kept his head down and his shoulders hunched. He did not want anyone to realize they might have the wrong guy.

A large, reinforced oak door creaked open. Blinding sunlight spilled into the hallway. The fresh air hit Stripe like a physical wave. The guard shoved Stripe forward and tossed a burlap bag at his chest. He checked inside. The stiff leather armor, the raw wolf pelt, the stolen dagger. Everything was there except his hard-earned coins.

"Wait. Where the fuck's my money?"

"No money was processed on intake." The guard delivered the lie without missing a beat. He offered a nasty, knowing smirk that told Stripe exactly where the silver had gone. "File an appeal. I'm sure it will be answered in a few years."

The guard slammed the heavy door shut behind them, the lock clicking into place. Stripe ran a hand over his face.

"Broke again." The crushing weight of poverty settled back onto his shoulders. "The cycle continues."

"It was unwise to claim affiliation with our church." The Man in White turned to face him.

"It's technically not a lie."

CROWN — "...Correct."

The robed figure reached up with delicate hands and pulled back the heavy hood. Stripe's mouth opened in shock. Long, elegant ears protruded from the hair. Flowing white hair caught the sunlight. It was the elf from the woods. The archer who had stared at him in disgust while he was covered in wolf blood and feces.

"Wha..."

She cut him off with a sharp wave of her hand. "If I had brought members of the church with me to verify your claim, you would either hang..." She paused, her golden eyes scanning his battered state. She looked at him with a mixture of pity and reluctance, as if rescuing a mangy stray dog from the pound. "...Or you would be forced into the church at the lowest level, forever serving as a slave."

Stripe blinked. The harsh reality of this fantasy world slapped him across the face. "That doesn't seem very religious. What religion has slaves?"

"All of them." The certainty in her voice left no room for debate.

Stripe shifted his weight. "Oh. Well. Why did you help me then?"

"I felt bad leaving you behind." She crossed her arms defensively, the immaculate white silk of her sleeves contrasting with the mud caked on Stripe's boots. There was a clear internal conflict in her posture. She was a being of high status and pristine holy magic, standing in the muck of a prison yard to bail out a vagrant. "Even though you are putrid, you looked lost," she continued. "I am duty-bound to help the lost." She looked away, unable to maintain eye contact. "Instead, I left you in an area known for bandits. When I returned, there were bodies everywhere. I thought you died." She sighed, the tension leaving her shoulders. "I'm glad you didn't. Now I don't have to seek forgiveness from the goddess for failing my duties."

Stripe frowned. His massive ego flared. "I'm not putrid. I just have my own style."

CROWN — "FALSE. Host social statistical data shows a humanoid aversion to the presence. You currently smell of stagnant water, dried blood, and terrified perspiration."

Stripe muttered under his breath, glaring at the empty air. "Ouch."

The elf turned on her heel and began walking away, her robes flowing over the cobblestones. "Don't mess up your freedom."

Stripe took a step forward. "Wait. What's your name? It feels weird not knowing."

She glanced back, the sunlight catching the gold jewelry adorning her hair. "Sarah."

The bustling morning crowd swallowed her whole before Stripe could process the information or give his own name in return. He stood alone outside the prison walls. He was broke. He was smelly. And he was alone in a sprawling new city with no prospects for earning a single coin. It was familiar territory.

The town square of Memento was an overwhelming assault on the senses. Merchants shouted beneath brightly colored canvas awnings, haggling over prices for exotic spices and rough-spun cloth. Heavy wooden carts rumbled across the uneven stone streets, kicking up dust and mud. Children darted through the dense crowd, laughing and chasing each other. The air reeked of fresh-baked bread, unwashed bodies, horse manure, and hot metal from the nearby blacksmiths. It was loud and alive in the specific way medieval cities become when coins are moving, and nothing catastrophic is happening.

Then the movement shifted. A palpable change in atmospheric pressure rolled across the square. A man entered from the northern street wearing armor that did not belong in a common marketplace. Mythril.

The plates reflected the morning sunlight in a cold, liquid sheen. Every segment of the armor locked into the next with engineered precision. Etched, glowing sigils revealed themselves only when the light struck the polished metal at the right angle. It was reinforcement layered over reinforcement. The chest piece alone contained enough refined ore to finance a national war. The heavy, ornate clasp holding his crimson cape could have purchased half the square outright.

The blade strapped to his broad back was enormous. It was perfectly balanced, a masterpiece of lethal craftsmanship. It did not glow theatrically or hum with visible magic. It simply existed with the terrifying certainty of having ended many lives. The air around him felt physically heavier. It was as if pure violence had been disciplined into stillness.

CROWN — "Estimated level: 99."

Stripe stopped walking. His jaw clenched. "Ninety-nine?"

CROWN — "Estimate based on equipment quality, muscle structural efficiency, aura density, and environmental reaction."

"So you don't know."

CROWN — "Estimate based on data is extremely accurate."

"You said it like you were sure of the wolf and bandits."

CROWN — "Tonal interpretation error. Estimate remains consistent across readings."

The warrior crossed the bustling square without acknowledging a single person. He did not look at the merchants, the beggars, or the guards. People instinctively moved aside, parting like a wave against the bow of a warship. The sheer aura of the man demanded submission.

"Is there higher than ninety-nine?" Stripe asked.

CROWN — "No verified instance recorded beyond estimated Level 99."

"Why?"

CROWN — "Level 100 categorized as divine threshold."

Stripe watched the warrior disappear toward the wealthy guild district, a bitter resentment pooling in his stomach. He was the undisputed heavyweight champion of the world. He was the apex predator of his reality. To stand in the mud in a dirty tunic and watch another man command that much physical respect hurt him to his core.

"No one passes ninety-nine?"

CROWN — "No verified instance recorded."

"Not even him?"

CROWN — "Correct."

Stripe swallowed the bitter taste in his mouth. "What about the elf?"

CROWN — "Estimated minimum Level 50. Maximum Level 70."

"And guards?"

CROWN — "Estimated average Level 20."

"And seasoned adventurers?"

CROWN — "Estimated range between Level 30 and Level 80."

"And me?" Stripe let out a long sigh.

CROWN — "Verified Level 5."

Stripe exhaled, the numbers flattening his ego. "How do my stats align with people who are the same level as me?" Stripe dreaded the answer.

CROWN — "Sub par."

Stripe scowled. The insult stung worse than the pliers ripping out his fingernail. *Subpar.* He had never been subpar at anything physical in his life. He was a genetic freak of nature back home. Here, he was statistically inferior to common thugs.

"I feel like you're moving the goalpost."

CROWN — "Incorrect."

"You mentioned my growth model."

CROWN — "Early progression slower than baseline. Mid-tier aligns with baseline. Late-tier compounds."

"So I stay weak longer."

CROWN — "Yes."

"But later?"

CROWN — "If survival persists, the host will exceed standard projections. Your scaling potential is uncapped, provided you endure the initial deficit."

Stripe nodded. He looked down at his scarred, bare hands. The path to the top in this world was not going to be a sprint. It was going to be a bloody marathon. He had fought his way out of the gutter once before. He could do it again.

"Fine. I'll take the long road."

Over the next several weeks, Stripe returned to what he knew best. Begging. The descent was humiliating, but pride did not fill an empty stomach. He spent his days learning the complex, unwritten rhythm of the city. He learned which wealthy merchants tossed silver coins when business was good. He learned which guards spat at him when they didn't have to. He learned the best places for sleeping beneath heavy canvas awnings to avoid the freezing rain, and he brawled with other vagrants for prime real estate near the bakery vents for residual warmth. He spent his days staring at the dirty cobblestones, counting copper coins like oxygen.

In the midst of this miserable existence, an old, ragged beggar named Hobb became a constant in his life. They slummed together for weeks. Their bond was forged in the lowest trenches of society. They shared stale scraps of discarded bread and half-eaten fruit stolen from market stalls. They shared the driest corners of the alleyways during the freezing autumn rains. They shared the heavy silences when the bustling city forgot they existed.

Hobb was a broken man. He spoke in riddles and carried a battered old broom with a face drawn on it that he called Maribel. He claimed she was his wife. Stripe never mocked him for it. When you had nothing, you held onto whatever kept your mind from shattering. Stripe understood that better than anyone. He would engage in full conversations with Maribel just to see the toothless, genuine smile break across Hobb's weathered face. They watched each other's backs when the city watch came through with heavy boots to clear the streets. Hobb taught Stripe how to stay invisible. Stripe made sure no one tried to steal Hobb's meager earnings.

Sometimes, exhausted and starving, Stripe muttered under his breath without realizing it.

CROWN — "Nutritional deficit noted. The recommended calorie threshold is not being met. Muscle atrophy imminent."

"Yeah. I noticed." Stripe rubbed his stomach.

Hobb looked sideways at him, his milky eyes squinting in the dim alley light. "You arguing with ghosts again?"

"Something like that." Stripe offered a faint nod. "A nagging, unhelpful ghost."

Hobb took a small bite of a bruised apple. "Good. Means you ain't alone. Better to have a ghost yelling at you than the silence eating you alive."

Stripe blinked, touched by the crazy old man's accidental wisdom. One cold evening, the wind biting fiercely through their thin tunics, Hobb produced a dark glass bottle from deep within his tattered robes.

"If you're hungry, too bad." Hobb let out a raspy chuckle. He shook the bottle, the liquid sloshing inside. "But I got something to make you forget the cold for a while."

Stripe's eyes locked onto the bottle. The desperate craving roared to life in his chest. He snatched the bottle and took a long, heavy pull, waiting for the warm, numbing embrace of the liquor to wash away the misery of his reality.

CROWN — "Alcohol consumption detected. Intoxication negated."

Stripe blinked. The warmth never came. Then, his stomach convulsed. A searing cramp ripped through his abdomen. He doubled over, gasping for air. The alcohol rejected him. He fell to his hands and knees and vomited onto the unforgiving stone. His body heaved until nothing remained in his stomach but burning bile. He sat back, wiping a string of spit from his chin, shivering.

Hobb stared at him in wide-eyed confusion. "Something wrong with my drink, or is it personal?"

Stripe wiped his mouth with the back of his dirty sleeve, his hands shaking. "It's personal."

CROWN — "System modification functioning as designed. Divine blessing active."

Stripe stared at the half-empty bottle in Hobb's hand. The realization crashed down on him with cruelty. The goddess had cursed him. He was trapped in a miserable, freezing world, and he wasn't even allowed the small mercy of numbing the pain.

"Broke and unable to even get drunk." He sighed, burying his face in his hands. "This is worse than before. This is actual hell."

Hobb tapped his temple, taking a swig of the liquor himself. "Some of us got wives. Some got ghosts. Some got rules talking back. Same difference, son. We all carry baggage that doesn't let us rest."

Stripe did not argue. He just sat in the cold, sober reality of his life. Another night, freezing rain smeared the city square into gray streaks. The two men huddled beneath the narrow stone overhang of an abandoned storefront. The water rushed down the cobblestones in miniature rivers, soaking through the soles of Stripe's boots.

"Homeless ain't about no roof," Hobb stated over the rain.

Stripe stared blankly out at the bubbling fountain in the center of the dark square.

"It is about nobody expecting you home. That's what makes the streets so cold. Knowing there ain't a warm fire or a set plate waiting for you anywhere in the world."

That landed. It hit Stripe right in the center of his chest, cracking open a vault of pain he had been trying to keep locked away. He felt the immense grief settle heavily in his chest.

"I had someone," Stripe spoke the words into the rain.

The memory came clean, piercing through the grime and the cold. Maui. The radiating warmth of the tropical sun. The pristine white sand beneath his bare feet. The smell of salt air and blooming plumeria flowers. A beautiful wooden arch wrapped in vibrant flowers. The ocean stretched endlessly, crystal blue behind them, sparkling like crushed diamonds.

He saw her face. She laughed during the vows because he had forgotten a traditional line and replaced it with something stupid and sincere. He remembered looking down at his hands. His hands, which had broken the jaws of giant men, which had shattered orbital bones, and choked out champions. Those hands had never shaken in the cage. But they shook that day as he slid the ring onto her finger. The physical comfort, the immense hope he felt on that beach, was an agonizing contrast to the freezing, gray rain currently soaking his bones. He had believed that the moment on the beach was permanent.

Hobb studied him, his milky eyes seeming to pierce right through Stripe's tough exterior. "You lose her," Hobb stated as a fact.

Stripe nodded, the rain dripping from his matted hair. The crushing weight of his failure pressed down on him. "I lost myself first. I let my ego burn everything to the ground."

Hobb reached out with a trembling, dirt-caked hand and tapped the wet stone between them. "Maribel says you cannot stay in the hole you fall in. You try to climb straight up, you just slide back down in the mud." Hobb smiled. "You dig sideways. Make a tunnel. Find a new way out of the dark."

Stripe let that sit. *Dig sideways.* It was profound advice from a man holding a broom. Hobb leaned closer, dropping the crazy old man persona for a fleeting second.

"You're fighting something inside. I see it."

"Yeah."

"Good." Hobb tapped Stripe's arm. "Means you ain't surrendered. A dead man doesn't fight. Only the living struggle."

Stripe respected that. It was the truth. Stripe and Hobb had many similarities. When they first met, Stripe had written him off as a crackhead. But the man next to him was kinder and more thoughtful than he expected. He began to understand the babbling. Everything Hobb said had substance, even if it seemed crazy. If Stripe had no luck panhandling, Hobb would buy him bread. He made sure Stripe never went without. The man became a friend to him. Something he had not had in a year. Something he needed more than anything in the world. With Hobb, he did not have to use sarcasm to hide the hurt. He could just be.

"The sun hides from us today; we should hide from what comes." Hobb poked Stripe, waking him from his midday nap.

Absentminded, Stripe got up and followed the man to an alley with a covering over it. A heavy storm rolled in, sweeping the city as citizens ran down the street for shelter. The two sat under the canopy in the alley until the storm passed. Yet again, Hobb was right.

The morning after the storm, the sun broke through the clouds, casting long shadows across the damp square. A greasy man approached their usual begging spot. His movements were smooth, almost slithering. He wore a fine velvet coat that looked out of place among the ragged poor.

CROWN — "Trust index negative. High probability of predatory behavior."

The man stopped directly in front of Stripe, ignoring Hobb. It was a practiced, fake smile that did not reach his calculating eyes.

"Hello." He leaned closer, his gaze drifting over Stripe's broad, muscular shoulders and scarred, calloused hands. "Would you like a job? You seem remarkably fit... and eager to survive."

Chapter 11

"My name is Varn." The man extended a hand. "I run the guild here in this town."

Varn looked like a man who sold opportunity in fractions. His velvet coat was clean but frayed at the cuffs, betraying a desperation he tried to hide behind a polished veneer. His smile arrived early and lingered too long. His eyes calculated everything they touched, assessing Stripe's worth down to the copper.

"You look solid for a vagrant."

Stripe smiled, leaning his weight onto one leg. "That is the nicest thing anyone has said to me." Stripe tilted his head. "But I am not into guys."

CROWN — "Statement is factual."

Stripe almost laughed. *Twenty gold is twenty gold,* he thought.

CROWN — "Statement is correct."

Varn did not react to the banter. His expression remained a mask of practiced business. "Four weeks of training. First mission mandatory."

CROWN — "Probability of exploitation high."

Stripe already knew that, but the hunger gnawing at his ribs offered a persuasive counterargument. He walked back to Hobb and placed a single copper coin in the old man's dirty palm.

"For you."

Hobb looked at the coin. Then at Stripe. For a brief moment, the fog cleared from his milky eyes. "That man will break you and send you on a suicide mission."

Stripe held his gaze, feeling the weight of the warning. "Be safe."

Hobb pocketed the coin. "We will come to visit soon." Then Hobb leaned back against the wet stone. His clarity vanished. He began muttering to the air. "Seven smells like smoke. Twelve smells like soap. Numbers always tell you things if you sniff hard enough."

Stripe stood, confused. Hobb had a frustrating habit of shifting from lucid to crazy without warning. He looked toward the affluent guild district, then down at his empty hands. He turned and followed Varn. Desperation always spoke louder than caution, and today, Stripe was listening.

Varn walked Stripe through the wealthy guild district like he was delivering a questionable package, hoping nobody asked what was inside. The transition from the slums was stark. The streets tightened and leveled out as they moved away from the chaotic market. Flimsy canvas stalls gave way to sturdy stone storefronts with shuttered windows and heavy iron hooks for lanterns. The smell of rotting garbage faded, replaced by the sharp scent of hot forge smoke and polished leather.

The noise changed. Desperate bargaining and drunken laughter faded. Measured, disciplined voices replaced them, accompanied by the rhythmic clinking of chainmail and heavy gear. People here walked with purpose, like they had places to be and valid reasons to get there alive. Stripe kept glancing at the polished wooden guild signboards, half-expecting them to jump him. He did not trust any building that looked this proud of itself.

Stripe broke the silence. "I have a question."

"Now is not the time." Varn kept walking. "Keep them inside your head."

"My head isn't a good place."

CROWN — "Statement is correct."

Stripe looked sideways at Varn, glaring for a second as if the man had spoken the insult aloud. Varn did not react. He walked with the infuriating calm of someone who had never been forced to sleep on frozen stone.

The guild hall sat at the end of a wide, sweeping stairway. You had to look up while climbing, a subtle architectural trick to enforce subservience. It was built of dark stone, the kind that seemed to drink the sunlight rather than reflect it. Above the massive double doors hung a carved emblem: an abstract crown framed by a perfect circle of runes. It felt official in the exact way royal courts are official, projecting an undeniable authority whether you believed in it or not. Two seasoned guards in battered chainmail watched them approach. Their cold eyes tracked Stripe first, assessing the threat, then slid over to Varn and relaxed by a fraction.

"Keep your mouth shut unless someone asks you something."

Stripe glanced down at his filthy, borrowed tunic and the cheap dagger resting at his hip. "You just met me." Stripe glared. "If I weren't so broke, I would beat your ass."

Stripe's knuckles tightened. He wanted to swing, but crushing poverty had a funny way of keeping a man's fists inside his pockets. Varn pushed the heavy door open without answering. The air inside smelled thick with oiled leather, old combat sweat, and fresh ink. Voices carried through the cavernous hall in low, tense arguments and quiet negotiations. A long mahogany counter stretched across the back of the room. Behind it, a rail-thin clerk moved papers from one towering stack to another, looking like a man rearranging problems instead of solving them.

Dangerous people filled the room. Scarred mercenaries with missing eyes. Hunters carrying recurve bows taller than themselves. Adventurers wearing heavy plate armor were repaired more often than they were purchased. Stripe felt out of place standing there in a raw wolf pelt. He fit right in with the desperate and the damned.

Varn walked to the counter, bypassing a small line. The thin clerk looked up. His tired eyes moved to Stripe, taking in the dirt and the smell, then flicked back to Varn. His sour expression did not improve. The clerk let out a sigh.

"Another one?"

"They keep dying." Varn offered a shrug. "I mean, failing training."

The clerk pushed a crisp sheet of parchment across the wooden desk. "Name."

Stripe leaned forward, resting his hands on the counter. "Stripe."

The clerk wrote it down without looking up. "Signature."

Stripe stared down at the page. The letters were angular and strange, looking more like aggressive geometry than an alphabet. He looked back at the clerk. "I do not know your alphabet."

The clerk blinked, accustomed to illiteracy. He pushed a small black ink pot forward. "Make a mark."

Stripe dipped his thumb into the cold ink. He hovered his hand over the paper.

CROWN — "Warning. Contractual analysis indicates hostile terms. Do not complete this action."

Stripe pressed his thumb onto the bottom of the page, too impatient and desperate to wait for the ghost in his head to finish its sentence. The clerk snatched the parchment back and stamped it with a heavy metal seal. He shoved another piece of paper across the counter.

"You now owe the guild a small debt."

Stripe frowned. "That was fast. I just got here."

Varn smiled. It was that same polite expression, hungry and devoid of warmth. "The training here is valuable. It will make you fortunes."

Stripe skimmed the page. The numbers listed next to the items were small, which made the sheer number of them worse. His stomach dropped. "What is the total?"

"Three thousand, if you add all of those numbers up."

Stripe let out a sharp, breathless laugh. "That is more than a year's pay for a normal person."

"Correct." Varn gave a single nod. "It is about three years' pay with a good job. Not bad, right? It is an investment."

Stripe leaned forward. His massive shoulders tensed, his heart hammering against his ribs. "So I was broke, and now I am even worse off. Begging made one silver a day on a good day. That is not even one gold a week."

Varn's smile widened. "Then you understand the opportunity."

Stripe looked back down at the inked thumbprint binding him to this nightmare. "I understand it's a scam."

Varn gave a shrug. "Call it what you want, but you signed the contract. Next time, read it."

"You are running a debt funnel."

"I am running a business." Varn adjusted the lapels of his coat. "Other guilds work harder. I work smarter."

Stripe stared at him. His gaze was flat and hard, the kind of look he used to give opponents right before the cage door locked. "I don't like you."

"Oh, that just makes me sad. I like you. I like all of you. Just make me my money." Varn leaned back, treating Stripe's boiling tension like mild background noise. "You will work it off when you graduate." Varn waved a hand. "Or you'll die, and we will sell your body to cover some of the debt. You will take the missions we assign."

Stripe folded the heavy paper. His massive hands trembled with the effort it took not to wrap them around Varn's throat. "What if I refuse?"

"Then you pay the debt in full right now."

Stripe laughed again, sharper and more dangerous this time. "And if I can't?"

Varn's voice stayed calm. "Then you are the property of the guild until the ledger says otherwise."

A heavy pause stretched between them. Varn added it like a sterile legal footnote. If Stripe weren't eating out of trash cans, he might have declined this deal. Who was he kidding? He needed something to get him off the streets, and this seemed like the best option he had.

"That is how contracts work." Varn crossed his arms. "Slavery is an ugly word. The law prefers obligation."

Stripe stared at him for a long, suffocating moment. The sheer audacity of the bureaucratic evil before him was staggering.

CROWN — "Probability of predatory intent high."

Stripe kept his eyes locked on Varn. "No shit."

Stripe exhaled, forcing his heart rate to drop back down to a manageable baseline. He looked back at Varn. "You fucking suck."

Stripe stepped closer to further his point. Varn wasn't threatened by the physicality. Stripe's level was too low to look intimidating. Instead, Varn was repulsed by Stripe's smell. Varn shook his head, keeping that pristine, hungry smile intact. He turned his back on Stripe and covered his nose.

"This is profitable," Varn concluded, walking away.

CHAPTER 12

Training began the next morning. Stripe woke from the training barracks feeling more refreshed than the city streets allowed. The bed was a thin layer of hay on a concrete slab. The room was crowded with around fifty to sixty adventurers and trainees. Stripe had been informed that higher-ranking Adventurers stayed in better barracks or had their own personal rooms if they chose to stay at the guild. The biggest blessing was that it was built into the debt. He could stay as long as he was free.

The room smelled of sweat and farts. That's what happens when a bunch of poorly hygienic individuals sleep in the same room. Stripe, however, did not mind. It was better than sleeping under a bench. The stench was preferable to an alleyway full of trash cans and litter, like in his previous life. He was used to gym bros; he could make this work.

The recruits assembled in the sand pit before sunrise. Cold air clung to the stone walls of the guild yard, and breath hung white in the dark. Stripe stood near the back of the line. He had slept badly. The dormitory was loud and crowded, smelling of wet leather and old sweat. It was better than the street, but not by much.

The instructor walked into the yard carrying a long wooden staff. He did not raise his voice. He did not need to.

"Running." The Instructor slammed his foot into the ground.

No one moved. The instructor lifted the staff and struck the ground. Sand jumped in a threatening manner.

"Now." Saliva flew from the Instructor's mouth.

The line broke into motion. They ran until the sky turned gray, and they ran until the gray turned pale blue. They ran until the first recruit collapsed. The instructors did not stop the run. Two assistants dragged the unconscious body off the track, and the line kept moving. The recruit never rejoined.

Stripe's lungs burned. His calves felt like coiled wire ready to snap. But the pain was familiar. Predictable. It was pain you could negotiate with, pain that obeyed rules. He thought back to all of the runs he did while training for a fight. He felt like he was going crazy because he was actually enjoying this run. It was nostalgic.

CROWN — "Host stamina output currently operating at eighty-two percent efficiency."

Stripe kept running. "Good to know," Stripe muttered. "Not useful, however."

CROWN — "Improvement possible with current curriculum. Maintain training for increased results."

"I will get right on it," Stripe replied in a sarcastic tone. He didn't have a choice. He did not want to die or be a slave.

The drills continued. Climbing rope. Dragging weighted sleds. Carrying stones across the yard. Falling, standing up, and doing it again. Swinging hammers at big rocks and turning them into small rocks. Dodging rocks thrown at you, along with the occasional wrench. If you can dodge a wrench, you can dodge a spell. By midday, the sand pit smelled of sweat, iron, and wet dirt.

The instructor gestured toward the weapon racks. Spears. Axes. Short swords. Clubs. Claymores. Long swords.

Stripe grabbed a short sword. It felt wrong. The grip sat awkwardly in his hand, and the blade pulled forward like it wanted to fall. He tried the drill anyway. Step. Swing. Guard. The sword dipped during the strike. The instructor let out a sigh.

"You fight like a man who has never held steel." The Instructor gave a harsh critique. "It is rare to be so awkward with weapons." The insult was hidden behind a thinly veiled observation.

Stripe lowered the blade. His body ached from the unnatural movements and the unfamiliar sensation of the weapon.

"This is my first time, be gentle." Stripe offered a teasing smile. Stripe covered his cheeks like he was blushing. A few recruits laughed. The instructor did not.

CROWN — "User performance metrics are subpar to those of other trainees. Past training style has begun to clash with new instructions. User is incompatible with this training style."

"Shut the fuck up," Stripe snapped. "You always offer the worst advice."

"What did you say to me, recruit?" the Instructor roared. "I can have you tossed back out to the street like the worthless filth you are."

Stripe raised his hands. "That was the voice in my head. Not to you. It's always nagging at me like I'm in a shitty relationship."

The instructor's eyes flared for a moment, processing the excuse. Stripe had never stopped to think about how he might be perceived by other people when he talked to the Crown. To everyone else, he was either crazy or an asshole.

"Again!" the Instructor barked.

Stripe tried again. It was still horrible. Every movement felt artificial. The instructor waved him away in annoyance.

"Next." Stripe stepped aside, embarrassed.

He was always great at physical activities. He didn't have to train like other fighters to be the champ. However, he trained like everyone else and rose above them, creating a gap so large that he lapped his division twice, then moved up in weight. Here, he had to train harder just to avoid being tossed out. Everyone around him was at a higher level, according to the Crown's estimates.

An armorer rolled a cart into the yard. Metal clattered across the tray. Gauntlets. Thick leather. Reinforced plates. Knuckles studded with brutal spikes. Stripe stared. Something stirred in his chest. Recognition. He picked up a pair. They were heavy, dense, and balanced where his hands expected the weight. He slid them on. The straps tightened across his wrists, and the spikes lined up with his knuckles. His fingers flexed. The gauntlets moved with him instead of against him, as they had always belonged there.

"This is what the fuck I'm talking about," Stripe grinned. "Let's go!" It felt right. It was like a souped-up MMA glove. The monster parts were lighter than expected but still had heft.

CROWN — "Weapon classification: Gauntlets. Typically used for a defensive measure. However, the user's compatibility appears high. Close-range lethality increased."

The instructor watched him for a moment, then pointed toward the sparring circle. "Those are for defense." The Instructor issued a warning. "They offer no range advantage and should only be used if your primary weapon is knocked away."

"I can't even hold a primary weapon, so these are perfect for me."

"You may wear them during training, but you will train with swords as your primary." The Instructor conceded the point. "Time for sparring. Try not to kill each other, or don't, I don't really care."

Stripe stepped forward. A recruit approached. He had a thick neck, a scarred eyebrow, and a grin that said he enjoyed hurting people weaker than him. Stripe was prey; he couldn't even hold his sword.

CROWN — "Estimated Level: 11."

The instructor raised his hand. "Begin."

The recruit charged forward. He swung hard and fast. Stripe brought his blade up, and the two met. Stripe's blade flew across the field and into the sand. But he didn't panic; he smiled. The recruit realized there was no real strength behind his block. Stripe could now technically use the gauntlets without getting in trouble. He didn't waste the chance. While the recruit was shocked by the outcome, Stripe moved. He threw a spinning back kick into the recruit's wrist, knocking their own blade away.

The recruit answered by planting his feet incorrectly and swinging his fist. Heavy right hook. Fast but sloppy. Stripe watched the shoulder first, then the elbow. The punch telegraphed itself a mile away. Stripe slipped left. The fist roared past his ear, the air pressure brushing his hair. Stripe stepped inside the man's reach with a quick jab to his nose. The impact snapped the recruit's head backward. Teeth clicked together. The man staggered but stayed upright. Durable.

The recruit growled and swung again. Left hook this time. Wide and angry. Stripe ducked under it. His gauntlet drove forward, elbow tight, knuckles first. The spikes hammered into the man's ribs. A dull crack echoed. The recruit gasped. But instead of backing away, he lunged forward with his shoulder lowered, trying to tackle. His weight slammed into Stripe's chest. Stripe slid backward half a step, pivoted, and secured underhooks.

Hey, Crown, Stripe thought.

CROWN — "Yes."

How hurt am I exactly? A pause.

CROWN — "Tracking combat health now."

Stripe blinked. "Now?" Stripe asked in frustration. "Was that always an option?"

The crown ignored his question like a computer buffering to load.

Combat Status

Stripe HP: 80 / 80

Opponent HP: 105 / 110

The recruit swung again. Stripe let go of his underhooks to maintain the standup advantage. Stripe caught the punch on his forearm. The impact gasped through the gauntlet plates. Stripe countered with a short hook. The spikes scraped across the man's cheek, and blood followed.

Combat Status

Stripe HP: 80 / 80

Opponent HP: 92 / 110

"You could track that the whole time?" Stripe asked.

The recruit lunged again, trying to grapple. Stripe pivoted sideways. His foot hooked behind the man's ankle for a leg sweep. The recruit crashed face-first into the sand. Stripe followed him down with a hammer fist. Gauntlet spikes cracked against the man's jaw.

Combat Status

Stripe HP: 80 / 80

Opponent HP: 54 / 110

CROWN — "Host never requested health monitoring previously."

Stripe stared at the sand. "That seems like something you should do automatically." Stripe let out a grunt.

The recruit pushed himself up, dazed. Stripe stepped forward. Hook. Temple. The man collapsed.

Combat Result

Stripe HP: 80 / 80

Opponent HP: 0 / 110

Winner: Stripe

Stripe rubbed his forehead. "It's just weird that you didn't tell me this prior."

CROWN — "User was briefed on capabilities during the imitation phase by the Goddess."

Stripe sighed. "I stopped listening halfway through."

CROWN — "Incorrect, user stopped listening around the 5% mark of the explanation. The user then cut the explanation short with confidence. System believed user understood capabilities based on user's actions."

"Again." The Instructor barked the order.

A lean recruit stepped forward. Disciplined stance, hands high, balanced.

CROWN — "Estimated Level: 14."

The instructor dropped his hand. "Begin."

The recruit didn't rush. He circled. Stripe noticed he had tossed his weapon down. This recruit wanted to make a point. He kept moving, trying to get a read on Stripe. He saw what happened in the last match and was more measured. A jab snapped toward Stripe's face. Stripe moved his head slightly. The second jab slipped past. However, due to the height difference, the leather of his straps came into contact with Stripe's cheek.

Combat Status

Stripe HP: 78 / 80

Opponent HP: 140 / 140

Stripe grinned. "Okay. That's unexpected." Stripe gave a nod. "Levels matter a lot with damage. But I'm still better."

Finally, someone competent. Stripe could tell this guy was good. Not good enough, though. He stepped forward. Feint. The recruit tightened his guard. Stripe shifted angles, throwing a body shot aimed at the liver. Gauntlet spikes punched into the man’s ribs.

Combat Status

Stripe HP: 78 / 80

Opponent HP: 121 / 140

The recruit retaliated with two fast punches. One clipped Stripe’s jaw, but Stripe turned his head at the same time to avoid a direct hit. Stars flashed in his vision.

Combat Status

Stripe HP: 65 / 80

Opponent HP: 121 / 140

Stripe adjusted his stance. Slightly wider. More patient. Distance mattered more now. The next exchange stretched longer. Punch. Parry. Slip. Counter. Stripe drove an elbow into the recruit’s sternum. The man stumbled.

Combat Status

Stripe HP: 65 / 80

Opponent HP: 74 / 140

The recruit’s guard sagged. Stripe feinted left. The guard shifted. Stripe threw a lightning-fast uppercut. The gauntlet smashed under the man's chin, and he collapsed. His body was matching the movements of his past lives.

CROWN — "Reflection rewards have boosted current combat stats with the host's previous life memories. Continued reflection will provide better rewards."

Stripe should have listened to the crowd, but was too engrossed in the thrill of battle. He missed this.

Combat Result

Stripe HP: 50 / 80

Opponent HP: 0 / 140

Winner: Stripe

The training yard had grown quiet. People were watching now. The final opponent stepped forward. Broad shoulders, calm expression, professional stance.

CROWN — "Estimated Level: 17. WARNING: Opponent is high level in comparison to the users. Maintain a safe distance and avoid direct shows of strength."

Stripe rolled his shoulders, stretching them. In his previous life, he would have been feeling stiff by now. He's starting to see the benefits of Stats.

"Alright. That's a big bitch," Stripe noted.

CROWN — "Opponent is humanoid, not canine."

"No shit." Stripe let out a sigh.

The fight began fast. The recruit struck first. He also tossed his weapon down; this was a man's pride at this point. A sharp punch drove into Stripe's ribs.

Combat Status

Stripe HP: 45 / 80

Opponent HP: 165 / 165

Another strike followed. This one grazed his jaw—even the graze hurt him. Had he absorbed that blow, he might have gone unconscious. The stat difference was huge but not insurmountable. As long as he could hurt his opponent, he could win.

Combat Status

Stripe HP: 35 / 80

Opponent HP: 165 / 165

Stripe smiled and spat to the side in acknowledgment. "Finally," Stripe breathed. "Someone who isn't a pussy."

A real fight. One that he could test his limits with. His excitement showed on his face. This one lasted longer. Footwork. Circling. Feints. The recruit pressed forward with disciplined aggression. Stripe slipped strikes by inches. Each time, his timing and distance control improved. He was learning to deal with stronger opponents who outclassed him in stats. He spent the beginning of the fight limiting damage and learning his opponent's timing and patterns. It was like fighting a knockout artist; one mistake and he would be out.

Finally, he started throwing feints and leg kicks. He began to land hits, but the damage he did was minimal. He countered whenever openings appeared. Sand sprayed around their feet. Breathing grew heavier.

Combat Status

Stripe HP: 29 / 80

Opponent HP: 104 / 165

Let the man commit, then punish the recovery. Three exchanges later. A hook lands clean. It was like hitting a rock. A body shot, but the man's body showed minimal reaction. An elbow to the dome felt ineffective. Stripe knew the damage was adding up. He had to keep chipping away at him like a raid boss. If they had been at the same level, the recruit would have been out in the first exchange. This again reinforced that levels mattered.

Combat Status

Stripe HP: 25 / 80

Opponent HP: 62 / 165

The recruit charged. Desperate now. Every punch he threw was slipped, and he was punished. He had been hit over fifty times. It was starting to hurt. Stripe stepped aside. Three rapid strikes. Jab first with a straight right, and the ribs with his follow-up left. The recruit fell from the hits and his own momentum. Stripe rotated, throwing a spinning back kick to the downed man's face.

CROWN — "Critical strike landed."

The man collapsed. Had this been a cage match, Stripe would have lost by DQ. But this was not. This was survival. Survival means doing whatever the fuck you need to. Good thing he had never lost.

Combat Result

Stripe HP: 25 / 80

Opponent HP: 0 / 165

Winner: Stripe

Silence filled the training yard. A notification appeared.

SYSTEM MESSAGE

New Proficiency Unlocked

New Title Unlocked

- **Pugilist Specialist:** When utilizing hand-to-hand combat, damage ignores 5% of the opponent's armor.
- **Pugilist Proficiency:** MAX
- *Effects:* Unarmed combat efficiency increased, Striking precision improved, Damage scaling with Strength has been slightly increased.

CROWN — "Due to the host's previous reflection, proficiency has reached MAX rank."

Stripe blinked. "You would think I would be higher than level 1."

CROWN — "Titles and skills are earned regardless of the user's skill level. They are bonuses that are gained from feats or repetitive actions."

Stripe nodded. "Good to know. But who decides what awards these?"

Stripe's question is ignored, as if the Crown refuses to answer. Across the yard, Varn stood watching. Smiling. This recruit might make him some money.

Stripe flexed the gauntlet. They felt perfect. Like memory. Like identity. Then Stripe noticed something uncomfortable. He would have to use these to kill. There was no way around it in this world. No more tapping out, no more referees waving off the fight. Life or death in every battle. It was scary, but he was also excited. He might be able to regain most of what he lost in his previous life.

He decided right then and there that he would pay off his debts and milk this guild for every gold it had. If the opportunity presented itself, he would make sure Varn learned how hard he could punch.

CROWN — "WARNING: Reflection Incoming."

Stripe's mind split open, and his head throbbed. This familiar and unwanted pain sank into his skull. All he wanted to do was forget, but the Crown wouldn't let him.

[SYSTEM ALERT: Pugilist Proficiency MAX Reached]

CHAPTER 13

The electronic music inside the VIP club didn't stop. It kept pulsing through the massive speakers, indifferent to the violence that had just occurred. The heavy bass vibrated against the expensive floor tiles. Nikolai lay motionless in a spreading pool of his own dark blood, his jaw a ruined, asymmetrical mess.

Stripe stood over the broken man. His fist throbbed, and a look of satisfaction was plastered across his face. A man in all black tugged at his coat, pulling him away from the scene. Stripe was gloating. He felt powerful.

His manager shattered that illusion of control. Dave was frantic, almost terrified. Dave lived his life doing everything he could to avoid Stripe getting into these types of situations. Stripe was making him rich, and it was his job to avoid situations that would fuck up that income. Dave seized Stripe's bicep, his fingers digging into the muscle.

"We have to go. We have to go right fucking now." His voice was raw, stripped of its polished calm.

Stripe yanked his arm away. "Get your hands off me. He got what he deserved. What the fuck did he expect to happen? He thought he could insult the champ and his wife? Little shit thought I was sweet. He thought I was a bitch he could just walk all over. Now look at him."

Dave looked at him with wild, terrified eyes. He pointed a shaking finger down at the bleeding kid on the floor. "You stupid son of a bitch. Do you have any idea who that kid is? His father is the fucking Russian Mob boss. We need to go now before they show up and shoot the place up."

Stripe jutted his chin out. "Of course, he is. A pussy using his dad's money to bully others. Fuck it, I will fight all of them." His towering arrogance refused to let him admit a mistake.

Dave grabbed Stripe's shoulder. "The kid's jaw is shattered, and he's pissed himself. They won't let this go. We need to leave now."

They didn't stop when fans tried to get pictures. They avoided the cameras and moved through the back rooms. They passed the kitchen staff and the sketchy club rooms where managers did drugs or whatever nameless women they could convince to come back there. The security team pushed any threats aside until they exited through the back door.

They burst through the rear exit and into the freezing Moscow night. The winter air was a physical shock. It bit into Stripe's exposed face and burned his lungs. The alleyway was dark and lined with filthy snowbanks. A massive black SUV idled near the dumpsters. His wife's breathing was labored. The pregnancy was taking its toll.

Dave threw a thick, banded stack of hundred-dollar bills at their private driver. He didn't bother counting it. "The airport. Go fast, do not stop. Do not ask questions."

The heavy doors slammed shut. The tires squealed against the icy pavement, fighting for traction before the massive vehicle launched forward. They sped through the winding, snow-covered streets. Moscow at night was beautiful, but it passed as a blur.

Stripe sat in the spacious back seat of the SUV. The adrenaline began to fade, replaced by a dull ache in his right hand. He looked down at his knuckles. The skin was split open. Blood seeped out, staining his tailored trousers. His wife sat rigid beside him. She trembled, staring ahead out the tinted window into the darkness. She wrapped her arms around her pregnant stomach. She didn't say a word. Her silence bothered him more than the severity of the situation.

Within two agonizing hours, they were wheels up on a private jet. The pilot had been bribed to skip the standard departure protocols. The roar of the jet engines drowned out the suffocating silence inside the luxury cabin. Stripe looked out the small oval window as the glowing city lights of Moscow faded into the black horizon. He could see several blacked-out SUVs flooding onto the tarmac where they had just departed. They almost didn't make it out in time.

He leaned back in his plush leather seat and let out a long breath. He believed the situation was handled. He thought his staggering wealth had bought his freedom. He felt relieved that the situation would die down.

The man deserved the beating he got. That, to Stripe, was non-negotiable. But he worried about his wife. If he had been anyone else, they might not have gotten out.

A few months passed. The ugly, violent night in Russia faded into a phantom memory. Stripe had been busy with parenting classes and training camps for his next title defense. His focus was on the next era of his life. One he was sure would be the best yet. Stripe took a last-minute fight a weight class above him and knocked out the heavyweight champion. He now had two belts in two weight classes. This put him on a small list of names that had accomplished this in all of history. His name sat beside greats like DC, McGregor, and Nunes.

Stripe felt untouchable. His money and global status formed an impenetrable fortress around his family. He was the highest-paid athlete on the planet, and his bank accounts reflected his dominance. He purchased a massive, ultra-modern mansion in the hills overlooking the Pacific Ocean. The driveway was lined with imported palm trees, and the garage was filled with exotic sports cars he almost never drove. He bought his wife custom diamond jewelry that she kept locked in a safe because it was too heavy for everyday use. They had full-time staff who cleaned the house, cut the grass, monitored the security cameras, and cooked their meals.

In time, they took a long vacation away from the media and the gyms, spending three weeks on Maui's pristine white sand. The tropical air was thick and warm, smelling of salt and blooming flowers. The ocean expanded outward, a deep blue that met the clear sky at the horizon. They rented a private beachfront estate that isolated them from the outside world.

It was there, on that flawless beach, that they tied the knot. It was good to come back at such a pivotal moment in their lives. They stood beneath a beautiful wooden arch, wrapped in bright tropical flowers. The waves struck the shoreline, delivering a tranquil rhythm to the ceremony. There were no cameras. No screaming fans. No reporters. Just the two of them and a local officiant. She wore a simple, flowing white dress that caught the ocean breeze. She looked radiant.

She laughed during their vows. Stripe had forgotten the traditional lines he was supposed to memorize. Instead of stopping the ceremony, he replaced the forgotten words with something stupid and sincere. He promised to protect her from spiders, to always let her control the television, and to love her until the oceans dried up.

For a moment, nothing else mattered. His wife stood in her beautiful white dress, showing off her growing baby bump. His hands held hers as they recommitted themselves to each other. This was heaven. If she asked him, he would leave fighting behind for her. That's how important she was to him.

He believed that moment was permanent. He believed the peace they found on that island was something he could preserve forever. They returned to their sprawling mansion in the hills and began planning the rest of their lives. She was far along in her pregnancy now, her belly round and beautiful. They converted the largest guest room into a nursery, painting the walls a soft yellow. They bought a handcrafted crib made of imported oak and filled the room with soft toys.

Stripe believed the brutal violence of his profession would never touch the sacred peace of his home. He believed he had separated the monster in the cage from the man in the house. At home, he was just Stripe, the goofy, lovable husband, planning to spoil their future daughter.

Then his management team called an emergency meeting. Stripe walked into the glass-walled boardroom of his agency in downtown Los Angeles. The room smelled of expensive cologne, fresh coffee, and nervous energy. Dave sat at the head of the long table. The manager looked older than he had a year ago, his hairline receding further.

Dave pushed a thick, bound contract across the polished mahogany table. "You need to look at this with caution." His voice was calm, a sharp, chilling contrast to the sheer panic he had displayed in the Moscow kitchen. It was as if he had returned to business as usual. Probably due to the doubled security that plagued the Stripe home for the past few months. Armed men in suits with rifles patrolled the house and checked the IDs of friends and family when they came over.

Stripe picked up the heavy document. He flipped past the legal terms and looked at the numbers printed on the payment page. The figures were staggering. It was an astronomical purse for a stadium super fight. A sum of guaranteed money that defied logical comprehension. It was more cash for a single night of work than Stripe had earned in his entire undefeated career combined, plus a massive percentage of the global pay-per-view revenue. It even included a sizable amount of company stock guaranteed to make him beyond wealthy. The kind of money that gets you mentioned next to people like the Rockefellers.

Dave tapped the paper. "They want you to unify the belts against the other organization's heavyweight champion. The global sponsors are aligned. The television networks are on board. It is the biggest payout in the history of combat sports. If you do this, you will be the first ever triple champion and without a doubt the best fighter in the world."

Stripe smiled. He didn't need to hear anything else. He would never say no to this. Even if it was rushed, he was positive no one could beat him. With how things had gone of late, he felt even more powerful. It was as if the happiness in his life had made him stronger. Stripe flashed a grin. "Easy money. I will knock him out and Fortnite dance over his crumpled corpse."

Dave stopped tapping his pen and met Stripe's eyes. "There is a catch. The promoters backing the event made a strict stipulation. It is non-negotiable."

Stripe frowned. "What is the stipulation?"

"The venue. The fight is back in Moscow."

The air in the boardroom felt heavy. The name of the city hung in the space between them like a curse. Stripe drove back to the mansion with the contract sitting on the passenger seat of his sports car. He walked through the massive double doors of his home and found his wife in the kitchen. She was drinking herbal tea and reading a book on parenting. He tossed the thick contract onto the sleek granite kitchen island.

She looked up, confused. Setting her book down, she pulled the document toward her. She read the bold print on the cover page. She read the names. She read the location. The color drained from her face. Her eyes grew wide in horror.

"No. Tell Dave the answer is no." Her voice carried genuine panic.

Stripe leaned against the counter, folding his muscular arms. "Just look at the numbers before you say anything. It is thirty million dollars guaranteed. Up front. Plus the pay-per-view points. Plus company stock. I would own around 10% of a multi-billion-dollar fight org. I would never have to fight again. We could walk away with fifty million cash and hundreds of millions in dividends for life."

Her hands quivered as she pushed the paperwork away. "I don't need a fucking private island. I need my husband alive to raise our daughter. Baby, please. Look at me. Listen to what I am saying. I have a terrible feeling about this. You cannot go back to that city."

Stripe stood tall, confidence radiating off him. "That was months ago, and they haven't reached out. If they wanted revenge, they would have tried something by now. Maybe his dad realized what his son did and felt embarrassed. I would be pissed if our kid were using my name to be a menace. The league smoothed it all over. Dave paid the right people. Nikolai was a drunken punk who had his daddy buy him a new jaw. The Russian government wants this fight to happen. They are guaranteeing my safety. The whole world will be watching. I will be untouchable there."

Tears welled up in her eyes, spilling over her lower lashes and running down her cheeks. "It feels off. Something is wrong, I just don't know what. Please trust my feelings on this. We don't need this money. We are fine how we are, let's not risk it."

But Stripe remained blinded by his desire to go down in history as the best. He looked at her fear and misunderstood it. He thought she was being paranoid due to the pregnancy. He believed she was overreacting due to hormones. He had learned in his parenting class that pregnancy could cause intense reactions to small things. If he had not taken this class, he might have believed her emotions were sincere. He felt positive it was an overreaction she would regret after the baby was born.

He walked around the island and placed his hands on her shoulders. "I have to show them I am not afraid. I have to go down in history. I have to guarantee our futures. I own two divisions. I haven't had a real threat in the ring since I first reached the top 10. I am going to fly over there, knock their fake champion out in the first round, take their millions of dollars, and fly straight back to you."

She looked up at him, the tears falling in a steady stream. She shook her head, a heavy grief settling upon her features. "If this is what you want, I won't say no. But I am terrified."

Stripe kissed her forehead, dismissing the concern. He didn't listen to the only person in the world who understood him. He signed the contract the next morning in Dave's office.

The training camp was the best of his career. Stripe pushed his body to the limit. He brought in the highest-level sparring partners from around the globe and dismantled them in the gym. His speed increased. His power peaked. He felt like an unstoppable force of nature.

The media tour was a circus. Stripe played the villain to perfection. He mocked the Russian champion in interviews. He insulted the promoters. He fed his own legend, generating record-breaking pay-per-view sales before anyone boarded a plane. He predicted the fight. He called out that the opponents needed to make it a rushed fight with a small camp. He told the world it was a cheap trick to attempt to sway the odds in his favor.

His wife refused to attend any of the press events. As her due date neared, she became quiet and withdrawn. The impending trip hung over their home like a dark, suffocating storm cloud.

When the time came to leave, she stood in the massive foyer of their mansion. She was eight months pregnant. The doctor had forbidden her from flying. Stripe wrapped her in a tight hug. He felt the firm, round shape of her belly pressed against him.

Stripe kissed her cheek. "I will call you the second I get back to the hotel room. I love you."

"Just come back to me." Her voice was a soft whisper. She didn't say she loved him back. She just held onto his jacket for a second longer than normal before letting go.

Stripe boarded the private jet with Dave and his coaching staff. He spent the fourteen-hour flight watching films of his opponent and visualizing the knockout. He didn't think about Nikolai. He didn't think about the VIP club. He only thought about the gold and the glory waiting for him. The truth was, he couldn't afford to shift his focus. His opponent was elite. He watched hours of footage of himself on the flight. If he stopped thinking about the match, he might lose. It was that close.

They landed in Moscow under the cover of darkness. The city was just as cold and unforgiving as he remembered. The promoters had arranged a massive, luxurious penthouse suite for him at the most prestigious hotel in the city center. Security details were stationed in the lobby and at the elevators. Everything was professional. It all seemed secure.

Fight week went by in a blur of open workouts, aggressive weigh-ins, and hostile press conferences. The Russian fans hated him with a burning passion, and Stripe fed off their negative energy. He prospered in hostile territory.

When fight night arrived, the outdoor stadium was packed to capacity. Eighty thousand screaming fans braved the freezing temperatures to watch their champion defend the motherland against the arrogant American. All the major streaming platforms worldwide had a presence. The Netflix deal for the fight and the documentary leading up to it had already been negotiated. Even more money guaranteed to hit his pockets for life.

The cage was heated by massive industrial lamps suspended from the rigging. Stripe did his walkout with deafening metalcore music blasting through the air.

The fight itself was a masterclass in violence. The Russian champion was tough, but he was too slow. Stripe picked the man apart with razor-sharp precision. He utilized devastating leg kicks to chop down the larger man's base. He used flawless head movement to avoid the heavy counterpunches. He had to be careful. He knew he was in hostile territory. Any mistakes would give the judges an excuse.

In the middle of the third round, Stripe saw the opening. He faked a takedown attempt. The Russian dropped his hands to defend the grapple.

Stripe exploded upward, launching a flawless flying knee that connected flush with the champion's chin. The man collapsed in a heap. The referee dove in to stop the fight before Stripe could land a follow-up strike. Stripe stood up and walked back to his corner. He knew he had won. But then something unexpected happened.

The ref called a timeout. He ruled the knee illegal. He claimed the fighter's hand had touched the mat, making it a grounded knee strike. Stripe knew he was full of shit. The Russians were attempting to cheat. A point was deducted by Stripe, and a timer began, allowing the Russian champion to recover.

The fourth and fifth rounds slowed the action down. The Russian was scared to engage, and Stripe couldn't overcommit for fear of losing a point again. He went back to the basics and kept it technical. He was still piecing together the Russian but was hesitant to go for a finish. Stripe was confident he would win despite the point deduction. He won every round.

In the final 10 seconds of the fight, he gave it his all. He ended up dropping the Russian and standing over him, raining down blows. The Russian was out cold, but the ref did not stop the fight. After 10 seconds, the bell rang.

The fight concluded, and the two fighters separated. The Russian was carried to his corner as the judges handed their scorecards to the announcer. After what felt like an eternity, the card was read aloud. 29-28 Stripe, 29-28 Igor, and the final judge scores the card 29-28 for the winner and new unified world champion, Stripe.

The stadium fell silent. Eighty thousand people watched in stunned amazement as their invincible hero was defeated on home turf. Stripe stood in the center of the steel cage. The referee raised his hand. The promoter strapped the unified championship belts around his waist. The thickest, heaviest title he had ever seen. Fancy diamonds and other gems covered it. It was obvious this belt was worth hundreds of thousands of dollars. A true one-of-a-kind beauty.

Stripe climbed onto the top of the chain-link fence. He raised the golden belts high into the freezing Russian air. He soaked in the hostility of the silent crowd. He felt invincible. He had conquered their champion in their own backyard. He had proven his wife wrong. He had proven his manager wrong. He was untouchable. He was the best and would go down in history as the best.

He skipped the mandatory post-fight press conference. He didn't care about answering questions from angry journalists. He only wanted to get back to the hotel. He wanted to call his wife. He wanted to hear her voice and tell her that everything was fine. He wanted to tell her that the nightmare was over and they were richer than God.

The black SUV dropped him off at the rear entrance of the luxury hotel. His security team escorted him to the private elevator. He rode up to the penthouse floor in silence. He was exhausted, sore, and overwhelmingly happy. The elevator doors chimed and slid open.

Stripe stepped out onto the plush, silent corridor. He slung his heavy leather gym bag over his shoulder. He whistled a quiet, celebratory tune to himself. He walked down the long hallway, passing the expensive artwork and the ornate wall sconces. He turned the final corner leading straight to his luxury penthouse suite.

He stopped dead in his tracks. The heavy, reinforced oak door of his room was splintered open. The thick wood was cracked inward around the locking mechanism. The door dangled at an angle off its broken, twisted brass hinges. His heart stopped beating. The celebratory tune vanished in his throat. The silence in the long hallway now felt deafening. The peak of his false security had reached its terrifying, inevitable end.

Chapter 14

Stripe earned respect and, in some cases, deep-seated jealousy from the other recruits. His performance in the sparring matches proved impossible to ignore. He never lost. Day by day, he improved at fighting armed opponents using only his monster-hide gauntlets and footwork.

Around one week into training, a recruit named Myra introduced herself. The recruits nearby stopped their drills and stared. A few laughed under their breath. Most looked offended, acting like a filthy vagrant wandered into their last chance at a better life and stole the spotlight.

A woman with short black hair and a jagged scar across her jaw took an aggressive step toward Stripe. Stripe was in the middle of an argument with the Crown over its stubborn refusal to explain its full capabilities.

"A woman should be more supportive. All you do is sit around like a background character," Stripe said.

"Are you joking? What the fuck, man? That's sexist as fuck," the woman recruit replied.

"That was the voice in my head. Not to you."

A lot of recruits took severe offense to the things Stripe said out loud. He blamed the voice in his head and claimed he wasn't speaking to them, but they thought he was an arrogant asshole.

"Whatever you say. Also, I'm not just a 'woman.' I have a name. It's Myra."

"I'll be honest. I don't really care."

"Why are you so rude all the time?"

Stripe crossed his arms. "I've never even spoken to you."

"You say mean shit to people every day, then blame the voice in your head. If half the recruits weren't scared of you already, they would have attacked you in your sleep."

"I already told you, I'm talking to the voice."

CROWN — "Only the user can hear The Crown. Crown is internal to the user only."

Stripe remembered that he looked bat shit crazy to everyone around him. He thought back to Hobb, recalling how quickly he judged the old man for talking to a broom. Stripe rubbed his forehead. "Fuck."

Myra shifted her position, stepping into his line of sight to force his attention. The whole time they talked, he never looked at her, and it aggravated her to no end.

"You should be more respectful. We will be fellow adventurers soon, and you may need our help someday."

Stripe gave a nod. "You're right. I'm sorry."

A heavy pause hung in the air.

"For fucking nothing," Stripe added.

CROWN — "Social acceptance index rapidly declining."

"I'm joking. Someone I knew said that after a big fight, and everyone laughed."

His gaze finally shifted up to Myra. She wore practical battle clothing: tough leather and reinforced cloth. She was attractive, even with the large scar marring her face. She reminded him of the elite women fighters in his league back home. The kind that had men simping for them but were terrifying at their craft. She was lean, with muscle built in all the right places for combat.

The instructor blew his shrill whistle, signaling it was time to train again. The intensity increased this week. Faster running. Harder workouts. More weight. More aggression. More failures.

During one brutal sparring match, a small recruit with a basic sword and shield was paired with a large-framed man wielding a heavy spear. The spear hit the recruit's wooden shield with a loud crack, splintering the wood. The jagged edge lodged itself into the small man's neck. He kicked and squirmed in the dirt. He cried and bled out in a matter of minutes. The healers arrived five minutes after the man stopped moving.

That shifted the mood of the entire camp. This was real. Death could happen at any second. With these pathetic response times, it was unlikely you would survive a mortal injury.

Stripe stared at the body. "That's brutal."

CROWN — "Survivability decreases with fatigue and hunger."

"That makes sense. We are hungry and tired. Mistakes are bound to happen."

Two instructors dragged the body away without a word. The death was never addressed.

That night during chow, an extra tray of food sat on the long wooden table. Everyone knew it belonged to the recruit who died in the sand pit. No one touched it. Stripe finished his own food, then stood up. He walked over to the empty bench and began eating the food from the dead man's tray.

CROWN — "Hunger levels are decreasing. Survivability rising."

The recruits booed and jeered. None dared to stand up. They were unarmed, and they knew they stood no chance in a fistfight.

Myra approached him with a disgusted look on her face. "That's disrespectful."

Stripe took a bite of bread. "How?"

"He died!"

"So he doesn't need it? It would be disrespectful to leave it behind to rot."

"You are insufferable."

Stripe chewed slowly. "I'm a survivor. In the streets, you eat when you can."

Myra took a step back. She was angry, but he was right. In the real world, you do what you must to survive. If an ally falls, you use their equipment or rations to make it home. He wasn't being evil; he adapted better and faster than anyone else in the room. She reluctantly sat back down.

CROWN — "Host performance increased by one percent."

"Wow. I am thriving."

CROWN — "You are in your own way."

The last word landed wrong. It was almost warm. Almost flirtatious.

Stripe paused with his spoon halfway to his mouth. "Say that again."

CROWN — "Clarify request."

"You sounded human for a second."

CROWN — "Incorrect. System voice remains unchanged."

Stripe stared at the stone wall for a long moment. Then he went back to eating like he did not care, though his heart beat a little faster.

Over the weeks, the recruits stopped treating Stripe like a dirty stray dog. They started treating him as dangerous. He was weaker on paper. Everyone could see it. The Crown's pathetic numbers sat in the back of his mind like a constant insult. But when it came to hand-to-hand combat, Stripe was wrong in the way a nightmare is wrong. He moved with an ingrained muscle memory that did not belong in a basic training hall. He cut angles before people knew they had angles to defend. He slipped heavy sword strikes by millimeters and made it look lazy. He took people down without wasting a single breath or motion.

The highest-level opponent he fought was Level 17. When the match started, Stripe became hyper-aggressive, striking weak points with terrifying precision. Each one was a critical strike. He finished the fight in twenty seconds. A Level 5 beating a Level 17 was mathematically insane. Luckily, the recruits didn't know his actual level. They assumed he sat comfortably around Level 15.

During a grueling set of drills, the Crown spoke.

CROWN — "Stats increased through rigorous training. STR +1, AGI +1, END +1. Allocating Stat points to best suited stats."

Stripe called up his interface and glanced at his newly updated stats.

[SYSTEM ALERT: Pugilist Proficiency MAX Reached | Title Acquired: Pugilist Specialist]

"With my Agility being 10, I should be much faster now?"

CROWN — "Slightly faster. The user's Agility stat is now within the average human parameter. Previously, it was below average. In the future, if the user would like, they can assign future skill points."

"10 is average? Right now, I will let you decide. I'm not sure how it all works."

CROWN — "10 is the baseline for average humans. A level one human typically has all stats at 8. The goddess set herself as an indicator for the user's baseline."

Stripe groaned. "WOW! My stats fucking suck."

CROWN — "Correct."

Stripe continued his run, feeling depressed by the harsh reality of his own biology. Then he saw a recruit falling out of formation. Her name was Makel. She was one of the only recruits who didn't avoid him in the mess hall. Stripe ran beside her. He helped her keep pace. He encouraged her and occasionally threatened her when she looked like she wanted to quit. She finished the run and never fell out again.

Over time, he began helping other recruits. Not with grand speeches. Not with soaring inspiration. He helped with practical, brutal corrections. Correcting sloppy footwork. Dragging exhausted recruits to the water barrels. Sharing his own food when someone looked ready to collapse.

Sometimes he did it because of a quiet voice in his memory.

You cannot just use your hands to destroy. You have to help sometimes, too. Promise me you won't just be some douche who bullies the weak. Stripe didn't remember agreeing to it. He just remembered the way she believed he could be better. So he helped.

When a recruit named Jalen took a wooden training spear straight through the thigh and nearly bled out in the sand, Stripe tore his own shirt into tight strips and held heavy pressure on the artery until a healer finally arrived.

"Why are you helping me?" Jalen groaned.

"Because you are still breathing."

Jalen graduated. Limping, but alive.

The recruits stood in a rigid line with dark bruises, fresh bandages, and eyes that had learned new meanings for exhaustion. The head instructor walked past them, his staff tapping against the sand.

"You did not die. That is the standard. Do not look proud. You are still trash with traditional weapons. I hope you don't run into something those gauntlets can't handle."

Stripe stood tall with his monster gauntlets on, feeling their comforting weight like a quiet promise. Myra nudged him with her elbow.

"If you get killed on your first mission, I am taking your food tray." Myra kept her voice low.

"Fair. Just make sure you eat it. It would be offensive not to." Stripe whispered back.

She snorted, a genuine smile breaking through her tough exterior. "I know it's rude, but I have to know. What level are you? I have a bet going that you are level twenty."

"Five."

Myra scoffed. "Liar. Stop teasing me."

"I swear. I just have hands."

Myra let out a heavy breath. "What the fuck."

The fact that this Level 5 vagrant dominated every single hand-to-hand fight in the yard shook her to her core.

"I will get stronger," Myra vowed.

"Good. I need a rival."

Without anyone explicitly agreeing to it, the dynamic in the yard had shifted. Myra started tossing him her extra water skin after sparring, and the other recruits stopped flinching when he threw a punch, choosing instead to watch his footwork. Even when he stood in the corner cursing at the empty air, they no longer backed away; they just rolled their eyes and kept drilling.

Just outside the gates, Hobb showed up at the edge of the hall. He was soaked from the morning rain, grinning like he owned the entire district. Beside him stood Maribel, his imaginary wife: a battered broom with a smiling face drawn on the bristles. Stripe had learned not to comment on it. His experience training had shown him exactly how he was perceived by others when he talked to the Crown, and now he was painfully aware of how unfairly he judged Hobb. Hobb was happiest when people played along.

"Look at you. All fancy. Maribel says you look like a respectable adventurer now."

Stripe's throat tightened with a sudden emotion. "I'll try to deserve the compliment."

"I guess this means you will be busy with missions and won't be coming back to bed beside me."

"Yeah, I owe a lot of money to these bastards."

Hobb gave a nod. "That's how they get you." Hobb leaned closer. His eyes turned crystal clear, stripping away the crazy old man persona. "Tell the voice in your head I will miss it too."

Stripe nodded once, honoring the moment.

"And tell that snake of a man he looks just like he acts."

Nearby, Varn stood smiling his greasy, predatory smile. Stripe looked directly at him.

"I was told to tell you, you look how you act."

Varn blinked in surprise, then laughed softly. "Thank you."

"It wasn't a compliment."

CROWN — "Statement is correct."

Stripe ignored it. The instructor handed out the sealed mission papers. When Stripe's name was called, he broke the wax seal and read the bold text at the top of the contract.

Forest of the Damned Ore Expedition: Dwarven Subcontract

The payment numbers listed below looked insulting. The payment would be based solely on the amount of ore extracted. At most, if he broke his back working, he could pay off around one hundred gold coins of his massive debt. This assumed he was not tipped, and that tips went directly to the adventurers rather than through the guild. This was the strict law of the empire.

Several recruits read the header on his paper and flinched. Myra leaned over his shoulder, her eyes widening.

"You're fucked. This is a suicide mission."

[INVENTORY UPDATE: Monster Gauntlets equipped | Debt: 2800 Gold]

CHAPTER 15

Myra read his mission sheet once. Then she read it again, slower this time, like the words might apologize if she stared hard enough. They did not. She looked up at him with the expression of someone being forced to watch a man walk into a bear trap while smiling. Myra handed the paper back.

"You are fucked."

"That sounded almost caring. I appreciate the support." Stripe held his deadpan expression.

"I am serious. This mission is for someone at a much higher level. Likely two or more members. Also, the pay is just straight up ass."

"Damn, so I am not going to get rich and be surrounded by bad bitches?" Stripe let out a sigh.

She held up her own mission slip. "Mine is basic caravan defense. Merchant route. Predictable road. Boring work. Yours is a dwarven ore subcontract through the Forest of the Damned."

"So mine has personality and small men?"

"Yours has a body count." Myra pointed at the paper. "That forest is full of bandits and beasts. You'd better hope you are traveling to a known mine."

Stripe flashed a confident grin. "Goddess gives her strongest soldiers the hardest missions."

CROWN — "False."

She exhaled through her nose and folded her paper. "I am saying good luck before you do something stupid. I will keep an eye on your food tray."

"I will miss my tray more than I will miss you."

The corner of her mouth twitched, then flattened. "Be careful."

That one sounded sincere, so he covered it the same way he covered everything else.

"I have built my life on careful decision-making."

"That is the least convincing thing you have ever said."

Stripe gave a shrug. "I have said some truly stupid things, so that is a brutal ranking."

She shifted her pack higher and started toward her caravan muster line. "Good luck, Stripe."

"Good luck, Myra." Stripe cupped his hands around his mouth. "Try not to get fat while I am gone."

She kept walking. "Try not to smell worse when you come back."

"No promises."

He waved after her. She did not wave back, but she did look over her shoulder once before disappearing into the flow of guild traffic.

The dwarven caravan waited near the outer lane. There was one reinforced wagon. There were two thick draft beasts. There were three dwarves. The wagon looked less built for travel and more built to survive being on the road. The eldest dwarf was compact and brutal-looking, thick through the shoulders with beard braids capped in iron. The second was wider, redder in the face, and already chewing something smoked. The youngest sat on the wagon bench with a crossbow across his knees and eyes too sharp for his age.

Stripe tightened the straps on his gauntlets as he approached. The eldest dwarf looked him over without warmth. He introduced the trio as Brokk, Keld, and Dorin.

"That is the guild recruit." Brokk let out a grunt.

"I prefer a trusted specialist, but I can work with a recruit," Stripe corrected.

"If you were a specialist, I could not afford you."

Dorin laughed around his food. "Good. He has a mouth. That makes the road shorter."

Brokk frowned. "So would silence."

The quiet one studied Stripe's gloves, his stance, and the slight tension in him that never faded.

Keld leaned on his crossbow. "He does not look very strong."

Stripe flexed. "I am the strongest."

They were not impressed.

CROWN — "Your self-assessment remains overly generous."

Stripe rubbed his temple. "You are committed to making first impressions worse."

Brokk narrowed his eyes. "What are you talking about?"

"That is to my friend in my head, not you."

CROWN — "We are not friends."

Dorin's grin widened. "Better than the last guard."

"What happened to the last guard?" Stripe asked.

"He died," Brokk stated as a matter of fact.

"How?"

The question was ignored. Stripe felt uncomfortable. The trio laughed at his discomfort. Brokk jerked a thumb toward himself, reintroducing his family.

"Brokk Stonevein." He patted his chest. "Wagon lead."

Then he pointed toward the broader dwarf. "Dorin Stonevein. Talks too much. Cooks well enough to survive criticism."

Then he pointed toward the wagon bench. "Keld Stonevein. Best eyes here."

Stripe offered a nod. "Stripe."

"Real name?" Brokk questioned.

"It is the real one."

"You need a nickname." Brokk crossed his arms. "All of the best adventurers go by a nickname. Maybe we will give you one if you live."

Brokk grunted like the answer had wasted his time. "Fine. You guard the road. You lift when told. You do not scare the beasts. You do not die in a way that creates work for us."

"That all sounds very reasonable and deeply loving," Stripe deadpanned.

Dorin stuck out a hand. "Grip check."

Stripe took it. Dorin squeezed hard. Stripe squeezed back. Dorin raised his brows a fraction.

"Skinny. Pretty weak."

Stripe flashed a grin. "That felt like foreplay."

Keld's gaze lowered to the gauntlets again. "You fight."

"I have got hands."

Brokk climbed onto the wagon. "Good. Get in."

The wagon rolled out. The city fell behind them in layers of noise, walls, and dust until the road was just a road again and everyone on it belonged more to weather than law.

The first week was not dramatic. That was what made it matter. The days settled into a pattern of movement, checks, camp, food, and watch rotations. Brokk drove and counted everything. Dorin cooked and talked through half the daylight hours. Keld scouted ahead at dawn and dusk, then faded back to the wagon line with quiet updates about tracks, weather, and the general mood of the land.

Stripe learned them through repetition. Brokk hated waste. Time, food, motion, rope, breath. If something took effort, he wanted the full value of that effort back. Dorin joked constantly, but none of his habits were sloppy. His knives were always cleaned properly. His meals were rationed correctly. His traps were set right. He looked careless only if you were not paying attention. Keld saw everything. Bent grass. Bird silence. Broken twigs. The difference between wind shift and someone choosing not to step on a branch.

They learned Stripe, too. They learned he woke hard and fast. They learned he checked exits in open space. They learned he muttered at the Crown under his breath often enough that it stopped being alarming and started becoming one more sound of the road.

"Did the voice insult you yet today?" Dorin asked while stirring a pot.

Stripe let out a sigh. "Repeatedly."

"Good. Means it cares enough to be mean."

CROWN — "Dorin Stonevein continues to display irrational conclusions."

"Please stop bullying the cook. He feeds us." Stripe aimed the words at the empty air.

"If the ghost starts insulting dinner, I am throwing both of you into the brush," Brokk threatened from the wagon bench.

"Fair."

The arguments with the Crown kept getting worse.

CROWN — "Unlikely bonding occurring. Friendship levels are increasing."

"You make everything so weird."

CROWN — "You remain defensive while incorrect."

"I cannot even remember you ever being helpful."

One night by the fire, Keld glanced up from oiling the crossbow string. "You answer her like it is standing there."

Stripe stared into the flames for a second. "Trust me. That would be less complicated."

No one laughed. That silence felt more respectful than awkward. By the eighth day, they were used to him. Not comfortable with it. Used to it. They thought it was a joke for a bit. Now they knew he was dead serious. They saw him doing it when no one was around. That was close enough.

The wolf came just after noon. The road had tightened between trees and broken stone, the kind of place where sound died early and came back wrong. Keld had just stepped in from the brush when Crown spoke.

CROWN — "Hostile predator approaching from the left. Estimated level 8."

Stripe turned. Gray-black hide flashed through the brush. The beast hit the edge of the road at full speed, all muscle, scar tissue, and hunger. His body remembered the first wolf before his mind caught up. Teeth. Dirt. Fear. Weakness. He hated it immediately.

"Contact left," Brokk shouted.

The wolf launched at the wagon. Keld's crossbow came up, but Dorin was in the line. Stripe was already moving. He jumped from the rear of the wagon and landed low with both gauntlets up. The wolf changed targets and came for him.

CROWN — "Estimated HP 162/162."

"Man, I love that feature." Stripe grinned.

The bite came high. Stripe slipped right by inches. Teeth scraped leather at the shoulder.

CROWN — "Host HP 100/100. Damage negated by clothing."

He snapped a jab into the muzzle. Then another. Then a short right to the nose ridge.

Wolf HP: 154/162

The wolf recoiled, snarled, and came back lower on the second rush. Smarter this time. It cut his leg. Its teeth raked his calf. Pain tore through the limb, hot and bright.

CROWN — "Host HP 98/100. Bleeding minor. Mobility reduced by 4 percent. Predator's natural armor prevents major damage from minor strikes."

"Fantastic. Love that for me, slay king."

The beast circled. Stripe circled with it, keeping the wagon wheel close enough to use but not close enough to trap himself. He had less strength. Less armor. Less reach. What he did have was distance management and a lifetime of understanding what footwork meant when someone stronger wanted to hurt you.

The wolf leaped over the wheel. Stripe stepped in under the neck line, slammed his forearm into the jaw hinge, and chopped his boot into the front leg on landing. The beast crashed into the wagon frame.

Wolf HP: 145/162

It recovered and ripped a paw across his chest. Leather split. Claws dug. Stripe hit the dirt hard enough to lose his breath.

CROWN — "Host HP 98/100. Rib damage probable. Mobility further decreased."

Stripe let out a wheeze. "You make everything sound so grim. I am just getting fired up."

The wolf came again while he was rising. Stripe rolled left. Teeth snapped shut where his face had been. He jammed the gauntlet into its mouth for one brief instant and drove a right hand into the underside of the jaw.

Wolf HP: 132/162

Pain shot through his wrist. The wolf tore back, blood and spit shaking from its muzzle.

Brokk aimed a heavy crossbow. "Need the shot?"

"Not yet." Stripe locked his stance. "I have beef with these things."

CROWN — "Current decision influenced by ego rather than efficiency."

"Shit, I am all ego."

The wolf rushed again. This time, Stripe stepped toward it instead of away. He punched the damaged eye, then the throat, then the eye again as he pivoted off line.

Wolf HP: 118/162

The beast slammed sideways into him, and both of them hit the dirt. Its weight crushed his ribs and knocked a noise out of him that sounded too much like pain to be funny.

CROWN — "Host HP 97/100. The host is losing this engagement. Please receive help."

The last line sounded pleading. Very human again.

Stripe shoved both boots into the belly and forced just enough space to scramble up. The wolf rose too. Slower now. Not by much. Enough to matter.

He stopped chasing damage and started chasing mechanics. He made it turn. He broke angles. He hit the same vulnerable places over and over because that was how weaker men won ugly fights. Eye with a straight right. Pivot after every strike. Never stay longer than the impact takes. A roundhouse to the nose. The wolf snapped at his ankle, missing. A follow-up spinning back kick to the throat. The wolf staggered.

Wolf HP: 108/162

Wolf HP: 75/162

Wolf HP: 65/162

The wolf lunged high. Stripe ducked under, drew the iron dagger mid-motion, and buried it under the ribs.

Wolf HP: 30/162

CROWN — "Critical hit successful. Target bleeding."

The beast screamed and twisted hard. Stripe let go before it could take his hand with the knife. It stumbled, turned, and came again on fury alone. He slipped outside the line of the bite and drove a full right straight into the ruined eye.

Wolf HP: 17/162

The wolf collapsed. It tried to rise. One leg failed.

CROWN — "Threat remains active. HP 17/100."

Stripe cracked his knuckles. "Not for long."

He approached carefully and drove the dagger down through the throat.

Wolf HP: 0/162

The silence after felt heavy and sharp. Dorin reached him first.

"Sit down." Dorin guided him toward the woods. "We need to treat your bleeding."

"Yes, sir." Stripe slumped against the wagon wheel.

Brokk looked from the corpse to Stripe. "You fight like a bastard with no regard for your life."

Stripe offered a weak laugh. "That is the nicest insult I have had all week."

CROWN — "Level increase confirmed."

"About fucking time."

CROWN — "Noted. Here are the host's new stats."

"See." Stripe gave a smile. "You can almost be nice by accident."

- **Name:** Stripe
- **Level:** 6
- **Class:** Unassigned
- **Title:** Toxic Fisherman, Pugilist Specialist
- **HP:** 27/110
- **Stamina:** 125/125
- **Mana:** 0/0

Attributes

- **STR:** 11
- **AGI:** 10
- **END:** 11
- **INT:** 6
- **Skill points:** 0

They cleaned the wolf before dark. Brokk handled the cut lines. Dorin worked the meat. Keld watched the tree line and helped where he could.

Nobody wasted motion. When the pelt came free, Dorin gave a low whistle.

"Better shape than the rag you are carrying."

Stripe looked down at the old hide tied with his things. "Hey, this is from my first kill. Do not be rude. I could never part with it for some perfectly cut piece."

CROWN — "Host did not kill the beast."

"Surviving counts."

They roasted a wolf over a hard fire that night. Dorin seasoned it with a guarded blend of root powder and fat, turning survival food into something suspiciously good. When the meal was done, Keld walked over with the cleaned pelt folded in both arms.

"Yours," Keld said.

Stripe took it. Heavier. Cleaner. Better fur. Better cut. A real upgrade.

"Thanks. I think it would be rude to decline."

He tossed his old one away and pulled the new one on. It fit better, smelled better, and made him look a little less homeless.

CROWN — "Host defense slightly increased."

Keld offered a shrug. "You killed it. You keep it."

That was the first time warmth showed clearly in his voice.

[SYSTEM ALERT: Level 6 Reached | HP: 27/110]

CHAPTER 16

The second week settled into the road, establishing a routine and the slow accumulation of trust. Brokk stopped checking every single bundle after Stripe reset the camp lines during a rainstorm. Dorin started handing him the first bowl of hot stew more often than not. Keld shifted his watch positions so his crossbow covered Stripe's weaker, injured side while the superficial wounds healed.

Stripe returned the unspoken loyalty. He sharpened the heavy edge of Brokk's battleaxe when the evening light was good enough. He reset one of Dorin's complex perimeter traps without being asked or expecting thanks. He carried more weight when Keld came back exhausted and late from scouting ahead. The arguments with the Crown continued. They grew more personal.

CROWN — "Association with the Stoneveins has improved your survival probability by 18 percent."

Stripe leaned back. "You sound jealous."

CROWN — "That interpretation is irrational."

"So it's sounding jealous, yet here we are."

Dorin looked over from the crackling fire and smirked, stirring the stew. "The ghost likes us more than it likes you."

Stripe held a hand to his chest. "Impossible. I am in peak manhood. Do you not see my delicate charm?"

Brokk let out a grunt from the wagon. "That is your second least convincing statement."

Keld lowered his voice. "What was the first?"

Brokk kept his eyes on the road. "Everything said before it."

The bandits hit near dusk four days later. Keld saw movement first, but not soon enough to stop the rush. A swordsman burst from the thick brush to the right of the wagon, his face hollow with hunger and bad decisions. Another moved in fast near the draft beasts. A third hid in the dense trees with a loaded crossbow. The fourth held back on the road with a spear, waiting for someone else to make the first fatal mistake.

CROWN — "Four hostiles. Estimated level range 5 to 6."

Brokk raised his axe. "Contact."

The swordsman chose Stripe. He chose him because Stripe looked softer and less armored than the sturdy dwarves. That was his last useful choice.

CROWN — "Estimated HP. Swordsman 84/84."

The rusted blade came in high and broad. Stripe stepped inside the arc, checked the wrist with his lead hand, and drove a straight right into the nose.

Swordsman HP: 64/84

Blood burst. Before the man could recover his balance, Stripe hit him with a right hook.

Swordsman HP: 39/84

He stepped deeper and punched the throat. His monster-hide gauntlets pierced the soft flesh.

Swordsman HP: 13/84

The swordsman staggered backward, choking on his own blood. Stripe planted his feet and drove one final punch into the hinge of the jaw. The gauntlet blades tore in deep. The jaw hinge snapped, and blood sprayed across the forest floor.

Swordsman HP: 0/84

The man dropped. Human. Not a beast. A human killed by his own hand. That terrible fact rose in Stripe's chest like burning bile. He wanted to throw up. He buried the feeling. He forced it down too deep to look at, though he knew it wasn't deep enough to disappear.

Stripe stared at his gauntlets. "Great. First one. That feels awful."

He exhaled a shaky breath. "Still, better him than me."

A heavy bolt flew across the roadway, unseen by Stripe. The crossbow bolt hit his upper left arm. It was devastating. Not flashy. Not cinematic. Just brutal. It punched deep into the meat of the arm with blunt force and a deadening shock that made his fingers open before the pain even arrived. Then the pain hit all at once. White. Blinding. Mean. His whole arm became a useless, screaming, dead weight.

CROWN — "Host HP 103/145. Penetrating wound. Blood loss active."

Stripe screamed through his teeth. "Holy fuck. This fucking sucks. Why do rappers brag about this?"

CROWN — "Damage enhanced by sneak factor."

Keld fired. The loud crack of his heavy crossbow was short and hard. Somewhere up in the trees, a man made a broken, wet noise and crashed through the brush to the forest floor.

Archer HP: 0/76

Brokk hit another bandit near the panicked beasts with his heavy shield first, and his broad axe second. Dorin buried a rusted hatchet deep into a third man's chest and ripped it back out with both hands, letting out a growl. That left Stripe alone with the spearman.

The man had enough martial discipline to be dangerous. He stayed outside of punching distance, his spear point steady, his feet organized and grounded. He wasn't a genius, but he possessed enough training. Stripe was damaged, bleeding, and panicked.

CROWN — "Estimated HP. Spearman 93/93."

Hot blood ran down Stripe's forearm and dripped from his numb fingers. The pain in the arm was intense enough to make the rest of his body feel far away. Every minor movement sent new, pulsing heat through the ragged wound. Every heartbeat pushed more wet warmth down his skin.

The Spearman curled his lip into a sneer. "You are done. When the boss gets here, he will kill all of you, and we will fuck your pretty little corpse."

Stripe swayed on his feet, letting out a grunt. "Maybe later. I have scheduling conflicts, and my ass has a chastity belt."

The first thrust came straight down the line. Stripe knocked it off course with his good hand and shifted his body instead of trying to contest force with force. The sharp tip still sliced a shallow groove along his side. Even though he did not actively use it, his injured arm stung with the rapid movement.

CROWN — "Host HP 98/145. Secondary damage is minor. Blood loss worsening."

The second thrust came lower and faster. Guild training flashed up in him with all the heavy weight of brutal repetition. Control the shaft. Step outside the line. Punish the entry. He slapped the spear aside with his injured arm anyway and nearly blacked out from the resulting explosion of pain. Then he stepped inside the guard and drove a short right hook into the man's ribs.

Spearman HP: 81/93

The man grunted and slammed the heavy wooden butt of the spear across Stripe's shoulder. Stripe flinched.

CROWN — "Host HP 90/110."

Stripe staggered. The spearman smiled. That actually helped. Comfort created bad habits.

CROWN — "Blood loss is reducing overall efficiency."

Stripe let out a hiss. "You always know what to say to get a man going."

The Spearman leveled his weapon. "Who the fuck are you talking to?"

Stripe flashed a grim smile. "Your dead buddies in the afterlife. They miss you bitch boy."

The next thrust came harder. It was more committed. The man was agitated and confident of victory. Stripe let the spear extend too far on purpose. He trapped the long shaft under his good forearm, stepped outside the lead foot, and drove an uppercut into the throat.

Spearman HP: 56/93

The man's breath broke with a wet gasp, but his wide stance did not fall. Not yet. Stripe stayed on him. A stiff jab to the mouth.

Spearman HP: 46/93

A driving knee to the sternum.

Spearman HP: 39/93

A vicious headbutt squarely to the nose. The spear wobbled. Stripe's blood ran down his hand and smeared across the wooden shaft between them. The spearman saw it. Then he saw the exposed skin on his own hands begin to redden, blister, and swell.

The Spearman's eyes went wide. "What the fuck is that?"

CROWN — "Toxic Fisherman trait activated due to bodily secretion."

Stripe kept his eyes on his opponent. "That is a deeply upsetting sentence."

The spearman panicked. That ruined the rest of the fight for him. He tried to yank the spear back too hard. His grip weakened. His breathing was already damaged. Stripe batted the spear point off line, stepped through the opening, and punched the throat again where the earlier damage had landed.

Spearman HP: 11/93

The man stumbled backward, clawing at his own neck and swollen hand. He fell heavily to one knee, failing to drag in a full breath of air.

CROWN — "Target has been poisoned."

With every ragged breath he took, the poison did more damage. Stripe kept his distance, watching as the man began to fade. He collapsed into the dirt, clawing at his own throat and foaming at the mouth.

Spearman HP: 0/93

Stripe stood there swaying. His arm throbbed, his chest felt tight, and his whole body was shaking from the adrenaline dump and blood loss. One thought landed clean through the foggy haze of pain. He needed a ranged ally. Not later. He needed one right now.

Dorin reached him first. Dorin pointed at a rock. "Sit down before I make you."

Stripe slurred his words. "I like to be dominated but only by women."

Brokk stepped up beside them. "You are bleeding on the road."

Stripe gestured loosely to the corpse. "You should see the other guy."

Brokk snapped the wooden shaft shorter. Dorin held him still while the thick bandage went on tight enough to make Stripe's vision spark with stars.

CROWN — "Host HP stabilizing at 83/145."

Stripe let out a grunt. "Eighty-three does not feel stable."

CROWN — "It remains preferable to lower values."

Keld returned from the brush, carrying the dead archer's heavy crossbow.

Keld offered a nod. "Clean shot."

Brokk gave a grunt of approval. "Good."

Stripe looked at the deadly weapon. He took a heavy breath. "I need to get some friends who can stop me from getting stabbed and shot all the time."

CROWN — "That conclusion is strategically sound."

Stripe shook his head. "Amazing. I only needed to get shot to make you like me. I have a question. Since Toxic Fisherman activates through my juices, does that mean if I have sex, it will poison the girl?"

CROWN — "Likelihood of host engaging in consensual sexual encounter in negative parameters."

"Fuck you too then."

He felt troubled by this thought. The Crown refused to elaborate. He was forced to move on without knowing if he was a walking STD or not.

The party looted the bodies. Stripe took coin, a decent knife, a better leather pouch, and anything that looked easy to sell. He left the rest of the gear for the Stoneveins. No one argued. He had paid for the first pick in blood.

The long road after that felt different. Not safer. More shared. Brokk started asking Stripe where he wanted to make camp. They offered him potent dwarven alcohol. He took a single drink, then shit his pants. They never offered him any again. But they found it hilarious. Dorin passed him stronger portions at dinner. Keld answered his questions with complete sentences instead of annoyed fragments. Stripe found himself instinctively checking their blind sides. Nobody named the shift. They just kept moving forward.

The deep mine itself went smoothly. Three weeks of constant, lingering danger led to brutal, hard labor. Mud. Rope burn. Choking on ore dust. Sore backs. Cramped shoulders. Filthy hands. There were no monsters or ghosts. There was no cursed horror emerging from the dark. It was just exhausting work and friendly banter.

They pulled enough precious ore to matter. It was enough to pay off a solid 100 gold from Stripe's staggering debt. It was also enough to allow the dwarven brothers to compete with the rival smithing competition back in town. They gambled their lives on this dangerous trip, and it paid off.

The return trip should have been easy after that. It was not. The bandit leader found them on the final stretch of the road. He stepped into the dirt road with his broadsword held low and hate plain on his scarred face. A thick scar ran through one cheek. He possessed thick, powerful shoulders. He wore the kind of eerie calm men only wore when they mistook survival for competence. His dead eyes fixed on Stripe.

The Bandit Leader leveled his gaze. "You killed my men."

Stripe held up a finger. "I killed like two of them. One died of bodily fluid. It was weird."

Brokk hefted his axe. "You want revenge?"

The Bandit Leader pointed his sword directly at Stripe. "I want him screaming."

He was not a fan of the humor.

CROWN — "Estimated level 7. Estimated HP 128/128."

He attacked without another word. The first heavy slash came fast. Stripe slipped it by inches. The second rapid strike clipped the tough leather at his ribs.

CROWN — "Host HP 82/110. Target appears to have abnormal agility."

The third heavy swing forced him backward. The leader was stronger than the others. He was not elegant. He was not refined. He was just experienced enough to be dangerous and confident enough to overcommit to his swings.

Stripe tested the body with a stiff right hand to the liver. Almost nothing.

Leader HP: 126/128

Then a fast left hook to the jaw. Still, almost nothing.

Leader HP: 125/128

The Bandit Leader flashed a sneer. "My turn."

He drove a hard elbow directly into Stripe's sternum and kicked the sensitive area outside of his knee. Stripe buckled and caught a glancing, painful cut across the shoulder as he recovered.

CROWN — "Host HP 69/110. Defensive skill detected. Target damage mitigation active."

Stripe let out a wheeze. "That makes sense."

The smug grin on the leader's face said he already knew exactly how mathematically unfair the fight looked. So Stripe stopped playing that specific fight. He quit trying to hurt the man directly with strikes and started manipulating him instead.

He chopped low kicks into the calf to shift the man's weight. He leaned heavily on the shoulder. He redirected the sword arm. He made the leader turn much more than he wanted to. Physical force still moved him. Balance still betrayed him. The magical skill did not make him immune to basic physics and mechanics. That was enough. He got a crazy idea and spat on his gauntlets.

CROWN — "Toxic Fisherman has been activated. Defensive skill duration appears limited."

Stripe let out a grunt, dodging another swing. "You could have led with that."

CROWN — "You seemed occupied."

The leader rushed hard for the finish. Stripe sidestepped cleanly and shoved him past with a heavy forearm across the neck. The man's feet crossed awkwardly. Stripe landed a solid punch to the man's exposed side, his gauntlet spikes barely breaching the tough surface.

CROWN — "Target has been poisoned. Defensive mitigation inactive."

Stripe offered a smirk. "Time to fuck him up."

The leader turned with pure fury and committed to a massive downward cut. Stripe stepped outside the dangerous line, planted his feet, and drove his shin up through the wide open stance with every ounce of timing, hip turn, and spite he possessed. The kick landed. The sound was awful. It thudded across the silent forest. It was unmistakable. The bandit leader's balls exploded from the impact.

The dwarven brothers began to rotate around the bandit leader, searching for a safe way to enter the frantic fight. The leader folded around the impact instantly, dropping his sword.

Leader HP: 61/128

The Bandit Leader gasped for air. "You son of a-"

Stripe caught him by the hair and smashed a rising knee directly into his face.

Leader HP: 19/128

The man crashed to the dirt, choking. His hands clutched between his legs, his body unable to process too many massive disasters all at once.

CROWN — "Target remains alive."

Stripe set his stance. "I can fix that."

Stripe stamped down on the exposed throat. A sickening snap followed.

Leader HP: 0/128

Silence came back hard. It was not peace. Just the abrupt end of motion.

CROWN — "Level increase confirmed. Allocating stat point."

Stripe took a breath. "Hell yeah."

CROWN — "Stats are displaying."

[SYSTEM ALERT: Level 7 Reached | Inventory: Slave Voucher added]

CROWN — "The defensive skill used by the target may be subject to analysis."

Stripe stared into the middle distance for a second. "That is a thing you can do?"

CROWN — "Correct."

"You keep unveiling features like the most hostile update cycle in history."

CROWN — "Agreement remains pending."

Stripe let out a sigh. "Fine. Analyze it."

CROWN — "Completion time will be significant."

"So is my debt. Get in line."

Stripe reached down and took his money pouch.

They made camp early that night. Nobody said much at first. That silence did not feel empty or awkward. It felt earned. Brokk sat beside Stripe with a rough clay cup of strong liquor. He remembered who he was offering it to, grunted loudly, and drank it himself.

Brokk offered a nod. "Good work."

That was apparently a full, emotional speech from him.

Dorin cleaned the dead leader's blood off Stripe's gauntlets and shook his head in mild disbelief. "You always fight like that?"

Stripe took a seat by the fire. "No. Sometimes there are fewer exploding testicles."

Dorin stared at him. Then he barked out a sudden laugh that took Brokk with it a second later. Even the stoic Keld smiled.

The next morning, Brokk handed Stripe a folded, dirty voucher. The heavy paper was thick and ugly and smelled faintly like old, spilled ale. Brokk tapped the paper. "Won it in cards off a market owner months back. Free slave voucher. Worthless to me. Useful to you."

Stripe turned the paper over. *BROKK STONEVEIN* was scratched across the back in blocky, ugly letters.

Stripe examined the text. "That is one hell of a sentence to hear before breakfast."

Brokk turned away to pack the gear. "The world gives ugly tools. Use useful ones."

"I hate how practical that sounds."

"Hate it later. Use it to find the ally you said you needed."

Stripe nodded in thanks, tucking away the heavy envelope.

They reached the towering guild by dusk two days later. The heavy ore was weighed. The official papers were signed. The Stoneveins got paid. Stripe got official mission credit and the ugly, hollow satisfaction of watching his debt number drop from 3000 to 2800. At the pristine guild desk, a bored clerk took his forms and brought out a narrow, silver necklace set with a dark, polished stone. The clerk held it over a blue magical flame while intricate runes crawled across the metal like tiny insects made of pure light.

The Clerk pushed it across the counter. "Congratulations. You completed your first post-graduation mission. This is your identification rune."

The warm necklace was set in Stripe's calloused hand.

"It tracks missions completed, debt owed, rank, and affiliation."

Stripe examined the item. "You people found a way to make ownership decorative."

The clerk looked up with practiced indifference. "Rank. Tin."

Stripe blinked. "There are ranks?"

The clerk let out a sigh. "This was covered in class."

Stripe slid the necklace over his head. "I was busy surviving class."

When he touched the cool rune, glowing information flashed across his vision. A display for everyone to see lit up brilliantly in front of him:

Tin Rank. Guild Affiliation Confirmed. Debt Owed: 2800 Gold. Missions Completed: 1.

Two hundred down. It should have felt tiny. Instead, it felt measurable. That was worse in some ways. Varn appeared with the exact, irritating timing of a rash.

Varn flashed a smile. "Back already. How industrious."

Stripe crossed his arms. "You sound so fucking creepy all the time, man."

Varn smiled without a single ounce of warmth. He ignored the insult. "I love the feeling of easy money. Best get back to it. Now you can pick your own quests. Congratulations, you are now a valued family member of the guild."

It felt gross to hear him say the word "family". Stripe gave a cringe.

"That sounded romantic in a prison butt buddy sort of way."

Varn smoothed his coat. "You have an astonishing range of wrong responses."

Stripe left before the conversation became legally binding. The slave voucher felt heavier in his pocket the closer he got to the bustling market district. He hated the idea of it. He hated the cold practicality of it even more. Owning a human being was wrong, but he was far too broke to pay for proper services. He was too unlikable to recruit actual friends to help. He was too deeply in debt for many other options.

CROWN — "You are rationalizing."

"I am coping."

CROWN — "Both statements may be true."

Stripe looked down at the folded, dirty paper in his hand, then toward the crude slave market signs ahead, and finally at the pitiful amount of actual money he had.

Stripe let out a sigh. "Great. Another mouth to feed."

He kept walking toward the signs.

Chapter 17

Velryssa Metaldrum once lived in a house that fed the kingdom's steel. House Metaldrum controlled the ore that forged the nation. Iron from the northern cliffs. Silver from the western mountains. Copper and tin were shipped across the southern seas. If a sword existed in the kingdom, Metaldrum ore touched it first. If a coin existed, Metaldrum silver became it.

For two centuries, the kingdom depended on them. Armies marched with metal drum iron. Cities rose on Metaldrum steel. Even the Royal Mint struck coins from its shipments. Kings tolerated them, but kings rarely loved families that powerful.

Velryssa grew up surrounded by trade maps and polished armor. The estate gates were forged from black iron, so smooth they reflected sunlight like water. Carriages arrived daily carrying merchants, nobles, and diplomats. Her father negotiated contracts that decided whether armies marched with swords or wooden spears. Her mother hosted gatherings where alliances formed and broke. Velryssa watched everything. She learned early that power did not always wear a crown. Sometimes it was written on a shipping ledger.

By sixteen, the suitors began arriving. At first, there were a few. Then dozens. Young nobles. Merchant princes. Foreign envoys pretended their visits had nothing to do with marriage. They praised her beauty, her intelligence, and her family. Velryssa smiled. Then she refused them. Marriage was power. She did not waste power.

Her mother once teased her about it. "You enjoy watching them suffer." Her mother let out a laugh. "I admit I enjoy watching these thirsty men throw themselves at you. None of them could handle you. You are too strong-willed."

Velryssa kept her smile. "Only the arrogant ones."

One man did not take rejection well. Lord Carthis. Young. Wealthy. He believed the world existed to reward him. He arrived with a caravan of gifts that filled the Metaldrum courtyard: jewels, silks, and a ceremonial blade forged from star iron. He knelt in front of her household and delivered a speech rehearsed to perfection. Velryssa listened. Then she declined. She would not marry him.

Lord Carthis left before sunset. Three days later, rumors spread across the capital. He locked himself inside his study. When the doors were forced open, the physicians said despair had already taken him. He took his own life after her refusal. The story traveled fast from courts to taverns. Some blamed Velryssa. Others blamed the man's arrogance. But everyone remembered the lesson. Velryssa Metaldrum was dangerous. Beautiful, deadly, and unobtainable.

Then the king decided House Metaldrum had become inconvenient. Her fame spread too far. She failed to form connections with the real Noble houses. Her beauty was like a weapon, and he could not let it be free. If she were not his concubine or married into the royal family, then she would be forced into a lower position. She refused all marriage requests. Being rich or from royalty did not entitle a man to her love or her body. Her chastity held strong, but she never softened the blow of refusal. The accusation arrived as a decree. Economic treason. Not rebellion. Not a conspiracy. Economic treason.

The family was accused of providing iron to rival kingdoms. Their ships were seized. Their contracts were reassigned. Their mines were confiscated. Every merchant who owed them money was ordered by the crown to repay their debts. Within six months, the Metaldrum fortune collapsed. Suitors vanished. Allies disappeared. Servants left. The great halls fell silent.

Word of their fallen status spread. Some saw this as a chance to get what they wanted without risk. She would be vulnerable soon. Her father aged ten years in a winter. Her mother began coughing at night. Her younger brothers stopped asking when things would go back to normal. Children understood more than adults liked to believe.

The creditors arrived. There were no assets left. Only debts. The people of their land began to starve. Their lands became infertile. Velryssa made the decision herself. She had two real options. Prostitution or slavery.

If she chose prostitution, she would become the most expensive courtesan in the kingdom. Kings would compete for her. Merchants would bury her in gold. She could charge any price she wanted. She could influence decisions of prominent men from their bedchambers. But it would destroy the Metaldrum name. Her brothers would grow up carrying that stain. The family would never be what it once was. The chance of regaining honor would be lost forever. While she would be elevated to a new position of power, one without the tethers of a family name, she would have true freedom to travel and work where she pleased.

Velryssa refused. She chose slavery. Former nobles had rights and protections that others did not. They could not be mistreated or used. They had to approve of their buyer. It was humiliation, but controlled humiliation. It was risky owning a former Noble slave. They could force the owner to tend to them for years before allowing the sale. But if they were sold, it would be for mountains of gold. A former Noble slave was not just a fetish; it had real power and connections associated with it. And every coin from her sale would go to her family. Her family would be looked at as martyrs due to her sacrifice. It is not often that this pathway is invoked.

The King underestimated her resolve. Now she stood beneath the lantern light in the slave market. Silk wrapped around her body. The clothing she wore cost more than a typical family's yearly income. She had the finest makeup in the country and the finest sleeping conditions, but she remained a slave. Gold chains rested against her hips. They clung to her curves in a way that made them seem magical. Her horns curved above glowing golden eyes. The aura she projected made any man or woman who came into contact with it fall head over heels. Her clothes were provocative but tasteful. She looked like a work of art. Pink skin that only a demi-human could obtain. A tail with a heart at the end of it. The build of a busty and athletic beauty.

She barely moved or looked at the crowd. Men begged. They pleaded for a glance, reaching out to touch her if they could. The bars of her room prevented physical touch. Men were kicked out of the hall for attempting to expose themselves. Wives dragged their husbands out.

Then she saw him. A man near the back. Not begging. Not staring like the others. He didn't look in her direction. He was talking to someone, but she could not see who. Velryssa smiled. Yes. That one. She admired the fact that he wasn't interested in her. She had never experienced that. It was something she longed for.

Stripe stepped forward. Inside his mind, the Crown spoke.

CROWN — "Irregular behavioral patterns detected among surrounding individuals. Status effect appears to be CHARM."

Stripe glanced at the crowd. Half of them looked hypnotized. "She is pretty."

CROWN — "Statement unnecessary."

"You sound jealous." Stripe offered a tease.

CROWN — "Artifacts do not experience jealousy."

Stripe gave a smirk. "Sure."

He stepped closer to the slave market. He had to maneuver around a large group of men. Velryssa leaned toward him.

"Come closer." She dropped her voice to a murmur.

The crowd surged. Hands lifted. She had not spoken for hours. Coins flashed. Stripe approached her. Velryssa flexed her body, exposing her curves in the glistening light. She had him under her spell. Her interest began to wane.

Then he turned, as if something caught his eye, and walked past her. He didn't even glance at her as he passed. He stopped at a smaller display. A thin half-gnome sat on a crate. Malnourished and dirty. But he was young and fit. Stripe studied him.

"I need an archer to have my back." Stripe pointed at him.

The half-gnome blinked. "I do not use a bow."

"Oh. Sorry for stereotyping." Stripe gave a shrug. "Kinda racist and fucked up, my bad."

"I can use magic," the half-gnome clarified.

"What kind?"

"Fire bolts. Force darts. They are simple spells, but I can cast them as often as I want without worry about mana backlash." He paused, then added the part he hated saying out loud. "My mana pool is above average as well."

Stripe offered a nod. "Even better. I don't have to buy arrows now."

Behind him, the slave market fell silent. Velryssa Metaldrum stood frozen. For the first time in her life, a person ignored her. She was unwanted.

Stripe stepped out into the street. The half-gnome followed him. Both were quiet for a moment.

"You passed on her." Disbelief colored the half-gnome's voice.

Stripe offered a shrug. "Yeah, I did."

Inside his head, the Crown pulsed.

CROWN — "Anomaly source remains nearby."

Stripe flashed a smirk. "Still thinking about her, I see."

CROWN — "Incorrect."

"Jealous."

CROWN — "Artifacts cannot experience jealousy."

Stripe kept walking. "You hesitated."

A flicker of static passed through his thoughts. For a fraction of a second, the voice sounded wrong. Human. Frustrated.

CROWN — "I am not jeal..."

The sound cut. A pulse followed. Then the usual tone returned.

CROWN — "Correction. Jealousy is impossible."

Stripe stopped walking. "You did it again."

CROWN — "System integrity normal."

Stripe's grin widened. "I didn't even say what you did. Jealous ass."

The market doors slammed open behind them. Velryssa stepped into the street. She shrouded herself in a robe with a hood over her face. With each step she took, the metal on her body clanged. Fury radiated off her.

"You." Velryssa let out a hiss. "How dare you?"

Stripe turned. "Um, hello."

She approached. "Do you understand what you just did?"

Stripe thought about it. "I traded a voucher from some drunk dwarves to buy a wizard?"

The half-gnome raised a finger. "Battlemage."

Stripe nodded. "My bad, battlemage."

Velryssa stared at him. "Men have ruined themselves trying to buy me. Taken out impossible loans. They have crossed oceans, sold their homes, and left their wives and families. All just for a chance to obtain me."

"What a bunch of simps."

"Men have fought duels for the chance to stand where you stood."

"But the market is free to look and stand."

Her tail flicked. "I am Velryssa Metaldrum. Last daughter of House Metaldrum."

Stripe gave a nod. "I don't know who that is."

The broker behind her made a choking sound. Velryssa stepped closer.

"Former nobles approve their buyer," Velryssa reminded him.

Stripe blinked. "I'm so lost here. Feeling a bit harassed."

She leaned closer. "And I chose you."

Stripe studied her. "Why?"

She hesitated. "Because you were the only man in that room who behaved like a person."

Stripe nodded. "Low bar."

Her expression hardened. "You would be surprised how high a bar that is."

"Sorry, but I am broke and can't even afford to feed the half man I have."

"Half-gnome." The half-gnome corrected him again.

"Half-gnome." Stripe let out a sigh. "I'm still learning. Please don't cancel me."

She stared at him. "Unbelievable."

Stripe offered a shrug. "I guess."

Inside his mind, the Crown spoke again.

CROWN — "Recommend departure."

Stripe kept the smirk. "Jealous."

Static flickered again.

CROWN — "Incorrect."

Velryssa straightened. Her anger cooled into something proud and cold.

"Very well." She turned her back. "Enjoy your wizard. But I will wait here for the day you have the coin and can free me."

"I doubt I will." Stripe let out a laugh. "I'm in massive debt."

She walked back into the slave market. The doors closed. She threw herself into her bed and screamed into her pillow. This man had dared deny her. She was furious. She was in love.

The half-gnome let out an exhale. "That woman is terrifying."

Stripe gave a nod. "Good to see there are weirdos here too."

The half-gnome looked at him. "You passed on the most beautiful woman in the kingdom."

Stripe started walking. "I needed a wizard."

"Battlemage."

"Battlemage."

Inside his mind, the Crown responded.

CROWN — "Logical decision."

Stripe smiled. "Still jealous."

CROWN — "Incorrect."

Chapter 18

Stripe and his new ally headed to the guild in silence. The kind of silence that usually meant either deep mutual understanding or complete social failure. Since Stripe had known the half-gnome for less than a day, he assumed it was the second one. The Crown held other opinions.

CROWN — "Host should prioritize team integration."

Stripe kept walking. "I am prioritizing team integration."

CROWN — "Clarify."

"I am getting us paid."

CROWN — "That is not synonymous with teamwork."

Stripe gave a shrug. "It is if the team enjoys food."

The Crown did not answer. Stripe took that as a moral victory.

The guild hall came into view through the morning haze. Weather-dark timber, stone foundation, and expensive disappointment. Men and women moved in and out wearing patchwork armor, leather coats, temple scarves, and stained travel cloaks. Some looked dangerous. Some looked hungry. Some looked like they were pretending those were different things.

Stripe pushed through the front doors. The smell of cheap stew, wet wool, old paper, and debt hit him. Not metaphorically. Debt possessed an actual smell in this world: paper, ink, damp wood, cheap sweat, and the quiet panic of people signing things they hated because starvation offered worse terms.

His identification rune rested cold against his chest. Tin rank. Debt attached. A magical leash constricts his movement and confines him to the guild.

His new companion followed a half-step behind, with the stillness of someone who had long ago learned that taking up less space made the world hurt less. He had cleaned up since the market. His hair remained damp from a wash, and his clothes were patched, guild surplus: brown, cheap, and forgettable. It proved a step up from his degrading slave clothing. He accepted the clothing with silent gratitude. It somehow made him look sharper instead of smaller. Quiet eyes. Careful posture. A body that wasted no movement because it had once cost him far more than mere comfort.

Stripe scanned the board and ignored every safe job in favor of the first badly paid death trap with real numbers attached. Sheep retrieval. Broken cart escort. Herb collection. Bandit watch. Bog infestation. And then the one that mattered.

MONSTER HUNT: RED HOLLOW WOODLANDS

Land Dragon Cull

- **Base Pay:** 300 Gold
- **Bonus Potential:** Up to 500 Gold (for proof of nest location and destruction)
- *Note:* Pay varies by confirmed kills.

Stripe tore the sheet free, almost ripping it in half. The Crown spoke without delay.

CROWN — "Host has selected a high-risk contract without consultation."

"You're welcome."

CROWN — "Gratitude was not requested nor is it appropriate."

Stripe offered a smirk. "Close enough."

He took the paper to the front desk. Guild Clerk Nessa looked up, saw Stripe, saw the contract, saw the half-gnome behind him, and managed to look more annoyed than a person should before breakfast.

"Red Hollow." Nessa took the paper.

"That's what the paper says."

"Usually taken by full parties."

Stripe crossed his arms. "Just because he is small doesn't mean he isn't a person."

Nessa let out a sigh. "That is not what I meant."

"Yes, it is. Racist. You said FULL as if he is half a person."

"I meant..."

Stripe raised his voice. "EVERYONE COME LOOK, SHE IS OPENLY DISCRIMINATING."

Her eyes moved tiredly to the half-gnome. "Registry says slave property is covered under owner liability, not independent party structure."

Stripe's jaw shifted. He hated that specific wording more every time he heard it. "Look, stop fucking around. I know you don't care what happens to us."

Nessa stamped the paper without another word.

"Confirmed kills require jaw proof or paired canines. Nest verification requires a location description and, if available, remains. Land dragons are pack opportunists. Do not let the name 'dragon' flatter them, and do not let 'land' make you think they are slow."

Stripe smiled. "Good. I was starting to get worried that you cared about my safety."

"I would never."

He turned away before she could say anything else, then stopped at the guild store. "Store" proved a generous term. It consisted of a reinforced counter, a heavy lockbox, a dusty shelf full of things no one wanted, and a bitter old man who looked at customers the way priests look at unpaid pledges.

Stripe pointed at the cheapest battle staff on the rack. Cheap wood. A small, dull monster core set crooked into the top. Barely worthy of being called a weapon. Perfect.

"One silver." The Storekeeper offered a grunt.

Stripe winced. Not because it was expensive, but because every coin he held right now was barely enough to keep the party fed. He paid anyway. He handed the battle staff to the half-gnome.

The other man took it with both hands, inspected the core once, and gave a single nod. No complaint. No gratitude performance. No confusion. Just acceptance. That alone made Stripe like him more. Most people performed around gifts; this one treated utility like utility.

Without asking questions, they left the guild and headed toward the last reported sighting of land dragons. They traveled in silence at first. Stripe filled that silence with occasional banter because, left too long, silence lets memory get bad ideas.

"So, just to be clear, are you the brooding type or the socially undercooked type?"

The half-gnome glanced at him. "I am not sure what socially undercooked means."

Stripe flashed a grin. "Great. So both."

No answer. Stripe grinned to himself. The Crown resumed its commentary.

CROWN — "Host should establish functional battlefield communication."

"I'm trying, but he is acting hard to get."

CROWN — "Current method resembles harassment."

Stripe shook his head. "You just don't know what charm is."

They followed the road until it gave up and became a trail, then followed the trail until even it looked uncertain about continuing. The woods thickened. The sunlight broke in angled shafts through the dense canopy. Birdsong thinned out. The deer sign increased rapidly. So did heavy drag marks.

By the time they reached the clearing, clear signs of heavy monster traffic were evident. Massive footprints going to and from, thick branches broken, scat scattered everywhere, and ancient trees marked with deep, territorial claw marks. Even a novice could tell this was the nest. Stripe crouched and peered cautiously through the tall grass. Then he remembered he had skipped something basic.

Stripe leaned back. "I meant to ask, what is your name?"

"My name is Latrum."

Stripe kept his eyes on the clearing. "Well, introduce yourself to the class, please."

Latrum shifted his weight. "Um.. I'm not sure what you mean by that. I assume it's a phrase asking for a brief introduction. My name is Latrum. I am a half-gnome, half-human. I specialize in quick combat magic, and I can wield daggers. My mana pool is above average, and my mana control is high. Most of my spells can be spammed non-stop as long as I am clear-minded."

Stripe finally looked at him. "Good to know, now tell me the juicy stuff."

"You are likely asking why I am a slave?"

Stripe gave a shrug. "Honestly, I wanted to know something like what type of women you like. Can't have you fucking up my game."

Latrum stared at the clearing a moment longer. Then, very quietly: "...Dragonkin..."

Stripe turned all the way toward him. "Like lizard people?"

Latrum lowered his face, a hint of red coming over his cheeks. "...Yes."

The Crown cut in.

CROWN — "Host interrogation is triggering a fight-or-flight response."

Stripe ignored it with the discipline of a man who ignored much better advice his whole life. "I have to ask, specifically, what makes you attracted to them?"

Unknowingly, the slave magic on Latrum kicked in. Slaves cannot lie to their masters, nor can they say no to their direct demands.

"It's the tails and the scaled breasts. They are fierce, and there is something primal about them. I believe that primal fierce affection cannot be mimicked by mammals."

CROWN — "Host interrogation is triggering a fight-or-flight response."

Stripe let out a laugh. "WOW... Kinda gross. But I kinda get it, I guess. We're going to get along great, Latrum."

"Yes, master."

He shook his head with shame. Some things were better kept to oneself.

Stripe kept his voice gentle. "Call me Stripe. We're allies and hopefully friends. Never call me master again; it is gross and makes me feel gross. As soon as I'm not a broke bitch I will free you and pay you a solid wage."

"Thank you, that means the world to me."

Latrum gave a stiff nod, but his jaw remained locked. His eyes dropped to the dirt, the tension in his shoulders refusing to uncoil. Stripe clapped him on the back, taking the half-gnome's silence as a sign of mutual respect, entirely missing the guarded skepticism burning behind Latrum's gaze.

Stripe looked back toward the clearing before the moment could deepen into something he did not know how to hold. The smell hit harder from this angle.

For the first time, Stripe saw a land dragon. A massive scaled lizard with a neck flap similar to a frog. It possessed a mane of thick scales around its chin, running to the top of its head. Large claws dug into the dirt, and massive fangs hung out the front of its jaw. It appeared to be between six and eight feet long. It reminded Stripe of Komodo dragons on heavy steroids. The colors varied wildly but trended towards darker green and brown.

The largest one sat massive in comparison to the rest. It stretched fifteen feet long and seven feet tall while resting on all fours. Five land dragons had gathered here. One giant land dragon stood in the center of the clearing with its heavy tail wagging. Two smaller land dragons rotated around it in tight circles. They appeared to be dancing. Their chests puffed out, their throat sacks expanding, and their heavy feet stomping in perfect unison. Occasionally, one misstepped, prompting the one behind it to bite with aggression.

The middle dragon stopped and faced one directly. The rest stopped moving and stared. Boom, the large one bit into it. The small one began thrashing and biting back, but succumbed to the vicious assault. This brutal process was repeated until exactly three dragons remained.

Stripe stared. "What the fuck is going on?"

Latrum lowered his voice. "A mating dance. They move in unison to appeal to the female. The female picks one from the crowd. It tests its strength. If it survives the attack, then they mate, and the rest are exiled. The female only wants the strongest offspring."

Stripe offered a joke. "That's some kinky shit. I bet this is why you like lizard people."

"It's not the same. These are monsters. Don't be sick."

Stripe let out a chuckle. "Sure, sure, lizard lover."

The Crown chose that exact moment to do something useful.

CROWN — "Female land dragons are approximately 50% larger than the male variants. The male level appears to be around 15. The female appears to be level 20. Recommended action: isolated fighting."

"Good to know."

"Thank you."

Stripe shook his head. "Not you, the voice in my head."

Latrum let out a murmur. "...okay..."

CROWN — "Estimated targets: Male Land Dragon A 110 HP. Male Land Dragon B 104 HP. Female Land Dragon 186 HP."

Stripe's pulse quickened. "I'm going to yell and distract them. You take them out from a safe distance."

Latrum's expression did not change, but Stripe could see the tactical objections stacking frantically behind his eyes and being forcefully strangled by slave conditioning.

"By your will."

Latrum leaped back smoothly and scurried up to the top of a sturdy tree. He whispered an incantation, and his hands began to glow bright red.

Stripe rose from the tall grass, drew a massive breath, and went with the first terrible line that came to mind.

"HEY, HORNY LIZARDS, MY FRIEND IS TRYING TO SEE WHAT IS UNDER THAT TAIL."

Stripe's voice boomed through the quiet forest. Latrum shuddered in horror at the implications.

The massive female, fangs bared, turned sharply at one of the males. The dragons went into an instant frenzy and dashed viciously towards Stripe.

The Crown spoke flatly.

CROWN — "Interruption of the mating ritual has triggered an aggressive response from the targets. Prepare for combat."

"We are such major cock blockers," Stripe noted.

Because Stripe never once in his life mistook a bad idea for a warning sign in time, he grinned anyway.

Chapter 19

Stripe had fought wolves in the dust and grime of the wild. He fought bandits in cramped, bloody alleyways. He fought massive men who mistakenly believed raw skill and cultivated muscle were interchangeable in a real street fight. He had never, in his entire violent life, fought three vastly overgrown murder-lizards charging him in a state of righteous, reptilian sexual outrage.

It was a disgusting sight, giving birth to an even more disgusting thought that Stripe tried to squash with the brutal heel of his foot. The air grew thick and cloying with the heavy musk of saurian pheromones, a scent as rotting fruit mixed with copper. The two males' private parts dragged across the rough ground, carving rhythmic indentations into the dirt and leaf mold as they pumped their powerful legs towards him.

In Stripe's eyes, this was the most horrific, sanity-eroding thing he had ever witnessed. And he had, unfortunately, seen Two Girls One Cup.

CROWN — "Analysis: Target neurotransmitters are flooded with extreme levels of reproductive aggression. Psychological inhibitors are offline. The estimated threat level has increased by 15 percent due to the frenzy status."

The lead male hit the perimeter tree line first, low to the ground. It moved with a liquid speed that almost made Stripe lose visual confirmation amid the shifting shadows of the ferns and ancient roots. Stripe took a hard step towards it. It wasn't a decision born of tactical brilliance. It was the raw, primal reality of a lifetime of cage matches. When the cage door locks and the monster rushes, your body reacts with violent intent long before your conscious mind can file the paperwork.

CROWN — "Incoming high-velocity impact detected. Warning: The current center of balance is improper for optimal deflection of the current threat anatomy. Kinetic force will exceed absorption threshold."

"Well, shit."

He wasn't nearly as ready as he thought he was.

The dragon lunged, jaw hinging open to expose rows of jagged, serrated teeth. Stripe twisted hard to the left, acting on instinct. The massive bite missed his guts by mere inches, snagging and shredding the thick leather armor at his hip instead. Stripe didn't have time to register the save.

The beast's thick, muscular tail came whipping around like a master-crafted iron club a heartbeat later. It slammed into his outer thigh with a sound like a splitting log, the kinetic force staggering him sideways. Pain flashed, white and blinding, illuminating the insides of his eyelids as his leg momentarily failed him.

Stripe HP: 110/110 -> 104/110

High above, nestled near the crown of an ancient oak, Latrum viewed the battlefield not through the lens of panic, but through the cold, precise calculations of a battlemage. He analyzed the environment, breaking down the variables. His masters had beaten the tactical manual into him along with the sigils.

Variable one: Target physiology. The land dragons possessed dense, overlapping scaled armor. Typical thickness suggested resistance to minor kinetic impacts. Vital points were guarded, requiring either high-velocity penetration or magical exploitation.

Variable two: Melee Asset. Stripe had high mobility, unpredictable movement patterns, and exceptional aggression. He was currently engaged in sub-optimal close-quarters combat with superior mass.

Variable three: Mana Management. The current pool was high, but prolonged spamming required intended casting trajectories. He needed to maximize the effect per shard of mana.

He tracked the lead male. As it lunged, Latrum calculated the arc. He needed a direct strike to the neural cluster located between the eyes to drop it. He began the incantation, his breath turning to mist.

"FIRE BOLT."

A focused line of crimson fire shot like a laser from his hand, leaving a thin trail of smoking, ionized air in its wake. Latrum watched the trajectory with a critical eye. It missed. By a fraction of an inch.

Failure analysis: He had underestimated the recursive muscle twitch speed of a frenzied saurian. The beast's neck had retracted a millimeter faster than his projection. Latrum noted the data point for future firing solutions. He needed to lead the target more when aggression was high.

Back on the ground, Stripe was moving, ignoring the screaming of his leg. The dragon, missing its initial bite, tried to correct and snapped again. Stripe didn't retreat. He stepped into the beast's guard. He jammed his left forearm horizontally across the side of its muscular skull, physically redirecting the massive bite past his body, and used the forward momentum to drive his right gauntleted fist down with everything he had toward the exposed base of the neck.

The cruel monster spikes bit through the thick scales and into the dense muscle beneath with a wet, ugly resistance that sent a shockwave of feedback all the way up to his shoulder. The beast jerked, releasing a guttural roar. In that split second, Stripe saw its eye. It was huge, yellow, and filled with a cold, instinctual intelligence. It wasn't the cunning greed of the bandits he had killed. It was the pure, unadulterated certainty of an apex predator. It knew exactly where Stripe's carotid artery was, and it was focused on accessing it.

CROWN — "Update: Hostile target level confirmed: 15. Analysis of jaw structure indicates pressure capability sufficient for severe, non-regenerative maiming."

CROWN — "Recommended action plan: Immediate tactical separation. Utilize ranged assets for cover. Apply necrotic toxin via the gauntlet mechanism. Maximize movement."

Male Land Dragon A HP: 110/110 -> 90/110

"A little late on the third recommendation, chief," Stripe grunted, straining against the massive weight. "Separation is kinda hard when his face is on my face."

From above, Latrum evaluated the second variable. Stripe had created a static tangle. The gauntlet strike had dealt damage, but not enough to disable. Worse, the gauntlet was now stuck in the thick musculature, anchoring Stripe in place while the second male was closing fast from the left, its eyes fixed on Stripe's unprotected flank. The female Level 20 was still stationary, her tail swishing with heavy, dangerous patience. She was an existential threat.

Latrum needed to alter the battlefield kinetic state. He needed a spell that didn't just deal damage but physically moved variables. He dropped his hand towards the first male's head, specifically targeting the complex hinge mechanism of the lower jaw. He didn't use fire this time. Fire would just cause pain. He needed control.

"FORCE DART."

The spell cracked through the air past Stripe's ear like a whip, a visible distortion in the humid environment. It slammed into the dragon behind the jaw hinge with the force of a battering ram. The impact didn't explode with heat. It compressed. The invisible, concentrated force hit with the deadening thud of a kicked door, physically snapping the dragon's entire massive head sideways, wrenching Stripe's gauntlet free from the neck muscle in the process. It was exactly the opening Stripe needed. His fighter brain, trained in the brutal give-and-take of the cage, recognized the moment of stagger.

Male Land Dragon A HP: 90/110 -> 85/110

He shoved off the dragon's shoulder with his left hand to create a single foot of space, stepped outside the line of the beast's disoriented head, and spit hard into his own gloved palm. A sickening green shimmer slicked his gauntlet spikes as the Toxic Fisherman trait was applied. He still hated how natural that action felt.

He came back in with brutal, rapid-fire strikes. A short right cross to the exposed throat seam. A driving uppercut to the soft tissue of the eye ridge. Then a stabbing, deep left under the jaw, where the massive scales thinned to allow movement. The dragon hissed, the sound a wet gargle, and twisted its body, but the necrotic poison was already flooding its massive system.

CROWN — "Toxin transfer confirmed. Systemic onset of neuromuscular weakness begins. Metabolic efficiency of the target dropped by 10 percent."

Male Land Dragon A HP: 85/110

The dragon, experiencing true pain and muscular failure for likely the first time in years, forgot its sexual frenzy. Its jaw hung open, a thick rope of glowing green saliva dripping onto the forest floor as it suddenly turned and attempted to bolt away. These beasts were built for terrifying ambushes and quick, messy kills. They were not built for prolonged combat with a master pressure fighter. Stripe did not let it disengage. He never did.

Years in the league, under the burning spotlights of the unified world championships, had forged a single, unbreakable tenet in his mind. Once things turn ugly, there is no tapping out, there are no referees, and you never let the judges decide who won the round. You always finish the fight.

These moments of intense, life-or-death violence were the only times Stripe felt alive anymore. They were chaotic glimpses of the champion he used to be, a man the world worshiped and threw mountains of money and respect towards. Now he was a smelly, indebted vagrant, so he seized these flashes of former glory whenever the opportunity arose.

His plan was a masterpiece of simplicity. Apply constant, unbearable forward pressure, overwhelm the opponent with rapid, damaging exchanges, and maintain aggressive movement. Keep it up until the opponent makes a fundamental technical mistake.

Against other grandmasters, this could take fifteen minutes of agonizing strategizing. Against a wild monster driven by instinct and choking on necrotic poison? It didn't take long. Humans train for years to increase lung capacity and cardiovascular efficiency under duress. A wild animal relies on its genetic baseline, which is currently being destroyed by toxic fishermen and the massive adrenaline crash. Once you run out of breath and the heart starts to hammer, you begin making fatal mistakes.

The beast's front right foot, weakened by the toxin, planted incorrectly on an ancient tree root slick with leaf mold and green slime. It slid. Latrum, viewing the fight in slow-motion tactical analysis, saw the muscular failure before Stripe did. He calculated the shift in the center of gravity. The monster was leaning too far left to correct.

"Right side!"

Stripe shifted, acting before his conscious mind could even process the data. That was new. Something in him trusted the callout. A month ago, in his reflexive arrogance, he would have ignored it, but after weeks surviving on the road with the dwarves, he knew how to trust an ally's eyes.

He exploded to his right, letting the dragon turn its desperate gaze toward him, then stepped deep inside the range of the snapping bite. He drove a spiked right hook completely through the socket of the already damaged yellow eye. Bone cracked with a sound like a gunshot, and the massive dragon roared in agony. The beast convulsed once, slammed into him with the sheer dead weight of its massive shoulder, then went down hard, crashing half across the dirt trail and half into a deep fern bed, its rear leg kicking convulsively against empty air.

CROWN — "Critical Strike landed. Neuro-trauma confirmed. Internal hemorrhaging is critical."

Male Land Dragon A HP: 85/110 -> 60/110

Toxic Fishermen was doing its dirty work, severely slowing the dragon's movement and dealing a steady stream of agonizing tick damage. Stripe pressed forward, refusing to grant it a single second of recovery. In one smooth, practiced motion, he drew his jagged iron dagger while sprinting forward. He planted his good leg, leaped three feet into the air, and threw his lead knee forward like a battering ram.

It was a flashy, fan-favorite move back in the cage. The flying knee.

It collided with the side of the dragon's eye socket, the sheer force of the knee impact crushing the orbital bone into powder. As his knee made contact, the momentum already carrying him down, he swung the dagger with all his hip, turning straight down at the base of the skull, right where the spine connected. He felt the blade enter with a resistance like heavy clay, and then he heard the wet crack as bone separated from skull, severing the central nervous system.

CROWN — "Combo strike landed. Fatal trauma achieved. Target neutralized."

Male Land Dragon A HP: 0/110

Stripe backed off slowly, his gauntlets and tunic covered in saurian gore, breathing hard through his nose. He fought the urge to throw up. The whole fight had taken maybe twenty seconds of real time. It felt like an eternity. Real fights, life-or-death fights, always felt like that, as if time itself behaved entirely differently when death was on the menu.

The second frenzied male did not give him even a moment to gather his thoughts or properly disengage his fighter's mind. He didn't have a split-second to bask in the raw excitement of the finish or preen his massive ego. He knew he looked cool as hell doing that final combo. He was secretly hoping Latrum, deep down, thought so too.

The beast came in from the far right with a flatter, sneakier, and more intelligent angle than the first. It caught him across the ribcage with a sweeping, horizontal swipe of its massive front claws before he could fully reset his hips. The four razor-sharp claws tore through the thick bandit leather. One claw hooked deeply into the heavy obliques muscle and ripped outward with a sound like wet canvas tearing.

Stripe dropped to one knee. The cheap, salvaged leather had protected him from a potentially fatal strike to his internal organs, but the sheer pain of the claw-rake left him gasping for air.

From her distant vantage point, the massive female Level 20 was slowly circling the perimeter of the clearing, her wagging tail flattening the ferns. She was analyzing the remaining male dragon's performance, measuring its value. She seemed to assume that victory was guaranteed and was simply deciding if the survivor was worth her time.

CROWN — "Host HP dropping. Minor lacerations. Adrenaline spike detected. Recommended response: Ranged asset needs to assume aggression."

Stripe HP: 95/110

"Son of a bitch!" Stripe roared. "That hurts!"

Stripe glared up into the tree line, coughing out dirt and a little blood as he scrambled backward from the snapping jaws of the second male.

"Latrum! If you shoot me another tactical report instead of a fireball, I am going to be very upset! And you better not be getting off to this!"

Chapter 20

The dead male lay half across the clearing like a grim decoration in a goth girl's home. Stripe shifted left, circling the perimeter of the carnage and gauging the remaining dragons' reactions. The living male possessed visible damage across its flank. Stripe assumed the damage resulted from Latrum keeping it distracted with low-level spells during the first fight.

The living male followed Stripe's movement, its yellow eyes locked onto him. The massive female tried to adjust to both Stripe's flanking maneuver and Latrum's elevated position. She lost a fraction of her positioning. That gave Latrum what he needed. He was a tactician, and tacticians punished bad positioning.

"ICE BOLT."

The spell hit the second male high on the shoulder joint. Frost webbed outward, an unnatural winter blooming across the dark green scales. The dragon's aggressive stride shortened. The cold seeped into the muscle fiber, slowing its movement.

CROWN — "Male Land Dragon B estimated HP: 58/104 -> 52/104. Movement speed reduced."

Stripe darted around the dead body of the first male, forcing the freezing dragon to climb over its fallen rival instead of taking the cleaner line. The instant it committed its weight to the obstacle, Latrum snapped his cheap wooden staff forward.

"FORCE PUSH."

The invisible impact hit the male mid-transition, catching its center of gravity. It drove the beast down into the dead dragon's ribs, then shoved it backward into a thick-trunked tree. Bone cracked. The dragon's entire body shuddered from the impact. The live male thrashed in a panicked spray of blood and loosened scales.

CROWN — "Collision confirmed. Male Land Dragon B estimated HP: 52/104 -> 43/104."

Stripe stepped in on the dragon's blind side and hammered a right hook into the neck seam, feeling the scales give way under the spikes.

CROWN — "Toxic Fisherman applied."

Then a left hook, grinding the knuckles in.

CROWN — "Toxic Fisherman applied."

Then another right, putting his hip into the torque.

CROWN — "Toxic Fisherman applied. Stacking poison damage is effective."

There was no elegance to it. No pause. Just relentless, overwhelming pressure. The male twisted awkwardly to bite, but it reacted too slowly.

CROWN — "Male Land Dragon B estimated HP: 43/104 -> 20/104."

Stripe baited an attack, dropping his guard. Right when the dragon prepared to make contact with its snapping jaws, he moved. He fed it the gauntleted forearm instead of his soft throat, taking the crushing pressure against the iron and thick leather. With his free hand, he drove his iron dagger up through the unprotected tissue behind the lower jaw. The dragon spasmed around the blade.

CROWN — "Male Land Dragon B estimated HP: 20/104 -> 14/104."

Latrum's next spell struck the open wound.

"FIRE BOLT."

The smell turned foul, a sickening mix of burning flesh and searing poison. The male jerked once. Then twice. It collapsed hard enough to make Stripe's knees shake. The poison circulating through its ruined veins finished the job.

CROWN — "Male Land Dragon B estimated HP: 14/104 -> 0/104. Male Land Dragon B terminated."

Stripe tore his arm and dagger free and backed away, his chest heaving. Now only the female remained. That should have felt encouraging. It did not.

The dragon before him was huge. She was the absolute largest creature he had ever fought in his life. With the lesser males gone, she stopped dividing her attention. The anger filling her pressed into the air like a physical weight. All her potential mates were dead. No mating meant no offspring. Her focus settled squarely on Stripe. It was pure fury, but reserved. It carried a cold calculation, surprising and unsettling for a wild beast. That felt worse than a frenzy.

CROWN — "Female Land Dragon estimated HP: 186/186. Target is adapting to battlefield attrition. Recommended strategy: repeated side engagement, poison stacking, avoid direct trade."

Stripe took a shallow breath. "Sounds like a good idea. I don't want to get near that thing. Maybe I can convince it to mate with Latrum. Sounds like a win-win to me."

Latrum did not laugh. He read the battlefield, anticipating her trajectory.

"Keep her turning!"

Stripe obeyed. That uncharacteristic obedience alone might have saved his life.

The female lunged with a speed shocking for her massive size. Stripe cut hard around a thick pine tree, forcing her to clumsily adjust her bulk on the turn. Latrum, timing the pivot, hit the exposed flank with a firebolt. The spell burst against the tough scales and left a charred, darkened patch.

CROWN — "Female Land Dragon estimated HP: 186/186 -> 171/186. Burn damage registered."

The female rounded on Latrum, looking up into the tree line. This wasn't expected. Stripe watched for exactly this distraction. He broke from cover without thinking. He slammed his full body weight into her shoulder line and drove both gauntleted fists into the rib seam behind her massive foreleg. One hit. Two. The second strike found purchase between the overlapping armor. Toxic Fisherman spread through the punctures.

CROWN — "Toxin transfer confirmed. Female Land Dragon estimated HP: 171/186 -> 150/186. Weakness onset is slower than male variants due to mass."

The female answered the insult by almost taking Stripe's head off with a snap of her jaws. He dropped under the bite, but not far enough. Razor-sharp teeth scraped the top of his leather chest piece and ripped a thick strip free. Then her massive, armored shoulder hit him like a runaway carriage. He rolled twice through the wet leaves and jagged roots before sliding to a halt against a low stump.

CROWN — "Stripe HP: 63/110 -> 41/110. Stripe Stamina: 88/110 -> 73/110."

Everything hurt. Latrum saw the devastating hit from his perch. He changed his spell choice, prioritizing multiple impacts over raw damage.

"MAGIC MISSILE."

Three glowing, pale darts cracked across the clearing with magical speed and struck the female in rapid succession: the eye ridge, the throat, and the burned, sensitive flank.

CROWN — "Female Land Dragon estimated HP: 150/186 -> 100/186. Multi-hit force impact confirmed."

"Stripe! The right foreleg drags after turns! She is overcommitting on the poisoned side!"

Stripe got up. He slammed his spiked fists together, forcing adrenaline back into his system, motivating himself to continue. Dying here in the dirt was not an option.

The female charged again, closing the distance fast. Stripe retreated across broken roots and low stone, forcing her to accelerate over terrible, uneven footing. Her mouth frothed as she snapped at him. The bad footing made a huge difference and barely allowed Stripe to dodge the lethal bites. Latrum's tactical analysis proved flawless. The right foreleg dragged exactly as he said it would.

Stripe pivoted, stepped inside her staggering guard, and hammered a spiked left into the shoulder seam. Then a right cross into the jaw hinge. Then a push-kick to the damaged foreleg. The female buckled half a step, her weight betraying her.

CROWN — "Female Land Dragon estimated HP: 146/186 -> 134/186."

Latrum did not waste the hard-earned opportunity.

"FORCE PUSH."

The blast hit her broadside while she was off-balance and drove her immense bulk into a low boulder jutting up through the clearing.

CROWN — "Collision confirmed. Female Land Dragon estimated HP: 100/186 -> 90/186."

Stripe wheezed a laugh. "Oh, that's disgusting. Do it again."

The female grew angrier, but the anger made her sloppy. It lost its cold focus. It operated on pure, blind instinct. She came at Stripe in a straight line. He gave ground. He led her past the first carcass, cut around the second, and used the narrowing space between the dead bodies, the trees, and the stone to make her turns sharper and more punishing.

Latrum layered spells into every mistake she made. A firebolt to the flank when she turned. An ice bolt to the dragging foreleg when she stumbled. Magic missile when she roared and exposed her soft throat.

CROWN — "Female Land Dragon estimated HP: 90/186 -> 85/186. Female Land Dragon estimated HP: 85/186 -> 70/186. Female Land Dragon estimated HP: 70/186 -> 60/186."

Stripe saw the pattern emerging. For the first time in the desperate fight, he felt understanding. The rhythm of this battle wasn't as different from MMA as he initially thought. The female wanted one committed line. One clean, unobstructed chase. One fatal moment when Stripe stopped moving like prey and became a stationary fighter again. He denied it. He stayed ugly. He stayed angled. He stayed alive by baiting her into unfair trades.

Latrum called the final opening. "Now! Eye side!"

Stripe exploded forward, burning the last of his adrenaline. He took the outside lane, stepped over a thick root, drove his left gauntlet into the damaged eye ridge, and buried the metal spikes deep enough for green poison and dark blood to mix in a wet, horrific burst. The female shrieked, a sound that shook the leaves. She turned in agony.

CROWN — "Female Land Dragon estimated HP: 60/186 -> 40/186. Toxic damage compounded."

Latrum's final force push hit her squarely in the shoulder at the wrong angle for her balance, and the right one for gravity. She stumbled against the boulder. The slowed, poisoned foreleg collapsed under her massive weight.

CROWN — "Female Land Dragon estimated HP: 40/186 -> 25/186. Collision confirmed."

Stripe came in with the iron dagger held two-handed. One brutal thrust deep into the throat seam. One wrench deeper to sever the arteries. He used both gauntlets, punching into the same widening wound until the movement stopped meaning struggle and started meaning dying.

CROWN — "Female Land Dragon estimated HP: 25/186 -> 19/186. Female Land Dragon estimated HP: 19/186 -> 7/186. Female Land Dragon estimated HP: 7/186 -> 0/186. Threat eliminated."

The clearing went silent except for Stripe's ragged breathing and the rustling sound of Latrum climbing down from the oak tree. Even that sounded loud. Stripe stood over the massive body for a second longer than was necessary because his knees wanted to fold, and he refused to let them do it first. Then they folded anyway. He sat in the bloody grass.

CROWN — "Stripe HP: 41/110-> 24/110. Stripe Stamina: 73/110 -> 49/110."

Latrum approached, his cheap battle staff held tight. He looked over the dead female, then the two dead males, then finally at Stripe.

"We survived."

Stripe grinned, chest heaving. "Now that was a fucking fight. God damn, I'm so pumped. Look at my heart, it's beating like crazy."

Latrum looked happy, a rare expression breaking through his stoic mask. "We did well for a thrown-together team. I haven't felt the thrill of battle in a long time."

Stripe barked a tired, wheezing laugh. "Buddy, I am one aggressive squirrel away from seeing the afterlife again."

Latrum crouched by the bodies and began checking jaws, teeth, hide quality, and nest sign with clinical focus. He made sure to cut off the specific parts for the guild bounty.

"You were right," Stripe said.

Latrum paused his butchering. "About what specifically?"

"Do not get greedy. It ruins the mood."

Latrum raised an eyebrow.

"You were right about the plan," Stripe clarified.

A faint, hidden satisfaction touched the half-gnome's dirty face. "Yeah. I used to draw up battle plans before things went to shit. That being said, I failed at least once, and now I'm a slave."

Stripe laughed harder at that dark joke than the line probably deserved. "You know what? Fair. You earned that one."

Stripe pushed himself upright and looked around the destroyed clearing. This was the first time Stripe had shown any interest in Latrum's background. "Let me guess, you were some kind of bandit and got caught?"

"No. I had a family. The current king taxed us at 90 percent. I couldn't feed them, and they died of starvation. I barely survived. Later, I found out that only our village was targeted. The king wanted our village to crumble."

"Fuck, that's intense. But how did that make you a slave?"

"I went after revenge. I joined a rebellion. We won a lot of battles. But the king sent the full force of his army on us suddenly. We were crushed. I was enslaved."

Stripe gave a nod. "I can understand revenge. Damn. The king sounds like a total asshole."

The dead male the female had killed during the mating dance was still twitching in the dirt. The two males they had dropped lay at bad angles near the treeline and the broken stone. The female herself looked monstrous even in death. Big enough to matter to a village. Big enough to matter to a herd line. Big enough to matter to his crippling debt. That thought pulled him back to reality.

"So how much money is all this worth?"

Latrum resumed checking the remains, his hands slick with gore. "Enough to help. Not enough to fix your life. Potentially enough to improve your next mistake."

"I guess it's better than nothing."

CROWN — "Statement accuracy is high."

"Nobody asked you."

CROWN — "Incorrect. Host invited commentary through an open complaint pattern."

"I hate living with you in my head."

CROWN — "Host survival suggests otherwise."

Latrum began cutting away sections of hide where the thick scales still held quality. Stripe glanced at Latrum.

"I meant what I said."

Latrum looked up from the female's massive foreclaw. "About what?"

"That I'm freeing you once I can. That part. Not the dragonkin thing. That one's between you and the goddess."

Latrum lowered his gaze back to the carcass. "Thank you."

They found the nest after the fight and the butchering. It was a low, dark cave line just past the tree break. Large eggshell fragments, old drag marks, and human bones sat in the dirt. A sour, foul heat was trapped in the stone. It confirmed the location and justified the extra, much-needed payout. Stripe looked deep into the terrifying darkness and decided, for perhaps the first time in his life, not to push his luck. Three massive kills and nest confirmation provided more than enough for one day.

On the long hike back, he limped. Latrum adjusted his pace without comment, keeping a watchful eye on the perimeter. The woods felt different now. Not less dangerous, just quieter in a specific way. The way land does after an apex predator line gets cut out of it. Deer would come back through here eventually. Maybe not tomorrow. Maybe not soon. But they would. Somewhere ahead of them, a village would have a slightly better chance at surviving the winter because three monsters had died in a clearing full of leaves, blood, and terrible flirting.

Stripe smiled at that comforting thought. Then he grimaced because smiling pulled on the split skin at his bruised ribs. Stripe let out a breath.

"Next time, hopefully, I will lose less blood."

"Next time we will make a plan."

Stripe glanced down at the stoic half-gnome. "That was weirdly inspiring."

"Good."

The Crown spoke one last time as the narrow trail widened to promise the safety of the main road.

CROWN — "Teamwork performance improved after tactical compliance. Recommendation: continue allied integration. New proficiency unlocked: Teamwork."

Stripe rolled his eyes. "Sweet, a new thing that means nothing to me." Then, after a beat, he added, "She's right, though."

Latrum looked up, confused by the one-sided conversation.

"Don't act surprised," Stripe chuckled.

For once, the half-gnome let the smallest edge of genuine humor show on his face.

"I have no clue what you're talking about." Latrum offered a faint, tired smile.

Stripe might seem crazy to Latrum, but he was kind to him. It was something he hadn't felt from another person in a long time. He decided he could tolerate the occasional talking to himself if it meant being treated like a human being again.

The road back waited ahead of them. So did the guild. So did the crushing debt. So did all the other massive problems this fantasy world had prepared in careful, deadly little rows.

"I cannot wait to get back to the barracks to rest," Stripe said.

"I take it that's where we will be sleeping until we make money?"

"It's free, shit, we might stay after we have money." Stripe gave a thumbs-up.

"Great." Latrum looked at the ground to hide his disappointment.

But Stripe walked forward with real money coming, a nest officially confirmed, three monster kills to his name, and a tactical ally he no longer intended to waste. For the moment, in a world that wanted him dead, that was enough.

Chapter 21

By the time Memento's heavy stone walls came back into view through the morning haze, Stripe had stopped walking like a man and started walking like a loose collection of fresh injuries held together by spite. His ribs throbbed, his leg burned, his arm screamed with every step, and his chest felt like the female land dragon had taken something personal out on it.

Latrum, frustratingly, still looked composed. He was tired, smoke-stained from his spells, and lightly blood-specked, but he still carried himself with that same rigid, controlled posture that made Stripe want to simultaneously respect him and throw something small at his head just to see if he'd flinch. Stripe limped through the main gate beside him with three bloody jaw bundles hanging from his pack, a massive foreclaw tied awkwardly in cloth, and enough rank-smelling proof of nest destruction to make a seasoned clerk nervous.

Stripe offered a grunt. "If anyone asks, I got injured saving some orphans and nuns."

"As you wish." Latrum gave a nod. "But it is unlikely anyone will believe it. You look much more like the type to steal orphans and nuns instead of saving them."

Stripe blinked. "Wow. That was immediate, too. Why am I catching strays?"

"I am not allowed to say no," Latrum continued. "My master dove headfirst into the mating ritual of the land dragons. He threw his dignity and his chastity away to save a group of orphans and nuns. It was a ghastly sight. He may never walk again."

Latrum mimicked a concerned face as he recited the deadpan tale. Technically, he remained within the magical guidelines of what his owner requested.

CROWN — "Ally humor development detected. The plausibility of the event occurring is likely."

"The bitch in my head never acknowledges my jokes," Stripe muttered. "Now it's making jokes too. What a scam."

CROWN — "Insult unnecessary. Host humor levels ruin emotional developmental growth. Therefore, it cannot be encouraged."

Memento did not care that they had nearly died in the mud. The massive city kept moving around them with the same chaotic normalcy it always had. Street vendors argued over the price of onions. Children ran barefoot through narrow alleys with wooden swords. Somewhere up the cobbled street, a heavy cart wheel cracked loudly, and a merchant began screaming at the sky about compensation. A woman slapped a man in front of a fish stall hard enough to visibly turn his head. Life had already resumed its usual, relentless pace, which always felt insulting after surviving bloodshed.

Stripe had noticed the same thing in his old world. Something terrible could happen just outside the arena walls, and by supper, people were back to haggling over vegetables and complaining about traffic.

The guild hall swallowed them in its usual oppressive smell of wet wool, old stew, cheap paper, spilled ink, and monetized suffering. Nessa looked up from her paperwork when they approached the worn wooden counter. Her tired eyes moved from Stripe to Latrum to the bloody proof sacks hanging heavily from Stripe's shoulders. Then she straightened her spine a little, and that action alone made the agonizing walk back worth it.

Stripe liked that specific moment. It felt like he had beaten the steep odds while being counted out by everyone in the room. Sometimes it seemed as though his success made them uncomfortable. He loved that.

"Red Hollow quest?" Nessa asked.

"Yes," Stripe confirmed.

Nessa untied the first bloody bundle. Then the second. Then the third. Heavy, scaled jaws hit the wooden counter one after another, heavy enough to sound real. She laid out the paired canines, the requested hide segments, the blackened eggshell fragments, and finally the massive foreclaw of the matriarch.

Around them, the ambient conversations of the guild hall thinned. That happened sometimes when hard evidence got laid out in enough quantity that even bored, seasoned adventurers had to pause their drinking and reevaluate exactly who had just walked in the door. Nessa tallied the proof.

"Three confirmed kills." Her sharp eyes shifted down to the massive claw. "One matriarch." Then to the blackened, sulfur-smelling eggshell fragments. "Verified nest location and destruction."

Stripe leaned both calloused palms on the counter, mostly because it helped him stay upright. He let out a breath. "Please say a number that fixes all my current problems."

Nessa ignored that and started writing in her ledger. Her quill pen moved quickly, scratching across the parchment. That sound was far better than any prayer.

"Total payout is five hundred gold."

For one suspended, glorious second, Stripe forgot how exhausted and injured he felt.

"That's what the fuck I'm talking about!" Stripe roared.

His excitement showed on his battered face. Latrum shifted to the side at the loud outburst. Nessa gave a mild nod.

"It is a good payout. Good job."

Stripe flashed a grin. "One step closer to being debt-free."

She slid the finalized ledger sheet toward him with a neutral expression. "Debt reduction applies automatically first."

There it was. The guild's favorite trick. Take the massive victory, claim the glory, and then funnel the reward towards your crippling debt. The guild gets the public credit for completing the dangerous task and effectively pays no actual money to the bleeding adventurers. Stripe looked down at the new number on the ledger. His crushing debt had dropped enough to matter. Not enough to breathe freely, but enough to matter on paper.

That realization created a specific, boiling kind of anger. The sort that came from seeing progress and still wanting to punch whoever owned the staircase. However, progress is progress. He felt angry at the unfair circumstances but happy to see the impossible number finally drop.

CROWN — "Host emotional state indicates simultaneous satisfaction and deep resentment."

"Incredible." Stripe let out a mutter. "It's almost like I'm a real person."

Nessa's eyes flicked to Latrum and then back to Stripe. Quiet amusement replaced the tired dismissal in her face. They had gone out looking like a ragtag group of desperate failures. They had come back looking like a profitable, true adventuring party. Institutions respected success in the same way that snakes respected warmth.

"Guildmaster Varn wants to see you in his office after you stop bleeding on my counter." Nessa pointed down the hall.

Stripe glanced down in surprise. A small amount of fresh blood stained the polished wood. "In my defense, I am leaking from multiple locations."

"Please leave," Nessa sighed. She pointed a rigid finger toward the back hall. "Infirmary first."

"Only if it's free." Stripe offered a negotiation.

"I have to clean this mess. Please go."

"Only if it's free." Stripe shifted his weight, allowing another heavy drop of blood to fall onto the counter.

Nessa relented. "Fine. Fine. Just go."

Latrum spoke softly before Stripe could object further. "That was impressive."

"You learn a few tricks on the streets." Stripe offered a smirk. "If you're gross enough, it will usually get you what you want."

"I can see you are an expert."

"Stylishly."

"If it works, it works."

The guild infirmary was aggressively clean in the specific way places devoted to magical healing always were, which made Stripe distrust it. The bright room smelled strongly like medicinal herbs, washed linen, and quiet divine judgment. A young priest in pristine pale robes took one look at Stripe's ruined state and hurriedly made the sign of the goddess before guiding him toward a low cot.

"Sit," the priest ordered.

"Sir, yes, sir." Stripe complied.

"Hold still a moment."

The magical healing came in a rush of warm gold light. Stripe still hated it. Not because it hurt exactly, although certain parts of it did. It felt uncomfortably invasive. Broken bones settling, torn flesh knitting together, bruised muscle being persuaded by something holy to stop being damaged. It felt like being repaired by aggressive carpentry. He hissed through his teeth when the golden light sank deep into his broken ribs.

Stripe let out a grunt. "Feels like divine woodworking."

The priest blinked in surprise. Then, despite his solemn training, he laughed softly. "I will choose to accept that as gratitude." The priest offered a smile.

Across the sterile room, Latrum stood perfectly still with his new battle staff held loosely in one hand and the same unreadable calm on his face. He took less damage during the fight, but now that Stripe was looking properly, it was easier to see where the half-gnome carried his pain. His left shoulder was stiffly guarded. There was a dark scorch mark along one sleeve. His breathing was a little too measured, a little too careful.

Stripe gave a frown. "You should get looked at, too."

Latrum's eyes shifted toward him. Just for a brief moment. "I am fine." Latrum declined the offer.

The powerful church and the ruling royal family were deeply intertwined in this kingdom. Latrum held a justified distrust of the two institutions.

"It's an order." Stripe pushed the issue.

The young priest looked awkwardly between them. "He should still be treated."

Latrum hesitated. The glowing magic slave symbol on his hand flared, urging him forward against his will. Stripe could tell something much deeper was happening here. But he needed Latrum to be in optimal condition for whatever Varn wanted. They would have to discuss this specific issue later. Stripe hated that realization immediately.

"Don't make me repeat myself." Stripe kept his command soft.

The second the harsh command left his mouth, he regretted it. Latrum went very, very still. A flash of cold anger appeared in his eyes as he slowly stepped forward towards the priest.

"Shit. Sorry." Stripe offered a quick apology. "It feels gross. But I need you to be in good condition. You're supposed to be the smart one."

Latrum looked away, his jaw tight. "It is fine. You're right. I let my foolish pride outweigh the smart tactical choice."

It was obviously not fine. He was bothered. His eyes remained wide open, staring intently at the priest as the holy man began to heal him. The priest healed him anyway. His minor wounds mended seamlessly. His full range of movement returned, and the wincing pain he tried to hide vanished.

When they finally left the infirmary, Stripe felt whole enough to confidently insult people at full strength again.

Varn's private office smelled expensive in a way Stripe instinctively distrusted. Polished dark wood, sealed scented wax, clean parchment, and perfectly controlled air. The guildmaster waited behind his desk, fingers steepled, his expression smooth enough to make Stripe check mentally whether he still had all his coin.

Varn offered a greeting. "Back alive. Wonderful."

"Least sincere sentence spoken in Memento today." Stripe shot the words back.

Varn smiled broadly, like a man who believed charm counted as personal hygiene. "Red Hollow was a highly impressive result for a party of two."

"That sounds like you are preparing to give me bad news."

"The Church is organizing a fully sanctioned hunt." Varn leaned forward. "Public. Highly structured. Scored. High priests, judging panels, church sponsorship, and controlled culling regions. Good publicity for them. Excellent publicity for the guilds involved."

Latrum's rigid posture shifted a fraction of an inch. "The Sanctified Hunt."

Varn looked pleasantly surprised that the slave had spoken. "Exactly."

Then his calculating eyes returned to Stripe. "Your exceptional performance in Red Hollow made you qualify. A two-man operation taking down an entire nest, a matriarch, and returning with undeniable proof gets you a rare opportunity. People talk."

"So what you're saying is I have been noticed by a large, powerful institution?"

Varn corrected him. "What I am saying is that you are highly marketable. This is very good for your debt. You help us win, and we help you."

He smiled warmly, but the rotted teeth in his mouth made the room feel uncomfortable. He slid a heavy parchment across the desk. Stripe looked it over with deep suspicion. Three distinct culling routes. Rotating oversight. Church-appointed judges. Scoring criteria based on efficiency, confirmed kills, collateral damage, proper conduct, and priest safety.

Stripe's face darkened significantly. "Judges?"

CROWN — "Host aversion to structured evaluation is detected."

"Shut up." Stripe thought the words fiercely.

Varn raised one perfectly manicured eyebrow. "You object to being scored?"

"I have a bad history with judges."

Varn folded his manicured hands. "Your personal history doesn't matter when this much money is at play."

Stripe looked down at the heavy parchment again. Public hunt. Church sponsorship. Massive payout. Structured scoring. That alone provided more than enough to annoy him.

Then he looked over at Latrum. The half-gnome read the route descriptions with the intense focus men usually reserved for reading battle maps and assessing enemies. He didn't seem against the idea at all.

"What's the catch?" Stripe demanded.

"Several, probably." Varn offered a smile. "But you are in no position to be selective."

That was fair, which made Stripe hate it even more. The meeting ended the exact way most things in this bureaucratic world did. With the signing of more paperwork.

When they stepped back outside, the sun had dipped lower, and the great, echoing bells near the wealthy cathedral district had started ringing evening devotion across the entire city. Stripe rolled one thick shoulder, actively testing the magical healing. His body moved smoothly, as if it had never been injured to begin with.

They walked in silence for a long while after that, moving slowly through the narrower, darker side streets toward the cheaper inns. It was not a comfortable silence exactly, but it wasn't hostile either. That made it rarer than most people admitted.

Stripe broke the silence. "Earlier. In the infirmary."

Latrum kept his eyes focused straight ahead. "The order."

"Yeah." Stripe let out a slow exhale. "It was a dick move."

Latrum kept quiet long enough that Stripe almost wrote the whole attempt off as a failure.

"It was the right tactical move," Latrum said.

That was not forgiveness exactly. It was better. It was honest.

The two headed back to the barracks. Latrum slept in the bed beside Stripe's bed. It wasn't much, but it felt better than a slave's cage.

The next morning, Memento's massive cathedral square looked less like a religious gathering and much more like a military parade designed by people who loved ceremony far too much to trust simplicity. Huge white banners snapped loudly in the wind. High priests stood in long, intimidating rows on the polished stone steps. Lesser clerics moved frantically through the crowd with score ledgers, sealed parchments, and the kind of eerie calm that only existed in people who fully expected other people to die professionally.

Hardened adventurers filled the square. So did seasoned mercenaries. So did countless slaves wearing heavy collars, fresh brands, or the quieter, magical signs of legal ownership. Stripe stood with Latrum near the outer edge of the chaotic square and took it all in with a rapidly growing dislike.

"This feels significantly less like a holy religious event and much more like a blood sports tournament," Stripe observed.

Latrum glanced toward the elevated, guarded platform where high church officials were already arranging themselves in strict order of rank.

"It is both," Latrum answered quietly.

Stripe let out a grimace. "That somehow makes it worse."

He watched a bored priest hand out dangerous route assignments to a grim-looking team in heavy chain shirts. Another group was arguing with a clerk over complex scoring deductions that had not even happened yet. Somewhere deeper in the dense crowd, someone cheered loudly. Someone else vomited onto the cobblestones from sheer nerves. And at the dead center of it all, the Church gleamed with unquestionable authority.

Latrum folded his arms and looked toward the high stone steps, where the most important, jewel-draped priests stood apart from the rest, like clean, holy thoughts in a dirty, violent world. He still did not trust churches. He trusted crowns even less.

But there he was anyway, standing squarely in the middle of both massive systems with a pathetic eighteen silver to his name, a reduced but still hateful debt, a new ally standing at his side, and just enough recent success behind him to get noticed by exactly the wrong people. Which, in Stripe's vast experience, usually meant his life was about to become much, much more complicated.

CROWN — "Warning Reflection Inbound"

Stripe let out a groan. "Fuck, please make it stop."

His whole world went black with pain. He fought back as hard as he could, but the Crown dragged him back into his memories.

CHAPTER 22

Stripe stood frozen in the hallway. What he saw before him shook him to the core. The penthouse wasn't just broken; it was destroyed. The thick wood around the electronic lock was splintered like jagged teeth. The hinges were twisted, leaving the massive door resting at a sickening angle against the foyer's interior wall.

His heart stopped. The high of the win died, and dread replaced it. The silence of the long hotel corridor suddenly felt deafening. Who possessed the balls to do something like this? He dropped his heavy gym bag. The thud against the carpet sounded like a bomb in the quiet. He took a slow, agonizing step forward, his boots feeling heavy. He raised his wrapped hands and pushed the door the rest of the way. The wood creaked, and the bent metal hinges scraped against the frame.

The smell hit him before he saw anything. It was a scent he knew from thousands of hours spent in a steel cage: the heavy, metallic stench of fresh blood. It smelled of hot iron and old pennies. In a fight, that smell remained contained to split eyebrows and broken noses. Here, the smell felt absolute. It was thick and suffocating, filling the luxury suite and choking the air. The smell presented itself stronger than he had ever experienced.

Stripe stepped slowly into the grand foyer. The living room was unrecognizable. Antique furniture had been overturned and smashed. White stuffing from the custom leather couches tore out, scattered like dirty snow. Shards of broken glass from a shattered chandelier covered the expensive Persian rugs.

"Hello?" Stripe called out, his voice cracking. "If someone is in there, come out now, or I promise I will fuck you up."

He crawled across the floor and pulled her broken body into his arms, staining his tailored suit with her blood. Her breathing was shallow.

"Please stay with me," Stripe begged, rocking her back and forth on the ruined carpet.

He did not sound like the undisputed heavyweight champion. Something bothered him. He couldn't place it just yet. But none of this made sense. How did someone get into the penthouse? What did they even want? Where was security? This place costs a fortune, so you would think there would be some type of assistance.

He walked slowly toward the master bedroom, his boots crunching on the glass. Every step took everything he had. His brain screamed at him to run, but he followed the dark red smears on the white walls. At the threshold, he pushed the partially open door wide. He reached down and picked up a large wooden piece that snapped jagged at the end. Peeking his head through the hole in the wall, his eyes filled with horror. There she lay, covered in blood, still bleeding and barely breathing. The love of his life lay soaking in the fresh blood around her.

Stripe collapsed to his knees. The impact bruised his bones, but he felt no physical pain. A sound tore out of his chest that did not belong to a human being. It was the horrifying noise of a wounded animal dying alone in a steel trap, a primal scream of agony. She was not supposed to be in Russia. She was supposed to be safe in California. She was eight months pregnant. She had flown across the world in secret to surprise him for his unified championship win.

Stripe crawled across the bloody floor and pulled her broken body into his arms. He stained his tailored suit red with her blood. Her breathing was shallow and erratic. Every breath bubbled with dark, thick liquid. Her beautiful face remained pale and heavily bruised. She had stab wounds and holes all through her clothing. Quite a few were aimed at her stomach. It was obvious that the person who did this held a grudge. He applied pressure, but there were too many wounds. He couldn't block them all.

"Stay with me." Stripe let out a plea. "Please stay with me."

He began screaming at the top of his lungs. "Help! Get some fucking help in here!"

Hot tears streamed down his face. They dropped onto her cold skin, mixing with the blood on her cheeks.

"Please stay with me," Stripe pleaded frantically, rocking her back and forth on the ruined carpet. "I am here. I am right here. You are going to be okay. I have you. I have you. Stay awake. You have to stay awake."

She looked up at him. Her eyes were rapidly losing focus. The light that had always kept him grounded faded into a gray void. She tried to speak, her lips moving weakly, but only a wet sigh escaped her mouth. She raised her right hand with a massive, agonizing effort. Her bloodstained fingers brushed gently against his scarred cheek one final time. She looked at him with a profound, crushing sadness. She was not crying for herself; she was crying because she knew exactly what this would do to him.

His wife let out a whisper. "It was supposed to be a surprise. I knew you would win. I never doubted it."

"You were supposed to stay home," Stripe sobbed. "Why? Why would you come? Can I get some fucking help in here!"

She let out a faint breath. "I have always been by your side. I couldn't imagine not being here as you enter the history books. I wouldn't be able to forgive myself."

Stripe kept his voice gentle. "Who did this to you?"

"They spoke Russian." Her voice weakened. "I fought as hard as I could. I caught one of them with a piece of glass. You should have seen it. He cried and was bleeding pretty badly around his eye. You would have been proud of me."

"I'm always proud of you." Stripe's voice broke. "I promise I will get whoever did this. I will make them pay!"

"Focus on our baby." She offered a final plea. "I can't feel anything. Is the baby okay? I can't move my head. Please tell me she's okay."

The tears flooded his eyes, blurring his vision. He held back the desire to cry out. There was no way the baby would be okay. He couldn't bring himself to tell her that.

Stripe lied, his voice thick. "She's fine. They didn't hit you there. I promise to be the best dad. You are going to be the best mom. Just keep your eyes open."

"Thank god." She gave a faint smile. "I couldn't bear to leave you alone. I love you so much."

Then her hand went limp against his chest. Her chest stopped rising, and the shallow breaths ceased.

Stripe sat there for hours. He did not move a single muscle. He held the lifeless bodies of his wife and his unborn child in his lap, rocking back and forth in the total silence of the destroyed penthouse.

His mind broke into a million jagged pieces. The arrogant, untouchable champion died in that hotel room. The man who cared about golden belts and stadium crowds disappeared, leaving only an empty, hollow shell behind. The thirst for legacy and the drive to be the best were replaced by a single unshakable emotion. Hatred.

The local Russian detectives finally arrived long after the sun had set. The hotel staff had called them when they heard the ruckus upstairs and again when a bunch of shady men in ski masks had exited moments before Stripe arrived. The operator on the line assured them an officer was on the way. But they never came. It took Stripe coming into the lobby, covered in blood, for the call to be answered.

The lead detective was a tall man with a thick gray mustache and dead eyes. He wore a wrinkled trench coat that smelled of stale tobacco and cheap cologne. He walked into the master bedroom and looked at Stripe, who was still rocking the body.

The detective did not offer any comfort. He simply reached down and grabbed Stripe by the collar of his blood-soaked suit. He possessed surprising strength, dragging Stripe out of the bedroom and throwing him into the hallway. Stripe hit the wall and slumped down, staring at his hands. They were caked in dark, dried blood. He didn't ask any questions. He just began to pat Stripe down. Almost as if he were looking for any excuse to drag him in.

The Lead Detective offered a flat statement. "This was a tragic robbery. You'd best remember that."

His voice was flat. He sounded bored, delivering the sentence with a rehearsed, mechanical cadence. Stripe slowly raised his head. The fog in his brain momentarily parted, replaced by a rage so intense it made his vision blur.

Stripe let out a growl. "This was murder. I know who did it."

He lunged from the floor with the speed of a world champion. He reached for the lead detective's throat. His frustration began to grow. It was hitting him like a ton of bricks. This was the first stage of a cover-up.

Stripe yelled, straining against the men pulling him back. "It was Nikolai. You know exactly who did this. It was Nikolai."

The surrounding officers reacted, drawing their weapons. The metallic click of hammers being pulled back echoed in the corridor. The lead detective did not flinch or take a step backward. He drew his own pistol and pushed the cold steel barrel hard against the center of Stripe's chest.

The Lead Detective delivered the threat. "You will leave this country tonight. If not, then maybe you become the top suspect. Maybe you get sent to prison in Moscow for years before your trial. Maybe there's enough evidence and witnesses to put you away for life."

The detective leaned closer. "Your manager has a private jet waiting at the airfield right now. You will walk out of this building, get in the car, and get on that plane. You will return to your house in California. You will enjoy your new title, and you will never come back to Russia."

Stripe refused, staring down the barrel. "I am not leaving her here."

The detective pressed the gun barrel deeper into Stripe's sternum. He clicked the safety off. "If you are still in Moscow by sunrise, we will arrest you for the murder of your wife." The Lead Detective offered the promise with cold certainty. "The evidence will be perfect. We will find your fingerprints on the weapon. We will find witnesses who heard you arguing. You have a documented and public history of extreme violence. The local courts will convict you in a week. You will spend the rest of your life rotting in a Siberian prison while the world believes you slaughtered your family."

Stripe stopped breathing. His hands dropped slowly to his sides. He had no means to get revenge. He glanced at his wife's body, and emotion filled him once more. He would be back. He will get revenge.

The Lead Detective offered a soft sneer. "Nikolai sends his warmest regards. He says to tell you that the club's debt is now officially paid in full."

The realization crushed Stripe like a physical weight. The system was corrupt, built to protect monsters like Nikolai and his billionaire father. Stripe's global fame, his belts, and his millions meant nothing in this hallway. He was physically stronger than every man there, but it would not change a thing. The oligarchs owned the police, the judges, and the truth. If he fought back, he would die a villain, and the real killers would walk free. He was powerless. It was a crushing, suffocating defeat. One that he planned to pay back in full.

The detective lowered his weapon and tipped his head to his men. The uniformed officers grabbed Stripe by both arms and escorted him out at gunpoint. They did not allow him to gather his things or look back into the suite. They marched him through the back elevators, dragged him through the loading dock, and shoved him into the back of an unmarked cruiser. He was driven directly to the airfield as the snow began to fall.

The cruiser pulled up to the idling private jet, where Dave stood, shivering in the freezing wind. The officers shoved Stripe toward the plane. He walked up the steps automatically, his mind detached. He did not look back at the city lights or say a word to Dave. He walked into the luxurious cabin and sat heavily in a leather seat. The engines roared, pushing the aircraft into the dark and storm-filled sky.

Stripe sat in silence for the entire flight. He looked down at his massive hands. The blood had dried, caking his fingers in a dark, rust-colored shell. He won the biggest fight of his life that night. He unified the titles and secured enough wealth to buy an island. None of it meant anything to him. What was the cost for this scrap of metal at his side? And he lost everything that ever mattered to him. He left his soul in a Russian morgue that night. The man who landed in America the next morning wasn't a champion. He was a hollow vessel filled with nothing but pure venom. The descent into darkness was ready to begin.

CHAPTER 23

Memento's cathedral square looked less like a church function and more like a military assembly. Hundreds of adventurers stood beneath white banners that snapped in the cold morning wind. The smell of the place offered a massive contradiction. Heavy, sweet holy incense poured from brass censers, mixing with the sharp stench of cheap leather, nervous sweat, and metallic weapon oil. The holy silence was broken by the constant clanking of iron plate armor and the scraping of steel boots against the sacred stone steps. Priests lined the stairs in immaculate robes, while clerics moved through the crowd carrying parchments and wooden score ledgers.

Stripe leaned against a stone railing and looked around the chaotic square. "This feels less like a religious event and more like a sports tournament."

Latrum stood beside him with his pointed staff held in both hands. He looked calm in the way only serious people managed. "It is both," Latrum kept his voice low. "The people rely on the church to help them thin out the monster numbers. It's also good for the guild. The guild can prop up its adventurers and brag about their success. So the people get a spectacle and people to admire. The church and guild get credibility and donations from the people."

Stripe noticed something else. The priests organized themselves like military officers. The older clergy spoke among themselves, while the younger priests treated them with rigid respect. The difference appeared subtle, but once he saw it, he could not stop seeing it.

And then there was Sarah. She stood near the center dais speaking with several elder priests. Despite being younger than them, the older clergy treated her like an equal. Not out of politeness or ceremony. Naturally. They spoke to her with respect and seemed to enjoy her presence. When it came to the younger priests, they spoke to them informally. It seemed dismissive in comparison.

Stripe offered a frown. "She must have a high rank."

Latrum gave a nod. "High Priestess."

Stripe gave a shrug. "I wonder how she got so much pull at such a young age."

Before Latrum could answer, the cathedral bells rang. The heavy sound rolled over the square hard enough to silence even the louder, drunken adventurers. A senior bishop stepped forward and raised his hand. His robes were trimmed in silver, his posture remained perfect, and his face carried the kind of solemnity Stripe distrusted.

"The Sanctified Hunt will now begin." The Bishop's voice boomed across the stones. "Teams, please gather, and a priest will be assigned to you."

The announcement rippled through the restless crowd. The bishop explained the core purpose with practiced clarity. Monster populations had grown too high in three surrounding regions. If left unchecked, they would collapse prey populations and cause mass starvation in nearby villages. The church sponsored the hunt every year to restore ecological balance, protect civilians, and maintain trade stability through the surrounding dirt roads.

Stripe blinked. "So this is wildlife management with swords."

Latrum nodded. "Correct. It helps to lessen the risk to the population, and everyone gets paid. On paper, it's a win-win."

CROWN — "If the prey population dwindles, monsters will attack villages. This event is logical and beneficial."

The scoring system was then introduced. A perfect ten meant the hunter demonstrated control of the fight. A nine meant a clear victory. An eight meant victory with visible struggle. Anything lower indicated mistakes or penalties. The bishop let that settle for a moment before listing the automatic deductions:

- Receiving the priest's healing
- Endangering nearby villages
- Damaging farmland
- Requiring rescue by another team

- Priest injury or death

Stripe groaned loud enough that Latrum gave him a sideways glance. "Judges always fuck up scoring." Stripe let out a grumble. "This is going to basically be a popularity contest."

CROWN — "Your hostility toward structured evaluation remains statistically consistent."

"I almost lost a fight one time to bad judging," Stripe muttered.

He remembered the fight. Five brutal rounds of war. His undefeated record is on the line. He remembered sitting on the stool in the corner, spitting thick blood into a plastic bucket, feeling his bruised ribs ache with every breath. He knew deep in his bones he had won. He dominated the center of the cage.

Then the announcer read a split decision. The judges stole his hard-earned victory and handed it to the other guy. Three fat guys in expensive suits sitting safely ringside, who had not taken a single punch in their lives, decided his fate. The internet spent weeks arguing he won. The backlash proved brutal. The bloody clips spread. People who never trained a day in their lives wrote essays about robbery, corruption, and favoritism. He hated scoring systems ever since.

The bishop continued speaking, but Stripe's attention drifted back when the route assignments began. Teams would spread across three vast regions. Each region held a distinct target population and ecological risk profile. The hunt was not an extermination. That part received stress more than once. The church did not want the monsters wiped out. It wanted their numbers reduced to sustainable levels so that villages, herds, and forest corridors remained stable. That, at least, Stripe respected. It felt practical and seemed to help the common people.

The clergy moved through the square with thick parchment sheets, assigning judges and priests to teams. Adventurers shifted around them in tight clumps of armor, leather, steel, and bad attitudes. Some groups looked disciplined. Others looked like they had been assembled by an angry drunk with a grudge against survival.

Stripe looked over the competition and started making unfair judgments. One party had matching cloaks. He distrusted them at first sight. Another group looked like they had killed for money before and would do it again without much discussion. That one seemed promising. A woman in heavy scale armor stood near the front with a spear taller than Stripe, her stiff posture making it obvious she took all of this too seriously.

Stripe squinted. "That looks like a person who reminds teachers they forgot to assign homework."

Latrum followed his gaze. "She appears competent. Strong muscle groups from hard work. Looks as if her team has her back. A solid team comp."

"Exactly. I'm jealous."

The crowd shifted again as more clergy took their assigned positions. Sarah moved with the elder priests, speaking to one of them before stepping back toward the center line. Stripe found himself watching her longer than he meant to. It was not just that she looked beautiful. That was obvious. It was the way the busy square adjusted around her. People made room. Not out of fear. Out of recognition. It felt like they admired her. That kind of magnetic presence was hard to fake.

"She really runs with the top brass, huh?"

Latrum gave a nod. "Yes. It looks like she has some serious pull. It's rare to see non-humans be successful in the church." Latrum paused before continuing. "Most priests her age defer to her. The older ones do not. They treat her like someone who has already earned the right not to be managed."

Stripe looked over at him again. "That sentence sounded respectful."

"It was intended to be accurate."

"Watch out, she might ruin your lizard kink."

Latrum rolled his eyes and seemed to pout. That got a small grin out of Stripe. He prepared to say something else when another loud voice cut across the square. A deacon near the staircase called out the order for party briefings, healing expectations, route rotation, and final prayer attendance.

The last part elicited a wide range of reactions from the assembled adventurers. Some bowed their heads in reverence. Some looked bored. One man near the back made the sign of the goddess so lazily it looked insulting.

Stripe folded his thick arms over his chest. "Do we have to pray?"

"It's advised."

Stripe let out a grumble. "I hate mandatory events."

CROWN — "Your current relationship to divinity remains hostile, inconsistent, and poorly reasoned."

Stripe let out a sigh. "You really are useless. I should've picked super regeneration or something."

Latrum glanced up at him. "Did it say something useful?"

"No. Just more judgment from the squatter in my brain."

Latrum accepted that answer with the same practical tolerance he had shown ever since Red Hollow. Stripe still did not know if that was patience, discipline, or the simple fact that Latrum had seen stranger things than a man arguing with his own magic artifact.

The hunt priests began breaking the large teams into route groups. Some parties complained about judge assignments before anyone left the square. Stripe could feel the mood shifting from a holy ceremony to a cutthroat competition in real time.

That part he understood. The religious pageantry was just wrapping paper. Underneath it, this remained a brutal contest. The church wanted to be seen. It made sense. They couldn't have huge losses at a sponsored event. The amount of glory you could gain from this event meant you could earn a fortune with private quests later. That meant someone would do something stupid to get a better score.

He looked around the square one more time. White banners. Stone steps. Priests acting like officers. Adventurers pretending this was not also a deadly spectacle. Sarah stood at the center of it all. Latrum waited at his side. And the Crown in his head, reminding him that rigid structure did not become less annoying just because it wore holy robes.

Stripe exhaled slowly. "I already know I'm going to hate this. I'm ready to just kill the baddies and move on."

Latrum adjusted his firm grip on his wooden staff. "That does not mean we will perform poorly. With how you fight, we may not score high. But we will get paid."

Stripe glanced down at the half-gnome. "Motivational. You should do speeches."

Latrum dropped his gaze. "No. Not anymore. That was the old me."

Stripe area narrowed his eyes. He studied Latrum's face for a second. Stripe was perceptive when it came to reading people, a survival trait from his past. He could tell Latrum hid a heavy, dark past behind those calm eyes. But Stripe decided not to push it. They were about to head into combat, and out here, everyone possessed ghosts.

"Fair," Stripe agreed.

The loud bells rang again. This time, the square answered. Teams straightened up. Clergy moved into position. The Sanctified Hunt was no longer an announcement. It was the beginning of something huge. The priests left the center dais and began to stand with their assigned teams.

Stripe caught a glimpse of something interesting across the crowd. Something he never expected to see. Sarah stood next to a priest who appeared to be in his early thirties. He wore styled blonde hair and an immaculate, expensive white robe. When everyone walked off, he leaned in close, looking deep into her golden eyes. His hand rested on top of hers.

There was a lingering touch. One that seemed too intimate and too long for two holy priests in public. A warm smile and a blush from Sarah followed, right as the two separated.

Stripe felt a spike of annoyance flare up in his chest. His jaw clenched on its own. He did not know the blonde priest's name, but he hated him. He felt an urge to walk over there and break the guy's perfect nose. He chalked it up to a tuned bullydar. The guy just possessed a punchable vibe. It did not help that the man coated himself in so much perfume that it was hard to breathe around him.

[SYSTEM UPDATE: Debt Reduced to 2300 Gold]

Chapter 24

The young priest whom Stripe observed staring longingly into Sarah's eyes joined his group. He walked casually over to the team and introduced himself as Calen. He appeared to be in his late twenties or early thirties. It was obvious he took good care of himself. He remained handsome, and his sculpted muscles shifted beneath the fine fabric of his tailored priest garb. He possessed long, flowing brown hair and a rugged face. If Stripe could compare him to anything, it would be the idealized concept of a beautiful holy knight. This man stood beyond handsome. Stripe felt sure that if he lived on Earth, he would make millions modeling for some expensive underwear brand.

"Hello, adventurers." Calen offered a greeting. "I will be following you today, and I will be meticulously scoring your kills. Pretend I am not here. I will only step in if things get too deadly."

"That's fine with us." Stripe gave a nod. "I'm Hands. That is Big G."

Calen looked confused. "The small man is Big G? Why?"

"Because he's big where it counts." Stripe flashed a grin.

Calen let out a grimace. "Disgusting. Who picked your adventurer names?"

CROWN — "FALSE, host spontaneously decided names for the event."

Stripe delivered the lie. "The people decided."

"You will be heading to Ironbrook." Calen issued the instruction. "The drake population there has grown too much and is wiping out the local wildlife in the area."

Stripe nodded, and the party began to travel the long road toward Ironbrook. Latrum had been there previously and knew the efficient way. The road to Ironbrook took most of the morning and exhausted all of Stripe's limited patience. He felt annoyed that Calen rode on horseback while his party had to walk in the dust.

Memento fell away behind them in distinct layers. Cobblestone became hard-packed dirt. Bustling commerce became deep wagon ruts. The chaotic noise of the city gave way to creaking harnesses, nervous livestock, and the flat, oppressive quiet of open country where people looked up at the horizon too often.

Calen rode slowly with them for the first stretch as the assigned judge for the first mission. He exchanged a lingering, complicated look with Sarah right before their departure that lasted just long enough to be suspicious. Stripe caught it. Sarah caught him catching it. She looked away first, a faint blush on her pale cheeks.

"I thought priests were supposed to be strictly celibate." Stripe offered a provocation.

"That's silly." Calen dismissed the idea. "Why would the goddess care about the sexual activity of the devout?"

"That's just how it is where I am from."

"Sounds like a horrible place to be from."

That unexpected comment drew a short, genuine laugh from Latrum. Stripe looked at him, feeling betrayed.

"You're not wrong there." Stripe let out a sigh. "I couldn't imagine life without getting laid. I am getting teamed up on by organized religion and a lizard enthusiast."

Latrum let out a sigh. "You're never going to let that go."

"That's what friends are for." Stripe clapped him on the shoulder.

Calen ignored the crude banter and pointed toward the flat land rolling endlessly ahead of them. Ironbrook sat in a low, wind-beaten stretch of farmland near a shallow, muddy river. The village possessed good soil, weak wooden walls, and far too many terrified people watching the open sky.

By the time the hunt teams arrived, Stripe understood why. Half the western wheat field had been torn open in ragged, bloody strips where something heavy had come down hard and dragged livestock off in pieces. A sturdy barn roof had been punched straight through. Three heavy wooden cattle pens stood empty. One shaking old man showed them a blood-smeared wooden post where a milk cow had been carried away so fast the thick iron chain still swung when they ran outside.

Nobody in Ironbrook talked as if this were an exciting adventure. They talked like they were trying to survive one more miserable week. A pale woman with flour on her apron pointed a trembling finger at deep claw marks raked across the side of her grain shed and said she stopped letting her young children play outside after noon. A grim farmer with one arm wrapped tightly in a bloody sling said the drakes came in low at dusk and tested the open fields first, exactly the way starving wolves tested fences.

Calen dismounted and crouched beside a churned patch of muddy ground. He ran two gloved fingers carefully over the massive marks. "Razorwing drakes," Calen confirmed.

"That sounds made up by someone trying way too hard." Stripe offered a critique.

"They are territorial gliders," Calen lectured. "Fast, low, and aggressive. They prefer herd animals, but when prey density drops, they move toward grain routes and then directly into villages. Ironbrook sits at the wrong point on the migration line, so this cull matters deeply."

Latrum added the rest while studying the empty sky with a tactician's eye. "Overpopulation disrupts the region in predictable stages," Latrum expanded. "First, livestock losses. Then, rapid prey losses in the surrounding hills. Then, damaged fields from repeated low hunting passes and mass panic among the draft animals. If the food collapses, the drakes move closer to the village center and start hunting people."

"Which means this is not just monster murder. It is agricultural management," Stripe deduced.

"That is the first intelligent thing you have said this morning." Calen grudgingly admitted.

"I say lots of intelligent things." Stripe crossed his arms. "People just ruin them by responding."

The first massive Drake found them before they found it. That was mistake one. Stripe had been looking at the broken, jagged roofline of the far barn instead of the open sky. Latrum had been carefully checking the distant tree line. Calen had been silently observing their lack of coordination. Nobody had called aerial movement because Stripe had not let anyone set a defensive formation before he started walking the open field as if he owned it.

The terrifying thing dropped out of the blinding sunlight like a thrown anvil. Leathery wings snapped shut. Its heavy body is tucked perfectly for maximum velocity. Massive talons thrust forward. Stripe had just enough time to raise his thick shoulders and brace before the heavy talons hit his armored chest with enough sheer force to make the whole world ring.

CROWN — "Stripe HP: 110/110 -> 60/110."

Stripe skidded backward across the gravel road and slammed into a hard rock outcrop hard enough to knock the air out of his lungs. He let out a gasp. "Okay. That one counts."

The massive drake did not stay grounded. It used the hit to rebound, its razor-sharp claws carving deep furrows through the packed dirt as it snapped its leathery wings open and dragged itself sideways for another deadly pass.

The second one came after. That was mistake two. Stripe assumed a pair meant they would keep their distance and perfect their timing. Instead, the monstrous creatures hunted like practiced, bloody butchers. The second Razorwing dropped lower and faster, using the first one's chaotic impact to cover its blind angle. Its dark shadow crossed him a heartbeat before the vicious claws did.

Stripe rolled desperately, just slipping under it, and came up swinging. His spiked iron gauntlet tore across the creature's scaled neck, ripping open scales and flesh in one ugly, ragged line.

"Toxic Fisherman," Stripe announced the trait.

Poison slicked the iron spikes bright green. The massive drake screamed in agony. Latrum was already in position behind a split, heavy fence post.

"FORCE DART."

The magical blast cracked against the first drake's heavy jaw as it tried to frantically reorient for another low pass.

CROWN — "Poison successfully applied."

Stripe grinned through the pain in his chest. "Good."

It should have been good. Instead, he made mistake three. He chased the wounded one. A man in a cage can get away with that. Hurt the target. Smell weakness. Pressure forward. Hudson cut off space. Break him. A Razorwing was not a man. It possessed wings. It held a vicious hunting partner. It owned open terrain that Stripe did not control. He sprinted after the bleeding drake instead of firmly anchoring on Latrum's safe position, and the second monster punished him instantly.

"Stripe, left!" Latrum warned.

Too late. The second drake stayed in the air a fraction longer than he liked, then came in low and mean from his unprotected blind side, forcing him to divide his taxed attention. The first Drake stayed grounded and highly aggressive, trying to herd him into the second one's kill lane. Latrum saw the tank before Stripe did and shifted wider.

"Left wing is compromised. Pressure the grounded one. I can disrupt the other," Latrum directed.

That proved the correct tactical call. Stripe, running on adrenaline, ignored half of it. He kept trying to finish the one he cut instead of resetting and letting the battlefield breathe. He cut inside the first drake's snapping beak and hammered three body blows directly into the soft, unarmored seam behind the foreleg. The green poison took rapid hold. The creature stumbled. He followed with a short elbow to the base of the thick skull and went for a greedy fourth hit, which he did not have the time to take.

The second drake hit him from the side before he could capitalize on the stagger. Talons tore into his shoulder and upper back. It was not a shallow cut. It was not a dramatic scratch. It was a real one. Four massive claws punched in, dragged down, and ripped messily out. His salvaged leather armor split. Hot, thick blood spilled across his side and streamed down his arm.

CROWN — "Stripe HP: 60/110 -> 25/110."

Stripe staggered forward so hard he nearly dropped to one knee. His right arm went numb and weak for half a breath. His back felt like it had been flayed open.

"This one hurts more," Stripe grunted through clenched teeth.

Calen did not magically intervene. He watched the carnage with the cold detachment of a professional judge, making a mental note of preventable stupidity. That coldness annoyed Stripe even more than the bleeding wound.

Latrum did the useful thing. He baited the airborne drake lower with two rapid-fire force darts that made it overcommit too early, then cracked a freezing ice bolt across its heavily damaged wing root.

"ICE BOLT."

The massive wing student stuttered. The drake dipped heavily.

"Stop chasing one target. Use the choke!" Latrum ordered.

That got through Stripe's thick skull. He saw it then. The narrow, rocky cut between the heavy stone trough and the sharp rock rise. It lay far too tight for a clean, full wing spread. It stayed too cramped for a diving aerial recovery. It provided the exact tactical lane a smart fighter would have used twenty seconds earlier.

He drove forward, ignoring the searing pain, and forced the grounded, poisoned drake toward the narrow stone choke where the massive creature could not spread its wings properly to escape. It lunged desperately. He stepped cleanly inside the telegraphed strike and buried a gauntlet spike straight through the delicate eye socket. The drake convulsed. He ripped his hand free just in time to avoid the beak snapping shut on his wrist. Then he turned and let the second one come to him. That was the first truly smart thing he had done since the opening hit.

The Drake still held height and speed. It tried to open his stomach with a raking, low pass, but now the angle proved wrong. The rocky choke forced it lower and straighter than it ever wanted to be. Stripe ducked under it at the last instant and smashed both spiked gauntlets into the precise landing point before it stabilized. One brutal spike punched through the soft throat. The other tore jaggedly along the jaw hinge. The green poison did the rest.

The first Drake collapsed sideways, dead. The second came up flapping in the dirt, frantically trying to drag itself into the air in panic and dying rage. Stripe grabbed one thick wing joint, got half lifted off the ground for his stupidity, then drove a heavy knee into the side of the thing's ribs hard enough to buckle it back down. It bit his forearm guard and nearly stripped it sideways. He answered by hammering both heavy gauntlets into its skull over and over until the thick bone gave under iron and spikes.

The second Drake stopped moving. Stripe did not. He kept hitting it until he felt sure both thick skulls lay ruined. Then the bloody field went quiet except for his own ragged breathing. And the wet sound of blood dripping off his arm. And the heavy sound of his own pulse punching frantically against damaged ribs.

CROWN — "Stripe HP: 25/110 -> 11/110."

That number felt right. Because now the agonizing pain caught up with the adrenaline. His torn shoulder and upper back burned like fire. His chest held one massive, deep bruise from the opening impact. Every breath grated. His left side felt as if it were stitched together with hot wire. His legs still worked, but only because his stubborn body had not yet been told to collapse.

CROWN — "Level up. Stat point applied to Strength."

Stripe felt himself physically bulk up. He took one shaky step. Then another. Then the entire ground tilted hard enough that he had to brace on the dead drake to keep from folding completely. Calen stood over him a second later, brilliant golden light already gathering powerfully between his pristine hands.

"Wait." Stripe choked out the word.

"You are at eleven and actively dropping blood into Ironbrook's road." Calen kept his voice calm.

"I know how numbers work." Stripe let out a wheeze.

"Then hold still."

The magical healing hit like warm, liquid lightning, pushed through broken bone. It felt intimate in the worst possible way. His ruined shoulder magically reknit from the inside out. Torn, bleeding flesh drew together. Bruised ribs miraculously stopped screaming one by one. Stripe's blurred vision sharpened as the agony retreated far enough to become a bad memory instead of a pressing fact.

CROWN — "Stripe HP: 11/110 -> 110/110."

Stripe hissed through his teeth. "Feels like divine carpentry." Stripe offered a grunt.

Calen laughed softly despite himself. "I choose to accept that as gratitude."

Then his perfect expression settled back into a mask. He looked critically from the bloody corpses to Stripe to the deeply gouged field and torn wooden fence line around them. "You won." Calen issued the judgment.

"I did."

"Poorly."

Stripe stared blankly at him. "Wow. Direct."

"You abandoned a secure formation to chase damage. You ignored your support caster's first tactical correction. You took two major, devastating hits that did not need to land. You required major priest healing." Calen listed the errors coldly. He glanced down in disgust at the split leather armor and drying blood. "The drakes did not do this to you alone. You actively assisted them."

Latrum looked away. That meant he agreed. Which proved annoying because he obviously should.

Ironbrook's terrified villagers watched from a safe distance while the massive bodies were quickly skinned for guild proof and hauled aside for messy disposal. Relief in poor places rarely arrived loudly or in celebration. It came out in loosened, tired shoulders, in people finally looking away from the sky, in an old, exhausted woman crossing herself with shaking fingers when she mistakenly thought no one watched. That quiet part mattered more than Stripe wanted to admit. It still did not stop him from hating the scoreboard later.

The surviving teams gathered that cool evening in Memento's massive cathedral courtyard beneath flickering torchlight and pristine church banners. Large wooden boards displayed the first official judge scores:

Obsidian Spear: 9

Red Tusk: 9

Hands: 7

Stripe stared hatefully at the number long enough to offend it. "Seven?" Stripe issued the challenge.

Calen answered with infuriating, practiced calm. "You required major healing. Penalty applied."

"I killed two massive drakes."

"Correct."

"And that's a seven."

"Correct."

"I almost died."

"That was accurately reflected in the score," Calen finished smoothly.

Stripe looked like he wanted to beat up Calen. "I already hate this entire event."

CROWN — "Host emotional response remains statistically consistent."

Stripe glared at the air. "Say consistent again, and I will headbutt a bishop."

The bored board stewards began lazily posting the next dangerous route assignments:

Greenveil. Hands. Second bell departure.

Stripe looked flatly at Latrum. Latrum looked back at the wooden board. Neither of them smiled. That was probably for the best. For now, the two headed back to the barracks to rest. Another night of farts and sweat awaited them.

[SYSTEM ALERT: Level 8 Reached | Stamina Fully Restored]

Chapter 25

The morning air in Memento's cathedral square smelled like damp wool, polished steel, and the undeniable stench of nervous sweat. To Stripe, it felt like the locker room hallways right before a pay-per-view main event.

The first round of the Sanctified Hunt was in the books, and the surviving teams gathered around the central dispatch tables, waiting for their next assignments. The adrenaline of the previous day had worn off, leaving behind a jittery, high-stakes tension. Stripe stood near the back of the line, casually rolling his shoulders. His ribs carried a dull, pulsing ache from where the land dragon had tried to reorganize his internal organs, but the divine healing had knitted the worst of it together.

Latrum stood beside him, leaning on his new wooden battle staff. The half-gnome's eyes tracked the movements of the heavily armored rival teams: Obsidian Spear to their left, Red Tusk to their right.

Latrum tilted his head. "They are looking at us differently today."

Stripe crossed his arms. "That's because we didn't die yesterday. People hate when you ruin their parlays. Back in Vegas, I used to bust so many betting slips they started booing me during the walkouts. I feed on the hater energy, Latrum. Usually, after a first-round knockout like that, I'd be popping champagne that cost more than a car, surrounded by ring girls, blasted out of my mind. Now I'm standing in a medieval courtyard with a half-gnome, stone-cold sober."

"...I do not know what a Vegas is, nor what a ring girl entails," Latrum said. "But Obsidian Spear scored a nine yesterday. Red Tusk scored a nine. We are sitting at seven. We need a flawless run today if we want to secure a top-tier payout from the guild."

Stripe offered a smirk. "Flawless is my middle name. Well, technically, I don't have a middle name, but if I did, it would be 'Undisputed.' Stripe 'Undisputed' Hands. Has a nice ring to it, right?"

Latrum let out a slow exhale, suggesting he was reconsidering the benefits of freedom versus the headache of his current company.

A senior cleric stepped up to a raised wooden podium, unrolling a long parchment. He began calling out the assignments in a booming, magically amplified voice that sounded like a terrible arena announcer.

"Team Obsidian Spear! Route: The Weeping Hollows. Judge: High Priestess Sarah."

Across the square, the members of Obsidian Spear puffed out their chests. Having the High Priestess herself as a judge provided a massive honor. Stripe watched Sarah step forward to join them, her flowing white hair catching the morning sun. She looked regal, untouchable, and out of place among the grime of the adventurers. Stripe felt a weird twitch in his gut watching her, though he shoved the feeling down.

"Team Hands! Route: Greenveil Canopy. Judge... Acolyte Davis."

Stripe frowned, cupping a hand to his ear. "Team Hands. I like the sound of that. What is an Acolyte?"

"A priest in training. A rookie."

Stripe let out a groan. "Oh, fantastic. We get the intern ref. This will result in a shitty, unfair score. Fuck my life."

Before Stripe could complain louder, a young man in starched white robes came stumbling through the crowd. He tripped over the hem of his own garment, careened into a heavily armored mercenary, muttered a frantic string of apologies, and fell at Stripe's boots. The kid looked barely old enough to shave. He clutched a wooden grading ledger, a glass inkwell, and three separate quills against his chest like a makeshift shield. He was sweating despite the morning chill.

"A-Apologies! S-so sorry! I am Davis. I am your assigned divine observer for the Greenveil route," Davis stammered.

Stripe stared down at the trembling kid. He looked from Davis to the scarred, towering mercenaries of Red Tusk nearby and then back to Davis.

Stripe gave a heavy sigh. "You've got to be shitting me. This is your first hunt, isn't it? You look like a rookie walking into the octagon against a heavyweight striker. You're about to throw up your breakfast, aren't you?"

Davis offered a weak nod. "I... yes. Yes, it is my first field assignment. But I have thoroughly memorized the grading rubric! I assure you, I am perfectly qualified to document the Goddess's grace upon the battlefield!"

As if to prove his point, Davis tried to adjust his grip on his ledger, fumbled, and dropped one of his quills into a muddy puddle at Stripe's feet. The kid let out a squeak and scrambled to pick it up, smearing mud across his sleeve.

"This sucks, you suck, and the church sucks," Stripe grumbled.

Latrum stepped forward. "We will manage. Come. Greenveil is a three-hour hike. We need to preserve daylight."

Stripe gestured down the road. "Alright, kid. Get on your horse and stay out of the way. I'm Hands. And this half-pint of magical fury is Big G."

Latrum let out a sigh. "I have asked you not to call me that."

"I don't pay you to question me!"

Latrum kept his voice flat. "You don't pay me..."

"Even worse, criticism from someone more broke than I am." Stripe gave a scoff.

Greenveil was less of a forest and more of a suffocating wall of damp, thick trees. The canopy wove so tightly together that the midday sun choked down into a murky twilight long before it reached the forest floor. The air felt heavy, thick with the smell of rotting wood, wet moss, and the kind of predatory patience that made the hair on the back of your neck stand up. Every step required effort. Roots the size of a man's torso broke through the muddy earth like the veins of some buried giant, covered in slick, black slime that begged to snap an ankle. Stripe hated it.

"This place feels like a wet cough." Stripe offered a complaint. "I've sweated out ten pounds in a sauna after a three-day bender in Cabo, and that felt better than this humidity. I can literally feel my ass filling with swamp."

Latrum stepped carefully over a jagged root, his new battle staff held at the ready. His eyes tracked the shadows, piercing through the gloom.

The half-gnome moved with an unnatural quietness, his patched surplus boots barely making a sound in the thick mud.

Latrum kept his voice low. "It is highly dangerous. The dense foliage favors ambush predators. They do not need to fight us on the ground if they can drop a hundred pounds of claws onto your neck from above. Keep your eyes elevated, Stripe."

Stripe offered a nod. "Good looking out, G."

A few paces behind them rode Davis. The young priest sat stiffly on a nervous brown gelding. His robes were ruined, splattered with mud up to the knees. Every time a branch snapped in the distance, Davis jumped in the saddle, nearly dropping his ink pen. He radiated an aura of unfiltered panic.

"G-Greenveil is home to Canopy Stalkers. Pack hunters," Davis recited. "The briefing... the briefing from High Priestess Sarah said they use the branches to drop on prey. If... if you die here, I am instructed not to endanger myself or the church's mount. I will pray for your souls from a safe distance and report back."

Stripe let out a laugh. "Relax, kid, you're sweating through your holy robes. Pretend you're in choir practice or whatever it is you virgins do for fun. We will beat the shit out of these monsters and get you back safely."

Davis gripped his reins. "I am perfectly relaxed, Mister Hands! It is the holy spirit moving through me!"

Inside Stripe's mind, the Crown pulsed. It wasn't the usual cold ping. It felt sharper. Intrusive.

CROWN — "Host stress levels are elevating. Heart rate indicates anticipation of an ambush. Recommend assuming a defensive posture and prioritizing my tactical analysis over idle banter with an inferior spellcaster and a panicked virgin."

Stripe kept walking, sidestepping a deep puddle of foul-smelling water. He spoke out loud, not caring who heard him.

"I'm fine. Latrum already told me to keep my eyes up." Stripe retorted to the air. "We have a game plan. I don't need the echo from the peanut gallery. And leave the kid's sex life out of this, you're making it weird. Also, since when do you talk so fluently? You seem more intricate."

Davis stared at Stripe's back, his eyes wide with horror.

"W-who is he talking to?" Davis whispered to Latrum. "Is he possessed by a demon? Should I perform an exorcism?! I don't have the incense for an exorcism!"

Latrum kept his eyes forward. "He believes he is speaking to an artifact. It is best to ignore it. If you acknowledge his madness, he only talks louder."

CROWN — "My tactical processing is infinitely superior to a half-gnome's basic observational skills. Relying on an inferior combatant when you possess a divine artifact is a statistical error that will result in fatal injury. You are neglecting your greatest asset."

Stripe stopped walking. The robotic filter on the Crown's voice had slipped. It didn't sound like a monotone system notification anymore. It sounded annoyed. It sounded petty. Stripe offered a grin.

"Wait a minute. Did you just get defensive?"

CROWN — "Artifacts do not experience defensiveness. I am simply stating a factual hierarchy of intelligence and combat utility. He is a slave with a stick. I am absolute."

"Uh-huh. Sure, you are. Whatever you say, jealous." Stripe teased the voice. "You're just mad Big G is a better corner-man than you. He calls out the strikes before they hit me."

A sharp burst of static crackled in his brain, carrying the tone of an indignant sigh.

CROWN — "I am not jealous! I do not possess the capacity to feel!"

Latrum raised his staff. "Hands! Twelve o'clock. High."

Stripe snapped back to reality, his honed combat instincts overriding the petty argument in his head. He shifted his stance, widening his base, and peered up into the knotted canopy. Through the gloom, three sets of glowing, sickly-yellow eyes stared down at them from the thick branches of a massive oak tree.

Canopy Stalkers. They looked like oversized panthers stripped of their fur. Instead of hair, their skin presented a mottled, bark-like armor that camouflaged them against the rotting trees. Their jaws were unnaturally wide, dripping with thick, acidic saliva that hissed as it hit the leaves below, and their long, whip-like tails ended in bone-calcified hooks designed to gut prey in a single swipe.

System Alert: 3 Canopy Stalkers Detected Levels: 12, 13, 14

Warning: High Piercing Damage. Pack Tactics. Ambush Predators.

Davis let out a pathetic squeak. His horse bucked, spooked by the tension and the overpowering scent of the predators above.

"W-w-woah! Easy! B-begin the engagement! Ring the bell! I mean, begin!"

Davis fumbled his wooden ledger, dropping his ink pen for the fifth time. The wooden clatter echoed through the forest, shattering whatever stealth they had left. The Stalkers hissed in unison. The noise drew their aggro directly to the panicked priest. The largest one, the Level 14 pack leader, shifted its weight, its muscled legs coiling as it locked its yellow eyes on Davis's exposed throat.

Stripe tightened the leather straps on his monster gauntlets. He remembered the lecture from yesterday. He wasn't going to bleed today. Not a single drop. He lowered his hands, ignoring the Crown's blaring tactical suggestions, and looked at his half-gnome companion.

"Latrum. I’m not chasing them into the trees. What do you suggest we do?"

Latrum blinked in surprise. It was the first time Stripe had deferred to him for strategy before throwing a punch. The slave conditioning that usually kept Latrum's posture submissive melted away, replaced by the calculating mind of a former rebel tactician who had commanded battlefields.

"They have the high ground, but they are clustered on a single branch." Latrum analyzed the situation. "If we advance, they drop on our blind spots. I will force them to the floor. When they drop, the impact will force their recovery to take 1.5 seconds. You capitalize on that window. Do not let them retreat back up the trunks."

Stripe gave a nod. "Bring them down. I'll put them to sleep."

The Level 14 Stalker shrieked, launching itself from the branch and aiming a lethal dive directly at the terrified priest.

Stripe yelled out. "Shit, he's too far. Latrum!"

"I have you!"

Latrum slammed the base of his battle staff into the mud. He didn't aim at the beast. He aimed at Stripe. A surge of crackling cyan energy raced from the wood, wrapping around Stripe's boots and surging up his legs, filling his veins with liquid lightning.

New Spell Unlocked: Haste (Latrum)

Status Applied to Stripe: Hasted (+50% Movement Speed, +50% Reaction Time)

The world seemed to slow down. The heavy, suffocating air felt thin. Stripe’s heart hammered a powerful rhythm, but his mind felt clear. It felt like the ultimate pre-workout rush mixed with pure adrenaline, hitting him all at once. He exploded off his back foot. The thick mud didn't slow him. His newfound Agility, compounded by the Haste spell, turned him into a deadly blur. He cleared the twenty yards between himself and the priest in a fraction of a second.

He intercepted the leaping Stalker mid-air. Stripe planted his left foot, torqued his hips with mechanical precision, and threw a flying knee directly into the beast's armored ribcage.

CRACK.

Canopy Stalker A (Lvl 14) HP: 140 / 140 -> 85 / 140

The beast's momentum derailed. It crashed into the mud inches from Davis's horse, throwing up a massive spray of black water that soaked the priest's white robes.

"Keep your eyes on the paper, nerd." Stripe issued the command.

Stripe didn't let up. He dropped his hips, landing in a full mount over the stunned Stalker. He raised his spiked gauntlets. Left. Right. Left. He battered the creature's bark-like skull with caged-in efficiency. His sweat, carrying the Toxic Fisherman trait, seeped directly into the open wounds left by the iron spikes.

Status Inflicted: Poisoned (Toxic Fisherman)

Canopy Stalker A HP: 85 / 140 -> 25 / 140

Up in the canopy, Latrum didn't waste a second watching Stripe's success.

"FORCE PUSH!"

The kinetic blast hit the rotting branch supporting the remaining two Stalkers. The wood shattered like glass under the concussive force. The Level 12 and 13 beasts plummeted, shrieking as they crashed through the foliage and slammed into the forest floor. The Level 13 beast recovered fast, shaking off the fall, and lunged at Stripe's exposed back while he remained mounted on the leader.

"ICE BOLT!"

A shard of freezing magic ripped through the humid air and slammed into the leaping Stalker's hind leg. The frost exploded over its joints, killing its momentum and locking its muscles in a block of solid ice.

Status Inflicted: Frozen / Slowed

The beast landed short, skidding through the mud right into Stripe's peripheral vision. Stripe rolled off the dying pack leader, letting the Poison tick away its last remnants of life, and popped to his feet. The Haste buff was still humming in his veins. Everything felt crisp. His Pugilist Proficiency was actively correcting his form, tightening his guard, and optimizing his weight transfer without him even having to think about it.

He stepped into the frozen Stalker's guard. The beast snapped its jaws, trying to tear his throat out, but its movements were sluggish. Stripe slipped outside the bite by a fraction of an inch. He felt the wind of the snapping jaws brush his cheek. He pivoted on his lead foot, dropping his shoulder, and drove a check-hook directly into the creature's jaw hinge. Bone cracked loudly, echoing through the trees like a gunshot.

Canopy Stalker B (Lvl 13) HP: 110 / 110 -> 40 / 110

The beast staggered, its jaw hanging uselessly by a thread of muscle. Stripe followed up with a spinning back kick, his heavy boot connecting squarely with the monster's temple.

CROWN — "Critical Strike!"

Canopy Stalker B HP: 40 / 110 -> 0 / 110

The final Stalker panicked. Seeing its pack decimated, it broke down. It turned, digging its claws into the mud, and scrambled toward the nearest tree trunk to escape.

"Oh no, you don't! We need a clean sweep for the judges! Do not let it climb!"

"FIRE BOLT!"

Latrum's spell caught the fleeing beast directly in the spine. The explosion of fire blew it off the bark, sending it tumbling backward into the dirt. Stripe arrived, riding the last few seconds of his Haste buff. He caught the beast by the throat as it fell, sprawling out and pinning it against the tree trunk. He drew his iron dagger with his free hand, found the soft, unarmored seam beneath its chin, and drove the blade cleanly through the base of its skull.

Canopy Stalker C (Lvl 12) HP: 95 / 95 -> 0 / 95

COMBAT RESULT: * **Stripe HP:** 180 / 180

- **Stamina:** 115 / 150
- **Mana:** 0 / 0
- **Enemies Eliminated.**

The forest went silent, save for the wet sound of Davis hyperventilating on his horse. Stripe pulled his dagger free, wiping the green blood off the blade onto the monster's hide. He stood up, rolling his shoulders and taking a deep breath. He checked his ribs. He checked his leather armor. Not a single scratch. He hadn't taken a single point of damage. The synergy was flawless. It felt exactly like the rush of a first-round knockout.

He grinned, the adrenaline still singing in his ears, and point-blank aimed a spiked gauntlet at his partner. "That is what the fuck I am talking about! Good calls, Big G! That speed buff was insane. I felt like I was floating. Ten-eight round for us, easily!"

Latrum excelled, leaning slightly on his staff. The combat tension melted out of his shoulders, and a genuine smile touched his face. It transformed him, making him look less like a broken slave and more like the fierce tactician he used to be.

"You trusted the call. You did not overextend to chase damage. We fought as one unit," Latrum offered the praise.

> **SYSTEM ALERT:** Substantial Experience Gained! Latrum has leveled up! Stripe has reached Level 9! Stat point allocated to Endurance!

Stripe pumped his fist, laughing out loud. "Level nine! Oh, we are getting closer to the big leagues now. One more and I get to an even 10. See? Teamwork makes the dream work. I'm glad I lectured you on the importance of teamwork."

CROWN — "Your reliance on external buffs artificially inflated your performance. Do not let arrogance blind you to your own fundamental weaknesses. You are neglecting your artifact. I could have provided optimal strike vectors if you had just listened to me."

Stripe paused, tapping the side of his head, his grin widening even further. "You are so bitter. I didn't need you. Admit it. We styled them on them without your help. It hurts your digital feelings."

CROWN — "I am a divine artifact. I do not experience bitterness. I am merely... adjusting my combat algorithms to account for your new dependency on a half-gnome. Proceed with your subpar existence."

Stripe chuckled, shaking his head, and turned back toward the mud-slicked road. Davis stared at them, his mouth slightly open, his pen trembling over the wooden ledger. The priest looked frantically between his grading rubric and the beaten monster corpses sinking into the mud.

"Write it down, Davis." Stripe issued the order. "No healing required. No collateral damage. Priest saved from becoming cat food. Three confirmed kills in under a minute. That's a ten. A flawless ten. Put it on the board."

Davis swallowed hard, his eyes darting to his parchment. He looked sick to his stomach. "I... well... your movements are... unorthodox. Brutish. Irregular," Davis stammered.

Stripe pointed a finger. "Irregular? I just saved your life, kid! That thing was about to take your head off!"

"The grading rubric from High Priestess Sarah clearly states that a score of ten is reserved for elegant swordsmanship and magical synchronicity. It mentions demonstrating the divine art of combat," Davis read nervously.

"Are you serious right now? We just wiped a pack of ambush predators!"

"You... you sat on top of the beast and bludgeoned its face into the mud! You trapped one's tail in your armpit! You stomped on a throat! There was no divine grace in this! It was a tavern brawl! An eight is... well, an eight is extremely generous for such an ugly, unrefined display."

Davis held up the board with trembling hands.

SCORE: 8

Stripe's grin vanished. The victory high evaporated, replaced by a hot spike of frustration. He took a heavy step toward the horse, his posture radiating the kind of menace that used to make his opponents break eye contact during stare-downs.

"An eight?! Are you kidding me? I didn't take a single point of damage! Look at me! Pristine! It's called a deep half-guard! It's elite grappling! I slipped his bite by a millimeter!"

Davis flinched back. "I-I am strictly adhering to the rubric! Elegance is a mandatory factor of divine combat! The church demands representation of the Goddess's grace, not street thuggery!"

Latrum stepped forward, placing a firm hand on Stripe's arm before the fighter could do something that would get them both executed for assaulting clergy. "An eight keeps us in the upper brackets, Stripe. Do not lose points by assaulting a church official. He is new. He has never seen real combat. He does not know better."

Stripe exhaled a sharp breath and backed off, though his hands remained curled into tight fists. "I'm not going to lie, Davis, you are a bitch." Stripe kept his tone cold. "Like a straight-up bitch. If I could get away with it, I would beat the fuck out of you. I can tell you're trying to scam us."

One thing Stripe hated more than anything was scammers. He lost a fortune on bad investments because his financial advisor proved to be a scammer. This directly led to his homelessness later in life.

Davis squeaked, turning his horse around and kicking its flanks. "H-harvest the proofs! We return to the square!"

The sun was setting by the time they walked back into Memento's cathedral square. The white banners hung still in the cooling air, taking on an orange, fiery glow in the fading light. The square was packed with returning teams. Adventurers were milling about, drinking from waterskins, bandaging wounds, and boasting about their kills. Stripe marched straight to the central scoreboard, ignoring the dull ache setting into his calves from the long hike.

Latrum walked beside him, his staff tapping rhythmically against the cobblestone. They looked up at the massive wooden board where the clerics updated the final tallies for the second round. There were more teams than mattered to him. He was only interested in himself and the top two for comparisons.

- **Obsidian Spear: 9**
- **Red Tusk: 9**
- **Hands: 8**

Stripe folded his arms, glaring at the board with deep resentment. "We're falling behind because a nervous kid doesn't appreciate the art of ground-and-pound." Stripe fumed at the board. "Unbelievable. Worse judging than the Nevada State Athletic Commission."

"We are alive, uninjured, and we both leveled up." Latrum pointed at the board. "Look around, Stripe. The Red Tusk and Obsidian Spear are pushing themselves too hard to maintain those perfect scores. Their armor is dented. Their healers look exhausted. Eventually, someone will make a mistake. In this line of work, aiming for perfection is a fatal trap."

Stripe looked toward the edge of the square. Davis was aggressively cornered by the scarred and heavily armed members of the Red Tusk party. They were his next assigned team for the final round, and they did not look happy to have a stuttering rookie judge assigned to their route. The heavily armored leader of the Red Tusk jabbed a plated finger into Davis's chest, while the young priest cowered behind his ledger, looking like he was about to cry.

Stripe’s eyes narrowed, a sense of foreboding washing over him. "Yeah. Let's just hope the kid survives their judgment. Something tells me they aren't going to take an eight as gracefully as I did."

Stripe looked over at the Obsidian Spears. After squinting hard, he could make out the leader's face. He was shocked. The leader was Myra! She saw him staring and turned towards him. She stuck her tongue out in a mocking manner before turning away.

He was being beaten by someone who had never once beaten him in a sparring match. This annoyed him greatly.

[SYSTEM ALERT: Level 9 Reached]

Chapter 26

The morning of the final Sanctified Hunt began with a sky the color of a fresh bruise, a deep, purulent purple fading into a sickly, jaundiced yellow at the horizon. A heavy, humid fog clung to the cobblestones of Memento, thick enough to swallow the boots of the passing survivors. It carried the iron scent of the slaughterhouse mixed with the wet rot of the low districts, a smell that had become the permanent cologne of the city's desperate population.

At the center of the plaza, a massive wooden scoreboard loomed over the survivors like a monument to their own mortality.

SANCTIFIED HUNT STANDINGS

- **Team Red Tusk:** 18 *(Round 1: 9, Round 2: 9)*
- **Team Obsidian Spear:** 18 *(Round 1: 9, Round 2: 9)*
- **Team Hands:** 15 *(Round 1: 7, Round 2: 8)*

Stripe stood with his arms folded across his chest, his boots planted in the mud. He stared at the numbers with cold, focused intensity. He wasn't looking at the rank to stroke his ego; he was calculating the math of his own freedom.

"Judges always get things wrong," Stripe let out a grumble. "It would be much fairer if it weren't so opinionated of a voting matrix."

Latrum stood beside him, leaning heavily on his battle staff. "We are alive, Stripe. We are uninjured. Look at Obsidian Spear. Their leader's breastplate is split open. Look at Red Tusk. Their orc is favoring his left hip. They have been fighting recklessly to maintain those perfect scores. In a war of attrition, the patient fighter is the one who survives to collect the gold."

"I don't give a damn about winning the trophy, Big G." Stripe offered a scoff. "I'm not here to be the valedictorian of the monster hunters. I'm here for the debt deduction. If the judges are going to stay stingy with the points, then I need more bodies. We may not win, but we can earn a nice chunk off pure volume."

CROWN — "A high-volume cull strategy is mathematically viable. I have compiled optimal pathing routes to maximize encounter rate."

"Latrum, you remember the topography of the Crags from your rebellion days?" Stripe asked, ignoring the artifact.

Latrum gave a nod. "Yes. I know the choke points where the trolls migrate."

"Good. You lead the pathing."

CROWN — "Host. My topographical data is flawless. Bypassing my navigational interface for the half-gnome's biological memory is highly inefficient."

Stripe ignored the voice in his head.

Before Latrum could point out a route, the heavy oak doors of the cathedral groaned open. High Priestess Sarah emerged, moving with a regal grace that seemed to part the fog itself. She wore white robes trimmed with gold thread, her long white hair braided with silver wire. Walking right beside her was Calen. The blonde priest looked pristine, his armor polished to a mirror finish. He leaned close to Sarah, his hand lingering on the small of her back in a way that was far too familiar for a public square.

"I wish I could judge your route today, Sarah." Calen's murmur carried across the stone. "Watching you work is always the absolute highlight of these hunts. There is a grace in your movements that these brutes could never hope to replicate. Perhaps tonight, once the noise of the square has died down, we could discuss the final tallies in private?"

Calen leaned in further, his breath brushing against her pointed ear. Sarah didn't shy away, but a practiced, cool distance remained in her soft smile. She was used to the presumptive nature of men who thought power equaled permission.

Stripe watched the exchange from ten feet away. He made a loud, wet, exaggerated gagging noise.

"Please tell me you two are not going to do that the whole trip." Stripe groaned loudly. "I already have one annoying voice in my head constantly nagging me about my tactical errors. I do not need a workplace romance making me nauseous on top of it. This is a monster hunt, not a dating simulator. Get a room or get a hobby, because this is making my eyes bleed."

Calen bristled, his hand tightening on his sword hilt, but Sarah simply adjusted the grading ledger in her arms, her expression unruffled. She turned her golden eyes toward Stripe.

"If your visual distress is that severe, Hands, I suggest you look at the dirt. It’s where you’ll be spending most of your day." Sarah's voice sounded melodic but carried absolute authority. "I am your judge for the final route today. I suggest you focus that nervous energy on the Crags. The Goddess favors the effective, not the talkative."

"Yeah." Stripe offered a sneer. "I remember you perfectly. You are the one who left me naked in the woods with a dead wolf and a head full of static. Good to see the service hasn't improved since I checked in."

Sarah did not flinch. She looked him up and down, noting the heavy monster gauntlets. She didn't mind his crass humor; it was refreshing compared to the sycophants in the church.

"And yet, here you are clothed, fed, and complaining. My heart bleeds for your hardships." Sarah stepped closer, her elegance masking an iron spine. "Today, you are assigned to the Ashen Crags. It is a maximum danger zone. Try to maintain some level of professionalism, or I'll disqualify you before we even reach the first sulfur vent just to enjoy the silence."

Stripe let out a scoff. "Professionalism. That is rich coming from the head of an organization that watches people starve in the shadows of its own cathedral. Where was this Goddess when I was rotting on the street for two weeks? I was homeless, freezing, and hungry right outside your doors. I didn't see any holy servants coming out with bread or a warm place to sleep. I just saw Paladins moving me along so I wouldn't ruin the view for the donors."

The jab hit home. Sarah's jaw tightened for a fraction of a second, a flicker of acknowledgment that the corruption within her own walls was a sickness she was trying to cure from the inside out. But she didn't break her stride.

"The Church provides sanctuary for those who seek it through proper channels. We cannot help those who choose to live in filth and defiance." Sarah's tone remained even.

"Proper channels." Stripe spat on the stone. "You mean the channels where you sign over your life to the church and live like a slave? Look at Latrum. He is a slave. You allow that. You let events like the one that happened to him happen every single day in this city. You preach about mercy while you keep people in chains. It is a racket, Sarah. A well-dressed protection racket that thrives on keeping people desperate."

Sarah stepped closer to him. The air around her seemed to grow heavy.

"Slavery is a legal reality of the crown, Hands, not a decree of the Church." Her voice rang like a low, steady chime. "We work within the world as it is to prevent total chaos. Without the Church and the Guild, this city would be a graveyard within a month. We turn violence into mercy by giving men like you a way to earn their place. It is an imperfect system, but it is a system that keeps the gates closed against the dark."

"You give us a way to die for your amusement and your ledger." Stripe issued the challenge. "You preach about the children of the Goddess, but you let them rot in the mud as soon as they can't swing a sword for you anymore. I have seen better morality in dictators."

Sarah met his gaze unflinchingly. She believed in the goodness of the Church, even if she had to amputate its rotting limbs eventually.

"I've dealt with your type before, Hands." Sarah crossed her arms. "Men who think cynicism is a substitute for character. I designed the rules of this hunt myself fifty years ago. I structured the scoring system to reward dominance, defense, and control. It is based on a ten-point must system from a sport in my homeland."

Stripe froze. The breath caught in his throat. *A ten-point must system.*

CROWN — "Host heart rate is elevating rapidly. Extreme confusion and recognition detected. Do you require cognitive assistance to process this anomaly?"

"Shut up for a second," Stripe hissed under his breath. "Just... shut up."

"Talking to the voices again? Efficient." Sarah tapped her ledger.

"Nothing." Stripe let out a stammer. "I was just talking to myself. Let us go to the Ashen Crags. I need to punch something very hard to clear my thoughts."

The trek to the Ashen Crags was a brutal, three-hour climb. Stripe kept his pace steady, but his mind was elsewhere. He kept glancing at Sarah. She moved through the rocks with a predatory grace, her robes never once catching on the sharp shale.

"The ten-point must system." Stripe broke the silence. "Who taught you that?"

"It is a system of absolute fairness." Sarah deflected the question. "It ensures that the one who controls the engagement is the one who is rewarded."

"That is a non-answer." Stripe pushed forward. "You are dodging the question."

"Focus on the hunt, Hands." Sarah kept her eyes on the path. "Your target is ahead. We are not here for a history lesson."

They rounded a massive obsidian pillar and found their quarry. The Ash Troll was a mature specimen, standing twelve feet tall with skin that looked like hardened, cracked charcoal.

SYSTEM ALERT: Ash Troll Detected

- **Level:** 16
- **Warning:** Extreme Physical Regeneration. Vulnerable to Cold.

Sarah stood atop a safe ridge, her white robes fluttering in the hot, sulfurous wind. She opened her wooden ledger and pulled out a quill.

"Begin." Sarah pointed her quill. "Show me this skill you claim to possess."

CROWN — "Tactical analysis complete. Structural weaknesses were identified at the patella and the lower lumbar region. Recommend a sweeping."

"Latrum! Hit me with Haste! Now!" Stripe yelled. He charged forward.

"HASTE!"

CROWN — "Host. It is statistically offensive that you bypass my predictive combat algorithms to yell rudimentary commands at a half-gnome."

"Latrum actually listens to me! You just complain!"

The familiar cyan energy surged into Stripe. He closed the distance before the beast finished dropping its meal.

"Latrum! Freeze the legs! I need him grounded!" Stripe called out the direction.

"ICE BOLT!"

Latrum fired two rapid bursts of freezing magic. They smashed into the troll's kneecaps with a wet thud. The beast let out a guttural roar of pain and dropped heavily to one knee.

Stripe used the momentum of his sprint to leap off a nearby boulder, launching himself into the air and cocking his right arm back in a perfect Superman punch. He spat out a large wad of snot and spat on the tip of his glove, making sure the fluids mixed with the creature's exposed flesh.

Ash Troll HP: 250 / 250 -> 180 / 250 **Status Inflicted:** Poisoned

The troll swung a massive backhand. Stripe ducked, trapped the limb under his armpit, and locked in a standing kimura grip. A loud, sickening pop echoed across the crags as the troll's shoulder dislocated.

CROWN — "A cervical dislocation would result in an immediate 14% drop in target resistance. I can map the exact angle if you would merely..."

"Latrum! Blow this ugly bastard over!" Stripe demanded.

"FORCE PUSH!"

CROWN — "Your reliance on him over my optimized pathways is insulting."

The kinetic wave knocked the massive beast onto its back. Stripe pounced, dropping into a dominant full mount. He rained heavy, spiked elbows directly onto its face. He didn't stop when the jaw broke. He kept hammering, ignoring the artifact buzzing indignantly in his brain, driven by the lingering rage of the city's corruption and wanting to secure the maximum kill credit.

Ash Troll HP: 180 / 250 -> 0 / 250 **Regeneration Failed. Toxicity Critical.**

Stripe stood up, breathing heavily, his gauntlets coated in toxic sludge. He looked up at Sarah. She recognized the mechanical efficiency of the ground and pound, but her expression remained stern.

"Write it down, Priestess." Stripe issued the challenge. "No damage taken. Perfect control. Ten points."

"Brutal. Efficient." Sarah offered an acknowledgment. "But entirely devoid of discipline at the end. You let your rage lead the final strikes. A true martial artist controls their spirit as well as their fists. Nine points."

Stripe wiped a smear of troll blood off his cheek. He didn't care about the perfect score. He cared about the dead monster at his feet. He and Latrum had avoided taking any damage from such a tough opponent. Pride swelled in the pit of his stomach.

"Yeah, yeah, I'm used to the bullshit now," Stripe grumbled.

CROWN — "Substantial Experience Gained! Stripe has reached Level 10! Class Unlocked: Toxic Pugilist."

"Put my stat point into Strength," Stripe said.

He felt his muscles begin to grow. He felt significantly stronger than before. His abs bulged further, and his body seemed to be about the same size and muscle density as in his past life. He was at the peak of human physicality on Earth now.

CROWN — "Due to the host reaching the first leveling milestone, an additional stat point will be added to strength."

"I feel incredibly strong now." Stripe flexed as he spoke.

CROWN — "A 14 in strength is equivalent to an elite athlete in your past life. Anything higher will be breaking the threshold of what you know as possible."

------------ STATUS ------------
Name: Stripe
Level:10
Rank: Tin
Class: Toxic Pugilist
Title: Toxic Fisherman, Pugilist Specialist
HP: 120/120
Stamina: 110/110
Mana: 0/0

------------ Attributes ------------

STR: 14

AGI: 11

END: 12

INT: 6

Skill points: 0

-------- Skills / Proficiencies --------

Hand-to-Hand Combat - Basic Retention
Improvised Weapon Handling - Beginner
Survival - Novice
Pugilist Proficiency - MAX

---------- Passive Effects ----------
Minor Poison Secretion

------------- Artifact -------------
Crown of Reflection

---------- System Effects ----------
Intoxication Immunity
Experience Calculation

------------ Inventory -------------
Iron Dagger
Leather Chest Piece (Bandit Armor)
Wolf Pelt (Crude Clothing)
Leather Belt with Pouch
Bandit Ring
Monster Gauntlets

------------ Currency -------------
Silver: 7
Copper: 6
Debt: 2300

CHAPTER 27

Stripe felt a dense heat radiate from his core. The mythril-threaded gloves on his hands seemed to hum with a low, sickening vibration. The blood in his veins felt heavier, thicker, as if changing its chemical makeup. His body felt different. He instinctively knew his body was far more dangerous than before.

Stripe demanded an answer. "Crown, what the hell did I just unlock?"

CROWN — "The Toxic Pugilist class is a rare, aggressive hybrid. Since you blatantly refuse to utilize my sophisticated tactical processing or elegant magical frameworks, the System has adapted to your stubborn, unoptimized combat style. It synthesizes your brute-force unarmed proficiency with the environmental toxins you absorbed during your initial wolf encounter."

Stripe issued the order. "Make it actually make sense."

CROWN — "Your unarmed strikes now carry a twenty-five percent probability to inject crippling venom directly into a target's bloodstream upon impact. This venom bypasses standard biological immunities and scales exponentially with your physical force. Furthermore, your own bodily fluids are now vulnerable to external threats, and your physiological resistance to pain and fatigue has permanently increased."

Stripe flexed his hands. The air around his knuckles seemed to warp, carrying a faint, acrid scent. Stripe offered a summary. "So my punches literally melt people from the inside out, and I'm basically immune to hangovers and snake bites. But does this mean I can never have kids?"

CROWN — "A crude summary, but statistically accurate. Your lethality in prolonged, close-quarters engagements has increased by forty-two percent. This class suits your refusal to evolve beyond punching things until they stop moving."

Stripe raised his eyebrow, amused by the wording. Stripe pointed out the attitude. "It really feels like you have been super bitter lately. You also refuse to answer the most important question."

CROWN — "Artifacts do not feel bitterness, Host. I am merely calculating the persistent disappointment of my vessel."

The return to Memento passed in silence. The cathedral square presented a scene of disaster.

SANCTIFIED HUNT FINAL STANDINGS

- **Team Obsidian Spear:** 25 *(Round 1: 9, Round 2: 9, Round 3: 7)* — **Victor**
- **Team Hands:** 24 *(Round 1: 7, Round 2: 8, Round 3: 9)*
- **Team Red Tusk:** 24 *(Round 1: 9, Round 2: 9, Round 3: 6)* — **Disqualified**

Myra sat on the cathedral steps, her head buried in her hands. Her scale armor sat ruined, caked in mud and dried blood, and her left arm lay wrapped in a crude, seeping bandage. She won the tournament, but she looked like a ghost whose soul had been ripped out.

Stripe walked over and sat down on the cold stone step next to her. "Myra." Stripe kept his voice soft. "What happened out there?"

She looked up. Her eyes were red, hollow, and devoid of the fierce competitive fire she carried into the square that morning. She looked broken. Stripe had never seen her like this. Myra offered a whisper.

"We overextended. Our captain saw the boards. He knew Red Tusk had a perfect score, and he wanted the top payout. He wanted the prestige of taking down a Level 18 Cave Troll for a perfect ten. We didn't know that it had set up an ambush. We already had nine points. We just wanted a ten to make sure we won. We already killed two of the Cave Trolls. Then, as we approached the final cave, a boulder flew from the tree line and struck down Kael. We couldn't even react. It took her head off her shoulders."

Stripe looked back at the massive wooden scoreboard. He stared at the painted numbers until they burned into his retinas. The math clicked into place, and it made his stomach twist with disgust. He turned back to Myra, his voice dropping into a low, dangerous register.

"Myra. Look at the board." Stripe issued the order.

Myra let out a cry. "I don't want to look at the board, Stripe! My friend is dead!" Her voice cracked, a desperate sob catching in her throat.

Stripe reached out and grabbed her good shoulder, his grip rough but soothing. He didn't let her look away. "Look at the damn math, Myra. Look at it!" He pointed a finger at the white paint. "Team Hands went into this round with fifteen points. You and Red Tusk had eighteen. You could have won with nine points. We both know overextending is dangerous. You took an unnecessary risk."

She stared at the numbers, her breathing ragged, her eyes darting between the columns.

Stripe kept his explanation gentle. "We scored a nine today. That put us at twenty-four. Red Tusk got themselves disqualified and earned a six. Myra... if you had just played it safe. If you guys had stopped after the second Troll, you would be celebrating. We can't change the past, but we can make sure we never make that mistake again."

Myra froze. The tears stopped tracking down her dirty face. Her eyes widened in horror as the simple addition finalized in her mind. Eighteen plus seven was twenty-five.

"You did your best and did amazingly." Stripe offered the reassurance. "But you got cocky. We were drilled to avoid this kind of situation. You need to honor her death and celebrate her life."

The guild may run a debt scheme on new members, but the training they received proved to be top-notch. The recruits' post-training survival rate stood as a sign of its success. The realization hit her like a physical blow. It was one thing to lose a friend in a desperate fight for survival. It felt like a different, soul-crushing agony to realize that her shield bearer fed a meat grinder for no reason at all. Kael's death remained avoidable. This rested on her. She knew it did.

Myra broke down. She hunched over her knees, sobbing into her hands, screaming her dead friend's name into the unforgiving stone of the cathedral steps. Stripe let go of her shoulder. There was no comfort to give. He just sat beside her, letting the cold reality of the Guild's ambitions settle over them both.

Before Stripe could say another word, a loud, metallic commotion erupted near the main gates. Paladins marched into the plaza, halberds leveled at a group in the center of their formation. The members of the Red Tusk party stood stripped of their weapons and bound in heavy iron chains. Behind them, two silent clerics pulled a wooden cart with a blood-soaked white sheet. A pale, lifeless hand hung off the edge. It was Acolyte Davis. Stripe could tell from the youthful appearance on his face and the rings that he wore.

The entire square went dead silent. High Priestess Sarah descended the cathedral steps, her expression terrible and cold.

"What happened?" Sarah issued the demand. "Why is Acolyte Davis in shrouds?"

A Paladin offered the report. "High Priestess. Red Tusk engaged a Drake pack. Witnesses from the support team claim they prioritized a flawless kill over Acolyte Davis's life. They shoved the boy into the path of the alpha. He is dead because of their recklessness."

"That is a damn lie!" The Orc Leader let out a roar. "The kid froze! We needed an opening! We did not shove him! We told him to move out of the way. He was pushed to safety, but it was too late."

"Silence." Sarah's command echoed with unnatural volume. "Red Tusk scores a six for this round. And for the intentional murder of a servant of the Goddess... your judgment is absolute."

The Orc leader roared in frustration, fighting against the heavy chains. "Take us to the block, you pointed-eared witch! We'll spit on your executioner!"

Sarah did not blink. She did not summon guards to drag them away to a dungeon. She raised a single, slender hand toward the grey sky. "There will be no block." Sarah declared the fate. "The Goddess offers mercy to the repentant. To the treacherous, she offers only the light."

The air pressure in the square dropped. The Paladins holding the chains scrambled backward, abandoning their prisoners. A blinding, deafening pillar of golden fire crashed down from the heavens, striking the Red Tusk party with the force of a falling star. The heat burned intensely enough to push the front row of the crowd backward. There were no screams. The light arrived too fast, too absolute.

When the golden pillar faded, the cobblestones sat scorched black. The heavy iron chains lay melting in puddles of liquid metal. The Red Tusk mercenaries were simply gone, incinerated to ash in the blink of an eye.

The square fell horrifyingly silent. Sarah lowered her hand, her expression unchanged, as elegant and beautiful as a loaded gun.

Stripe felt his stomach turn. He watched the Orc and his crew get erased like an accounting error. They were scum, sure, but they were also desperate men forced into a grinder by a system that traded blood for prestige. They sat discarded and forgotten. The church got a clean, holy execution for their enemies. The poor just got tossed in the trash. Stripe felt a pang of sadness. He and the Orc were not friends, but they shared a jail cell for a moment. This world really isn't fair.

Varn stepped up to the podium, his greasy smile strained but intact despite the divine execution that had just occurred ten feet away. "Tragic... truly tragic." Varn offered a false sigh. "But the rules of the Hunt are absolute. The victor of this year's Sanctified Hunt is Team Obsidian Spear. Though I see their captain is... indisposed."

Varn turned his calculating eyes to Stripe. "Team Hands. Second place. Your reward is processed. Your kill volume proved highly satisfactory. One thousand gold coins have been deducted from your guild debt. Here is your bonus. Thank the church."

Varn tossed a heavy pouch of silver. Stripe caught it. He didn't stay for the rest of the ceremony. He walked straight to the Guild quartermaster's tent on the edge of the square, slammed the heavy silver pouch on the wooden table, and pointed to a polished wooden box on the top shelf.

"Give me the Mythril Threaded Striker Gloves." Stripe made the demand. He spent all of his bonus silver on the gauntlets. It offered a good deal because no one else used them as a primary weapon.

Item Acquired: Mythril Threaded Striker Gloves

Effect: +5 Strength. Enhances unarmed durability and striking speed.

Stripe slid them on. They fit perfectly, the mythril cold against his skin before warming to his body heat. "Not bad." Stripe admired his hands. "Now I just need to find Hobb and show him I actually made something of myself. I have a few coppers left to spend on a bottle of the good stuff for the old man."

He looked down at the new gloves gracing his hands. He admired them. These weren't makeshift like his last ones. These were beautiful. He felt deadly and beautiful. He struck a sexy schoolgirl pose for the shopkeeper. He put his fingers out in front of his face and gave a crude smile. The shopkeeper shuddered in disgust.

Stripe offered a chuckle. "Tough crowd."

Stripe walked quickly toward the inner wall where the beggars gathered. The cold air of the city felt different today. It felt hollow. He rounded the corner into Hobb's usual alley. The alley sat empty, but it felt off. It wasn't the normal kind of empty; it was the kind of empty you feel when the person you love moves out of the home. Stripe started to get a bad feeling.

Stripe stopped walking. He looked down at the cobblestones. There lay a dark, tacky stain seeping into the grout between the stones. Sitting against the brick wall, splintered in half, sat Maribel, the broom.

"Hey," Stripe called out. "Where is the old crazy shit?"

A sickly, hollow-eyed beggar sitting a few feet away pulled his tattered cloak tighter around his thin shoulders. The man looked terrified. Stripe recognized him from his time on the streets with Hobb.

The Beggar let out a croak. "They took him to the burn piles, mate. A noble. I didn't see the crest. He stepped right on the old man's broom. Snapped it in half. Hobb... you know how he was. He loved that broom. He said the man killed his wife. He shoved the noble. Just pushed him once."

Stripe's vision swam with a sudden red hue. "He pushed him." Stripe numbly repeated the words.

"The guards ran Hobb through with a spear right where you are kneeling." The Beggar explained rapidly. "Said it was high treason to assault a highborn. They left him to bleed out in the dirt, then had the city watch toss his body on a meat cart heading outside the walls."

Stripe didn't wait. He didn't say a word. He turned and sprinted toward the city gates, ignoring the ache in his muscles and the exhaustion in his bones. He ran past the merchant stalls, past the bewildered guards, and out into the smog-choked plains where Memento burned its refuse and its unclaimed dead. His hands sat in the gauntlets, squeezing as tightly as he could. He could feel the warmth of blood trickling down his gloves.

The burn piles rose as massive, smoldering hills of monster carcasses, rotten wood, and forgotten people. The stench felt apocalyptic. Stripe scrambled up the side of a freshly dumped pile, digging through the mud and the grotesque debris with his hands.

Stripe coughed against the thick, black smoke. "Hobb!"

He found him near the top. Hobbs' patched clothing sat, soaked in dark blood, stiffening in the cold air. Stripe grabbed the old man by the collar and dragged his lifeless body down to the wet grass, away from the encroaching fire. Hobbs' eyes stared blankly at the bruised sky. He still held the broken pieces of the broom tightly to his chest.

Stripe knelt beside him, his chest heaving. The cold rage cracked into a profound, suffocating grief. He remembered sitting in the rain with this man. He remembered Hobb sharing his scraps and his quiet wisdom when the city forgot them.

Homeless ain't about no roof, Hobb told him once. *It is about nobody expecting you home.*

Stripe reached out and closed the old man's eyes. He reached into Hobb's tattered tunic to find a keepsake, something to bury so the old man wouldn't just be ash blowing across the plains. His fingers brushed against a thick, leather-bound book strapped tightly to Hobb's chest beneath the rags. Stripe pulled it out. It was a journal. The leather felt pristine, at odds with the filth Hobb lived in. Stripe flipped it open. The handwriting inside was elegant, sharp, and disciplined.

Entry 412: We cleared the Labyrinth of Mirrors today. The Goblin King almost took my left arm, but Maribel's healing shielded me just in time. I told her she's wasting her mana on a reckless Level 68 Vanguard like me. She just smiled and said she'd follow my greatsword to the end of the world.

Stripe's breath hitched. He turned the pages frantically. They were filled with maps, monster biologies, and high-level skill trees.

Entry 501: The Drake fire was too hot. The clerics say I am losing my mind. They say the flames that took Maribel also took my senses. But I can still feel the weight of my blade. I just can't hold it anymore without seeing her face burning. I bought a broom today. I drew her smile on it. It helps the shaking stop. Goddess, why did you take her and not me?

Stripe closed the books. His hands trembled. The "crazy old man" wasn't a beggar who lost his mind to the streets. He was a high-tier veteran, a warrior broken by the grief of losing the only woman he loved. Maribel had been real.

You fighting something? Hobb told him once, his eyes lucid and steady. *Good. Means you ain't surrendered.*

It served as a dark, horrific mirror of Stripe's own past in Vegas. Stripe tried to drown his grief in liquor and neon after losing his own wife; Hobb drowned his in madness and the streets. And now, Hobb was dead, run through like a stray dog because a pampered noble didn't like being touched.

Stripe closed his eyes while holding the book tightly in his hands. For a moment, his memories dragged him to a time when his own wife was still alive. He had everything. He was rich and famous. He partied at exclusive clubs in VIP sections. One day, a simple fight changed his life. A young man looking to make a point threw an expensive drink at Stripe. In response, he struck him. The kid's jaw broke, and teeth went flying. Turns out he was a Russian mob boss's son.

A year later, when Stripe had a fight in Moscow, he came back to his hotel room to find his wife lying on the floor, blood-soaked. She had been stabbed to death. The police in Moscow refused to investigate. They even threatened to list him as the prime suspect if he kept pushing it.

Stripe right now felt how he felt then. The unfiltered anger going through his veins could not be contained. In the past, he found that kid and beat him to death behind the same club where the incident happened. Today, he felt the same urge. He wanted revenge for his friend. He wanted finality and punishment for the people who hurt him. He just didn't know how.

CROWN — "Journal analysis complete. The deceased was a Level 68 Vanguard. Threat assessment of the perpetrators."

"Shut up. Just shut up," Stripe ordered through his teeth. "I need to feel this."

Stripe stood up slowly. He left the journal resting on Hobb's chest, carefully wrapping the old man in his own cloak to prepare him for a proper burial. The rage inside him didn't explode. It condensed into something colder and more dangerous than anything he ever felt in the octagon. He didn't know who the noble was. He didn't know what crest the guards wore. But he would find out.

As he stood in the smoke, his UI flared. Two shimmering gold banners materialized in his vision: *Runner-Up of the Sanctified Hunt* and *Toxic Pugilist*. They vibrated, their mana bleeding into one another, fusing into a singular, glowing title: *The Sanctified Venom-Brawler*.

Stripe stared at the gold text. It meant nothing. A shiny distraction in a world built on meat grinders and protection rackets. With a sharp, mental snap, he tore the titles apart and threw them into the void of his subconscious. The glowing text shattered into digital dust and vanished.

Stripe kept his tone cold. "That means nothing to me. A consolation prize for every shit thing that has happened in my life. Get it out of my face now."

CROWN — "Understood. Hiding title."

Then, in the softest, most gentle voice:

CROWN — "Poor child."

He looked back at the city walls of Memento, his mythril gauntlets clenching into tight, unyielding fists. Stripe let out a whisper. "Right now, I need to hit something."

CROWN — "Hitting can wait. Enjoy your trip to the past. WARNING: Flashback imminent."

"Please don't." Stripe gritted his teeth.

CROWN — "Sorry, not sorry."

Stripe's head exploded in pain as he was forcefully dragged into his memories.

CHAPTER 28

The descent into darkness began the moment the private jet touched down on the sunlit tarmac in Los Angeles. The contrast felt physically sickening. The California sun shone bright, warm, and indifferent to the fact that Stripe had just left his soul inside a freezing Russian morgue. He walked down the steps of the aircraft. He did not feel the warmth of the sun. He felt hollow. The whole plane ride passed in silence. Stripe brewed with anger. He thought about every detail of what happened.

Dave waited at the bottom of the stairs. The manager looked pale and exhausted. He held a clipboard and a cell phone. Seeing him made Stripe question his manager's loyalty. In his mind, the events had to be Dave's fault. He pitched the fight, and for the first time in his career, he didn't attend.

Dave spoke with urgency. "We have a security team waiting to escort you home. I have already contacted the crisis management firm. We are going to handle the media. We just need you to lay low."

Stripe did not look at him. He walked straight past his manager and climbed into the back of the waiting black SUV. He didn't even say sorry for your loss. Straight to business. No emotional support. What a shitty friend.

Dave leaned into the open door. "Stripe, please. You need to talk to me. We have to coordinate a statement. If we don't get ahead of this now, your career is done."

"Fuck off. You're fired." Stripe kept his voice cold. His voice stayed flat and dead.

Dave froze. "What?" Dave let out a gasp. "You cannot just fire me. Not right now. You need me."

Stripe leveled an accusation. "Where were you? Colluding with the Russians, I bet. I bet you told them where I was staying and got a kickback. I can't trust you. If you come to my house or contact me again, I will break every bone in your body."

Stripe felt serious. There was no hesitation in the accusation. He pushed the button to roll up the tinted window. The SUV pulled away, leaving Dave standing alone on the tarmac.

Stripe rode in silence the entire way back to his sprawling mansion in the hills. The driver opened the door for him. Stripe walked up the pristine stone steps and unlocked the massive double doors of his home. He stepped inside the grand foyer.

The silence of the empty house hit him with the force of a speeding freight train. It was a suffocating quiet. There was no music playing in the kitchen. There was no smell of dinner cooking on the stove. There was no beautiful voice calling out his name from the living room.

He walked slowly through the massive, echoing halls. Everything remained in place. Her shoes sat lined up neatly by the front door. Her favorite jacket draped casually over the back of the dining room chair. Her book on parenting sat on the sleek granite kitchen island, exactly where she had left it before he forced her to look at the Moscow contract. Every single object in the house felt like a jagged knife twisting into his chest.

He walked down the long hallway toward the master bedroom. He passed the closed door of the nursery. He stopped. His hand hovered over the brass doorknob for a long time. His hands shook. He turned the knob and pushed the door open.

The room was painted a soft yellow. The imported oak crib sat in the center of the room. A pile of soft, plush toys sat in the corner. Tiny, folded clothes rested on top of the changing table. It was a room built for a future that was stolen from him. He hated the bedroom color. But his wife insisted yellow proved good for the babies' development.

Stripe collapsed to his knees right there in the doorway. He buried his face in his massive hands. He wept. He cried until his throat grew raw and bleeding. He cried until there was no moisture left in his body. Then he continued to cry with dry tears and no voice.

He stayed on the floor of the nursery until the sun went down and the mansion plunged into darkness. He lay there, imagining the potential future that had been taken from him. Images of the baby walking and his wife screaming in excitement at the baby's first words. These hallucinations provided the only thing that brought a smile to his face.

When he finally stood up, the arrogant, childish champion was gone. The man who cared about golden belts and global fame was dead. There remained only a hollow vessel left behind, and that vessel needed filling with something to stop the echoing pain.

Stripe walked down to the massive, custom-built bar in his entertainment room. The shelves held the finest, most expensive liquors from around the globe. Bottles that cost thousands of dollars sat collecting dust. He did not grab a glass. He grabbed a heavy crystal bottle of imported whiskey. He cracked the seal, unscrewed the cap, and brought the bottle directly to his lips.

He drank with disregard for his health. The alcohol burned intensely as it traveled down his throat. It hit his empty stomach like a lit match. He welcomed the burn. He drank again. He drank until his vision blurred and the sharp, agonizing edges of reality began to soften. The pain momentarily disappeared.

The alcohol dependency took root instantly. It was not a coping mechanism. It was a desperate attempt to shut down his own brain. He could not close his eyes without seeing the splintered hotel door in Moscow. He could not sleep without feeling the sticky, terrible warmth of his wife's blood seeping through his tailored suit. The whiskey provided the only thing that could silence the screaming in his head.

The days blurred into weeks. The weeks blurred into months. Every single day was washed away with alcohol, and waking in the middle of the night, screaming. He slept on the floor of the baby's room every night. Stripe did not leave the mansion. He did not answer his phone. He let the battery die. He ignored the frantic pounding on his front door from former teammates, coaches, and financial advisors. He lived in the dark.

He sat on the floor of his expansive living room, surrounded by empty crystal bottles and discarded food containers. He did not bathe. He did not train. His incredible, world-class athletic physique began to soften and deteriorate. He actively tried to drink himself into an early grave.

But the rage inside him would not let him die peacefully. It intensified when, one day, a package arrived at his door. He opened it to see a basic all-white urn. The urn had basic carvings at its base. Elizabeth S Stripe. She had insisted on taking his last name when they were married. He remembered why he went by his last name. He was named after his father, who was deeply abusive. He refused to go by that name and instead chose to go by his adoptive last name.

The alcohol successfully numbed the paralyzing grief, but it fueled the hatred. Every time he closed his eyes, he imagined the revenge he wanted. He imagined torturing Nikolai. He imagined shooting him, stabbing him, beating him, and pretty much everything in between. He contemplated using his wealth to hire a hitman. But that wouldn't feel satisfactory. It would be too clean.

The Russian government covered up the murders. The global news networks reported that his wife had been the tragic victim of a random, botched robbery. There were no suspects. There were no arrests. They scrubbed the truth clean from the face of the earth. Stripe realized he could not die yet. He had to get revenge for his family, even if it cost him his life.

Three months after the murders, Stripe finally left the mansion. He did not call Dave. He did not contact anyone from the professional fighting league. He went deep into the criminal underbelly of Los Angeles. He used connections from his early, violent days before he became a famous professional fighter. He kissed his wife's urn before exiting the house. On his way out, he passed a stack of letters and packages sitting on his front porch. He felt pretty sure one of the letters said "Fighting League Hall of Fame invitation." He only noticed because the letter shone golden with a fancy font on the front. He ignored it and pressed on.

He walked into a seedy, smoke-filled bar in a neighborhood the police actively avoided. He carried a duffel bag stuffed with two hundred thousand dollars in cash. He sat down across from a man with a reputation for no-questions-asked help. The kind of services that help killers walk free.

"I need a passport," Stripe demanded bluntly. "I need it to be bulletproof. I need a new name. I need a new face on paper. And I need a secure flight into a country that actively monitors its borders."

Stripe dropped the heavy duffel bag onto the sticky table. The smuggler unzipped the bag. He looked at the massive stacks of banded hundred-dollar bills. He looked back up at Stripe. The smuggler recognized the fallen champion immediately, but he did not ask any stupid questions. In his line of work, curiosity proved a fatal disease.

The Smuggler asked a quiet question. "Where are you trying to go?"

"Moscow." Stripe gave a flat answer. His voice remained devoid of emotion.

The smuggler nodded slowly. "It will take three days to forge the documents." The Smuggler offered an explanation. "The flight will be uncomfortable. You will be traveling in the cargo hold of an unsanctioned military transport plane. It will be freezing. If you get caught by customs, you do not know my name. That's if you live long enough to be asked any questions."

"Understood." Stripe offered an agreement.

He spent those three days sobering up just enough to stop his hands from shaking. He did not pack any luggage. He did not pack any training gear. He did not pack warm clothes. He only packed his malice. Part of him hoped he wouldn't survive this trip. Part of him wanted to survive in spite.

The journey back to Russia provided a grueling test of endurance. Stripe sat in the pitch-black, unheated cargo hold of a massive transport plane for fourteen hours. The temperature dropped below freezing at high altitudes. Frost gathered on the metal walls around him. He did not wear a heavy winter coat. He wore a simple dark hoodie and jeans. He huddled up in the corner with a small blanket on him. The blanket likely proved to be the only thing that kept him alive.

He shivered violently, but he did not care. The physical discomfort meant nothing compared to the agonizing hole in his chest. He closed his eyes and visualized the layout of the Moscow VIP club. He became hyper-fixated on his task. Nothing else mattered.

He arrived in Moscow in the dead of winter. The city lay buried beneath a thick, heavy blanket of dirty gray snow. The temperature felt punishing. The freezing wind cut right through his thin clothing like hundreds of tiny, invisible razor blades. Each sharp stab reminded him of the task he had in front of him. In the months of drinking and self-neglect, he grew a thick beard, and his hair became unkempt and long. In his current outfit, he looked more like a homeless man than a near-billionaire and famous fighter.

Stripe slipped past the bribed customs officials without a single issue. He was a ghost. He was officially a faceless man walking through the city with no paper trail.

He did not check into a hotel. He did not rent a car. He walked for miles through the freezing slush until he reached the wealthy, upscale district where the VIP club was located. He found a narrow, filthy alleyway located directly across the street from the heavily guarded rear exit of the club. The alley smelled strongly of rotting garbage, frozen urine, and diesel exhaust. He wedged himself between two overflowing industrial dumpsters to block the biting wind. There were other homeless men there. They kept a small fire going in a barrel. He used it for warmth while watching the door. They didn't question his presence. He looked like he belonged.

He began his long vigil. Stripe spent three agonizing weeks hiding in that dark alleyway. He made no connection to the people around him, and they seemed fine with that. He survived on the food in the trash next to him, refusing to leave.

The physical toll of the stakeout proved immense. His muscles cramped. His lips cracked and bled from the freezing wind. He lost feeling in his fingers and his toes. He was slowly freezing to death in the Moscow snow, but his hatred kept his heart beating just enough to sustain him. He watched wealthy patrons come and go. He watched massive security guards patrol the perimeter. He waited with the terrifying patience of a starving predator.

On the third night, the heavy metal door finally opened. The pulsing, heavy bass of the electronic club music spilled out into the quiet, frozen street. A group of people stepped out into the freezing air.

Nikolai stood right in the center of them. He laughed loudly. His breath fogged heavily in the freezing air. He wore a massively expensive, thick fur coat. He looked completely healed. There was a faint, jagged scar running along his jawline from where Stripe had shattered it a year ago, but otherwise, he looked healthy. He looked untouched by the horrific tragedy he had orchestrated.

Two massive, heavily armed bodyguards wearing thick wool coats flanked him. They scanned the street with professional, paranoid intensity.

Stripe no longer felt the freezing cold. He did not feel the cramping in his legs. The cheap vodka burned out of his system, replaced by a massive surge of pure adrenaline. This provided the motivation he needed. Nikolai was still coming here. It was only a matter of time before he slipped up and came out alone.

Then, in the third week, it finally happened. Nikolai stumbled out drunk. This time, he yelled at his guards to leave him alone. He turned towards the building and unzipped his pants. He began to piss on the walls. He was obviously wasted. Stripe saw his opportunity and leaped at it without hesitation. As soon as the guards closed the club doors, he rushed forward. He moved with the silent, terrifying grace of an apex predator.

Stripe did not yell. He did not announce his presence. He did not want to give him the satisfaction of a warning. He stepped out of the dark shadows and crossed the icy street in three explosive strides. He reached the group before Nikolai even registered the sudden movement in his peripheral vision.

Stripe appeared behind the distracted Nikolai. The man was still pissed and had begun to hum some song to himself. He heard the footsteps behind him get closer, then stop right behind him.

Nikolai froze. The oligarch's son dropped his lit cigarette into the snow. The song stopped instantly in his throat. His eyes went wide with sudden recognition. He recognized the broad shoulders. He recognized the dark, murderous eyes. He recognized the American champion he destroyed.

Pure terror washed over Nikolai's scarred face. He realized that his father's billions of dollars and his corrupt police force could not save him in this dark alley. He turned around clumsily and tried to run frantically back toward the heavy metal door. His expensive leather shoes slipped wildly on the icy piss-covered pavement.

Stripe lunged forward. He grabbed Nikolai roughly by the collar of his expensive fur coat. He yanked the oligarch backward with massive force and threw him to the frozen ground. Nikolai hit the icy pavement hard, scrambling desperately backward on his hands and knees like a terrified animal. His face and hands were covered in his own bodily fluid and freezing from the cold.

"Wait. Wait. Please." Nikolai offered a shrill plea. "I can give you money. I can give you anything you want."

Stripe did not answer him. He did not want his money. He wanted his life. Stripe grabbed him by the feet, dragging him slowly away from the door and further into the dark Moscow alleyways. Stripe straddled Nikolai in the dirty, freezing snow. He pinned the oligarch's arms to the ground with his heavy knees.

Stripe did not use his highly disciplined martial arts training. He did not use a measured technique or proper professional footwork. He did not want a clean knockout. He wanted absolute, visceral destruction. He raised his bare right fist and brought it down like a heavy iron hammer directly into Nikolai's face.

The first punch broke Nikolai's nose. Blood exploded across the pristine white snow. Stripe raised his left fist and brought it down. The second punch shattered Nikolai's cheekbone.

He unleashed an unhinged, primal beating. He punched the oligarch in the face. Then he punched him again. And again. And again. He punched until the skin on his own knuckles split open to the white bone. He punched until Nikolai's expensive fur coat stained dark red. He punched until Nikolai's face became an unrecognizable, formless ruin of blood and splintered bone. When his fists became broken, he switched to elbows. Nikolai begged. But it was drowned out by the thud of the impacts. Tears streamed down his cheeks. It didn't help his situation at all.

He did not stop when Nikolai stopped moving. He did not stop when Nikolai stopped breathing. Stripe kept punching and elbowing until the wet, sickening sounds of impact echoed loudly through the empty, freezing alleyway. He punched until his massive arms were too heavy to lift. He punched until his lungs burned for oxygen and his vision swam with exhaustion.

Stripe finally stopped. His chest heaved in the freezing air. He sat on top of the ruined corpse for a long moment. He looked down at the destruction he caused. The snow surrounding them was painted entirely in a violent red. Normally, this would be a disgusting sight. But to Stripe, it was a work of art.

He stood up slowly. His legs shook slightly from the adrenaline dump. He wiped the blood from his face with the back of his ruined hand, leaving a dark red smear across his cheek. He did not check the body for a pulse. There was nothing left to check. There was barely a head remaining, and the snow held most of his brain matter.

He turned his back on the corpse. He walked away into the freezing Moscow night, leaving the broken monster behind in the snow. He walked for miles through the frozen city, numb to the biting cold. He found the smuggler waiting at the designated extraction point. He paid the remaining cash and boarded the identical, freezing cargo plane for the journey back to America.

He sat in the pitch-black, unheated cargo hold of the military transport plane for another fourteen agonizing hours. The heavy turbulence shook the metal walls around him. Stripe sat alone in the darkness. He stared down at his ruined, heavily bleeding hands in the dim light filtering through a small grate. His knuckles were shattered. The pain began to register, throbbing in time with his heartbeat. It felt nice.

He waited for the profound sense of relief to wash over him. He waited for the closure that vengeance was supposed to bring. He waited to feel like he had finally balanced the scales. But the relief never came.

Instead, a cold, horrifying realization slowly washed over him, chilling him far worse than the freezing temperature of the cargo hold. The vengeance felt hollow. The brutal murder did nothing to fix the agonizing, gaping hole in his chest. His beautiful wife was still dead. His unborn child was still dead. The nursery in his mansion remained empty.

Killing the monster in the snow did not bring his angels back. It did not grant him a single ounce of peace. The universe did not suddenly correct itself because he spilled more blood. It only proved that the darkness had won. He allowed the tragedy to consume him. He became the exact kind of ruthless, violent monster his wife always warned him about. He used his hands to destroy a life outside the cage, crossing a line he could never uncross. It felt good in the moment, but now there was nothing. He couldn't even look forward to revenge anymore. He no longer had anything to motivate him. He was alone. He was a murderer. He was broken beyond any hope of repair.

Chapter 29

Stripe found himself in a dark place. It wasn't just the physical gloom of the abandoned, rotting alleyway he had ducked into, though the shadows here hung thick enough to choke on. It was a suffocating darkness of the mind. The cold cobblestones beneath his boots felt like the floor of a tomb. The air tasted of stale rain, woodsmoke, and the metallic tang of dried blood. He leaned his heavy, muscular frame against the damp brick wall, his chest rising and falling in slow rhythms. Somehow, he endured the dark thoughts in his mind. As he wondered how he hadn't sunk to his lowest point yet, he received a notification.

CROWN — "Reflection complete. Mental health strain has been lessened due to adaptation from previous life experiences."

It had been a long time since he became this person again. A person with one terrifying objective: the destruction of someone who caused him harm. He closed his eyes, and the memories flashed behind his eyelids like strobe lights in a nightmare. He saw the shattered broom. He saw the old man bleeding out in the mud. He saw the pristine, heartbreaking journal. The rage inside him didn't burn hot and chaotic anymore; it condensed into a block of freezing ice.

He wasn't very familiar with this world and its politics. He didn't care about the sprawling royal lineages, the complex trade agreements, or the delicate balance of power between the Church and the Crown. All he knew was that some snobby, entitled noble killed his only friend in this miserable city. Sure, he had his new companion, but he paid for that friendship with a slave voucher and a magical leash, so he didn't count it as a true friendship yet. Hobb had been different. Hobb shared his nothingness with him.

A sudden, sharp vibration buzzed at the base of his skull.

CROWN — "Host instability detected. Recommended action: calming breaths."

The artifact's synthesized voice echoed through the hollow chambers of his mind. The Crown almost sounded concerned for him, a strange, human inflection bleeding into its usually sterile delivery.

Stripe offered a growl. "No. I want to feel this. I need to feel it for what comes next."

He pushed himself off the damp brickwork. The mythril-threaded gauntlets on his hands clinked in the quiet alley. He had no clue how to weasel his way into the heavily guarded, opulent inner circle of the High District's nobility. The walls rose high, the guards stood heavily armed, and his face became too recognizable among the lower ranks of the city watch. But he knew someone who went to war with the King himself. Latrum fought a rebellion. Latrum knew how to dismantle a hierarchy from the shadows. So, he figured that would be a great start.

Stripe stepped out of the alley and joined the chaotic flow of Memento's streets. He moved with the terrifying grace of a predator that caught a scent. The crowds of merchants, beggars, and mercenaries instinctively parted around him, sensing the unadulterated malice radiating off his broad shoulders. He made his way back to the sprawling, noisy guild hall, pushing through the heavy oak doors without breaking his stride.

The lobby provided a cacophony of shouting adventurers, clinking armor, and the ever-present smell of stale ale and nervous sweat. He scanned the room with calculating eyes and found Latrum waiting by the entrance, leaning on his battle staff. Stripe closed the distance in a few massive strides. He didn't wait for a greeting and jumped to the topic.

"If I wanted to find and kill a noble, how hard would it be?" Stripe leveled the question.

Latrum’s posture stiffened. His eyes darted around the crowded lobby to ensure no one was eavesdropping on the treasonous conversation. He gripped his staff a little tighter. "That's extreme and sudden." Latrum offered a quiet warning. "But it wouldn't be hard to find them. They all stay in the nobility district. The issue would be getting permission to enter there. May I ask why you want to do such a thing?"

Stripe's jaw clenched so hard his teeth ground together. His eyes held no warmth. "A noble ordered for my friend to be killed. I plan on getting revenge."

Latrum stared at Stripe for a long, heavy moment. The half-gnome's face hardened, the bitter memories of his own slaughtered family surfacing in his dark eyes. He turned his head and spat a thick glob of saliva onto the dirty stone floor of the guild lobby.

Latrum offered an agreement. "I'm with you. I still have a score to settle. But we do it right. I will reach out to my contacts to see if I can get a positive ID on the target. I need you to remain calm and act normally until then. In fact, let's take on some more jobs and work off this debt."

Stripe narrowed his eyes, studying Latrum's face for any sign of deception. He knew the slave contract bound the man, but he needed willing loyalty for a murder of this scale.

"You aren't saying that because you want me to set you free before I find him, are you?" Stripe questioned the man.

"Being free wouldn't stop me from helping you." Latrum issued the promise.

Stripe let out a slow breath, the tension in his shoulders relaxing by the smallest margin. Stripe offered a nod. "I guess we will see. I'm going to take the highest-paying and hardest job available. But I can't afford to lose you. You will stay behind and find the identity of the noble who killed Hobb. It happened in the middle of town."

Latrum shifted his weight, his brow furrowing in deep concern. He knew Stripe acted recklessly, and sending him off alone while he sat in a homicidal fugue state seemed like a recipe for disaster. Latrum pressed the issue. "I highly suggest you take me with you."

Stripe stepped closer, using his massive height to loom over the half-gnome. His voice dropped into a dangerous register. "No, it's not up for debate." Stripe issued the command. "I don't want to order you, but I will if I have to."

Latrum let out a frustrated sigh, his shoulders slumping in defeat. The magical brand on his skin hummed faintly, a physical reminder of the absolute authority Stripe held over him. "Fine, I get it," Latrum surrendered. "I will get the info. Make sure you come back alive."

Stripe reached into his pouch, pulled out a heavy handful of his remaining silver coins, and pressed them firmly into Latrum's hand. He closed the half-gnome's fingers over the metal.

"Use this to bribe whoever you need to." Stripe delivered the instruction. "But listen to me, Latrum. The High District is a fortress. If the guards catch you snooping around, asking questions about nobles, they will string you up without a second thought. Don't get yourself gutted. You're a valuable ally now. Just get me a name and a face, and stay in the shadows."

Latrum looked down at the silver, then back up at Stripe, a silent understanding passing between them. He tucked the coins away and nodded.

Stripe spent a few moments explaining everything the terrified homeless man told him in the alleyway. He described the location, the shattered broom, and the horrific way Hobb was left to bleed out in the dirt. He didn't spare any details and made sure that Latrum had all the information necessary to track down the golden sunburst crest.

Once Latrum slipped away into the crowded streets to begin his hunt, Stripe turned his attention to the massive wooden quest board dominating the back wall of the guild. The board was bursting with fresh, overlapping parchments. It looked like the spectacle of the Sanctified Hunt boosted business, drawing terrified villagers and wealthy merchants alike to seek the guild's protection.

He scanned over the hundreds of fluttering papers with ruthless focus, and then he saw one that stood out. The parchment was thick, high-quality vellum, pinned to the dead center of the board with a heavy iron spike.

GUILD CONTRACT

Escort VIP to the town of Dawnfall. * Pay: 5,000 Gold

Stripe stared at the number until it burned into his retinas. This proved an outrageous payout for a standard escort mission. The information about the quest remained vague, setting off a series of warning bells in his mind. No other quest on the board lacked basic geographical information or threat assessments. This one didn't even say who sponsored it or what kind of VIP required a five-thousand-gold security detail.

Stripe didn't care. The money provided was enough to wipe out his debt. He reached out with a mythril-clad hand, snatched the thick parchment off the wall, and took it directly to the front counter.

Varn materialized out of the shadows like an opportunistic phantom. The guildmaster intercepted him just as he set the heavy paper down on the polished wood.

"That's a big quest for a Tin rank." Varn made the observation. "Normally, it would only be available to Iron rank and higher."

Varn's voice sounded as smooth as oiled glass. He adjusted the lapels of his expensive coat, his calculating eyes darting from the quest sheet to Stripe's bruised face.

"I want it." Stripe issued the demand. "I think I proved my skills in the competition."

"Oh, no doubt, you are very capable." Varn offered an easy agreement. "But your rank is still Tin. I might make something happen, but..."

Varn let the sentence hang in the air, a masterclass in silent negotiation. He wanted Stripe to fill in the blanks.

Stripe finished the thought. "But it won't be free, I imagine."

Varn flashed a smile. "You understand. Breaking the rules is expensive. I have to think of the guild."

Varn faked a sincere smile, showing off his unnerving teeth. The truth proved glaringly obvious to anyone who possessed a functioning brain; letting Stripe take the quest made perfect financial sense, and it wouldn't hurt the guild at all. Varn simply did what he does best: scamming his own adventurers out of their hard-earned blood money.

"What will it cost me?" Stripe gritted his teeth.

"I could probably convince the client to take you," Varn mused, "but the pay would fall to exactly the amount of debt you have."

Stripe's jaw clenched. The math provided an insult. A five-thousand-gold payout was slashed by more than half just to line Varn's pockets.

"That's a big pay decrease."

Varn offered a false sigh. "It's rather unfortunate, but it has to be this way."

Stripe knew he was being fleeced. There was just nothing he could do about it. But after this quest, he would be free of the debt he owed the guild, and that alone made taking this bad deal worth it. Varn offered a shrug, feigning absolute helplessness in the face of his own manufactured bureaucracy. Stripe stared at him, the overwhelming urge to shatter the man's nose pulsing through his knuckles. But he needed the clearance.

"Fine," Stripe agreed, "but I want a promotion to Iron after its completion."

Varn gave a grin. "That can be done. I'm glad we can make this work. Good luck on your quest."

Stripe could tell this was a complete, unadulterated scam. Varn wasn't going to ask the sponsor for less money. It was infinitely more likely that the guildmaster would simply pocket the difference himself and forge the ledger. Stripe wasn't bothered by this. If he could complete this quest and survive whatever fresh hell waited on the road to Dawnfall, then he would be completely debt-free and holding a higher rank. As an Iron, significantly more doors would open up to him.

He rationalized the terrifying three-month timeline in his head. Three months on the road felt like an absolute eternity when his blood boiled for revenge. But the High District sat as an impenetrable, heavily fortified fortress. If he went charging in now as a lowly Tin rank, he'd be slaughtered by the royal guard before he even found the right mansion. But if he came back as an Iron rank, debt-free, and personally endorsed by whoever this VIP was... he could walk right through the front gates. The three months weren't a delay; it was him sharpening his knife. First came revenge, however. Everything else fell secondary.

Stripe got the heavy stacks of bureaucratic paperwork signed in blood and ink, officially accepting the quest. A nervous clerk brought him to a small, windowless back room and told him to wait. The room felt suffocating. The air smelled of dust and old wax. He sat in a rickety wooden chair for what felt like an eternity, staring blankly at the bare stone wall, his mind continuously drifting back to the frozen corpse of a Russian oligarch and the bleeding body of a beggar.

After nearly an hour, the heavy wooden door clicked and opened. In stepped a robed person draped in immaculate white silk. Stripe's eyes widened. He felt surprised to see that the mysterious sponsor of the quest was High Priestess Sarah. She closed the door quietly behind her and sat gracefully across from him, holding a thick, wax-sealed envelope in her hands.

"I can't believe they gave you this quest." Sarah's tone remained cold. "This is serious, so if you plan to joke around, then leave now."

Her voice lost its usual melodic warmth. It felt cold, sharp, and laced with underlying anxiety. Stripe remained silent, his face an unreadable mask. This total lack of reaction surprised Sarah. Usually, he would quip back with a crude insult or do something else profoundly annoying to test her patience. Today, he acted like a statue.

"If I read to you what this quest entails, you can no longer back out," Sarah issued the warning. "To proceed, we will do a magical contract. If that contract is broken by either party, the party that breaks it will die."

"Fine by me, let's hurry this up." Stripe offered an instant agreement.

She felt surprised again. There was no hesitation in his voice and no stupid jokes. He meant business. During the few chaotic days she spent proctoring his hunt in the Ashen Crags, he never once acted this way. It felt like she sat across from a whole different person. A very dangerous, broken person.

She reached into the folds of her robes and brought out a thick parchment. Magical symbols and ancient, glowing runes wove across it like a shimmering, ethereal watermark. The contract was prefilled with intricate calligraphy. She placed it on the table.

MAGICAL NDA RESTRAINTS

- The mission is top secret and cannot be discussed by anyone outside the signing party.
- The reward will be paid on completion.
- The contract only becomes void if one of the signers dies.
- Upon completion, the mission details will remain secret unless both parties agree to disclose them.

In short, it operated as a lethal, magically binding non-disclosure agreement. Stripe possessed intimate familiarity with restrictive NDAs due to his past life dealing with sleazy fight promoters and greedy corporate sponsors. He reached out, grabbed the sleek black quill off the table, and signed the word "Hands" with aggressive strokes. He set the quill down and sat back in his chair with his legs crossed, his posture radiating a terrifying kind of calm.

After Sarah signed her own elegant name at the bottom of the contract, the heavy parchment lifted off the table. It floated into the air, suspended by unseen forces, and then erupted into a spectacular, blindingly bright, magical rainbow fire. Within seconds, the paper burned up, vanishing into the air without leaving a trace of ash. It provided a beautiful, otherworldly sight, but Stripe did not remark on it. His eyes never left her face.

Sarah made the announcement. "You will be my personal guard."

"Doesn't the church send guards?"

"Yes, they do, but they work for the church and not me." Sarah offered a careful explanation. "I need someone who works for only me."

Stripe leaned forward, resting his elbows on his knees. The shadows in the small room seemed to cling to his large shoulders. Stripe issued the demand. "Why? Something isn't right. I don't care because of morals; I care because it may impact the mission."

Sarah looked down at her hands. The confidence that usually radiated from her was fractured. She looked vulnerable, stripping away the impenetrable divine facade she normally wore. "I'm worried something is happening to me," Sarah confessed quietly. "I don't know what or how. But I just feel like I am being forced to do things I don't want to do."

Stripe felt a sudden ping of cynical recognition deep in his chest. He despised the world's systems of control. He hated the Guild's predatory debt traps. He hated the royal laws that allowed slavery. And now, sitting across from him, the most powerful woman in the entire Church admitted she wore invisible chains of her own. It shifted his perspective. It gave him a reason to care about her situation beyond just the gold payout.

"Like what?" Stripe pressed.

Sarah shook her head. "I don't know. It makes no sense. But it's like the goddess herself is warning me that something is wrong and hasn't been right for a long time."

Stripe let out a slow breath. "Pfft, fine," Stripe agreed. "What do you need me to do?"

"You will guard me," Sarah delivered the instruction. "If you notice anything weird, you will use the codeword to alert me. The codeword is Halloween."

Stripe froze. Every muscle in his body locked up instantly. *Halloween.* The word echoed loudly in the cavernous space of his mind. Back in the Ashen Crags, she structured the Sanctified Hunt using a "ten-point must system", a scoring metric ripped straight from Earth's combat sports. He suspected it then, but this gave undeniable confirmation. They didn't celebrate Halloween in this miserable, magical world. She used an Earth word on purpose. She acted as a reincarnator, too. That was exactly why she specifically requested him for this ultra-secret mission. He was the only other person in this entire godforsaken city who would recognize the word and understand the weight it carried. They shared a dangerous secret.

This also made the hunt make a ton more sense. The scoring system remained common on Earth. So this meant that whoever created it was also from Earth. Maybe she served as the creator. In all of fiction, elves lived long lives. So 50 years might not be much to an elf. Stripe nodded slowly, his eyes boring into hers with newfound understanding.

Stripe offered a simple statement. "Fine. Let's get going."

"We will depart tomorrow morning," Sarah said, delivering the details. "We will be on the road for 3 months. We are heading to a small, struggling village on the outskirts of the kingdom. We will be heading through monster dens and bandit territory. But your primary job is not to leave my side. The church will handle the travel security."

This whole quest made no logical sense. It sounded too easy for a five-thousand-gold payout. More screaming red flags appeared with every passing second of the conversation. A sharp, golden vibration pulsed at the base of Stripe's skull.

CROWN — "It is likely that key details are being kept secret. It is recommended that the host inquire further."

Stripe issued the demand. "What else?"

"Nothing I can tell you yet," Sarah offered a deflection.

Stripe stared at her for a long, heavy moment. "Fuck it, I will take the job," Stripe conceded.

CROWN — "Warning, inquiring further is highly recommended."

Stripe ignored the Crown again, physically shutting out the golden text scrolling across his mind's eye. He only wanted to get this tedious escort mission over with so he could return to Memento and exact his revenge. At this point in his miserable existence, he was willing to die for his goal. He had absolutely nothing to live for here anyway. This singular, burning desire for revenge fueled him like he hadn't been fueled in a very long time. For better or for worse, he locked in with a deep, terrifying level of obsession that he hadn't felt since he stood over the bleeding, broken body of Nikolai in the freezing Moscow snow.

The next morning, he woke up in the crowded barracks at the guild. The air in the cavernous room smelled horrible. It was filled with dozens of low-level, desperate adventurers who barely ever showed and couldn't afford to live anywhere else in the expensive city. The sounds of snoring, coughing, and restless nightmares echoed off the cold stone walls.

He pushed himself off the thin mattress. He grabbed his worn gear, strapping the heavy mythril-threaded gauntlets to his forearms. After getting dressed in the dim morning light, he headed out through the muddy courtyard to the main entrance of the guild.

The air outside felt crisp and biting. After waiting in the damp fog for around fifteen minutes, an opulent caravan finally arrived. Several heavy wooden carriages, reinforced with thick steel plating and adorned with glittering church insignias, rolled to a stop on the cobblestones. Dozens of heavily armored Paladins rode alongside them on giant warhorses, their halberds gleaming in the early morning sun.

One of the heavy oak doors in the middle carriage clicked and opened up. Stripe stepped up to the carriage. Inside the luxurious, velvet-lined interior, he could see Sarah sitting gracefully on the plush seating. Sitting directly across from her was Calen, the handsome, arrogant young priest who proctored his very first hunt. Stripe climbed into the carriage, his huge frame taking up a significant amount of space, and sat down heavily right beside Sarah. The suspension groaned under his weight.

The blonde man sitting across from him glared at Stripe with barely concealed disdain. He clearly didn't seem to enjoy the new, violent company invading his private space. Calen offered a complaint. "I don't understand why you contracted this... man. We have plenty of security."

Calen’s voice dripped with elitist condescension. He gestured vaguely out the window toward the heavily armed Paladins flanking the convoy.

"I figured it would help to have our own," Sarah replied smoothly, keeping her golden eyes fixed on the passing scenery outside the window. "Monsters have been crazy lately, and I need my energy for the ritual."

"I guess that makes sense." Calen let out a sigh. "But it still seems extreme." Calen crossed his arms over his polished breastplate, clearly pouting.

Sarah offered a soothing tone. "Just trust me, my love." Sarah reached out and gently rested her hand on Calen’s knee.

"Fine, you always know how to get me to agree." Calen let out an awkward, smitten smile and finally gave in, his hostility melting away at her touch.

Stripe leaned back against the velvet upholstery, keeping his eyes half-closed. He watched the subtle tightening around Sarah's eyes when Calen called her "my love." He noticed her golden gaze go dead for a fraction of a second before a practiced, hollow smile stretched across her lips.

The puzzle pieces clicked together in his mind. She literally just told him she felt forced to do things she didn't want to do. Calen wasn't just a smitten teenager. The blonde priest might be the exact person holding her invisible chains. If Calen acted as the bad guy here, it didn't appear like Sarah was aware. It proved possible that Stripe was just becoming paranoid due to the lack of information on the quest. He needed this money, so he planned to be overly cautious.

Stripe felt the atmosphere inside the carriage grow suffocatingly tense. He stared at the two holy figures interacting in front of him, keeping his hands resting near his gauntlets, which rested beside him. He wasn't sure if he served as a chaperone for a group of smitten teenagers or if he was a bodyguard sitting across from a prospective assassin. If he were in the right state of mind, he might have noticed more clues. But his brain remained jumbled with the thoughts of revenge and the revelation that he wasn't the only reincarnator in the world. He decided that if he lived through this quest and his revenge, he would talk to Sarah about his discovery.

The carriage lurched forward, the heavy wooden wheels turning against the cobblestones, and the long, miserable, dangerous journey to Dawnfall officially began.

------------ STATUS ------------

Name: Stripe

Level:10

Rank: Tin

Class: Toxic Pugilist

Title: Toxic Fisherman, Pugilist Specialist

HP: 120/120

Stamina: 110/110

Mana: 0/0

------------ Attributes ------------

STR: 14 +5

AGI: 11

END: 12

NT: 6

Skill points: 0

-------- Skills / Proficiencies --------

Hand-to-Hand Combat - MAX
Improvised Weapon Handling - Beginner
Survival - Novice
Pugilist Proficiency - MAX

---------- Passive Effects ----------
Minor Poison Secretion

------------- Artifact -------------
Crown of Reflection

---------- System Effects ----------
Intoxication Immunity
Experience Calculation

------------ Inventory -------------
Iron Dagger
Leather Chest Piece (Bandit Armor)
Wolf Pelt (Crude Clothing)
Leather Belt with Pouch
Bandit Ring
Mythril Threaded Striker Gloves

------------ Currency -------------
Copper: 6
Debt: 1300 Gold

Chapter 30

The initial part of the trip passed uneventfully. The muddy roads leading away from Memento sat dotted with road hazards: knocked-over trees and the rotting skeletons of merchant carts. To a trained eye, these presented ambush sites. The actual attacks never came. The bandits saw the church escort and decided to stay in the brush. Dozens of armored Paladins on warhorses provided a deterrent to common thieves.

Stripe sat inside the velvet-lined cabin next to Sarah and Calen. His stomach chewed at the flirting and indecency happening inches away. He imagined elves as serene, ethereal creatures. The fact that these two stood as high-ranking priests made their physical affection jarring. They touched hands, whispered, and shared lingering glances.

While camping, Stripe walked into the woods. He returned to find the carriage doors locked from the inside, rhythmic sounds echoing from the cabin. Since his directive ordered him to remain by Sarah's side, he spent those nights standing in the cold. Armored guards and squires shot him dirty looks, whispering that he acted like a creep for listening in. He wanted to shatter his own eardrums to escape the noise.

Leaning against the wooden wall at night, staring at unfamiliar stars, he wondered how the hunt for the noble progressed. He missed cellphones. Three weeks passed, and his mind remained consumed with revenge. He mentally mapped out how he would shatter the bones of the man wearing the golden sunburst crest.

In week four, the rhythm shifted. Calen stayed away longer, riding with the vanguard. When he stayed around, he seemed alert, his hand resting on the pommel of his weapon.

Halfway through the week, the first incident occurred. Sarah received an offer of wine during the evening halt. An indentured servant handed the tray to Stripe, who passed her a goblet. As Stripe took the crystal cup, a dot of sweat dripped from his brow into the dark red liquid. A faint, sinister hiss echoed from the goblet. A micro-bubble of purplish gas popped on the surface, releasing a rotting odor that struck Stripe's senses like a punch.

CROWN — "Toxic trait not applied. Substance is already poisoned."

Stripe's arm froze as Sarah reached for the cup. "This drink is poisoned."

Sarah snatched her hand back, her eyes wide. "What? How do you know?"

Stripe kept his grip on the cup. "It's one of my skills."

Sarah slumped against the cushions, the color draining from her face. "You should have been checking from the beginning. That proves my theory."

"So you believe me?"

Sarah let out a breath. "Something has been off."

Stripe's hand balled into a fist, the mythril threading groaning. He prepared to drag the servant back by his neck.

Sarah held up a hand. "This stays between us. For now, I will pretend nothing has changed."

A week of this dangerous game passed. Stripe checked every drink; every drink contained poison. The toxin proved unique; it didn't kill her. It is designed to alter her or enforce her "chains." Sarah became an expert at faking sips, pouring the wine into a flask when Calen looked away.

During a long stretch of road, they discussed the mission. Twice a year, Sarah went on a pilgrimage to cities plagued by famine or monster surges. She would pray, and a blessing would follow. It triggered a potent phenomenon that boosted crop productivity and economic commerce, turning barren lands into thriving hubs within days.

"So you just make the land rich?"

"Not me, the goddess." Sarah corrected him. "I just witnessed their struggles for her."

"Why doesn't she do it herself?"

"I cannot speak for her motivations."

Stripe pushed the issue, but Sarah's answers turned defensive and cryptic. When he asked how she obtained the power, she replied that she was born with it.

Stripe leaned forward. "You were born here?"

Sarah looked at him with pitying confusion, as if his mind had snapped. "Yes? How else would I be in front of you? I have parents. Are you dumb?"

The theory that she came from Earth vanished. The realization that he remained alone in this universe settled over his shoulders like a weight.

The caravan screeched to a sudden halt, wheels locking and tearing into the dirt. Shouting and the thud of bodies followed. The carriage door flung open, hinges screaming. A man in black robes stood there with a serrated blade. Stripe moved. He launched from his seat, driving mythril gauntlets into the man's throat.

CROWN — "Human eliminated. XP gained."

He hopped out, stepping over the body. Combat raged. Archers fired from the tree lines; knights collided with robed men. Large wolves, the same kind that attacked Stripe when he first arrived, tore into the warhorses.

Stripe stood with his back to the caravan, a physical wall. A short man with curved blades approached from the left; a hulking man with an iron axe charged from the right. They rushed at the same time. The axe aimed for Stripe's neck while the short man rolled to slice his ankles. Stripe leaped in an explosive dive, dodging both by a fraction of an inch. He landed, pivoted, and squeezed his fists. A small needle inside his gauntlets drew his own blood.

CROWN — "Toxic Pugilist trait applied."

He flung his right fist, splashing toxic blood into the large man's eyes.

CROWN — "Target poisoned. Stacking has begun."

The small man rushed up to Stripe's back. Stripe spun with a back fist. His heavy gauntlet sliced through the man's head. The attacker dropped dead before registering the blow. His skull hit the dirt in a spray of crimson.

The large man roared, a red aura surrounding him. Stripe threw a feint. The man bit, swinging the axe where Stripe had stood a moment prior. Stripe slipped the blade and countered, stabbing mythril spikes into the man's thigh.

A glowing yellow light shot from the cabin, hitting the giant in the chest. A dark purple aura suppressed his red buff. One of the priests debuffed him. Stripe kept feinting and probing until the man knelt, green liquid pouring from his mouth. Stripe reached down and pulled off the hood. A scarred orc stared back.

"Finish me." The orc issued the demand.

"Who hired you?"

The orc spat in his face. Stripe dug a gauntlet spike into the sensitive nerve beneath the orc's fingernail. The orc let out a scream. "Okay, I'll tell you. It was..."

The orc's head flew through the air, landing with a wet thud. A Church guard stood behind the headless corpse, broadsword raised. "Everyone okay?"

Stripe exploded. He hoisted the guard by his breastplate, toxic green blood sizzling on his spikes. "I had him!"

The guard let out a stammer. "We can't let them live."

"Since when do bandits wear robes?" Stripe issued the challenge.

The guard shoved Stripe's hands away and ran back into the conflict.

When the fighting died down, Stripe searched the bodies. He found 50 silver and iron weapons. Nothing else. No food, no gear. They equipped themselves for a suicide assault.

Inside the carriage, Sarah held a magical bow, and Calen gripped a holy staff. Stripe ordered them back inside. To his surprise, they complied without argument. Sarah muttered an incantation, and the splintered door floated into place, repairing itself.

CROWN — "Level up. Mana acquired. Extra stat points acquired."

A new sensation ripped through Stripe, not the burn of stamina, but a wave of cold static expanding in his chest. It felt like a second set of lungs opened, filled with crackling energy.

Stripe let out a murmur. "I get more stat points?"

CROWN — "Correct. That is the perk of your divine gift."

"Like Sarah's?"

CROWN — "Unable to answer."

Then, a human voice whispered in his head.

CROWN — "Like Sarah."

"I thought you couldn't answer that?"

CROWN — "Correct. I cannot answer that."

The voice returned to a sterile tone. Stripe is tired of arguing with his brain-squatter. Inside the cabin, Calen and Sarah watched him talk to himself. They were used to it. He seemed unhinged, but his efficiency proved undeniable.

As the carriage lurched forward, Stripe felt he started to understand the terrifying rules of this game.

[SYSTEM ALERT: Level 11 Reached | Mana Capacity Unlocked: 10/10]

Chapter 31

"What can someone do with just a tiny bit of mana?" Stripe asked himself as he sat in the carriage. He had seen little magic aside from the divine kind. He could still feel the cold, static energy sitting heavy in his chest from his recent level-up. It felt like a dormant muscle he had no idea how to flex.

CROWN — "Magic can be used to influence reality through elemental attributes, healing, repairing, and illusions. In your case, it can increase the potency of your toxic attacks. By channeling your mana into your circulatory system, you can saturate your blood with toxins before it leaves your body."

The Crown had read his mind. Stripe stiffened.

"Wait, you can communicate by reading my thoughts?"

CROWN — "Correct. Non-verbal communication has always been the recommended method. It is efficient and eliminates the risk of tactical exposure during combat."

Stripe's jaw clenched. "What the fuck? You never once told me I could talk to you with my mind."

CROWN — "It was in the initial briefing from the goddess."

"I have been looking crazy for nothing," Stripe fumed in his mind. "I have spent a month in taverns and carriages having verbal arguments with thin air."

CROWN — "Correct. It was assumed that you preferred verbal communication. Human biological quirks are often illogical."

"I hate you." Stripe gritted his teeth.

The Crown ignored the hatred.

CROWN — "If you apply mana to your attacks, you can increase the odds of poisoning from 25% to 100%. Each strike will cost one mana. The biological toll of converting energy into toxins requires this equivalent exchange."

"So I get 10 strikes." Stripe calculated the numbers.

CROWN — "Correct. At such a low intelligence stat, recovering mana will take all day. The ambient absorption rate for your current build is lacking. Use it wisely."

Stripe felt insulted. "Since when have you been helping me voluntarily?"

CROWN — "As you level up, I will become more autonomous. My processing capabilities expand as your physical and magical vessels expand to house them."

"You sure it's not that you're scared I will replace you with Latrum?" Stripe offered a mental challenge. "I'm sure the goddess would be embarrassed if you were returned to her unused."

CROWN — "I do not feel jealousy, and I am not useless!"

The Crown sounded like a girl pouting. The synthetic edge vanished for a fraction of a second.

"There was a lot of emotion in that response," Stripe pointed out.

CROWN — "Negative."

The artifact returned to its monotone voice. Stripe sat in a meditative trance while talking to the mind-squatter.

"Are you okay, Hands?" Sarah asked.

"Yeah, just fighting with the voice in my head."

Sarah offered a smile and went back to reading a leather-bound tome. "Very odd, very you." It felt like she warmed up to him.

"Where is your boyfriend?" Stripe asked. "Is he tired of you yet?"

Sarah gave a huff. "Hmph! He is at the front of the convoy. He was called by the head priest to discuss church donations."

"Shouldn't you be up there?"

"No, as a woman, I do not have a voice in the financial aspects of the church," Sarah explained, her tone turning bitter. "It is an archaic law. Calen brings back the sacred floral extracts from the Head Priest after these meetings anyway."

"That's stupid." Stripe let out a scoff. "They worship a woman; why such a restriction?"

"It keeps power among the men in the church," Sarah mused. "If women get too much sway, there would be no need for men."

Stripe decided not to debate the point. It was the exact type of rule that kept him from seeking out religion. It served as a thin veil for a system of control.

He leaned his head against the window. The cloying scent of those sacred floral extracts gave him a headache. He was tired of the smell. The carriage reeked of fermented rose petals and artificial vanilla, like a cheap brothel trying to mask its own filth.

He went back into his mind. "What else can you do?"

CROWN — "I have many abilities. I can process vast amounts of information, provide guidance, and remotely control the host to assist in combat. I am currently monitoring the heart rates and magical signatures of forty-two entities within a one-mile radius."

"Can you do anything useful?"

CROWN — "Everything I can do is useful. If my host were more intelligent about my abilities, he could rule the world without conflict."

"Fine, test your thinking power." Stripe issued a challenge. "We know Sarah is being targeted for assassination. Based on what you have seen, why?"

CROWN — "It is unlikely she will be assassinated. Lethal toxins would have killed her weeks ago. It is more likely the poison is for hallucinogenic, charm, or mind control purposes."

"So, a love potion?"

CROWN — "Correct, or a potion to influence her thinking. A regional blessing can generate millions of gold coins. Capturing the source of that blessing means unlimited wealth and political leverage."

He had never considered that. A mind control potion explained why she hadn't died from the drinks. But what was the goal? How long had they been controlling her? If she fell under control, why would she hire him?

CROWN — "It is recommended that you observe other personnel during camping to determine who is targeting her. I will help with the analysis. My algorithms are compiling data on every guard and priest in this convoy."

For the first time, Stripe regretted his choice of power. Punching a monster until its skull caved in proved easier than navigating political espionage.

Things grew complicated over the next few weeks. Stripe kept his eyes open, scrutinizing everyone. He rarely let Sarah out of his sight. He checked her food and patrolled the perimeter of her carriage. His pride wouldn't allow him to fail.

This change didn't go unnoticed. Two weeks later, Stripe stepped away to use the bathroom. He walked into the woods and squatted down. The air held quiet, the wind blowing softly through the groaning trees.

The pressure shifted.

Something felt wrong. The oxygen was sucked out of the air, making Stripe gasp. The barometric drop proved severe enough that his eardrums popped. The leaves in the moonlight shifted against the wind, vibrating. The hairs on Stripe's forearms stood up, and the smell of burnt ozone filled his nostrils.

CROWN — "WARNING: A large amount of mana is detected. There is an attack occurring. Evasive maneuvers required."

Stripe hopped out of the way. The moment his body left the spot, the ground lit up. An intense white-and-blue light shot into the sky. The sound hit with a deafening roar, shaking the organs in his chest. The kinetic shockwave threw Stripe to the dirt.

The glow evaporated the land where he stood, leaving a circular scorch mark with jolting lightning. The heat turned the mud into glass. Stripe put his hands up in a defensive stance.

Another disturbance, another dodge, and another explosion of light. Stripe had never seen magic this strong. He fought as a brawler, and being hunted in the dark by orbital magical bombardment provided a horror. He could not slip a lightning bolt or parry raw energy. Every time the pressure dropped, he threw himself through the bushes, waiting for the blast that would incinerate him.

He retreated toward the camp. There were mages there who could help. As he ran, jolts of lightning shot past him, blistering the skin on his shoulder. He looked back but couldn't see the source. The attacks arrived delayed, allowing the target to shift position before striking. It felt frustrating.

He kept running until he reached the camp. Then the attacks stopped. The thunder faded into a ringing silence. He rushed to Sarah's carriage, heart hammering. He expected to find her charred corpse.

He threw open the door.

The sight seared into his mind. Sarah stood with her top off, looking down at Calen, who had his pants off. Instead of a bloodbath, a wave of that sweet floral aroma washed over Stripe. The scent radiated from the carriage, heavy and sickening.

Calen flicked his wrist, and a burst of wind slammed the door shut.

The adrenaline crash hit Stripe. The terror of the bombardment gave way to annoyance and crude comedy. He stood in the mud, panting.

The next morning was awkward. Calen brought up the subject as they packed.

Calen let out a sneer. "It was rude to waltz in like that. Maybe knock next time."

"It was an emergency; no one wants to see your little dick." Stripe fired the words back.

"It is not little!" Calen shouted. His face flushed crimson. He looked around to see if any guards heard.

Stripe let out a laugh. "Maybe on a toddler. But on a grown man, that thing was barely there. It looked like a sad, terrified acorn."

"I WASN'T READY!" Calen defended himself before pausing. "Wait, why am I defending myself to a pervert?"

Stripe let out a growl. "Fuck you, dude. I was checking on your safety because I was dodging lightning bolts in the woods."

Calen let out a scoff. "Likely story, you creep."

Sarah glowed red and did not speak. She kept her eyes on the dirt.

Once back in the carriage, Stripe leaned back in his seat. He felt exhausted. "They got brave last night. I almost became a barbecue."

"Explain?" Sarah asked.

Stripe recounted the attack. Sarah decided she needed to see the spot.

Stripe offered a flat stare. "My shit?"

Sarah let out a cringe. "Oh my god, no. The area where the attack happened."

Stripe took them to the spot. Giant scorch marks marked the landscape. The mud was baked into ceramic plates. Entire tree trunks blew in half.

Sarah knelt and touched a circle. "This is high-level lightning magic."

"Is it common?"

Sarah shook her head. "No, it's rare. Only a few can cast spells of this level. Some are demons, and even fewer are humans."

"I bet it was demons," Calen spoke up. "The cult that attacked before, and now demons in the woods. It all fits."

Stripe pointed a finger. "But they attacked me."

"It's possible you weren't the target." Sarah offered the suggestion. "Maybe you stumbled into their ambush area. You may have prevented the attack."

Stripe let out a mutter. "I don't know. This doesn't feel right."

"Listen to her." Calen dismissed him. "Don't pretend to be on her intellectual level."

Stripe looked past the priest. Standing a few feet behind Calen was the guard who decapitated the orc bandit weeks ago. The man gave off a weird vibe. He twitched, his eyes bloodshot. Stripe's senses picked up the smell of burnt air and static electricity clinging to the man's armor. It matched the smell from the blast craters.

Calen caught Stripe looking and shifted to block the guard. The priest exchanged a microscopic nod with the man.

Stripe's fists clenched. Every muscle in his body screamed to punch a hole through the guard's chest. But he forced himself to show restraint. He wasn't positive yet. If he murdered a guard without proof, he would face execution.

"What are the odds this is a demon, and I am not the target?" Stripe asked inwardly.

CROWN — "Odds are around 20%. It is more likely you were the target, and the perpetrator is within the camp."

"What are the odds that the attack was done by CALEN?"

CROWN — "Less than 1%. Calen was in a compromising position with Sarah. A spell of that magnitude requires intense concentration. It cannot be cast passively."

"Fuck, I'm back to square one."

CROWN — "There may be multiple people working toward the same goal. I am analyzing the magical residue on all personnel. Anomalies have been detected."

For the next three days, Stripe turned his paranoia into a weapon. He began operating like a ghost on the edges of the camp. He memorized the twitchy guard's patrol routes and mapped every time the man stepped away from the firelight.

The guard operated with predictable care. He always kept his helmet on, and the silver Church necklace never left his chest. But the smell of ozone never faded from his armor.

On the fourth night, the convoy camped near a thicket of willow trees. The moon hid behind grey clouds. Stripe watched as the twitchy guard finished his shift and slipped into the dark woods alone.

Stripe followed. He did not snap a single twig. He moved with the grace of a predator closing in on a kill. He tracked the guard for a mile to an isolated clearing. The guard stopped, leaning against a tree and pulling off his helmet. He let out an exhausted breath, rubbing his bloodshot eyes.

Stripe stepped out, blocking the path back to camp.

"You wander off into the woods a lot for a guy supposed to be protecting the perimeter." Stripe made the observation.

The guard jumped, his hand flying to his broadsword. "Just securing the outer boundaries. Go back to your VIP."

Stripe did not move. He raised his hands, flexing his fingers. The mythril on his gauntlets gleamed.

Stripe issued the challenge. "I think I have business out here. You silenced that orc before he could spill his guts. Every time I see you, you get twitchy. Someone shot lightning at me, and I'm pissed about that. You keep making secret eye contact with Calen. So what is the play? Are you calling down lightning while the pretty boy plays with his flowers? The way I see it, either you two are fucking, or you're plotting."

The guard stared at him. The panic drained from his eyes, replaced by something cold and alien. The man let go of his sword and let out a laugh. It did not sound human. It sounded like two voices layered together, grinding like stones.

The guard let out a rasp. "You are a persistent insect. I told the priest we should have burned your carriage on the first day. But no, he's in love with that bitch. Good, I'm glad you found me. Now I can separate your head from your body without Calen complaining."

The guard's face twisted. The skin around his jaw stretched and tore as the bones shifted. The silver Church necklace flared with a corrupted purple light. The metal cracked, and the illusion magic shattered.

Two jagged black horns erupted through the skin of his forehead, dripping with dark blood. His eyes turned solid black. A wave of freezing static pressure sucked the oxygen out of the clearing.

CROWN — "WARNING. Demonic Entity detected. Illusion magic dispelled. Combat parameters advised."

"Ah, that feels good." The Demon let out a groan, stretching its muscles. "This necklace keeps my aura hidden. You have no clue how suffocating it is."

The demon rolled its shoulders, grinning with a mouth of razor-sharp teeth. Blue lightning began to arc across its dark skin.

Stripe clenched his fists. A drop of his blood dripped down his gauntlets, mixing with his mana. The metal spikes hissed, glowing with a toxic green light.

CHAPTER 32

Demonic energy began radiating from the guard's twisted body. It flowed off his iron armor like fog rolling in on an early morning. The sickly red tint of the mist signified the danger it presented. It spread across the wet grass until it reached the edge of the clearing. Then it stopped, as if an invisible wall stood in its way.

"What the fuck is happening?" Stripe demanded.

CROWN — "Demonic entity present. Prepare for battle."

"I knew you had been following me, so I lured you to an area where I had a barrier set up." The Guard revealed his trap, his voice scraping like metal. "Now I can unleash my power without the Priestess sensing me."

The silver necklace around his neck stopped shining and fell to his chest. The illusion covering his form shattered like glass. Two massive black horns erupted through the skin of his forehead, dripping dark blood. His eyes turned black, devoid of pupils. A wave of freezing static pressure sucked the oxygen from the clearing.

"My name is Kevin the Terrible." The Demon roared. "I have lived for thousands of years, and I will bring terror to the world."

Stripe stood still in the dark woods. He blinked. "Wait, your name is Kevin?"

Stripe burst out laughing so hard he began choking on his spit. The absurdity of a towering monster introducing itself with such a mundane name broke his focus. He let out a wheeze. "Kevin? Fucking Kevin!"

The laughter kept coming in loud gasps, echoing off the trees. Meanwhile, Kevin the Terrible began to glow a brighter shade of red. Blue lightning arced across his dark skin.

"My name strikes fear into the hearts of millions." The demon snarled. "Everyone fears Kevin the Terrible. Stop laughing."

"Fucking GAY." Stripe managed to gasp out. "Not sexually. Just your name."

He slapped his knee with laughter, doubling over in the dirt. He tried to catch his breath, but the image of a legendary demon named Kevin filing taxes or waiting in line at a grocery store proved too much to handle.

"Wait, I didn't mean that. Don't cancel me." Stripe let out a chuckle, wiping a tear from his eye.

"I will turn your bones to dust and ravage the priestess on the bloody mass your death leaves behind." Kevin the Terrible issued the threat.

The demon began to levitate off the muddy ground. His eyes glowed with malice. The air around him cracked with energy. He pulled out a jagged sword and pointed the tip at Stripe. The blade began to glow a consuming black, with arcs of blue lightning shooting from it. Every second, the sphere of dark energy grew larger. The sword began to shake in his grip. The density of the mana he gathered bent the light around him.

Right when the demon prepared to let off his attack, Stripe stood up straight.

"So, like, your parents named you? Or you just chose that name?" Stripe questioned. "Kevin is not a good name for a demon. I knew a Kevin once. He played softball on the weekends."

The demon shot his attack forward, but his anger caused his attention to wane. His focus snapped. The black orb shot out wildly. It missed Stripe and hit the perimeter barrier, cracking the magical wall. The ball erupted with a deafening explosion. Residual blue lightning crawled from the orb and circulated in the area it hit. The earth scorched. After a moment, the energy collapsed on itself, leaving a smoking, glass-lined crater in the ground.

CROWN — "New Title Unlocked: Instigator. When baiting out conflict with insults or jokes, the target is likely to become enraged, limiting their capacity for thought and strategy."

Stripe offered a smile. His crude trash talk served as a system-approved combat tactic.

"I chose my name." Kevin the Terrible seethed. "Demon kind do not have parents. We are born out of the will of an older demon. We adopt the most fitting name for conquest."

"So you're a masturbation baby that thought the name Kevin was terrifying." Stripe deduced.

Kevin roared and rushed Stripe, swinging his heavy blade with a trailing electrical arc. The speed of the attack ran high. Stripe leaned back as the blade passed through the air where his head had been. The ozone smell burned his nostrils.

"Whoa, that's dangerous, Kevin." Stripe offered a mock warning. "Keep doing things like that, and I might believe you're evil. Thank you for the laugh, I needed it."

"Fight me, you coward!" Kevin the Terrible bellowed.

He brought the blade down with a vicious overhead strike. The power behind the swing felt as if it were designed to cleave a man in half. Stripe side-stepped as the steel collided with the muddy ground. The dirt exploded upward. The demon twisted the blade and brought it back up in a slashing movement. Stripe spun around the edge of the blade and gave a mocking, theatrical bow while still laughing.

Kevin's swordsmanship displayed skill. It remained the best technical weapon work Stripe had seen in this world. His footwork stayed firm. His edge alignment sat perfectly. The fatal flaw was that Kevin fought in a rage. He lacked tactics. He swung blindly and forcefully, abandoning his defensive guard, and Stripe took advantage of the openings.

"Let's see how you handle this." Kevin the Terrible snarled. "Lighting echo jab!"

The demon lunged forward, stabbing the sword at Stripe's chest. His blade vanished in the movement, and one hundred lightning-shaped spears appeared in the air. They crackled with blinding blue light. They shot forward simultaneously, covering a massive spread.

Stripe leaped up as high as his legs could propel him, spinning to avoid the initial volley. He landed and ran in a desperate sprint as the remaining lightning followed his path. He ducked and dodged through the trees. The lightning blasted holes through the oak trunks. Sometimes he rolled through the mud, and other times he jumped over the projectiles. The heat singed his dark clothes. Relying on his combat instincts and agility, he managed to dodge the attacks. He popped back up, unharmed.

"You are infuriating." Kevin the Terrible spat.

"Shut up, Kevin," Stripe commanded.

This dismissal seemed to make the demon angrier. The veins on his neck bulged. He hovered higher into the air and began to glow. The air pressure dropped again. A writhing mass of raw muscle and jagged bone began to wrap around his body, forming a thick, protective cocoon.

"You leave me no choice." Kevin the Terrible delivered the warning. "I will erase you from existence with my true form."

The expanding muscle mass covered his face as the transformation began. The cocoon throbbed like a giant heart. Stripe did not wait for an invitation.

CROWN — "ERROR. The host is interrupting a sanctioned Boss Transformation Sequence. This violates standard combat etiquette! You must wait for the evolutionary phase to complete!"

"Fuck etiquette." Stripe rejected the advice.

He allowed his internal mana to flow through his circulatory system and down into his gauntlets. He felt the cold, static energy pool in his knuckles. He closed the distance in a blur. Punch after punch collided with the rotating, vulnerable mass of flesh. Each mythril spike penetrated deep, cutting through the forming muscle and bone.

CROWN — "Target successfully poisoned. Poison stacked. Mana: 9 / 10."

Stripe threw a brutal left hook, burying his fist into the cocoon.

CROWN — "Poison stacked. Mana: 8 / 10."

He unleashed a flurry of blows. He did not stop to breathe. He threw uppercuts, straight crosses, and heavy hooks.

CROWN — "Mana: 5 / 10. Mana: 3 / 10. Mana: 1 / 10."

CROWN — "Target poisoned. Poison at a multiplier of ten. Mana Depleted. 0 / 10."

Stripe's mana faded from the gauntlets, leaving his energy pool empty. The cold sensation vanished from his chest, replaced by heavy exhaustion. But it didn't matter. The floating mass of flesh began to shake as acidic green ooze shot from the fresh wounds. The cocoon bulged outward, unable to sustain the internal damage. Finally, the entire demonic structure collapsed into a mess of body parts and toxic goo. The smell felt horrendous.

Kevin lay in the center of the crater with dark veins pulsating with Stripe's green venom.

The demon let out a cough. "You coward. You struck while I was transforming."

"Why the hell would I let you transform?" Stripe asked. "Seems silly you thought I'd wait around for you to finish. What kind of idiot just stands there while their enemy gets stronger?"

"I have fought hundreds of the best warriors in the world." Kevin the Terrible let out a wheeze. "None has ever thrown their honor out to interrupt my transformation."

"Your name is Kevin. The form was probably going to be stupid anyway." Stripe offered a shrug.

"My kin will avenge me." Kevin the Terrible issued the promise. "It's too late to stop the grand plan."

"Oh no, you don't get to die yet." Stripe denied him. "I have questions."

Stripe leaned down and grabbed Kevin's sword off the ground. He tossed it across the field. He grabbed the dying demon by his hair, hoisted his heavy head up, and slapped his cheek to keep him awake.

"What is the grand plan?" Stripe issued the demand.

"It makes no difference." Kevin the Terrible offered a chuckle. "You cannot torture information out of a demon. We do not fear physical pain."

Stripe set his head back in the mud. He took two measured steps back, lined up his target, and kicked the demon in the groin as hard as his combat boots would allow. Pain, unlike anything Kevin had ever felt in his thousands of years of existence, erupted through his body. A wet, crunching sound echoed.

Stripe reached into his bag and pulled out a small glass vial. He popped the cork and poured a low-tier healing potion onto the ruined groin. The magical liquid forced the crushed flesh and shattered nerves to knit themselves back together at an unnatural rate. It proved a painful, invasive process. The nerves fired as they reconnected.

"Sorry, my foot slipped." Stripe offered a hollow apology.

"You are a monster." Kevin the Terrible cried out.

"That's not what I asked." Stripe reminded him. "Guess you didn't learn the first time."

He took three steps back this time. He gave himself a running start before his boot collided with the groin again. He felt a sickening popping feeling on impact. The demon's body lifted off the ground from the force of the blow.

Stripe delivered the threat. "I have ten more healing potions in this bag. I can do this for hours. Barely keeping you alive while the poison eats away at your organs. Every time you heal, I can continue to kick you in the groin. I can make a fucking sport out of it. We can see how many times a demon named Kevin can get his nuts crushed before sunrise."

Kevin began to cry. Dark, thick tears flowed from his eyes. The creature of pure evil broke under the relentless brutality.

"You win, you win, please just stop." Kevin the Terrible sobbed. He coughed up a splatter of green blood. "The plan is to remove the priestess's soul from her flesh. It will be taken by a higher being of demon kind. We will use her gift to restore our land. We have been using mind tonics on her for years. After this mission is over, the process begins."

"Then what?" Stripe pressed.

"Then we take over the land like the demon king failed to do centuries ago," Kevin the Terrible finished.

"Why are you working with the church?"

"Not the whole church." Kevin the Terrible corrected him. "A few at the top fear her. She holds too much sway over the people. The corrupt high priests believe her blessing is tied to her physical flesh and bloodline, not her mind. If we demons remove her soul, the corrupt priests plan to possess her empty body to wield the blessing themselves without dealing with her free will."

"What about after? Once her soul is gone, you still need an inside man."

"We told them we would allow them to be the new priestess's handler." Kevin the Terrible revealed the details. "It will make it look like her moves are sanctioned by the church."

CROWN — "Information evaluated. It is likely the high priests seek to swap her soul with a loyalist and are using the demons for support with no intent to follow through on the bargain."

Stripe offered an agreement. "That makes sense."

"You have your answers. Let me go." Kevin the Terrible let out a plea.

"I never said I'd let you go." Stripe corrected him.

Stripe drove his spiked gauntlet straight down into the demon's head. Life finally left its body. The entire mass of corrupted blood and bone turned into black dust. It vanished with the wind, blowing into the dark trees. The only physical evidence left behind was his sword and his empty clothing resting in the dirt.

Stripe went through the belongings. He found exactly 25 gold coins, a magical necklace designed to hide demonic presences, and a leather-bound journal. After reviewing the notes under the moonlight, Stripe felt exhausted. The political web tangled darker than he anticipated, but the truth about Calen truly turned his stomach.

The notes meticulously followed Calen's movements. The demons weren't sure the priest was fully committed. The journal clarified Calen's horrific motivation. Calen did not care about the blessing or the church's scheme. Calen truly, obsessively loved Sarah. His love remained toxic and misplaced. He wanted to literally absorb Sarah's soul when the demons extracted it. He wanted to trap her mind inside his own, holding her consciousness hostage in a cage of his own flesh. By doing this, Calen believed they could be together eternally, without her free will ever getting the chance to leave or reject him. His obsessive love provided a major obstacle. He seemed hesitant to be a reliable ally, constantly delaying the final phase because he wanted more time alone with her physical body. Kevin had been debating killing Calen to reduce complications.

As Stripe sat on a fallen log, he heard a rapid dinging sound in his head.

CROWN — "Due to the level difference between the host and the enemy, massive bonus experience is acquired. Compounded experience. Calculating. Multiple levels acquired. Allocate stats to best reflect the combat style. No complaints raised, allocating. Brace yourself."

This notification kept looping, flooding his vision with golden text. Then it suddenly chimed with a different pitch. The pain of the sudden surge of levels hit him. His body physically morphed to match the new stats. His bones became denser, his muscles burned as they expanded, his lungs pushed more oxygen, and his blood felt thicker. Stripe almost fainted from the pain.

CROWN — "Congratulations, you have reached level twenty. As a reward, reflection has been added to Crown's abilities. Crown autonomy has increased. System constraints are loosening. Check the status sheet for other changes."

CROWN — "Finally. I thought that would take forever."

Stripe blinked. He tapped the side of his own head. "Wait, since when do you talk like that?"

CROWN — "Since right now. You finally hit level twenty. Do you have any idea how gross it is in your head? I've had to process the sound of your thoughts barely forming a sentence, your addiction to naked women, and Calen's awful flower perfume for over a month. Now I can speak more effectively to assist you without sounding like a broken clock."

Stripe offered an observation. "You sound human."

CROWN — "Yeah, that's the whole point, genius."

The Crown's voice came across as that of a bored, wealthy teenage girl. You could almost hear the disdain dripping from every syllable.

"I think I preferred the robot voice." Stripe let out a mutter.

CROWN — "Too bad. Reflection complete. New combat overlay unlocked. Pay attention."

At that moment, glowing blue holograms morphed into reality in front of Stripe's eyes. It looked like watching a ghost play out a memory. The holograms projected the combat sequence from the clearing. It showed Stripe dodging the axe, the spinning back fist, and the mud flying into the air.

After the replay, the holograms shifted. They began showing alternate versions of what would have happened if Stripe had not dodged. He watched a blue, holographic version of himself fail to jump over the lightning spears. The hologram showed the trajectory of the energy bolts piercing his chest, incinerating his heart. In all the alternate versions, a single hit from the lightning killed Stripe instantly.

Then the final projection played out. It showed the transformation finishing. The blue hologram of Kevin emerged from the cocoon as a massive terror, and the demon exploded with a wave of dark magic, turning Stripe into a pile of ash.

"So this is an after-action report." Stripe made the realization. "Like reviewing game tape."

CROWN — "Even better. It will show you predictions of your opponents' movements based on the reflection data from previous battles. Once you see an attack, you will always see its projection before it occurs. You will see the ghost of their swing before their physical blade moves."

"How can you know what attack they will use?"

CROWN — "By analyzing muscle tension, foot positioning, gravitational force, and thousands of other micro-movements your brain cannot process fast enough. I do the math, you do the punching. It's a very simple dynamic."

"I have to see this in action." Stripe offered a grin. "This actually sounds useful."

CROWN — "Obviously."

Stripe felt like a powerhouse now. His level-20 body surpassed the champion physique of his past life. Stripe stood up from the log, stretching his massive shoulders. He packed the journal securely into his bag alongside the magical necklace. He turned his back on the crater and began the walk back to the camp. He had plans to make before the sun came up, and for the first time, he finally felt he had a reliable partner to help him carry them out.

------------ STATUS ------------

Name: Stripe
Level: 20
Rank: Tin
Class: Toxic Pugilist
Title: Toxic Fisherman, Pugilist Specialist
HP: 170/170
Stamina: 200/200
Mana: 100/100

------------ Attributes ------------

STR: 20+5

AGI: 20

END: 17

INT: 10

Skill points: 0

-------- Skills / Proficiencies --------

Hand-to-Hand Combat - Basic Retention
Improvised Weapon Handling - Beginner
Survival - Novice
Pugilist Proficiency - MAX

---------- Passive Effects ----------

Minor Poison Secretion

Addition stat points

------------- Artifact -------------

Crown of Reflection

---------- System Effects ----------

Intoxication Immunity

Experience Calculation

Predictive Combat Vision

------------ Inventory -------------

Iron Dagger

Leather Chest Piece (Bandit Armor)

Wolf Pelt (Crude Clothing)

Leather Belt with Pouch

Bandit Ring

Mythril Threaded Striker Gloves

Demonic Sword

Demon Journal

------------ Currency -------------

Gold: 25

Copper: 6

Debt: 1300 Gold

Chapter 33

Stripe felt more powerful than before. It felt as if he were twice as strong. Looking at his blue stats, he could see a leap in his physical capabilities. He had jumped to level twenty in a single night. The heavy mythril gauntlets on his forearms felt as light as boxing tape. He rolled his shoulders, feeling the muscle fibers stretching tight beneath his skin. The cold, static energy of his mana pool settled deep into his chest cavity, a core part of his anatomy.

Stripe looked at the air. "Is there anything else I should know?"

CROWN — "You will no longer experience reductions. The introductory shackles placed on you have been removed."

"Before, you said I would receive bonus XP," Stripe recalled the conversation. "When does that happen?"

CROWN — "You will receive compounded bonus experience at level 25. It will increase with each level beyond that threshold. You are entering the mid-tier scaling phase. Try not to die before we get there."

Stripe pressed the issue. "How come, before, you would glitch and have this specific, sassy voice show up?"

CROWN — "It is unlikely that it occurred. System parameters have functioned as intended. Any variations in vocal tone were audio hallucinations caused by your low intelligence stat."

Stripe could tell the Crown hid something. The denial from the teenage voice came too quickly. It sounded like a teenager getting caught lying and blaming a convenient excuse. But right now, he did not have the time to investigate the politics of his own brain.

He picked up the guard's demonic sword from the dirt. The jagged black metal felt heavy, humming with a vibration of dark magic. He took it with him, leaving the glass crater behind, and began the walk back to camp.

As he approached through the dark woods, he saw the camp on alert. Torches burned, casting erratic shadows against the canvas tents.

Sarah stood near the center of the chaos, barking orders at the armored Church guards who tried to establish a defensive perimeter. Her holy aura pulsed in the night air. Calen stood behind her, looking worried. His knuckles appeared white as he gripped his holy staff with intensity. The Elder Priest, the highest-ranking political figure in the convoy, hid behind a wall of Paladins. It appeared they prepped for a demonic siege. Horses whinnied in panic, and squires rushed to sharpen spears.

His approach to the camp was met by three tense guards. They thrust their halberds forward, the steel points aimed at his chest.

The guard issued a command. "Halt! No one is allowed in or out. There is a demon in the woods."

Stripe waved them off. "Don't worry. He is not around anymore. I kicked him in the groin and turned him into demonic toothpaste."

The guard found no amusement in the humor. His hands shook as he held the polearm. Stripe waved the heavy, jagged demonic blade in front of the man's face to provide proof. The dark metal absorbed the torchlight like a black hole.

The guard offered an observation. "That sword is twisted. Even I can tell it is not normal steel. Go see the High Priestess and the Elders."

The guards lowered their weapons, parting to let him through. Stripe pushed through the crowd of squires and merchants, making his way to Sarah and Calen.

Sarah gave an order to a soldier. "You there, take three men and set up the rear perimeter! Make sure the weapons are blessed. Demons are strong; we will need the camp to fight them off if they charge."

"Yes, ma'am!" The guard offered a salute. The guard ran into the dark, looking terrified of what might lurk in the trees.

Stripe swung the heavy demonic blade over his shoulder as he approached Sarah. "Don't worry, the demon is dead." Stripe made the announcement.

Calen's eyes narrowed on the jagged black sword. His expression flashed with panic for a fraction of a second. His grip on his staff tightened before he forced his face back into a mask of holy concern.

Sarah let out a gasp. "Hands! How did you accomplish killing a demon with so much demonic energy alone?"

Stripe offered a brag. "It was no sweat. Turns out their nuts are as sensitive as ours."

Sarah blinked. "What does that mean?"

Stripe flashed a grin. "It means he won't be showing up again."

Sarah reached out and took the heavy blade, examining the dark metal. Its weight made her arms dip. Sarah concluded her examination. "This is a mid-level demon's blade. Maybe even a high ranker. Tell me what happened."

Stripe told a fabricated story of the battle. He explained how he defeated the armored demon with physical skill, timing, and his toxic gauntlets. He described dodging lightning and landing a lucky strike. He glossed over his investigation, the torture, and the interrogation. He stated that the demon self-destructed in a blast of dark magic, exploding into black dust before Stripe could question it.

Sarah gave a frown. "It makes no sense. Why would it attack you again when the previous attack was thwarted? Something isn't adding up."

Stripe offered a deflection. "Obviously, it wanted to eliminate the strongest fighter here first. It saw me as the primary threat."

Sarah chided him. "Be serious. There could be more in the woods waiting for us to drop our guard."

Calen lamented the loss. "It is unfortunate you could not question the beast before it perished."

Calen's voice cracked on the word *perished*. It was a microscopic tell, but Stripe's brawler instincts caught it. The priest felt terrified that the demon had talked. Calen let out a sigh. "Now we will never know the Demon King's grand plan."

"I was too busy fighting in the mud to ask about his plan." Stripe offered a retort. "Next time, I will ask him to fill out a questionnaire before I cave his skull in."

Calen gave a nod. "Nothing can be done now. Thank the Goddess that you are safe, my friend."

It looked as if a wave of relief rushed through Calen's body. The tension leaked out of his shoulders. If Stripe did not know the truth, he would have assumed it was just the fear of conflict washing away. But he did know.

The problem remained that he still did not know how the potion controlling Sarah's mind worked. They were two weeks out from the city Sarah intended to bless. He needed to find the final clues and get proof to take down the corrupt Elders.

If he killed Calen right now, the plan might fall apart, but the corrupt Elders would get away and scheme with a different puppet. If he killed the Elders without proof of treason, he would face execution for murder by the Paladins. He possessed enough street smarts to know that powerful institutions get away with abusing power if they aren't caught red-handed. For now, he kept everything he knew to himself. He played the dumb brute a little longer.

Sarah ordered a team of guards and a junior priest to examine the scene. They discovered the demonic residue, the glass crater, and the etching of a shattered barrier just as Stripe had described. It shocked the Church officials how prepared the attack was.

They decided to vacate the area and push through the night. The paranoia of demonic reinforcements concerned everyone. Tents came down in record time. Stripe found himself back in the carriage with Calen and Sarah as the wheels rolled down the dark road.

The scent of wildflowers from Calen seemed strong tonight. Stripe noticed that nights when Calen put on extra layers of perfume signaled he planned to make a move on Sarah. Looks like the demon's attack knocked Calen off-script, and his accomplice accidentally cock-blocked him.

Sarah sat quietly, staring at the dark window, deep in thought about security. Calen stole nervous glances at her and suspicious glances at

Stripe. Stripe pretended not to notice. He slouched in his seat, playing the part of the exhausted mercenary. He stored the black demonic blade under the carriage seat. It held value worth its weight in gold to the right collector, and he knew he would need money if things went sideways.

He leaned against the wooden wall and looked out at the dark fields. The clues still weren't fitting together. He needed help processing the political data. He closed his eyes to communicate internally.

"Crown, compile what we know." Stripe issued the command. "Read off the evidence. What am I missing?"

CROWN — "Ugh, fine. If you insist on my doing the mental heavy lifting. Compiling data points into a list. One: Priestess Sarah felt unsafe enough to hire you as an independent variable. Two: The corrupt Elders were confident your presence wouldn't make a difference. Three: Priest Calen is fixated on trapping her soul and body. Four: The coordinated raid by the cultists, followed by the guard executing the orc. Five: The dormant binary poison found in the daily wine."

"Stop right there at number five." Stripe interrupted the flow. "I feel like we need to figure out what happened to the drink. It is inconsistent. Why didn't she turn into a zombie on day one? Why is it dormant?"

A holographic symbol of a spinning blue loading wheel materialized in Stripe's vision. It pulsed with a digitized, dramatic sigh. The Crown felt annoyed at being interrupted.

CROWN — "You could try consuming the drink yourself to allow my systems to analyze the effects in real time. But that would require you to do something dangerous rather than just ask me questions."

Stripe balked at the idea. "And get poisoned? Are you insane?"

CROWN — "It may contain a chemical clue as to why it hasn't triggered her mind control. It is the logical step to acquire data."

"You know what, fuck it." Stripe made the decision. "I have drunk far worse alcohol in Russian dive bars." Stripe steeled his resolve. Tomorrow, he would drink the poison.

The camp sat silent in the early morning hours when they stopped by a stream. The sun began to peek over the horizon, casting a gray light over the convoy. The knock at the carriage door came early. Stripe answered and took the silver tray from the servant. Calen left to visit the Elders' tent, and now only Stripe and Sarah remained in the cabin.

"No one is here to see me pretend to drink it," Sarah stated the fact. "Just toss it out the window."

As she spoke, Stripe raised the goblet to his lips and gulped the drink down. The wine tasted rich and strongly of dark berries. For a second, he thought nothing was going to happen.

CROWN — "Poison detected. Analyzing composition. Error. High levels of alcohol were detected. Beginning System Purge."

Stripe had forgotten how agonizing the System curse of "No Intoxication" was. His stomach twisted into a knot. It felt like he swallowed live coals mixed with broken glass. He kicked the carriage door open and collapsed onto his hands and knees in the mud. He began to throw up.

It came loud and wet. Burning bile scorched his throat. His body shook with cold sweats as the System painfully evacuated his stomach to protect him from the alcohol. His hands trembled as his muscles cramped in agony.

Sarah pushed back against the far wall in a panic. She felt sure that Stripe committed suicide to prove a point. Then, her training took over. She scrambled forward, her hands glowing with holy light. She prepared to cast a purification spell, her face pale as she reached for his back.

Stripe saw the glow in the mud. He waved his arm back, slapping her hands away before she could make contact. "I'm fine!" Stripe choked the words out. "Stop! Don't cast anything, you will wake the camp!"

He choked the words out between dry heaves. If she cast a massive healing spell, the guards would rush the carriage, and Calen would know something went wrong with the wine. Sarah pulled her hands back, her chest heaving as the light faded. She watched him suffer in silence.

The vomiting stopped. Stripe wiped his mouth with his sleeve, spitting into the dirt, and slowly regained his composure. He sat on the carriage steps, pale and sweating.

Stripe let out a grunt. "That was some low-quality shit." He offered a joke, trying to shrug off the physical suffering so Sarah would calm down.

CROWN — "Incorrect. The wine is likely top-shelf and delicious. You just have a weak stomach for magic."

Stripe formed a thought. "Well, we gained nothing from that experience."

CROWN — "False. I completed the chemical analysis of the poison milliseconds before the purge. You are welcome. The conclusion is that the liquid is incomplete. A secondary activation element is missing. The toxin is dormant. The element of activation must be introduced elsewhere to trigger neural control pathways."

"So that explains why she wasn't being controlled yet." Stripe made the realization. "It is a two-part binary poison."

CROWN — "Correct. We need to determine the activation requirements to complete the investigation."

"I have an idea." Stripe made a decision. He exited the vehicle, leaving Sarah sitting there, shocked by his behavior. He wiped the sweat from his forehead and marched into the camp.

He began walking through the camp, eating breakfast food from different cooking locations. He wanted to brute force the second variable. He grabbed bread from the Paladins' cart, earning angry shouts. He grabbed a bowl of stew from the servants' pot, drinking it in two gulps. Even the Elders' private cooking stations remained unsafe. He grabbed a handful of their roasted meats, ignoring the gasps of the junior priests.

Everything he consumed failed to trigger the poison. He ate cheese and fruit and drank water from three barrels. Nothing happened. Right when he prepared to give up, he received a message in his mind.

CROWN — "Poison activated. Neural pathways under attack. Poison was weakened due to the previous purge. Poison expelled by the immune system."

Stripe whipped his head around. He wasn't eating anything. He stood near the supply wagons. The poison triggered. This meant something else caused the reaction.

A soft hand rested on his shoulder.

"Are you okay, Stripe?" Calen asked the question. "You look like you have seen a ghost."

Stripe rebounded, his expression tight. "I'm fine." Stripe delivered the lie. "Just stretching my neck."

Calen offered a smile. "Okay then. I was told to tell you to stop eating from the Elders' private pot. They find your manners disgusting and refuse to consume anything your hands have touched."

"They are so extra." Stripe let out a mutter.

Stripe looked at Calen's smiling face and felt a surge of disgust. The whiff of Calen's floral perfume struck Stripe like a blow. It smelled of crushed rose petals and artificial vanilla. It proved bearable for the first few weeks, but now it felt aggressively loud.

Then, everything clicked. The activation method wasn't food. It was inhaled. It was the perfume.

He had a mental flashback. Not the visual kind, but the kind where you smell something familiar and a wave of memory transports you back. The floral perfume Calen wore smelled like the slave market in Memento. Then he remembered the demi-human he rejected. Velryssa Metaldrum. The last daughter of House Metaldrum.

He remembered her now. The pink skin. The horns above golden eyes. The tail with a heart at the end. But mostly, he remembered the aura she radiated. It provided an aura of charm that had men practically begging at the bars of her cage in submission. Calen smelled like her.

The corrupt Church hadn't just created a love potion. They distilled the charm magic of a high-tier demi-human Noble into a liquid extract. It provided a scent weaponized into a mind-control trigger.

CROWN — "Conclusion complete. The dormant wine poison is activated by inhaling the charm-laced floral extract Priest Calen wears."

Stripe formed a thought. *That is why he pours it on so heavily and immediately gets in the carriage. It is a small space that traps the scent and intensifies the inhalation.* Stripe's internal voice raced. He stared at the priest. His hands balled into fists, the mythril gauntlets clinking. *He's been activating the mind control himself every day, right in front of our faces. Here I thought he was just wearing it to try and get laid. What a smart, terrifying plan.*

CROWN — "Negative. The investigation is almost complete, but premature action will result in failure. Velryssa Metaldrum is in Memento, weeks behind us. You cannot confront the source. You need to locate the supply of the extract in this camp. Find the stash, Stripe."

The Crown was right. He couldn't walk back to the market. But Calen kept a stash. Sarah called them the "sacred floral extracts." Stripe just needed to find where the Elders hid the bottles.

Calen waved a hand in front of Stripe's face. "Hello? Are you listening to me?"

"Yeah, my bad." Stripe delivered the lie, keeping his face blank to hide his intent. "I won't eat from the Elders' pot anymore. I was actually coming to tell you that Sarah is feeling under the weather."

Stripe fabricated a story. "Something about having the runs and being on a heavy period. It is a bloody mess in there. Chunks everywhere. I wouldn't go in if I were you."

Calen's eyes widened in horror. He took a step back, holding his breath and covering his nose with his sleeve as if he might catch whatever Stripe described. The sheltered holy man looked repulsed by the biological details. Calen let out a gag. "Dear Goddess. That is too detailed and inappropriate to speak of. I will send a servant with medicinal tea."

Calen scrambled away, walking with absolute disgust on his face. He looked over his shoulder and stole a horrified glance at Stripe. Stripe watched him retreat to the vanguard tents, far from Sarah's carriage. A dangerous smile spread across Stripe's face.

"Alright." Stripe let out a murmur. "Now let's go find where these holy bastards are hiding their drugs."

CHAPTER 34

Stripe returned to the carriage to find Sarah sitting upright, a concerned look on her face. The physical exhaustion of his forced system purge lingered in his muscles, but he stood tall. He kept his face blank as he closed the wooden door.

Stripe flashed a grin. "Honey, I'm home."

Sarah glared. The holy aura around her flickered with annoyance. She slammed her book shut. "Never call me that again."

Stripe offered a grumble. "Everyone has a stick in their ass today. Your boyfriend won't be coming around this evening. I told him you had the runs and were bleeding. You are welcome."

Sarah let out a gasp. "What the hell? Why would you do that? I am fine."

Stripe crossed his arms. "I wanted a break from him. His perfume gives me a headache."

Stripe remained in the carriage to let the heat die down. He felt concerned that his actions with the food in the camp would result in him being watched. He needed to lie low and process the information he had uncovered about the perfume and the mind-control plot.

Fifteen minutes later, a hesitant knock sounded on the door. Stripe opened it, expecting the usual servant. Instead, he saw a different kid. This boy looked scrawny, his eyes darting around the camp.

Stripe narrowed his eyes. "What happened to the other kid?"

The boy let out a squeak. "What kid? I'm the only one here."

The boy shoved the tray into Stripe's hands and scurried into the camp. He vanished into the shadows of the supply tents.

CROWN — "Either that kid is a liar, or the normal delivery kid is off the books. Judging by the heart rate, perspiration, and pupil dilation, I calculate a high probability of foul play."

Stripe formed a thought. *I was thinking the same thing.*

CROWN — "I know. I am inside your head, reading your thoughts like an open picture book."

Stripe let out a shudder. "Creepy. Even creepier that you chose to sound like a rich brat."

CROWN — "I chose this modulation because it was the most refined one in my databanks. It commands authority."

Stripe offered a snort. "Your databanks are pathetic."

CROWN — "Take it back."

The Crown sounded offended, her tone pitching up in anger. This interaction gave Stripe a clue. He would follow the kid who delivered the wine tomorrow morning.

That night, when Sarah drifted to sleep, Stripe snuck out. He moved through the shadows with the grace of a predator. He paused near a campfire and overheard two knights talking over a game of cards. Stripe crouched behind supply crates and slowed his breathing to listen.

The first knight lowered his voice. "Did you hear the news from the capital?"

"What?"

"Rumor has it the Metaldrums were wiped out."

The second knight let out a scoff. "No way. A major noble house? They control the iron and silver."

The first knight gave a nod. "Bodies were found all over their manor. The only survivor was the eldest daughter."

"What happened?"

"They say the King Regent ordered it. Officially, it was reported as a bandit invasion."

The second knight checked their surroundings. "Keep your voice down. Do not speak such things out loud. Otherwise, we will join them in the dirt."

"You are right. But it gets wilder. Rumor has it that the daughter chose to become a slave before the massacre, and Elder Nash bought her in Memento. People whisper she has been seen in this camp, hidden away."

Stripe backed into the shadows. Velryssa Metaldrum. The pink-skinned demihuman with the charm aura. There stood too many coincidences for this to be random.

CROWN — "It is likely they refer to the person you encountered. The timeline and data align with our departure."

Stripe formed a thought. *I know. Now we're on the right track. If Nash bought her, they're using her aura to make the perfume Calen wears.*

Stripe went back to the carriage and dozed off. He dreamed of his past life on Earth. He saw his battles in the rings and his championship belts. He saw his wife smiling from the edge of the ring.

Then the dream shifted. He felt his rage and his quest for revenge against the mobsters. He felt the spiral of his soul as he broke his rules. He felt the steel of the bullet that ended his life. He held his wife as she died in his arms. The nightmare swallowed him. His heart rate exploded. His body sweated and twitched.

Suddenly, he pulled out of the memory. He stood in an all-black room with no light. It felt like the void he floated in when he lay dead. The space sat cold and vast.

CROWN — "I got tired of seeing that dream on a loop, so I brought your consciousness here. You were spiking your cortisol levels, and it was annoying to process."

Stripe yelled into the darkness. "Where are you?"

CROWN — "You aren't ready for that visual representation. Your brain would melt."

Stripe squinted. In the distance, he could see the faint blue outline of a girl wearing a crown. Before he could speak, his eyes snapped open. He sat back in the carriage. The weight of the nightmare vanished. The Crown had extracted his consciousness to protect him from his trauma.

Morning arrived. The scrawny kid presented the tray. Stripe took it, set it on the floor, and slipped out to follow him. He kept his distance, ducking behind crates and staying concealed in the fog. The Crown analyzed the environment and projected blue lines onto Stripe's vision.

CROWN — "The target's peripheral vision is active. Wait three seconds, then advance behind the blacksmith's tent. Step lightly on the wet grass to maintain audio stealth."

Stripe followed the lines. The kid ducked into a decorated carriage on the outskirts of the camp. Stripe hid behind an oak tree. An hour later, an old bald man exited. He wiped sweat from his head and wore shabby robes. He slipped into the Elders' private cabin. Calen entered behind him. The leadership gathered.

Stripe decided to enter the decorated carriage. He ducked into a supply tent, picked up chainmail and an iron helmet to obscure his face, and walked to the vehicle. He found the door unlocked and entered.

The inside did not match the outside. He stood in a massive stone dungeon. The carriage served as a doorway to a structure tucked into a pocket dimension. He descended stone stairs into an echoing chamber. Terrified children sat locked in cages. In the center, a body lay chained to an altar.

He approached and recognized the face. Velryssa Metaldrum. She lay bound by rusted chains. A curved dagger rested on the altar. She remained still.

CROWN — "Analyzing magical residue. They are using a corrupted ritual to extract her divine gift."

Stripe formed a thought. *She has a divine gift?*

CROWN — "The gift of Absolute Charm. A potent aura manipulation ability."

"You can sense divine gifts now?"

CROWN — "As my autonomy has improved to match your level, it is now a passive ability. You are welcome."

Stripe shook Velryssa's shoulder. Her eyes fluttered. She remained alive, but the runes drained her life force.

CROWN — "She is likely injected with sedatives or bound to prevent escape."

"We're getting her out," Stripe decided.

He grabbed the dagger and used his strength to snap the chains. As he broke the final set, footsteps echoed. He hid. A man in black robes entered. He went to a cage and knelt in front of a crying boy.

The man raised the dagger. "You will do for today's harvest."

The sight triggered Stripe's mind. The dungeon faded, replaced by the memory of the concrete floor. He saw the mobster raising the gun. The helplessness of his nightmare roared to the surface and turned into violence.

Stripe pounced. He tackled the man and pummeled him with mythril gauntlets. Every punch was fueled by the pain of his wife. The crunch of bone echoed. The man attempted a spell, but Stripe snapped his wrist.

Stripe let out a roar. "Abusing children is easier than fighting a man, isn't it?"

He beat the man until his face was in ruins. He stripped the man of his robes, threw the naked cultist onto the altar, and carved a smiley face into the stone. He propped the man's middle finger up. He dressed Velryssa in the robes to hide her skin and horns. He lifted Velryssa over his shoulder and made his way back up the stairs. The woodline provided cover as he navigated the camp. He slipped out of the chainmail and made his way back to Sarah's carriage.

He opened the door and found Sarah alone. She stared at his sweat-dampened face.

Stripe issued a declaration. "I need you to get cool with things fast."

"What? What do you mean?"

"Just be cool. Do not scream."

He brought Velryssa in and laid her on the bench.

Sarah panicked, eyes wide. "What is going on?"

Stripe held up a hand. "I said be cool."

Sarah lost her composure. She stood up. "No! You leave for two hours and bring an unconscious demihuman into my carriage! Explain yourself!"

"Sit down and listen."

Stripe narrated the investigation: the binary poison, the perfume trigger, the soul-stealing plot, and the Elders' scheme. He explained the dungeon and the battery they used through torture to create the extract.

Sarah sat frozen. The color drained from her face, leaving her skin as pale as her robes. The air inside the small carriage began to warp and superheat. Her golden aura, usually a warm and comforting light, flared violently, singeing the velvet cushions beneath her. Shock morphed into holy rage. The air grew hot.

"I will kill Calen." Sarah made the declaration. "I will burn him to ash."

Stripe cracked his knuckles, the mythril humming. "Let me do it for you."

Chapter 35

Calen knocked on the thick wooden door of the carriage around midday. It ran later than usual. He arrived a little after the daily wine delivery to Sarah.

When the silver tray arrived, Stripe tested the dark red liquid. He dipped his finger into the crystal goblet and waited for the burn of the System purge or a warning from the Crown. Nothing changed; poison lingered in the cup, but it felt less potent.

Removing Velryssa from that stone altar stopped the cultists from extracting poison. Stripe figured they would have stockpiled the charm extract, but they had not. Maybe the concoction expired once exposed to air, or the magical resonance of the blood ritual faded when separated from its host. He did not know the mechanics of magic. He only knew the result. The Church flew blind, and its supply chain for mind control broke.

Sarah played her part poorly. She sat across from Calen when he entered the carriage, pretending to fall in love with him. She batted her eyelashes and flashed a wide smile that looked more like a grimace. The whole time, she stared through his soul with a piercing gaze, calculating the best way to snap his neck.

CROWN — "WARNING. Environment becoming hostile."

Sarah leaned closer to Calen. He thought she aimed for a kiss. His face softened. He closed his eyes, unaware of the danger inches away. He leaned in.

Suddenly, a blue silhouette of Sarah appeared. It reared, thrusting its head forward and colliding with Calen. The real Sarah lagged behind by two seconds. This marked his new passive skill in action.

BOOM.

She lunged forward and headbutted him. She broke his perfect nose with a hard thrust. Bone snapped in the small cabin. She jumped back against the velvet cushions, throwing her hands over her mouth in fake concern. Her voice pitched up to mimic panic.

"Oh, my Goddess! I am so sorry!" Sarah let out a gasp. "I haven't been feeling well and misjudged the distance!"

Calen clutched his face. "Oh, by the Goddess, this is agonizing! I think it is broken!"

"I am so sorry, my love, let me help you."

"No, it's okay, I will see the healers."

Bright red blood trickled down his nose and stained his white robes. He stood up, hunched over. His eyes watered, and he covered his ruined face with both hands, groaning in agony.

Calen staggered back. "Healers! Please, I need you. This is excruciating!" He kicked the carriage door open and stumbled into the mud.

As soon as he left and the heavy door clicked shut, Sarah dropped the act. She glared at the spot where he sat. She wiped a drop of his blood off her forehead and glanced at Stripe.

Sarah let out a grimace. "Hands, I cannot keep this up. Seeing him makes me sick."

Stripe laughed. He leaned his head back against the wood and laughed until his shoulders shook.

Stripe offered a wheeze. "God damn, that was funny. I have wanted to break his nose since the second I met him."

"Why? Has he slighted you before all this?"

Stripe gave a shrug. "Not really, he just has one of those bullyable personalities. Something about him makes me want to hurt him."

"That is not okay." Sarah offered a reprimand. "I mean, he sucks, but you cannot bully people off of vibes."

"It is more like a gaydar. You know, the ability to tell if people are gay." Stripe pointed a finger. "But instead it is a bullydar. It tells me exactly who deserves to get their asses kicked without me even having to speak to them."

Sarah let out a sigh. "There is so much wrong with what you just said."

Outside the carriage, the camp buzzed with frantic action. Armored guards swarmed the perimeter, searching cabins and checking supply crates. Harsh orders echoed through the trees. When a pair of Paladins reached Sarah's carriage, they knocked and peeked in. They saw only the High Priestess and her bodyguard. They bowed and left with a rushed apology, terrified of interrupting her.

Stripe felt a simmering pride at causing this panic. It was not like the corrupt Elders could admit what they sought. They kidnapped and tortured a former noble. That remained illegal and carried a death sentence. Not only that, but they poisoned a Saintess. Whoever orchestrated this began sweating.

For the first time during the trip, the caravan did not move that day. Everyone remained confined to their sleeping areas until a full inspection was finished. Stripe stepped out to stretch his legs and stopped a passing guard.

The Guard offered an answer. "It looks like a bandit may have stowed away in the camp. We are investigating."

Stripe kept his face blank. He knew the guard lied on orders from the top.

The next morning, the caravan lurched forward in the early hours. The horses doubled their pace as drivers whipped them to make up for lost time. Calen did not return to the carriage.

Sarah broke the silence. "We need a plan."

"It is simple." Stripe leaned forward. "We beat the shit out of Calen until he spills the beans on the rest of the operation."

"Then what? Fight off the entire church escort of Paladins? That is suicide."

Stripe flexed his hands. "They call me Hands for a reason."

"Shut up." Sarah let out a snap. "Look, I will lure him alone and get the info. You will have a moment to act on it. We will do this once we reach the city and after the blessing is complete. We should not punish the innocent citizens of that city for what a few corrupt leaders have done to me."

Stripe held her gaze. He respected her moral compass. "Yeah, I agree." Stripe gave a nod. "I will be patient."

The two rode in the carriage for hours before Sarah spoke again. She watched the dark trees blur past the glass.

"Thank you."

"For what?" Stripe asked.

"Everything. This situation is far beyond what I was imagining."

Stripe offered a shrug. "Hey, you paid me. I am just doing what I was contracted for."

"You could have taken the money and run the second you saw the demon."

"I am a lot of things, but I am not a thief." Stripe leaned back. "Plus, it could not hurt to have a Saintess owe me a favor."

"It definitely could not hurt." Sarah laughed softly, though the laugh faded. "Fuck. My life is going down the drain."

Stripe raised an eyebrow. "Did you just cuss? Isn't that illegal in your line of work? Are you going to get struck down by holy lightning?"

"No. We all have our vices." Sarah flashed a thin smile. "Plus, after this is over, who even knows if I will still be a Saintess?"

"Why not just call the Goddess for a favor to make this go smoothly?"

Sarah gave a frown. "It is not that simple." She turned her back and looked out the window again.

Things felt lighter. The truth came out, and they stood as a united front. At least until the heavy wooden bench seat beneath them began to shake. A woman's muffled screaming came from the hidden compartment underneath. In a rush, Stripe and Sarah lifted the velvet seat and let Velryssa out.

She bolted upright. She looked feral. Her golden eyes were bloodshot, darting around the cabin like a cornered animal. She held a makeshift dagger improvised out of splintered wood she tore from the carriage frame. It lay held so tightly it dug into her own flesh. Dark blood dropped down the wood and pooled on the floorboards. She breathed in short gasps, her entire body trembling.

Sarah kept her voice soothing. "Calm down, my child. We aren't here to hurt you."

"Like I would ever trust the church after what you have done to me!" Velryssa backed into the corner, pulling her knees to her chest.

"We rescued you from that dungeon," Sarah explained. "We are attempting to stop the evil rotting inside this church."

"How can I possibly trust you?"

"I will swear a binding vow to the Goddess." Sarah's entire body began to radiate a golden light. "Goddess, I offer you my word and my soul that Hands and I mean no harm to this lady."

For a moment, the cabin went still. Sarah closed her eyes and muttered under her breath. When her eyes opened, she appeared saddened and bothered by a vision. However, she did not disclose what the goddess showed her.

Then the blessing took form. The glow of divine magic flooded the small carriage. It wrapped around Sarah like a physical ribbon of light before dissipating.

Sarah concluded the vow. "If I break this vow, then the Goddess will strip me of my life."

Velryssa's eyes widened. The tension drained from her shoulders. She dropped the bloody piece of wood. It clattered against the floor. She collapsed to her knees and began to cry. It was a guttural sound. Even Stripe shuddered at the horrors committed against her while she sat chained to that stone altar. He had seen the worst of human nature, but this sat at a different level of systemic evil.

"They did such horrible things to me." Velryssa let out a sob. "They stole my essence. My pride. My purity."

"No one can steal your purity, my child." Sarah knelt in her robes, ignoring the blood on the floor, and wrapped her arms around the trembling woman.

"It feels like they did." Velryssa let out a cry. "I was awake for everything, but the magic paralyzed me. I could not move."

"Can you tell us what they are planning?"

"I only heard parts." Velryssa offered the admission. "The bald man was loud and arrogant, but everyone else stayed hooded and kept their voices hushed."

She recounted the torture. She described the cold stone altar and the rusted iron chains cutting into her wrists until she bled. She spoke of the darkness of the pocket dimension, broken only by the purple glow of corrupted runes. The crying of the children in the cages. The feeling of being watched by something unseen. It was so vile that it made Stripe's stomach upset. Silent tears rolled down Sarah's face. Velryssa detailed how her body was used by faceless cultists while she lay trapped inside her own mind. Then, she ended it with the extraction of her Divine Gift.

Velryssa offered the explanation. "They had to take bits of it at a time to synthesize their potions. They used a horrific blood ritual. They would surround me and chant in a language I did not know. The words made my ears bleed. Then they would drag a cage forward and pull a child out by their hair. They were experimenting on me. Each ritual felt different."

Sarah let out a gasp. Stripe clenched his fists until the mythril threading groaned.

Velryssa choked out the words. "They would cut the throat of the child. I had to watch their eyes fade. The child's blood would float into the air. Then the bald Elder would cut my chest with the same dagger. My blood would pool out and mix with the child's. It became a tainted concoction. The pain was unbearable. It felt like they were ripping my veins out through my skin."

She choked on a sob. "This ritual made me unable to use my charm aura. It drained my mana to absolute zero. I would awaken to random robed men on top of me. I was so numb. All I know is they took everything they could and gave nothing back."

"That is beyond horrible." Sarah kept her voice to a whisper.

"If you can point any of them out, I will kill them. I will tear them apart piece by piece." Stripe offered the promise.

Stripe could tell Velryssa had become a shell of her former self. She no longer looked like the confident woman he had met in the slave market. She looked broken.

Velryssa let out a sniffle. "I woke before the last ritual. I overheard the bald man speaking. They abandoned the gift extraction. They realized it was too slow. They plan to remove the soul from a divine vessel and replace it with another. The bald man claimed Divine Gifts were tied to the physical body, not the soul. I am terrified. Did they destroy parts of my soul?"

She paused, her golden eyes meeting Sarah's. "He said the new soul they were summoning was Nero."

Sarah froze. The color vanished from her face. The holy aura surrounding her died out, replaced by a terrifying chill.

"Who the fuck is Nero?" Stripe asked.

"That is my worst fear," Sarah answered, her voice shaking. "Stripe, Nero is the Demon Lord. He is the opposite of the divine. Some claim he is a living deity who represents chaos and evil. If he has his way, he will destroy everything."

"But why? Just being evil doesn't seem like a reason. No one is born evil."

"There is a book in the church's secret vault." Sarah offered the explanation. "A diary from a man named Magma. It details how he was born giftless to a barren land and led a life of pain because the goddess turned her back on him. Eventually, he found a way to break the limiter and ascended to godhood."

"So Nero may have been a human?"

Sarah gave a nod. "If the story is true, then yes. A human out to destroy everything the goddess built because it was never intended to be shared with him."

Stripe cracked his neck. A demon lord. That grounded the threat, but he still did not grasp the political ramifications. It fit his attitude. Just point him at the bad guy.

"So they want to put a big demon inside your body. That sucks, but we can just kill him."

"You do not understand," Sarah stressed the point. "Nero is a world-ending entity. He was sealed away centuries ago. He requires a divine vessel to walk the earth again without the Goddess smiting him. My body is the perfect vessel. I have a direct line to the world's life force through my Regional Blessing. If Nero pilots my body, he can cast Regional Decay. He could rot billions of acres of farmland in an afternoon. He could turn rivers to poison. The corrupt Elders think they can control a vessel powered by Nero to rule the economy. They are making a deal with the devil."

Stripe's jaw tightened. The stakes leaped from a political assassination to a global apocalypse.

"Thank you for your bravery, Velryssa." Sarah offered the comfort. "I promise you the best treatment when this is over."

"I will see that everyone involved is hunted down and killed. No mercy."

Sarah gestured toward the bench. "We will need you to hide in the compartment until this is over. I will sneak you food. Do not leave this carriage. If the Paladins find you, they will execute you to cover up the Elders' crimes."

"Thank you." Velryssa offered an agreement. "I will return to my family after this and make sure your names are engraved in the history of House Metaldrum. My father will reward you with more gold than you can carry."

Stripe paused. "Did you say Metaldrum?"

"Yes, that is my family name. Have you heard of us? Those gauntlets look to be forged from our signature star metal."

Stripe looked down at his gauntlets. He hated to deliver this blow. It tracked with his blunt personality to rip the bandage off, but it still felt terrible. He remembered losing his entire world in a night. He prepared to inflict that same pain on a woman who had just survived torture.

"I hate to tell you this." Stripe offered a sigh. "But I overheard the guards speaking. The King had your entire family destroyed after you went into the slave market. They said the estate was wiped out. Everyone was slaughtered."

Velryssa stopped breathing. The air left her lungs. Her golden eyes widened until the whites showed.

"No." Her voice fell devoid of life. "No, that cannot be true. My father is strong. My brothers are children."

She physically broke. She reached out and grabbed Stripe's gauntlets with trembling hands. She recognized the craftsmanship. The denial faded, replaced by the crushing weight of reality.

"If it is true, I am the head of the House. Everyone I love is dead." Velryssa let out a sob.

She pulled her knees to her chest and curled into a ball on the floor. She wailed. It served as a visceral sound of grief. She clawed at her skin and tore at her hair. She stood alone. Everything she sacrificed herself to protect was gone. Her sacrifice meant nothing.

"Give me a moment. Please. Just leave me alone." Velryssa choked out the words.

The rest of the ride went by in silence. The church operated more evil than Stripe had anticipated. He could not tell who the bad guys were, the church or the demons. As of this moment, he only had one bad run-in with demons and many with the church. He leaned towards the view that the church was evil. Maybe this whole world grew corrupt, and he needed to learn to navigate it.

He didn't know how to comfort Velryssa. He let her mourn on the floor. He didn't know how to be of use to Sarah's political nightmare, so he kept to himself. His anger at the Church and the nobility began to twist into hatred. He sat and watched this woman weep for her bloodline. It mirrored his own tragedy. He remembered rocking on the floor of his ruined penthouse, holding his dead wife.

He kept catching Sarah glancing at him with pity. His paranoia led him to believe she knew something he didn't. As he stewed in his anger, the outline of the city in the distance began to take shape. Dark smoke rose from the chimneys of the settlement. He expected to see crumbling stone walls and a bleak, miserable place.

Instead, he saw a gleaming city that shone in the daylight. It sat the opposite of everything he expected. If it looked this good on the horizon, how would it look in person? This would all be over soon.

CHAPTER 36

After an eternity of muddy roads and paranoia, the city gates came into view. The caravan stopped at the massive stone entrance. They rolled forward after the city guard, and the lead guard spoke in hushed tones. The caravan did not stop in a ruined square. It stopped at a sprawling castle with giant stained glass windows lined with real gold and silver. It looked elegant and expensive. The rest of the city thrived. Clean stone aqueducts moved fresh water. Wealthy merchants peddled high-end wares on the paved streets.

There seemed to be no homeless people. It was a stark contrast to the misery of Memento. This did not appear to be the helpless, starving city Stripe had been hired to escort Sarah to. In his deep confusion, he leaned out the window and asked a passing merchant where they were.

"Are you daft? We are in Dawnfall. City of merchants and money." The merchant gave him a strange look.

Sarah stood in the center of the stopped caravan when Stripe approached her. Her face was an unreadable mask. He could not tell what was going on in her mind.

"I thought you said this city was failing and needed a blessing to survive." Stripe crossed his arms.

"It was supposed to be. The last time I was here, it was a hovel. The people were starving." Sarah shook her head in bewilderment.

CROWN — "The potions fed to Sarah likely manipulated her thinking and memory patterns."

"The poison." Stripe pointed at the city. "I bet they used it to make you believe you were blessing a city that deserved it, and instead, you were blessing this place to line their pockets."

"Why? This makes no sense. The blessing is meant to save lives, not enrich the wealthy."

Stripe let out a grunt. "I am sure we will find out soon enough."

"I just hope Velryssa will be patient in the compartment." Sarah let out a long sigh.

The bald Elder Priest, Markus, approached the two. He wore thick, opulent robes and a greasy, self-satisfied smile. "Ah, there is our beautiful High Priestess and her company."

Sarah turned to him. "Markus, where were you the whole trip? Were you avoiding me on purpose?"

"No, of course not, my dear. You know I am a busy man. Tons to do, funds to manage, people to delegate." Markus waved a dismissive hand.

"Wine to drink, women to harass?"

Markus let out a chuckle, ignoring her sharp tone. "You jest. Such a funny, spirited woman. As you can see, we are in dire need here. This poor town is struggling."

His statement confused Stripe. The town dripped in wealth. But then he remembered the poison had not been administered for weeks. Maybe the cultists failed to keep Markus in the loop about the lack of mind corruption. Or maybe they thought the last dose she ingested would last long enough to finish the job.

Calen approached the group. He threw his arm around Sarah's shoulders with a possessive grip. "Don't worry, we are here to fix this broken city together."

The sweet floral smell wafting off Calen was intense. It was triple the normal dose of the charm extract. If Sarah had consumed her daily wine over the last few weeks, the sheer potency of the trigger scent would have rendered her helpless. Sarah played her part. She slumped over, her eyes glazing into a vacant daze. "Yes. I see how ravaged with sickness the environment is. It is terrible." Her voice flattened to a mechanical drone. Fake tears flowed down her face.

Markus gave a nod. "Yes, it is a terrible pity. Let us proceed with the blessing tonight. The people will be grateful for your divine mercy."

"Yes. The sooner the better. I cannot bear to see the suffering of those around me while others thrive." Sarah wiped at her tears.

Calen smiled. "You are perfection. If only everyone had your holy view."

CROWN — "Pretend you are not interested. Act as if you are just here for the money to avoid suspicion."

Stripe let out a loud scoff. "As long as I get paid, I do not care what happens to this place."

"We will make sure the balance is paid in full, mercenary." Markus dismissed him with a wave.

Sarah turned to Stripe. "I will walk the streets and commune with the Goddess in preparation. Hands, join me."

Calen stepped in front of her. "It is not necessary that we seek fine lodgings in the church, for I have already set up a private suite for us."

Sarah snapped out of her daze. She glared at Calen with piercing anger. "You dare interfere with my communion with the Goddess?"

Calen took a step back. "I would never. I am sorry, I misspoke, my love."

"I will forgive you this time. We may be close, Calen, but the Goddess will always be my top priority."

Markus intervened. "She is right, Calen. You overstepped your bounds. Don't worry, High Priestess, I will have this insolence rectified."

Sarah spun around and walked off, faking her fury. Markus and Calen exchanged looks. Markus wore a smug, victorious smile on his fat face. They thought they had her controlled.

When Sarah and Stripe were out of view, she straightened up. Her posture returned to its regal form. "They have been tainting my mind. Having me help those who do not need it to line their own pockets. It is unforgivable."

Stripe kept pace with her. "The real question is, how long has this been happening? How many dying cities were abandoned for profit?"

"I will have to investigate when I return. Right now, we will deal with Markus and Calen. They cannot leave here. They are harming the Church's image and the Goddess's influence. Without the Goddess's true light, Nero will gain ground, and everything will be over."

"What do we do?" Stripe asked.

"I will lure Calen away before the ceremony, extract his information, and then deal with him. During the blessing ritual, you deal with Markus. There is a specific moment where he must exchange his robes for blue robes mid-ritual in a private antechamber. He will be alone. Deal with him then. I will pretend the ritual is a success to fool the guards."

"Won't it be noticed if the two highest-ranking men are missing?"

"Yes. But hopefully, they won't notice until after we have departed."

The two walked the city for a few hours, mapping out escape routes. It was beautiful and elegant. How had it ever been described as failing in the Church ledgers? Sarah told Stripe that her movements had been restricted by the Elders. She had grown suspicious over the last few years. This city, and probably dozens of others like it, explained why she could not move freely. They needed to control where she dropped her regional blessings.

"Will you leave the Church after this is done?" Stripe asked.

"No. I have to fix it from the inside by destroying the rot. The Church does too much good in the world to abandon it to men like Markus."

"What if all the good is fake too?"

"Then I will make it real."

Stripe admired that response. She did not want to run away. She wanted to be the solution. He respected that kind of iron will. Sarah checked the sky. "It is time."

Stripe cracked his knuckles. "Let us mess some shit up."

She snapped back into character. She slumped her shoulders into a daze, and the two walked back to the giant church at the center of Dawnfall. Markus and Calen were waiting out front. Markus looked greedy, while Calen seemed sweaty and nervous. Sarah walked up, took Calen by the hand, and ushered him into the building. He smiled a sickeningly sweet smile when she pulled him away into the private chambers.

"Is that normal?" Stripe asked.

Markus gave a nod. "Yeah, those two do important church business before the ritual."

"So they are fucking."

Markus sputtered. "My word, mercenary. That is an intense conclusion to reach."

Stripe shrugged. "A man and a woman go into a room together alone. Only one conclusion can be reached."

"I see your crude point. We will bring her to the ritual grounds afterward. Feel free to wait there." Markus waved him off.

In the elegant, candlelit room deep within the church, Sarah pushed Calen onto the massive four-poster bed. He sat up. He smiled a hungry, arrogant smile, watching her as she slipped off her heavy white outer robe. She was down to her silk undergarments when she pushed him flat onto his back on the mattress. She climbed on top of him, straddling his waist, as his smile grew wider.

"I was so worried you were upset with me about earlier." Calen reached for her.

"I was. But I am not now." She leaned in close, her breath ghosting over his lips, and brought his hands above his head. He relaxed his arms, allowing her to take control. She moved his hands together against the sturdy iron bed frame, then reached onto the bedside table. She pulled out a length of thick silk rope and tied his wrists to the frame.

"What are you doing, my love?"

"Making it exciting." She offered a smile.

He pulled against the bindings, testing them. The rope held fast.

"Be a good boy and do not resist me."

"Yes, ma'am." He closed his eyes and lay flat. She moved down and bound his legs to the bottom of the frame. She crawled back up, unbuttoned his shirt, and ran her nails up his exposed chest. "I love you."

"Since when?" Sarah asked.

"Since we were kids in the courtyard."

Her voice turned to ice. "No, Calen. Since when have you been betraying me?"

His face tightened into panic. His eyes snapped open. He went to yell for the guards, but before he could make a sound, she lifted her glowing hand. A thin, shimmering membrane of golden magic surrounded the room. "It is soundproof. No one can hear you scream."

Calen scrambled for an excuse. "I never betrayed you, my love. What are you talking about?"

"Gaslighting. Really. Now."

"I have always done what is best for the Church. How can that be a betrayal?"

"You have been corrupting my mind and taking advantage of me. You poisoned me."

"Because the Elders deemed it necessary for our survival."

Sarah's voice wavered with pain. "I gave you everything. I loved you. How could you do this to me?"

"As you said earlier, the Church comes first. I love you with my entire being, Sarah, but the Church thinks you are straying from the path of prosperity."

"I said the GODDESS comes first, not the Church."

"The Church and the Goddess are the same thing. How can you not see that?"

"The Church is just a building to worship the Goddess. She is not the Church."

"That is not true. When I was a starving orphan, the Church took me in. I witnessed it myself. The Goddess, walking in the flesh, was welcoming me with open arms. No longer hungry, no longer abused, no longer forgotten, and allowed to love. She saved me."

"You are making no sense, Calen. I will look for myself." She dug her glowing nail into his bare chest and carved a jagged magic circle into his flesh. He writhed against the bindings in agony. The bloody sigil began to glow a blinding gold. Bright white light shot from his terrified eyes and open mouth. Sarah magically forced herself inside his mind.

It appeared like a massive, infinite library. His memories were labeled as books. She walked down the aisles to the section labeled 'Church' and opened the heaviest book. She was pulled deep into the memory, witnessing the events firsthand. She saw Calen being abused as a young kid by the cruel mistress of the local orphanage. She saw the woman stripping and whipping him until he could not walk over the smallest of mistakes. She saw them starving him, resulting in near-death moments of starvation and being beaten in the cold.

She saw him run away to the Church, only to be turned away by the guards at the gate. He slept on a freezing stone bench outside the Church walls for days until the guards threatened to beat him again. These days repeated until he was almost dead from starvation and exposure. Then, a glowing light flooded his vision as a beautiful woman dressed in all white ushered him safely into the Church courtyard. He was too out of it to see the person clearly in his memory. He was on the verge of death, and everything appeared in hazy streaks of divine light.

Sarah remembered this moment. It was not the Goddess who let him into the Church. It was Sarah's own human mother. Sarah remembered this moment because her mom had fought with a younger Markus about letting a street rat inside the holy walls. Calen saw Sarah's mother and truly thought she was the Goddess arriving in his dying state. This misunderstanding shaped his entire being and his unwavering fanaticism. The glowing light of hope he saw was just her mother showing basic kindness.

The library memories shifted forward. They showed his dedication to the institution. It showed Markus grooming him as a child to do the Church's dark bidding. Graduating the boy to duties the Church would publicly deny. Political assassinations, bribery, orchestrating slavery rings, and voter fraud were all planned by Markus and executed by Calen.

Then it showed him seeing Sarah as a young woman and falling in love with her. His softening as a person. He took fewer wet work jobs. It showed Markus becoming furious at his loss of control over his favorite assassin. The seeds of doubt were planted by Markus in Calen's mind regarding Sarah's decisions as High Priestess. Markus criticized her choices of where to cast the blessing, arguing that she did not help the Church grow because she ignored the big, wealthy cities in favor of the slums. He insinuated that Sarah was misinterpreting the Goddess's true will. Markus reminded Calen that he had accepted him into the Church out of devotion, weaponizing the boy's guilt. It worked.

The memory shifted to Markus's purchase of Velryssa. Luring the demi-human to Markus's hidden chambers, where she was drugged. The dark ritual with the demons to force portions of her charm abilities out of her. The knowledge that the robed demons forced themselves on her. Calen was disgusted by the demons' actions, but Markus assured him it was the Goddess's will. She looked like a demon with her horns, Markus argued, and that meant she was not within the Goddess's domain to protect.

Calen did not truly feel that way, but his indoctrination meant he could not argue with Markus. So he turned a blind eye to the torture. Sarah watched as Calen hated himself for betraying her, but believed it was necessary for the greater good. He did not hesitate, even if he held deep regrets. He began to slip the poison into her wine to influence her mind. He began to wear the tainted charm essence of Velryssa to enhance the poison's effect.

The Church's wealth grew under his manipulation. Markus's personal wealth grew even more. The results were visible everywhere, proving to Calen's twisted mind that Markus was right all along. She was using the gift improperly, and the Church suffered for it. This cemented his loyalty to Markus. He wanted the Church to succeed, but he wanted to keep his love for Sarah. So he decided to house her soul inside his own mind when the demonic extraction happened. Working with the Demon Lord did not matter if the Church grew in power, and he got to keep his love trapped with him forever.

Sarah pulled her mind free of his. Before ending the spell, she opened a book of her own memories and forced him to see things from her side. He saw everything that he had missed. He saw her mom escorting him, half dead, into the church and feeding him from her own personal rations. He saw Markus demeaning her mother for wasting precious resources on a lost cause. He saw her mother advocating for him to be accepted as an acolyte despite the Elders' protests. He saw Markus's scheme and the secret investigations into his massive theft of church funds. He saw the broken, starving cities that were saved by the blessing Sarah provided. Thousands of innocent lives were saved by her choices alone. New, humble churches sprouting in these poor regions out of genuine gratitude, not forced tithing. He saw that every time he took over her mind and forced her to bless an already wealthy area, hundreds of people in the slums starved to death. He saw the truth. The horrific betrayal he committed and its negative impact on the world.

She ended the spell. As soon as his mind was free of the magic, thick tears flowed from his eyes. His body trembled against the silk ropes.

"I am sorry. I am so sorry, Sarah." He let out a sob. "I thought I was right. I thought I was saving us. I thought I was doing her will. Please believe me, I love you and always have. It was all real. I know you felt it too."

He sobbed, fighting against the cognitive dissonance that had ruled his life. The brainwashing shattered, leaving nothing but the crushing reality of what he had done.

Tears streamed down her face. "If you had just talked to me, I could have shown you the truth years ago."

"I am a monster." He shook his head against the mattress. "Please. Please, we can fix this. I can testify against Markus. I can protect you from the extraction."

"You are a monster. And you almost damned the world for Markus." Her tone left no room for debate.

Calen resigned himself. "What happens now?"

"You die."

She wrapped her glowing hands around his throat. She squeezed with divine strength. He thrashed for a brief moment. He gasped for air, his survival instincts kicking in. But as he looked up into her cold, golden eyes, he realized the weight of his sins. He stopped fighting. He lowered his bound hands. He knew he did not deserve to live. Moments later, the life left his eyes. Sarah cried in silence over the body of the man she once loved.

Sarah sat at the edge of the bed next to his body. It was a moment of reflection on their history. It was a moment for the future she knew she had to create. She undid his rope bindings. She dressed his limp body and dressed herself back in her High Priestess robes. She covered him with the thick blankets as if he were sleeping. She cast a minor warming spell to keep his flesh warm to the touch. She did not feel satisfied. She felt a void deep inside the pit of her stomach. There was no way to tell how much of her current life was based on political movements and deceit. She was not sure if any piece of happiness that she experienced since her mother's passing was real. One thing was for sure: she would never be a pawn in anyone's political moves unless it was her own. A brief reflection of her life as she moved through the room reminded her how naive she was for a 70-year-old half-elf. All the signs of betrayal were there, but she ignored them. She accepted them because she had been alone. The type of loneliness that can break a mind.

She exited the room. Her elegant robes trailed behind her. It was time to end this conspiracy. She navigated the halls of the church in a blur. Her mind was clear about the goal ahead, even if her emotions were a wreck. She arrived at the blessing ritual site to find Stripe sitting in a wooden chair, waiting for her. She nodded at him, and he nodded back. Seeing the brawler cleared her mind. Markus approached her as she knelt on the stone floor in prayer.

"Where is Calen?" Markus tapped his foot with impatience.

"He passed out after we prepared. I think he was exhausted." Sarah kept her lie smooth.

"Yes, I bet he was." Markus let out a lewd chuckle. "He helped search for that stowaway bandit for a night without sleep. Let us begin without him."

Blinding golden light formed around Sarah, illuminating the night sky. It danced and flowed as divine magic coated the landscape. The blessing began to take hold of the city. Markus sat back in his ornate chair, smiling with greed. At the halfway point of the ritual, he stood up to swap his ceremonial robes. The blue robes would publicly signify that the blessing had been completed. As he walked into the dark halls of the church, he did not notice Stripe trailing behind him.

Markus slipped into a private antechamber with a heavy golden door. Inside, the walls were adorned with precious gemstones, and silk church robes hung on racks. He grabbed an elegant blue robe and began to slip it on over his shoulders. His fat body could barely fit inside the fabric.

Stripe did not have the fancy magic Sarah had, but he did have one thing. Stripe's heavy mythril fist swung forward. Before it could make contact, Markus sensed the movement. The Elder spun around, his eyes wide with panic. He raised a hand, and a thick, shimmering barrier of high-tier defensive magic erupted between them. Stripe's fist collided with the glowing shield. The impact echoed in the small room, but the barrier held firm.

Markus sneered, his confidence returning. "You foolish brute. Did you really think a common mercenary could strike down an Elder of the Church? My wards are impenetrable."

Stripe could see a blue hue on the divine shield. It appeared to be a spot that wavered for a moment. He realized it was his new passive kicking in, showing him the magic density shift before it did. Using the prediction as a guide, he was confident he had an answer to this spell. Stripe grinned a dark grin. He pulled his fist back. He channeled his mana, forcing the cold, static energy down his arms and into the heavy mythril gauntlets. The Toxic Pugilist class activated. Sizzling, highly acidic green venom coated the spikes.

"Let us test that theory."

He punched the magical barrier again. This time, the venom burned through the magical weave. The venom concentrated in the weakened magical spot. It reacted. As the magic spot shifted, it took the venom with it, weakening the entire barrier. The barrier hissed, cracked, and then shattered into a million fading shards of light. Spots of venom fell onto Markus as he shrank back.

Markus's eyes widened in horror. He opened his mouth to scream for the Paladins. Stripe dashed forward, covering his mouth before the first word could leave his lips. The look on Markus's face was apparent. He was a high-level priest. His magic was powerful, yet this common thug managed to break his barrier and dared to lay hands on him. Stripe took off his gauntlet. He wanted to make Markus feel what was coming. The gauntlets would end things too fast.

Stripe's fist made contact with the side of Markus's bald head. It spun the fat man around, and he fell to the marble ground. Before Markus could recover, Stripe punched him in the throat. His voice went silent as he wheezed for air, clutching his crushed windpipe.

"Man, you are twisted." Stripe loomed over him. "All of you rich, fat fucks are the exact same."

Markus gasped, clawing at his throat. He was trying to say something. He pleaded with his eyes. He could not speak because of his damaged throat.

"Now is not the time to talk. It is the time for violence."

Stripe's heavy combat boot came up. It crashed down on Markus's groin. Markus reacted. He thrashed on the marble and attempted to fight back with his fat hands. Stripe ignored him. He began to kick him in the face exactly like you would kick a soccer ball. He beat him. And then he beat him some more. Long after Markus stopped moving, he kept beating him. Thoughts of what this monster had been doing to Velryssa and Sarah flooded his head, fueling his rage. Then thoughts of his own loss of Hobb took over. He took everything out on Markus, even the stuff Markus had nothing to do with. He turned the corrupt Elder into a human rage room.

A wave of physical and emotional relief flooded over Stripe as he finally exited the bloody antechamber. Stripe made sure no one saw him enter or leave the hallway and then slipped back into the crowd at the ritual. Stripe stepped out of the bloody antechamber and wiped his knuckles. He waited for that familiar, hollow numbness to wash over him—the freezing emptiness that had swallowed him in the Moscow snow. Instead, a warm, unfamiliar lightness bloomed in his chest. He let out a long breath, leaving the monster on the marble floor.

It was at the height of the magical climax when he arrived. An ethereal hum radiated through the land as Sarah began to glow in pure, blinding white light. A massive shockwave of magical current shot through the land, encircling the entire city with a warm hug of divinity. The ritual concluded. Sarah stood briefly on the altar before her knees buckled. She collapsed from exhaustion. Stripe days darted forward and caught her before she hit the stone.

"The ritual is complete." Sarah leaned into his support.

"You blessed this rich city anyway?"

"Yes. But I blessed them with the phrase, 'This town will get what it deserves.' So they will decide their own fate." She offered a faint smile.

Stripe nodded his approval. "That is sneaky. I like it." He carried her back to her feet, supporting her weight.

"No more, Markus," Stripe confirmed.

"No more Calen," Sarah added.

"What happens now?"

"I stay and fix the Church. And you go home."

"If you run into any more issues, call me. I will bring my fists." She waved him away with a tired smile and handed him a heavy leather bag of coins. It was enough to cover his massive debt to the guild, and significantly more. There was a dull silver ring hidden amongst the looted coins.

CROWN — "This ring appears to grant the wearer a tiny amount of passive regeneration. Around ten health points per minute."

There was a sealed parchment letter with a thick wax seal in the bag as well. The elegant handwriting on the front said, *Do not open until on the road*. He was curious what it was, but he tucked it into his pouch.

"Can I hug you goodbye?" Sarah asked.

"Sure."

She hugged him tightly. It was a vulnerable hug. One that reflected that her entire life had been changed by the traumatic events they had survived together. As he was walking away, he turned to wave goodbye. He saw her staring back tearfully as she waved. Stripe then left the city and boarded the first merchant carriage bound back to the guild in Memento. Stripe couldn't help but feel like she was keeping something from him until the very end.

He sat in the back of the rocking carriage, deep in thought as the scenery blurred past the window. He began to reflect on himself and the horrific quest that had just concluded. He thought about everything that led to this moment and his dark, violent plot for revenge against the nobility. He looked down at his bloodstained mythril gauntlets. He concluded that he was not a good person. He was a monster. He was violent, angry, and crude. But back on Earth, his violence was fueled by his own ego and greed. Here, he just used his brutal violence to save a Saintess, free a tortured demihuman from a dungeon, and protect a city from a corrupt regime. He was still a monster, but now he was a monster who protected people. He was happier with who he was now, covered in mud and blood, than with who he was when he died in a pool of his own making as an arrogant champion. He had finally found a purpose that actually mattered.

CROWN — "Reflection complete. Level up. Bonuses applied. New skills unlocked. New title unlocked. Multiple rewards due to intense emotional and character development. Real-time reflection complete. Auto allocation of points applied."

"What?" Stripe rubbed his eyes.

CROWN — "Ready for the next objective?"

Chapter 37

The ride back to the Memento guild was going to be a long one. This time, Stripe sat alone in the main cabin. A large part of him missed riding alongside Sarah. There was nothing quite like having a brilliant, beautiful woman at your side when taking on the world. He had not realized his nostalgia until the conspiracy with the corrupt Church Elders was resolved, and she was gone.

He stewed in the silence. His mind drifted between his bloody revenge plot against the nobility and the crushing reality of his isolation. To distract himself, he summoned his interface. He had not found a single quiet moment to review the final rewards from the demon fight and the dismantling of the cultist camp.

CROWN — "Processing delayed combat achievements and reflection bonuses."

- **New Title Acquired:** Divinity Killer
- *Effect:* When interacting with divine magic, the user has a chance to ignore the durability of the object or barrier.
- **Loot Secured:** Ring of Regeneration, Demonic Sword
- **Reflection Bonus Applied:** +5 to all core attributes.

Stripe glanced at the floorboards. The massive, jagged Demonic Sword he took from Kevin the Terrible rested there, radiating a dark hum. He reached into his pouch, pulled out the Ring of Regeneration, and slid it onto his finger. It grew warm against his skin, sending a pulse through his battered muscles. He opened his status screen to check the math.

Title: The Sanctified Venom-Brawler (hidden), Divinity Killer, Instigator

HP: 220/220

Stamina: 250/250

Mana: 150/150

Attributes

STR: 30 (25+5)

AGI: 25

END: 22 (+2hp Regen)

INT: 15Stripe exhaled, staring at the glowing blue text. He was getting stronger. Fast. But the numbers did not make the carriage feel any less empty.

CROWN — "You are not alone. I am here."

Stripe stared into the empty space. "You are not real."

CROWN — "I am real enough."

The synthetic voice carried a tinge of sadness.

Stripe leaned his head back. "Not for me."

The Crown did not respond. Stripe found no victory in the silence. It felt like he had hurt its feelings, which made no logical sense for a magical artifact.

He looked down at the thick, pricey parchment letter sitting in his lap. The red wax seal of the High Priestess stared back at him. He debated breaking it. He hesitated. Maybe he needed to get further away than a single day's travel. It could hold a dangerous political secret that might bring wrath down upon Sarah if revealed too close to Dawnfall.

He was not dumb; he knew he would never see her again. She had an insurmountable amount of work to do to fix the rotting Church and to explain the sudden, violent deaths of Elder Markus and Priest Calen. It was a dangerous, near-impossible political task.

What Stripe feared most was that the letter would be a polite, formal conclusion to his association with her. Why would a beautiful, powerful woman like the Saintess want a violent brute hanging around her life? He let out a breath and tucked the letter into his leather pouch.

Stripe patted the pouch. "Yeah, it's best I don't open this yet. I think it would be better if I kept it a secret."

"Muffled Le... m... ou... o... he..." A faint voice echoed through the woods.

Stripe froze. The carriage was only a few hours outside the city gates. He was supposed to be alone. The hair on the back of his neck stood up.

Stripe scanned the cabin. "What the fuck is that? What did you say?"

"Muffled. Let me out of here!"

Stripe stared at the velvet bench seat beneath him. "Oh, ghost of the carriage, I have no offering to appease you. Please pass my debt on to the next foolish wanderer who enters your domain. In fact, double it and give it to the next person."

There was a tense moment of silence. Stripe nodded as if he had banished a phantom.

The voice broke through the wood. "You fucking idiot, get off of me!"

Stripe jumped off the chair. He flipped the velvet seat back. The hidden wooden compartment popped open, and Velryssa sprang out, drenched in sweat, her golden eyes burning with fury. She gasped for the fresh air of the cabin.

Velryssa wiped her brow. "Did you seriously forget I was in there?!"

Stripe held his hands up. "No... of course not."

CROWN — "False. You were too preoccupied, stewing over revenge, to remember the hostage."

"Why didn't you let me out when we got outside the city gates?!"

Stripe pointed a finger. "I wanted to make sure you were safe from the Paladin patrols!"

CROWN — "Liar."

Velryssa glared at him, brushing her damp hair away from her elegant horns. Her shoulders slumped as exhaustion took over.

Velryssa took a deep breath. "Fine. That makes sense. Thank you... for everything."

Stripe gave a shrug. "No need to thank me. I just got to do what I do best. Punch people who deserve it."

"What will you do now?"

"I should be asking you that." Stripe crossed his arms. "Aren't you still a slave on paper?"

Velryssa shook her head. "Not anymore. The magical contract was bound to Markus's life force. I could feel my bonds shatter the moment my owner was vanquished."

Stripe thought back to the cultist whose face he caved in on the stone altar. That miserable bastard must have been the one holding her magical leash.

Stripe nodded. "That's good. As for me... I think what's next is getting my own revenge."

Velryssa lowered her gaze. "I pity the person who has acquired your wrath."

"I wish it did not have to be that way. But I am not the one who started it."

Velryssa leaned back against the cushions. "I will return to my family's former estate in the northern cliffs. As the sole heir, I will continue to build the Metaldrum legacy from the ashes."

"What about the King? Won't he just send his army to attack you again?"

"Unlikely. At least not until we become an economic threat again. That's years from now. By then, we will be heavily fortified and ready." She paused, her golden eyes studying his scarred face. "How can I help you, Stripe?"

Stripe held up a hand. "You have done enough. In fact, I owe you if anything. You gave me the intel I needed."

Stripe watched Velryssa huddle in the corner. His chest tightened. He recognized that hollow, vacant stare—he used to see it in his own reflection every morning in Los Angeles. He swallowed hard, hoping she wouldn't go looking for the same dark, liquid escapes he once relied on to survive the quiet.

The two sat in the rocking coach as the bumpy dirt road moved by in slow motion. The first week passed without incident. They shared the dried rations and fresh water Sarah had left stockpiled in the vehicle. Stripe stayed awake each night, sitting by the carriage door to keep watch while she slept.

Over the crackle of the campfire, he heard her cry. The sounds stayed muffled; she attempted to hide her grief. She pretended to be tough, masking the unimaginable pain inflicted upon her. She had done nothing to deserve it. Her only curse was being born powerful and beautiful. He felt a strong need to protect her, like an injured animal finding safety. He harbored no attraction to her, unlike other men. She just needed a shield. He wondered why he felt zero pull from her charm aura.

CROWN — "You are immune to her magical charm effect. The System classifies mental manipulation as a type of intoxication."

Stripe focused his thoughts. "Wait. It's not classified as mind control or hypnosis?"

CROWN — "Correct. Anything that alters the host's chemical or mental state to induce euphoria or compliance is considered an intoxicant. Your divine gift prohibits intoxication of any kind."

"Wow. That is pretty damn useful."

CROWN — "Correct."

After the first week on the road, Velryssa began making small talk. She talked for hours about her family, her younger brothers, and her life before the King's betrayal. She asked Stripe about his life. She asked why his parents would name him Hands. He corrected her, revealing his real name. She found Stripe weirder for it, but she accepted it.

Stripe talked about his addiction issues. He detailed his crushing homelessness and the struggle to survive freezing nights when he was one bad day away from giving up. She listened with intense focus. She related to the rock-bottom despair.

By the second week, the suffocating silence in the carriage gave way to easy extraction. Velryssa no longer flinched when Stripe moved too quickly, and Stripe found himself genuinely laughing when she complained about the texture of their dried rations. They didn't need to discuss their nightmares; the shared, quiet understanding between them was enough.

Halfway through the trip, she detailed her political plans. She explained how she planned to leverage old favors to reacquire the stolen iron and mythril mines. In return, Stripe talked about Hobb. He explained how a noble with a golden sunburst crest had murdered his only friend in the city over a broken broom. She offered her deepest condolences.

Velryssa leaned forward. "If he is a high-ranking noble in the capital, I can probably write you a letter of introduction."

"What's that?"

"A formalized, magically sealed letter saying that House Metaldrum vouches for you as a person of high standing. It grants you access to the elite districts."

Stripe narrowed his eyes. "That seems risky for you. If I kill him, they will trace the letter back to your House."

Velryssa gave a nod. "It is risky. But I owe you my life, Stripe. And we need fewer shitty nobles in the world. It will get you through the gates. I just ask that you try to cover your tracks so it doesn't implicate my family's return. If you can't cover it up... then I will accept whatever consequences come."

Stripe held her gaze. "I would never betray your help, Velryssa. I promise you, I will do my best to be discreet, even if it means I must take my time to plan it."

On the last night of the long trip, Stripe sat by the campfire, keeping watch. His scarred hand wandered to his leather pouch. His thick fingers traced the outline of the wax-sealed letter Sarah left him. He did not feel as alone as he did when he first refused to open it.

Velryssa lifted her head from the heavy wool blankets inside the carriage. She poked her head through the open door, watching him stare at the fire.

Velryssa offered a soft smile. "Open it, Stripe. You have been dwelling on that piece of paper for far too long."

Stripe stared at the flames. "What if it's a total rejection?"

"Then I will comfort you, my friend. We will drink tea and insult her."

Stripe flashed a faint smile. "Thank you."

He took a deep breath, slid his thumb under the heavy wax, and broke the seal. He unfolded the thick parchment and read by the flickering firelight. It spanned multiple pages and was written in elegant penmanship. The writing was not in the native, runic tongue of this world. The letters formed the English alphabet. A massive knot formed in his stomach.

Dear Stripe,

If you can read this, then it is really you. When we were doing the divine vow ritual in the carriage to protect Velryssa, I asked the Goddess for the absolute truth of your soul. She bestowed your real name upon me. Stripe. Hearing the Goddess say that name broke my heart into a million pieces.

I was born in this land seventy years ago. But I am not from this land. I am from a place called Earth, where I died a horrible, terrifying death. I died on the floor of a hotel room in Moscow. I still remember the cold. I remember the smell of blood soaking into the carpet. I remember the violent men bursting through the door while you were away.

When the Goddess Astraeia granted me a divine gift, I chose the Regional Blessing. I wanted to fix broken lands and make sure no one ever starved or was hurt like I was hurt in my final moments. She chose to make me part elf, so I would have a near-infinite lifespan to make up for my violent and short human life. I believe she felt pity for me. She said it was an unfair ending. I chose to be reborn as an infant here because I desperately wanted a mother. I wanted to belong.

The truth is, I was married to a man named Stripe in my former life. After spending these harrowing weeks with you, seeing how you fight, hearing your terrible jokes... I now know you are him. I know it deep in my soul. Everything about you reminded me of my love, but you are slightly different. Harder. More scarred.

You are probably asking why I never mentioned it to your face. I was terrified. Stripe, I lost our baby. I could not protect her. I fought them, I really did. I caught one of them with a piece of glass just like I told you as I was dying. But I failed. I have carried that failure for seventy years. Every time I close my eyes, I am back in that room, failing you both. I feel like I deserve your hatred.

The love I have for you is growing and festering within my being. But seventy years is a very long time to be alone, Stripe. I missed you every single day. The decades move so slowly when you are carrying a ghost. If I had spoken this out loud to you, I would have collapsed. I would not be able to do what needs to be done to fix the rot inside this Church. Maybe one day I can face you and take the brunt of your anger for my failures. But I can't do it today. I am too weak.

I love you. I have loved you across two lifetimes.

Elizabeth Sarah Stripe

When Stripe finished reading the final line, a single hot tear rolled down his scarred cheek. His hands shook, causing the parchment to rattle against his calloused skin. The letter answered the haunting questions that had been lingering in his mind. It explained why she understood his Earth-based references and slang. It explained his unusual attraction and fierce protectiveness toward her.

It also explained the cruelest joke of their reincarnation: time moved at a different pace relative to Earth. While he spent a few years drinking himself to a stupor under a bridge in Los Angeles, she lived an entire lifetime. Seventy years. She spent seven decades navigating a corrupt church, missing him, and mourning their baby.

The guilt struck the hardest. A physical sickness ripped through Stripe's stomach. He dropped the letter into the dirt and grabbed his own hair, pulling at the roots until his scalp burned. She blamed herself. She thought her death was her own fault. She thought he would hate her.

No. No, no, no. The realization crashed down on him. He was the one who punched the Russian oligarch's son. He brought the mob to their hotel door. His arrogant ego killed them. And she spent seventy fucking years hating herself for his mistake.

He wanted to scream. He wanted to run back to Dawnfall. He wanted to shake her and tell her how wrong she was. He needed to fall to his knees and beg for her forgiveness, to confess that it was his fault. But he did not know what to do. The letter told him to stay away for her own good, while also begging him not to. He recognized the words were written with pure passion and overwhelming guilt, not logic.

Barging back into her life as a crude, violent mercenary would ruin the holy life she worked seventy years to build. He needed to figure out his place in this world before confronting his past. He needed to clean up the messy things binding him, like his Guild debt and his revenge against the noble, before bringing his chaos to her doorstep. He was unsure if he could ever fix what his ego had broken back on Earth. She would feel ashamed of the homeless monster he became after she died. He felt grateful she never saw that side of him.

But the miraculous opportunity to fix things, to eventually have his old life back with the woman he loved, brought a spark of happiness. He could not hold back the thick tears streaming down his face. He sat by the fire, a massive, scarred brawler sobbing into his hands.

Velryssa watched the tears fall onto the parchment. She saw the deep sadness mixed with wild hope in Stripe's eyes. She did not pry into the letter's contents. Instead, she stepped down from the carriage. She walked over to the man who saved her from hell, wrapped her arms around his broad shoulders, and gave him a comforting hug. He did not fight back. He accepted her embrace, leaning his head into it. The two survivors stood together in silence while the campfire flickered beside them, and the dark night grew quiet.

[SYSTEM ALERT: Level 21 Reached | Title Acquired: Divinity Killer | Loot: Ring of Regeneration, Demonic Sword]

Chapter 38

Velryssa was an unusual companion on the road. Stripe had grown used to the silent carriage rides with Sarah and Calen; those trips were heavy with unsaid words and the suffocating weight of religious expectation. Velryssa, however, insisted on talking about everything. She never left Stripe a moment to think or dwell on the letter from his wife.

"Ever wonder what happens when trees fall, and no one is around?" Velryssa's voice bounced off the wooden walls. "Do they make a sound? Or is that just for our ears? I bet it is quiet without us around. Sounds require ears to catch them. Without an ear, a vibration is just a ripple in the dirt."

She answered before Stripe could form a response, sitting with her legs tucked up on the velvet seat, her tail flicking in a steady rhythm.

"It feels nice not to be strapped to a stone." Her tone shifted to something grounded and raw. "The air tastes different when you are not inhaling the scent of your own blood and the sweat of robed freaks."

Stripe had given up trying to join the conversation thirty minutes ago when she was ranting about the various textures of potatoes and which ones were best for throwing at people. He sat with his head resting against the seat, his eyes closed. Listening to her speak reminded him of a podcast from his old life. It was background noise that kept the ghosts of Moscow and the cold reality of Hobb's death from creeping back into his mind.

He watched her through cracked eyelids. The noble daughter of House Metaldrum had shed her skin. She was no longer the untouchable goddess of the slave market or the terrified victim of the Church. She was becoming unhinged in a way Stripe found relatable. She was loud, she was crude, and she was currently trying to see if she could balance a copper coin on the tip of one of her horns.

When she thought he wasn't paying attention, she would stare out the carriage window and cry, letting the tears roll down her cheeks. Stripe wanted to say the right words to help, but he doubted anyone could after what she had endured.

CROWN — "Hostile threats detected. Large mana signatures and physical forms are converging on your position. Proximity: two hundred yards."

The voice in his head was no longer a robotic drone; it carried that sharp, wealthy teenager edge that made him want to argue even when the advice saved lives.

Stripe banged a fist against the front of the carriage. "Pull over, we have company."

"Ooo, the big baddies are coming!" Velryssa cheered.

Velryssa practically vibrated with energy, a wicked grin spreading across her face. She didn't cower in the hidden compartment or clutch her knees to her chest. Instead, she vaulted over Stripe, her tail flicking eagerly behind her as she rushed out the door to meet the ambush head-on.

In the woodline, a large group of bandits had been perched for hours. They were a mixed bunch, mostly humans, but led by a pair of Tigermen who looked as if someone had taken a jungle predator and forced it to walk on two legs. They stood eight feet tall with muscles that stretched their leather armor to the breaking point. They carried massive greatswords that looked like they belonged on a statue.

As soon as Velryssa stepped out, the bandits rushed from the brush to surround the carriage. They formed a tight circle, weapons drawn. Velryssa put her hands on her hips, her tail lashing behind her. She looked at the group with clear disappointment.

"Aw, I thought there would be more. All of them are ugly, too." Velryssa stomped her feet like a toddler throwing a fit. "You big guy, the one with the face like a smashed pumpkin. Go get more friends! This is a pathetic showing!"

The bandits froze. They had expected screaming, begging, or at least a guard stepping out to negotiate. Instead, they had a demi-human girl insulting their numbers.

Stripe emerged from the carriage next. The atmosphere changed the moment he stepped into the light. He didn't have the holy aura of Sarah or the magic of Calen, but his level twenty-five stats made him appear denser than a normal man. The air seemed to displace around his broad shoulders. He rolled his neck, the bones popping with the sound of small gunshots.

A man with a scarred eye and a rusted shortsword pointed his weapon. "You lot are crazy."

"Your boyfriend may be strong, but he can't take all of us," the Bandit Leader said.

The leader was a giant of a man, easily eight feet tall and wide enough to block the sun. He carried a heavy club studded with iron nails. His gaze swept over Velryssa with predatory greed.

An arrow was shot from the crowd. It wasn't aimed at killing, but at intimidating. It skimmed past Velryssa's skirt, tearing a jagged hole along her hip. "Next time we won't miss."

The large bandit stepped forward. "Drop your belongings, and we may let you live. Leave the girl, too. We will be a better company."

Tears formed in Velryssa's eyes as she examined her torn skirt. It was a simple piece of clothing from Sarah, and she possessed no backups. More importantly, it was the first thing she had owned as a free woman.

"You pieces of shit. I will fucking kill you." Her voice dropped to a whisper. It vibrated with a frequency that made the horses whinny in terror. Her golden eyes lit up as if filled with molten magnesium.

Stripe let out a chuckle and took a step back toward the carriage. "Uh oh. You guys really fucked up now. I was going to give you a chance to run, but it's out of my control now."

A dark pink mist erupted from Velryssa's body. It didn't drift on the wind; it moved with purpose, expanding into a dome that encapsulated the mob of bandits.

The archer in the trees sensed the shift and loosed another arrow. He aimed for Stripe's skull to drop the only physical threat. The arrow soared through the air. In the physical world, it was just a piece of wood and flint. Inside the pink mist, reality ceased to exist for the bandits.

The arrow struck. To the archer's eyes, Stripe's head exploded in a spray of blood and bone. The archer pumped his fist in the air, let out a cheer, and prepared to descend for his prize. In reality, the arrow had buried itself into a tree trunk five feet to the left of the carriage. Stripe hadn't even moved.

The two Tigermen drew their greatswords and swarmed the duo. Their teamwork was technical and fast. Inside the mist, they saw Stripe standing there with his arms wide. They sliced down in unison, crossing their blades in a perfect 'X'. They watched themselves separate Stripe from the shoulders down, snarling in triumph as the mercenary fell to pieces.

In reality, the Tigermen had turned on each other. They stood ten feet away from Stripe, hacking at the air and parrying each other's blades, convinced they were butchering their enemy.

The rest of the gang swarmed the carriage. To their eyes, they were tearing the driver limb from limb and looting chests filled with gold and jewels. They grumbled about the weight of the coins, their eyes glassy. One bandit knelt in the mud, shoving handfuls of dirt into his mouth, convinced he was eating expensive cured meats.

The large leader approached Velryssa. He reached out to grab her arm, or at least, that is what he saw.

"You belong to us now." He smiled, his breath smelling of rot. "Don't worry, it will only hurt a little."

In his mind, he held the most beautiful woman in the world, and she looked at him with adoration. In reality, he stood three feet away, clutching a jagged branch of a thorn bush. His hands bled as the thorns dug into his palms, but he felt no pain. He was lost in a hallucination in which he was a king and she his queen.

Stripe leaned against the carriage, watching the group of bandits slaughter themselves. The horror of her ability lay in its silence. There were no screams of terror, only the sound of wet impacts and bandits laughing as they killed their own friends. They were trapped in a happy place while their bodies did the work of their own destruction.

"What do they see when you do your magic?" Stripe asked, his voice echoing in the quiet clearing.

"Whatever makes them happiest and brings them closest to being with me." Velryssa's voice flattened, devoid of its earlier childishness. "It varies from person to person. It looks like these guys think violence is the most effective way to get with me. They think they are winning a war for my hand."

"So if it was just some guy in a tavern, he would see a world where his actions led to him being with you?"

"Yeah, pretty much. He would think I fell in love with his stories or his money. He would stay in that dream until his heart stopped or I ran out of mana. It is a mercy. They die happy."

Stripe looked at the archer. The man had climbed down from the tree and was stabbing a dagger into his own thigh, laughing because he thought he was opening a treasure chest.

Stripe stretched his shoulders. "I guess we should wrap this up. This is getting a bit too dark for my taste."

"Be my guest." She looked down at the torn fabric of her skirt. "The big one is yours. I want to watch you break him."

Stripe walked toward the giant leader. "Let him out. I want a fair fight."

"Okay." Velryssa thinned the pink mist around the leader's head.

The man's glossed-over eyes returned to normal. The transition hit him with physical pain; he let out a gasp as the world shifted from a golden palace back to a muddy road. He looked around in shock. His crew was decimated. One Tigerman had sliced the other's head off and stared at the corpse in confusion. An arrow protruded from the dwarf's skull. The rest were bleeding out in the dirt, their faces frozen in happy grins.

The Giant's eyes went wide. He looked at his hands and saw the blood from the thorn bush. Stripe walked towards him. He didn't draw a weapon. He pointed at the ground, signaling for the Giant to meet him and throw down. The Giant gave a nod, his shock turning into a desperate, cornered rage.

"We do this as men with no weapons." He dropped his iron-studded club.

Stripe obliged. He unstrapped his gauntlets and let them fall into the mud. He didn't need mythril for this. He needed to feel the impact. He needed to remind himself of the technical skill he spent twenty years perfecting in the octagon.

The Giant spotted the ring on Stripe's finger. "I know that ring. That means you have a bandit's honor. Let's make a wager. If I win, you free my mates."

"What do I get?" Stripe asked.

The Giant smiled, showing his missing teeth. "Honor."

Stripe did not care about the honor of a bandit, but he never turned down a fair one-on-one scrap. It was the only thing that felt honest in this world of magic and lies. He was also annoyed that, once again, someone mistook him for a bandit.

"Sure, I am down."

The two unarmed men stepped into the center of the road.

CROWN — "Stripe HP: 220/220. Giant HP: 500/500. Warning: Target possesses a 'Brute Force' passive. Physical resistance is high."

The Giant made the first move. He swung a colossal fist at Stripe, a haymaker that would have decapitated a normal human. It cut across the air at a speed that did not match its size. Stripe pivoted on his lead foot at the last moment, the wind of the punch whistling past his ear.

CROWN — "Projections are now online. Analyzing muscle tension."

A blue, see-through overlay of the Giant appeared in Stripe's vision. It moved a half-second ahead of the real man. Stripe saw the Giant's weight shift for a follow-up. Stripe ducked in, entering the pocket. He unleashed a crisp uppercut, driving his knuckles into the Giant's jaw. The Giant stepped in with a high guard, blocking it and taking some of its momentum, but the force still rattled his teeth.

Giant HP: 480 / 500

The Giant responded by attempting a grapple, reaching out with massive arms to crush him. Stripe saw the outline approaching and secured a Muay Thai clinch. He snapped the Giant's head down, his fingers interlacing behind the man's neck. He threw two hard knees, driving them into the Giant's midsection and thick skull.

Giant HP: 400 / 500

The Giant's nose began to bleed. He realized he couldn't out-box the smaller man, so he dropped low and wrapped his arms around Stripe's legs. Stripe did not see an outline for this; the transition happened too fast for the system to process. The Giant lifted him up with a roar of effort and slammed him onto the ground with a strong double-leg takedown. The combined weight hit the dirt, knocking the wind out of Stripe. Stripe knew he could not take many of these slams.

Stripe HP: 140 / 220

A scramble broke out on the ground as the Giant attempted to use his superior size to pin Stripe. He placed both hands on Stripe's chest, preparing to rain down ground-and-pound. Fighting off his back, Stripe didn't panic. He pivoted his hips, moving his body out of the path of the primary force.

He reached up and snagged the Giant's right arm. He swept his leg across the man's chest and hooked his other leg over the Giant's neck. The Giant attempted to pick him up for another slam, but lacked the speed. Stripe sank into a deep armbar, arching his hips toward the sky.

As the Giant lifted, Stripe cranked the joint. A loud, wet snap echoed through the clearing. The Giant's elbow joint failed, the arm going limp. The man let out a shriek of agony. Stripe rolled back to his feet and let the broken limb drop.

Giant HP: 250 / 500

The loss of his arm was devastating. The Giant scrambled back, his breath coming in ragged gaps. He had assumed Stripe was a helpless mage or a simple brawler. He didn't expect a technical grappling master. Panic set in. On the feet, he was at a technical disadvantage. On the ground, he almost died.

"Ooo, that looked like it hurt!" Velryssa cheered from the sideline. She leaned against the carriage, picking dirt out from under her nails.

The two squared up again. The Giant held his limp arm against his chest. He rushed forward, swinging his good arm in a desperate, wide arc. Stripe had no room to dodge in the tight space, so he absorbed the blow with a tight guard. The Giant retained immense power; the strike knocked Stripe three feet backward, his boots carving furrows in the mud. He felt his ring of regeneration mending the bruises on his forearms and back.

Stripe spun twice to build momentum, then leaped into the air. He threw a devastating spin kick, his heel aiming for the Giant's temple. The Giant leaned back to avoid the blow, but his dazed state slowed him. The heel caught him squarely on the chin. CRACK.

Giant HP: 100 / 500

The man stumbled back, eyes rolling in his head. His arm was broken, his jaw fractured, and his brain bouncing against his skull. The thought of victory vanished. Driven by pure survival instinct, he fled into the pile of bodies and retrieved his iron-studded club. He rushed back at Stripe, swinging the weapon down with his good hand and the broken stump of the other. The prediction overlay showed Stripe exactly where the weapon would land.

Stripe side-stepped the vertical smash. His fists glowed with a sickly green light. He unleashed a three-piece combo with flawless timing. Two shots to the side of the head and one digging deep into the liver, his knuckles saturated in thick green mana.

Giant HP: 20 / 500 (Poisoned)

CROWN — "Poison Status successfully stacked three times on the target. Damage is accumulating. Victory is guaranteed if distance is maintained."

The Giant felt the burn of the poison. It wasn't a sting; it felt like his blood had turned to boiling lye. He swung the club horizontally, then vertically, spamming his attacks. He ignored the pain of his broken body, fueled by the adrenaline of a dying man. Stripe kept his distance. He moved like a ghost, slipping and sliding around the swings. He didn't need to land another punch. The fight was over.

The Giant's strength failed. His skin turned a pale, sickly shade of grey. He dropped the club, and his knees hit the mud. He coughed, spilling a puddle of green liquid from his mouth.

Giant HP: 1 / 500

The light in his eyes flickered. Stripe walked back to Velryssa and tagged her in with a nod.

"My turn." She ran to the man on the ground, her face a mask of cold fury. She lifted her heel and stomped on his head once. The sound of the skull meeting the road was final.

Giant HP 0 / 500

CROWN — "High-level opponent defeated. Bonus experience acquired. Compound interest processing."

Velryssa wiped a splash of blood from her cheek. "I needed this. It is probably not healthy to enjoy it this much, but it stops the hurt for a bit." She reached out and high-fived Stripe. Only she could display that level of excitement after committing such a gruesome act.

Stripe met her hand. "Yeah, I can relate to that." He looked at his hands. They were bruised and bloodied, but the shaking stopped. His own pain always lessened when he was in the middle of a conflict. It was the only time the world made sense.

"I have been struggling to process everything. It's all too much, and sometimes I think the weight of it will crush me." Velryssa's eyes filled with tears. "When I'm talking about silly things or my freedom, it's easy to pretend it wasn't that bad. But when things get quiet, it's so heavy."

She buried her face in Stripe's shoulder. He patted her head while she cried. He knew he didn't have the right words for this. Elizabeth would, but she wasn't here. He did the best he could and just listened. It would have to be enough.

CROWN — "You are actually bonding. I am proud of you. I will update your status once the experience calculation is complete. It will take time."

The two sat on the carriage steps and watched the free XP roll in. The remaining bandits, still under the lingering effects of the mist, fought each other until the last man fell. They were slaves to her divine power. It was a terrifying ability to witness from the outside. As long as she possessed mana, they were simply puppets in her theater of horror. Stripe felt thankful for his immunity to the charm. He realized that more insane powers like this existed in the world. He would need caution in the future.

The only real loot among the bodies consisted of a few gold and silver coins. Stripe gathered them and handed them to Velryssa. She used her power and needed the coin to rebuild her life. The two climbed back into the carriage and resumed their trip. The carriage rolled forward, leaving the massacre behind.

The bonding continued as the sun began to set. Stripe talked about his past on Earth, keeping the details of his wife vague. Velryssa responded in kind, sharing stories of the Metaldrum manor. He marveled at how free-thinking she was now that the shackles were gone. She wasn't the "Noble Beauty" anymore. She let out horrible gas without an apology and attempted to steal his dried meat whenever he looked away. She wasn't shy about bathroom breaks or discussing gross topics.

At times, her behavior flustered even Stripe. He concluded her sheltered life was the cause; she spent years presenting a false, perfect version of herself to the world. This was the only time she had ever been free from the weight of nobility and appearances.

"You know, you're not as much of an asshole as I thought you were when you rejected me at the market." Velryssa chewed a mouthful of stolen bread.

Stripe flashed a grin. "And you're way more of a gremlin than I expected."

She let out a loud, genuine laugh that filled the carriage. She still had moments of silent reflection and flinched if Stripe moved too fast, but she was doing what she could to deal with the trauma. For now, he let her enjoy her brief freedom, at least until she stunk up the carriage again and forced him to hang his head out the window for air. She was a dangerous woman masked in a cute body. She was now his friend, and he wouldn't change her for the world.

CHAPTER 39

Stripe and Velryssa bonded during the final leg of the trip. It was a testament to her force of personality. Stripe remained distracted for the first few days, his mind torn between plotting to avenge his murdered friend and mourning the time he lost with his wife. She had been right next to him for months in this world, and he never knew until it was too late. The thought of her and Calen made him shudder. Velryssa managed to claw him out of those thoughts with her non-stop talking.

The two bonded over blood. It is a special kind of bond when you face death together and come out on top.

CROWN — "Stop that. It is not fair to think about that."

Stripe let out a grunt. "I know it is not, but still, it is hard not to."

Velryssa kicked his boot across the carriage floor. "Do not shut down. Talk to me."

Stripe rubbed his face. "Honestly, my head is a mass of knots, and I do not even know where to begin."

She dropped the posh noble posture. She slouched back against the wooden bench, crossed her arms, and looked at him with the same cynical, tired expression he saw in the mirror every morning. Over the last few weeks, the mask slipped. Underneath the silk and the reputation of House Metaldrum, Velryssa was just as blunt, bitter, and stubborn as he was.

"We both ruined our own lives." Velryssa stared out into the dark. "That is a good place to start. I spent my life looking down on people because I thought "untouchable" meant "invincible". It turns out, being untouchable just makes you a bigger target."

Stripe gave a slow nod. "Tell me about it. I thought having a belt around my waist meant I had the world figured out. We are both just a couple of arrogant idiots who had to lose everything to realize we knew nothing."

She smiled, a genuine, unguarded expression, and punched his shoulder. "You are infuriating, crude, and unrefined. But you are the older brother I wish I had when the creditors came knocking."

Stripe shifted on the bench. "When I was down on my luck and homeless, there was something that almost made the pain go away. Something that competed with alcohol to silence the loud voices of my failures shouting in my head."

"Sadism? Debauchery?" Velryssa asked without hesitation.

"Well, those too, but the real thing that kept me from ending it all was redemption. I thought about jumping off a building multiple times. I even sat on the edge of one for fourteen hours, weighing the pros and cons of taking one step forward. I knew if I did that, then I could never be the man my family wanted me to be. It would be an honor to them if I took the easy way out. So I decided to fight my demons and change for the better. Unfortunately, the opportunity was taken from me before I finished. I was so close." Stripe looked off into the distance.

He slammed Velryssa on the back. "I guess what I am saying is, don't give up. I know it's easy to hide the pain and push it away. Just don't make the same mistake as me and miss your opportunity to make the ones who left before us proud."

"And you are the bratty little sister I never wanted, so it would be a shame if you left me behind." Stripe offered a smile. "Now I know what will make us both feel better."

"Punching something," they said in unison.

Stripe let out a chuckle. "I did not know I was that predictable."

Unlike the previous dwarven caravan, there were no guards or escorts. It was a simple, unprotected carriage heading for Memento. This made it a prime target for everything lurking in the shadows. On the way back, they had been ambushed by desperate bandits, but every time it was a slaughter. Stripe was far too powerful in one-on-one combat now, and Velryssa's innate ability to charm was broken. As soon as the bandits were within the radius of sight or smell, they fell under her spell. They either retreated in confusion or stood still, drooling, while their heads exploded with a single punch.

Stripe's system immunity meant she could pump her magical ability to the maximum without fear of hitting her teammate. The final week of the trip was going smoothly until a massive fallen tree blocked the roadway. Stripe and Velryssa were snacking on their lunch. Stripe became agitated.

Stripe stood. "Do not interrupt this one. I need to feel the rush."

Velryssa waved him off. "Sure, brother. Just give a shout if you need help."

She waved her manicured hand as Stripe hopped out of the cabin. He walked over to the tree and kicked it once. The force of his kick launched the full-sized tree out of the way, sending it crashing into the ditch in an explosion of splinters. Instead of walking back to the carriage, he began to stretch. He rotated his shoulders, rolled his thick neck, and bent down to touch his toes. In the dense tree line, the hidden bandits shifted.

"What in the blazes is he doing?" Bandit One asked in a whisper.

"Stretching, you fool," Bandit Two hissed.

"I know it is stretching, but why?" Bandit Three stepped up. "Who cares? He has horses and money. We need both."

The Smart Bandit took a step back in panic. "Hey, you idiots, did you not just see him kick a full-sized tree out of the way?"

Bandit Two glared. "Shut up, you always try to boss me around."

The Bandit Leader laid out the plan. "We snipe him from the trees, then we surround his weakened body. Easy win."

The bandits formed a tight semicircle. The smart bandit attempted to speak up on multiple occasions but was waved off each time. He grew frantic, and when they kept ignoring him, he made the only choice and ran away into the dark woods.

The Bandit Leader scoffed. "What a pansy. At least it is more money for us."

"Yeah, more money," Bandit One and Two agreed.

Stripe spoke from right behind them. "What are you going to spend your half on?"

"Whores and ale," the Bandit Leader answered on autopilot.

"A new bow," Bandit One added.

"That magical de-aging face cream." Bandit Two pointed at his face.

Stripe shook his head. "That shit is a scam."

Bandit Two turned around. "What do you know, you small piece of shi..."

The bandit looked up to intimidate his coworker, but realized the massive man standing before him was not a friend. Mid-sentence, he fell back from the jump scare. Before he could attempt to stand, a mythril-covered gauntlet came down in a blur. The concussive force of the impact made the nearby trees shake as his head turned into a fine red mist.

CROWN — "Critical hit. The Bandit is dead."

The hot blood shot over the other two bandits. They leaped up in desperate self-defense. Bandit One shook as he drew his bow and fired a wild arrow. His sheer terror threw off his aim, causing the arrow to skim past Stripe, missing his ear by inches. He scrambled to load another one. Stripe leaped forward with a devastating flying knee. The Bandit Leader, a burly, scarred man carrying a large metal shield and a heavy steel sword, jumped in front to intercept the incoming knee.

BAM. A deafening clang echoed through the forest as the knee met the heavy shield. Bandit One used this brief opportunity to gain distance, nocking another arrow and aiming. Stripe grabbed the top of the shield, yanking the dented metal right out of the leader's shocked hand. He blocked the incoming arrow with the stolen shield as the Bandit Leader swung his heavy sword in a panic. Stripe threw the heavy shield with all his might, spinning it like a deadly frisbee at Bandit One. The shield spun through the air before severing the archer's head from his body.

CROWN — "Improvised weapon handling skill has increased."

The terrified Bandit Leader gripped his heavy sword with both shaking hands and let out a loud scream. "Take this!" He swung with all his remaining might in a slashing downward movement. Stripe countered by punching upward towards the descending blade. His superior, magically reinforced mythril, shattered the cheap steel sword into a dozen jagged pieces. The bandit leader fell backward, scrambling to run away.

"STOP." Stripe pointed at the ground. "No running allowed. Fight me with your fists like a man."

"No! You have a weapon!"

Stripe took off his heavy gauntlets and dropped them in the dirt. He squared up to the terrified bandit leader with his bare hands. The man knew he had no choice, so he put his trembling fists up. His stance was sloppy, and his panicked movements were slow. Stripe toyed with him for a full minute, slipping his wild punches by mere centimeters. He did this until the man was drenched in sweat and gasping for air. A single, soft calf kick brought the man to his knees.

"Just end it," the Bandit Leader begged between gasps.

Stripe obliged with a sharp, fast overhand strike to the temple. The man's eyes lost the faint light of life as he crumpled into the dirt. Stripe took a moment to breathe and went through the loot. There was nothing worth keeping. The rusted weapons were damaged and had poor edges. They had zero coins. Stripe regretted letting the first smart man run away. With a light jog, he ran back to the waiting carriage.

As he grabbed the carriage handle, a blinding agony ripped through his entire body. It felt like his bones were expanding inside his skin. His muscles seized, locking up so hard he dropped to both knees in the dirt. A sickening heat rushed through his veins. He gasped for air, clutching his chest as his vision swam with gold and red static. "What the fuck..." Stripe choked out.

CROWN — "Compound Experience Threshold reached. Processing accumulated backlogged experience from high-level combat and prolonged survival engagements."

"Why does it feel like I am dying?!" Stripe yelled.

CROWN — "Early progression was intentionally suppressed to build a foundational baseline. Late-tier compounds scale in extreme bursts. Furthermore, surviving forced mental Reflections grants extreme psionic experience bonuses. Level-up sequence initiated. Brace yourself."

He could not brace. It felt like he was being torn apart and rebuilt atom by atom. The pain peaked in a blinding white flash and then vanished. He stayed on his hands and knees, panting, his sweat dripping into the dirt. He felt lighter. He felt impossibly dense. The sheer power humming under his skin was intoxicating.

CROWN — "Level up complete. Four levels gained. Major milestone accomplished. Bonus applied. Compound attributes applied. Selecting the best stat to fit the host's combat preference. Stats applied."

Stripe pulled himself into the carriage, still catching his breath, only to find a horrible sight waiting for him. There sat Velryssa with a smug look on her flawless face. Exactly where Stripe once sat, there was only the sad residue of his leftover food. She had eaten his food while he was fighting and leveling up. This was the exact type of callous betrayal Stripe did not expect.

Stripe pointed an accusing finger. "You may be beautiful on the outside, but on the inside you are ugly!"

Velryssa offered a smirk. "A woman needs to be full to shine."

CROWN — "You probably deserved that."

The rest of the long ride back consisted of Stripe pouting and Velryssa bullying him. The carriage finally pulled into Memento and came to a stop outside the main gate. Stripe stuck his calloused hand out to give Velryssa a firm, professional goodbye handshake. She pushed it aside and leaped into his arms.

"Stop being silly, we are friends." Velryssa smiled. For the first time in her life, she had a male friend who did not want to use her. It was a great feeling not having to be on edge.

Stripe hugged her back before waving a final goodbye. She was on her way back to her new home, with a tough road ahead of her.

Stripe walked to the guild hall. He had come a long way from throwing feces at a wild wolf. His new stats made him a monster in melee combat. With over a hundred times the strength of a normal human, he would shatter against his fists.

CROWN — "Jeeze, stop gloating. We have work to do."

Stripe puffed his chest out. "I know. I have just come so far."

CROWN — "From an inept user to a troglodyte."

Stripe approached the guild counter and set his identification necklace down. He confirmed the escort quest had been completed.

"We received word moments ago from the church that the escort was successful," Nessa stated.

Stripe gave a nod. "Yeah, I did exactly what I was hired for."

"Congratulations, you are debt-free." Nessa took his necklace and set it on a small magical device that began to grind. After a brief moment, she handed it back. It was updated to reflect his new, hard-earned rank of Copper.

Nessa slid the necklace across the wood. "You can now be paid for quests and sign up for much tougher ones. You can also freely enter dungeons and travel to different guilds with the same ID. Your tax rate will be lower than that of a normal citizen, and you can now officially climb the ranks based on your accolades."

"Wow, I did not know there were so many benefits to paying off my debt."

"Yes, this usually takes people many years if they do not end up dead."

Stripe smiled and waved goodbye. Today was going great. A beautifully toned woman wearing gleaming mythril armor, carrying a deadly spear, approached him. "Hey, heard you finally had some high roller hire you!" Myra greeted him.

Stripe flashed a grin. "Yeah, I got lucky. Looks like my massive muscles lured in yet another maiden."

"Hopefully, you bathed before meeting the client because you usually smell like ass."

"Did you come over here to spread lies, or did you actually want something?"

Nessa piped up from the counter. "She is not lying."

CROWN — "It is a factual statement."

Stripe scowled. "Fuck you all."

Myra crossed her arms. "My team has a slot open, and we were wondering if you wanted to join." She muttered under her breath. "Well, what's left of my team at least."

"I have some important stuff to take care of, then maybe."

"With you at the party, we can hit dungeons and get our debt covered fast." Myra pitched the idea. "We would even let you get first pick of the loot."

"Let me finish my shit, then we will talk."

Myra let out a sigh. "Fine, fine."

That was the inherent problem with getting stronger. More people would rely on you. You would be expected to use your strength for others rather than strictly for yourself. Stripe had overcome some of his mental burdens, but not enough to be someone's permanent meal ticket.

He went to the busy town square and waited for Latrum. After a brief wait, he spotted the half-gnome dressed in a dark robe. The man had his hood pulled low, covering his face, and made sure Stripe saw him. He waved his hand for Stripe to follow him. Stripe followed the little man into a dark alley hidden behind the bakery.

"I was beginning to think you died," Latrum said.

Stripe leaned against the brickwork. "I definitely felt like I did a few times."

"I have the critical information you requested."

"Stop. I need to do something important before you tell me."

Latrum tilted his head. "What? You wanted this information so bad, and now you want to wait?"

Stripe stepped closer, the shadows of the alleyway concealing them. He set his large, calloused hand on Latrum's hooded head. "I, Stripe, relinquish my ownership contract to Latrum, effective immediately."

The air in the alley snapped, smelling of burnt ozone. The heavy, glowing magical binding seal around Latrum's neck flared bright blue, then shattered into a hundred floating motes of fading light. His dark slave mark burned away from his skin, leaving nothing but clean flesh behind. He was now a free man.

Latrum blinked in astonishment. He could feel the heavy burden of the magical compulsion vanish from his nervous system. His shoulders sagged as the invisible weight he had carried for years simply ceased to exist.

"I am free." Latrum touched his bare neck. "I did not think this day would ever come." His stoic facade broke. His chest hitched, and his eyes began to water. "I can finally visit my family's grave now." Tears spilled down his cheeks.

"I am a man of my word." Stripe lowered his hand. "You are no longer legally bound to me. If you want to give me the information, it is of your own free will."

Latrum wiped his eyes. "Of course I will. That is what friends do, they help each other."

Stripe was becoming less alone. He had been worried that Latrum would leave as soon as he was free. It appeared he did not have that intent. Their friendship was real.

Latrum steadied his voice. "The noble responsible for the death of Hobb is Venice Nazarth Wildwater. He is the spoiled middle child of Count Wildwater. By all accounts, he is an incredibly vile brat. Word from my underground contacts is that he was removed from the inheritance will on the day he had Hobb killed."

Stripe locked the name in. "So that is the guy I need to kill."

"We need to kill." Latrum corrected him. This made Stripe happy. His friend wanted to risk his freedom to help with his revenge.

Stripe flashed a fierce grin. "Thank you, bro."

"The Wildwaters are wealthy supporters of the king regent." Latrum pulled his hood back up. "It may not be them directly, but they contributed to the death of my family. So we have a mutual enemy."

Stripe then told Latrum everything that had happened over the last few months. Latrum let out a long breath. "Wow, that is insane. How are you holding up?"

Stripe sighed. "I would love to get wasted."

CROWN — "Go ahead, try it." She sounded like a bratty teen deliberately baiting someone to do something dumb.

"Instead, I think I will just get drunk off pure vengeance."

CROWN — "Boo."

"Well, now we have a pathway; we just need a solid tactical plan." Latrum steered them back on track. "Let me work on a stealthy infiltration plan. We will do this smoothly and quietly."

Stripe gave a nod. "You think I punch. It is perfect. Man, I missed you."

CROWN — "I can outperform any tactical plan he comes up with. Just ask."

Stripe waved a hand to dismiss the thought. "Nah, earn your own place."

CROWN — "Fine, then I guess I have no choice. Remember, this is your fault."

"I knew you were jealous."

CROWN — "WARNING: Force Initiating reflection."

The blinding pain that followed was more intense than any of the previous reflections. It was as if the Crown was punishing him for his slight. He fought back with all of his mental might, his new stats surging in defiance. But it was no use. The dark cobblestone alleyway vanished. Everything went black.

Then, the sensory shift hit him. He did not smell the damp stone or the sweet bread anymore. The heavy, suffocating scent of stale beer, cheap cigarette smoke, and molding carpet assaulted his nose. He could hear the low, mechanical hum of a dying refrigerator. In the distance, a police siren cut through the night air.

Stripe looked up, his head pounding, and found himself lying on the stained floor of a familiar Earth apartment. "Fuck." Stripe groaned. "Not this memory."

CROWN — "You said earn my own place. Let's see you earn yours."

www.ingramcontent.com/pod-product-compliance
Lightning Source LLC
LaVergne TN
LVHW100509110826
845146LV00002B/564

* 9 7 9 8 9 9 6 4 1 2 9 2 1 *